BREAKTHROUGH!

Near the end of the 20th century occurred the most epochal scientific breakthrough in the history of man: the discovery of the macroscope. In resolving and making coherent the information carried on macrons, it brought the entire universe within man's range of vision, revealing levels of technology vastly beyond anything dreamed of by man.

But there was peril—when men attempted to unlock the secrets of the macroscope, it destroyed the minds of the best of them. . . .

Other Avon Books by
Piers Anthony

MACROSCOPE

PIERS ANTHONY

AVON
PUBLISHERS OF BARD, CAMELOT AND DISCUS BOOKS

AVON BOOKS
A Adivision of
The Hearst Corporation
959 Eighth Avenue
New York, New York 10019

Certain astrological passages used in the text are quoted
and/or adapted from ASTROLOGY, *How and Why It Works*
by Marc Edmund Jones, copyright 1945, and *The Sabian Symbol*
by Marc Edmund Jones, copyright 1966, both published by the
Sabian Publishing Society. Reference is also made to *Astrology
and Its Practiced Application* by E. Parker, translated from the
Dutch by Coba Goedhart: P. Dz. Veen, Publisher,
Amersfoort, Holland, 1927.

First Avon Printing, October, 1969
Tenth Printing

Printed in the U.S.A.

The author wishes to express his appreciation for the kind assistance given in aspects of the research and drafting of this novel to Alfred Jacob, Joseph Green, Marion McIntosh and Glen Brock. Without their diligence the scope would have been less macro. And special thanks to Marc Edmund Jones for permission to quote from his texts on astrology, though the treatment of that subject in this novel should not be taken as in any way official or definitive.

MACROSCOPE

...vival dictated hatching within the body: live birth.
...en then the tiny newborn were vulnerable, and natural
...lution brought forth at last the successful compromise:
...-laying mammals. This was the stem stock for the
...of animal that was to dominate the planet. From an
...emendous new radiation emerged its successor. The

CHAPTER 1

Ivo did not realize at first that he was being followed. A little experimentation verified it, however: where Ivo went, so did this stranger.

He had seen the man, pale, fleshy and sweaty, in a snack shop, and thought nothing of it until repetition brought the matter to consciousness. Now it alarmed him.

Ivo was a slim young man of twenty-five with short black hair, brown eyes and bronzed skin. He could have merged without particular notice into the populace of almost any large city of the world. At the moment he was trying valiantly to do so—but the pursuer did not relent.

There was less of this type of thing today than there had been, but Ivo knew that people like himself still disappeared mysteriously in certain areas of the nation. So far he had personally experienced nothing worse than unexplained price increases at particular restaurants and sudden paucities of accommodations at motels. There had been disapproving frowns, of course, and loud remarks, but those hardly counted. He had learned to control his fury and even, after a time, to dismiss it.

But actually to be followed—that prompted more than mere annoyance. It brought an unpleasant sensation to his stomach. Ivo did not regard himself as a brave man, and even one experience of this nature made him long for the comparatively secure days of the project. That was a decade gone, though, and there could be no return.

His imagination pictured the stout Caucasian approaching, laying a clammy hand upon his arm, and saying: "*Mister* Archer? Please come with me," and showing momentarily the illegal firearm that translated the feigned politeness into flat command. Then a helpless trip to a secluded spot—perhaps a rat-infested cellar—where . . .

Better to challenge the man immediately, here in the street where citizens congregated. To say to him: "Are you following me, sir?" with a significant emphasis on the "sir." And when the man denied it, to walk away, temporarily free from molestation. Around the corner, a short hop in a rental car, somewhere, anywhere, so long as he lost himself quickly.

Ivo entered a drugstore and ducked behind the towering displays of trivia, temporizing while he covertly watched the man. *Would* a direct challenge work—or would the bystanders merely stand by, afraid to get involved or just plain out of sympathy? Outside the glass he saw a harried white woman with two rambunctious little boys, and after her a Negro teenager in tattered tennis shoes, and after him the follower dawdling beside the entrance and mopping the sweat from his pallid complexion. A plainclothes policeman? Unlikely; there would have been none of this furtiveness.

The dark suspicion flowered into certainty as his mind dwelt upon it: once this man laid hands upon him, his life would never be the same. Life? Worse; within hours Ivo Archer would vanish from the face of the earth, never to be—

He *had* to face down this enemy.

"Yes?"

He looked up, startled. A clerk had approached him, no doubt having observed his aimlessness and become alert for shoplifting. Her query was impatient.

Ivo glanced around guiltily and fixed on the handiest pretext. He was beside a rack of sunglasses. "These."

"Those are feminine glasses," she pointed out.

"Oh. Well, the—you know."

She guided him to the masculine rack and he picked out a pair he didn't need and didn't want. He paid a price he didn't like and put them on. Now he had no excuse to remain in the store.

He stepped out—and knew as he did so that he lacked the valor to make his stand. Stubborn he was, in depth; courageous, no.

The surprisingly solid hand extended to touch his arm. Coarse black hairs sprouted from the center links of three fingers. "Mr. Archer?" the man inquired. His voice, too, was somewhat coarse, as though there were chronic phlegm coating the larynx.

Ivo stopped, nervously touching the right earpiece of the sunglasses. He was furious at himself but not, now, frightened. He did know the difference between reality and his fantasies. He looked at the man, still mildly repelled by the facial pallor and the faint odor of perspiration. Fortyish; clothing informal but of good cut, the footwear expensive and too new. This man was not a professional shadow—those stiff shoes must be chafing.

"Yes." He tried to affect the tone of a busy person who was bothered by being accosted in such fashion, but knew he hadn't brought it off. This was plainly no panhandler.

"Please come with me."

It was not in Ivo to be discourteous, even in such a situation; it was a weakness of his. But he had no intention of accompanying this stranger anywhere. "Who are you?"

Now the man became nervous. "I can't tell you that here." But just as Ivo thought he had the advantage, those hairy fingers closed upon his forearm. They were cold but not at all flabby. "It's important."

Ivo's nervousness increased. He touched the useless glasses again, looking away. The long street offered no pretext for distraction: merely twin rows of ordinary Georgia houses, indistinguishable from Carolina houses or Florida houses, fronted by deteriorating sidewalks and slanted parking spaces. The meters suggested monstrous matchsticks stood on end, heads up. Would they explode into fire if the unmitigated glare of the sun continued, or did it require the touch of metal, as of a coin? His fingers touched a warm disk in his pocket: a penny. Thou shalt not park in the noonday sun . . . ?

"I'm sorry," he said. "Good day." He drew his arm free and took a step forward. He had done it! He had made the break.

"Swinehood hath no remedy," the stranger whispered.

Ivo turned about and waited, eyes focused on nothing.

"My car—this way," the man said, taking his arm again. This time Ivo accompanied him without protest.

The car was a rental electric floater, no downtown runabout. The hood was as long and wide as that of any combustion vehicle: room enough for a ponderous massing of cells. The pressure-curtains were sleekly angled. This thing, Ivo judged, could probably do a hundred and fifty miles per hour in the open. His host was definitely not local.

They settled into the front compartment and let the upholstery clamp over chests, abdomens and thighs. The cab bubble sealed itself and cold air drafted from the floor vents as the man started the compressor. The vehicle lifted on its cushion of air so smoothly that only the fringe turbulence visible outside testified to its elevation. It drifted out into traffic, stirring up the dry dust by its propulsion.

There were angry and envious stares from the pedestrians trapped in the wash. Inches above the pavement and impervious to cracks and pebbles, the car eased into the center lane reserved for wheelless traffic.

"Where are you taking me?" Ivo inquired as the car threaded through the occasional congestion, selecting its own route.

"Kennedy."

"Brad's there?"

"No."

"Who are you?"

"Harold Groton. Engineer, Space Construction."

"At Kennedy?"

"No."

Irritated, Ivo let it drop. The key phrase Groton had spoken told Ivo all he really needed to know for the present, and it was not his style to extract meaningful answers piecemeal.

The last leg of the journey was routine. The car moved down the interstate under self-control at almost a hundred miles an hour, and the flat expanse of marsh and scrub was monotonous.

Ivo studied his companion discreetly. Groton no longer seemed quite so fleshy or pallid. Somehow it made a difference that the man had been sent by Brad. Actually, there had been no reason for his initial aversion.

Well, yes, there *had* been—but not a valid reason. Once Ivo had been free of prejudice; he had allowed some to creep into his attitudes. That was not good. He, of all people, should know better.

"That's what you might call coasting on ninety-five," Ivo remarked, glancing at the speedometer after an hour's silence.

Groton's heavy head rotated slowly, brow furrowing. "Interstate 95, yes," he said. "But we're not exactly coasting."

"What I meant was, we're doing ninety-five miles per hour down the Florida coast," Ivo explained, chiding himself for a puerile attempt at wit. Groton wasn't stupid; it was the pun that was at fault. He had tried to make a friendly overture, perhaps in apology for his initial suspicion, and had bungled it.

Coasting on ninety-five, he thought, and winced inwardly. About time he learned that that kind of complicated punning was not amusing to most people—people past twenty-five or so, anyway. Brad, of course, would have picked it up and shot it back redoubled—but Brad was scarcely typical, even in their age group. Ivo suddenly felt extremely young.

"Oh," Groton was saying. "Yes, of course."

Ivo turned away in the awkward silence and brooded upon the landscape again. They were well below Jacksonville, and the slender palmettos were increasingly evident, though still outmassed by the southern pine. A sign promoted ST. AUGUSTINE—OLDEST TOWN IN AMERICA—NEXT EXIT EAST. He wished it were possible to travel for any distance anywhere without constant commercial importunings, but he knew that industrial and other pressures had forced an increasingly liberal interpretation of permissible billboard advertising along the interstate system. Motels, gasoline, batteries, restaurants, points of public interest (as defined, mainly, by private enterprise)—these had seemed justified originally. But once the precedent had been set, erosion had been continuous until public interest was assumed to include even hard liquor, soft hallucinogens and intimate feminine hygiene.

Ahead he spied one of the old-fashioned series signs, clumps of words printed upon each square. He read it sleepily:

> WHAT THE CLOUD DOETH
> THE LORD KNOWETH
> THE CLOUD KNOWETH NOT

Ivo smiled, wondering how this was going to relate to the public service of smoother shaving.

> WHAT THE ARTIST DOETH
> THE LORD KNOWETH
> KNOWETH THE ARTIST NOT?

He snapped awake. Groton sat stolidly beside him, reading a newspaper. Nothing but brush and gravel and occasional plastic containers lined the highway here. That had been no series sign, even in his imagination; it was an excerpt from a poem he knew well, by a poet he had studied well.

Yes, man possessed free-will, unlike the cloud. The artist was responsible for his creation. Predestination did not apply to the sentient individual.

Yet Ivo Archer was traveling to a place he had never seen, obedient to the subtly relayed directive of another person. Free-will?

THIS TOO SHALL PASS, a sign said, a real one this time. He sighed, closed his eyes, and gave in to sleep.

He woke over water: Groton had assumed manual control and was driving across the bridge toward, presumably, the cape. Though Ivo was not enchanted by the mystery surrounding his summons to this place, he could not repress a feeling of excitement. If the end of this journey were not the cape, it had to be—

One of the orbiting space stations?

They were on State route 50. A sign at the far end of the bridge identified Merritt Island; then, shortly, the Kennedy Space Center Industrial Area. This was a neat layout of city blocks with parklike landscaping and elegant buildings, the whole reminding him somewhat of a modern university campus.

"Newest town in America—next exit up," he murmured.

"Close enough," Groton agreed, again mistaking the reference. "There's a post office here, and a telephone exchange, bank, hospital, sewage conversion plant, power station, railroad yard, cafeterias, warehouses, office buildings—"

"Any room for the spacecraft?"

"No," Groton said seriously. The man seemed impervious to irony. "Fifty thousand people work here daily. The vehicles are constructed and assembled elsewhere, and of course the launch pads are safely removed. We're just stopping here for the normal red tape—security clearance, physical examination, briefing and so on. Necessary evils."

"I'm healthy, and I can't be much of a security risk because I was born in Philadelphia, raised hydroponically, and have no idea what I'm doing here."

"Want to gamble that you're in condition to withstand ten gravities acceleration? That your system can sustain intermittent free-fall without adverse reaction, such as violent nausea? That you're not allergic to—"

"I never gamble," Ivo said with sudden certainty.

"As for the security clearance: it isn't what you know now that counts, but how you'll react to what you learn. Good intentions and partial information can lead to the most extraordinary—"

"I get the point. When's liftoff?"

"Just about six hours from now. The shuttle is already being assembled."

"Assembled! What happened to the regular one?"

Groton ignored the question, this time evidently taking sincere uneasiness for humor.

Four hours and a multitude of tests later they were conducted to the Vehicle Assembly Building, a structure of appalling volume. "Largest single building in the world, at the time it was built," Groton said, and Ivo could believe it. "We have two of them now. The Saturn launch vehicles are put together here—"

"Saturn? I thought the Saturn shot took off three years ago."

15

Groton paused to look at him, then smiled. "You're thinking of the *planet* Saturn. You're right; that was an instrumented economy mission set up in '77. A one-shot bypass of all four gas giants. It's adjacent to the planet Saturn right now, and will terminate at Neptune in six years. The same goes for the concurrent Soviet shot, of course."

"So what's with Saturn *here*?"

"The Saturn VI is the name of our *vehicle*. Its major components are assembled here in an upright position, then carried on its mobile launcher to the pad. That enables us to use our facilities efficiently."

"I see," Ivo said, not seeing, but hesitating to blare out his ignorance again. Why was Groton giving him this little lecture-tour, instead of taking him directly to the shuttle?

Away from the giant gray and black Assembly Building he saw a peculiar structure with caterpillar treads. It stood about twenty feet tall and was approximately the size and shape of half a football field. "What's that?"

"Crawler-transporter. Weighs around six million pounds, travels loaded at a good mile an hour."

"I like that space-age speed." Then, before the man had another chance to miss the humorous intent: "Where does it crawl? What does it transport?"

"It crawls over the Crawlerway. It transports the Mobile Launcher."

Ivo refused to give up. "Where does the crawlerway expire? What does the mobilauncher launch?"

"The pad. Us."

"Oh."

A short drive beside the pebbled Crawlerway—a handsome dual track resembling the interstate highway, except that its surface was loose—brought them to the Pad: an irregular octagon over half a mile across. In its center was an elevated pedestal of steel and concrete with a deep trench running through it. Perched upon it, squatting over the trench like a man about a private call, was a platform and tower of metal beams, steadying a rocket three hundred fifty feet tall.

"The Mobile Launcher," Groton said. "With a standard Saturn VI workhorse booster. Rather old design, but reliable."

"And that booster is—"

"Our shuttle."

Somehow Ivo had visualized a pint-sized rocket, a space-dinghy built for two. He should have known better.

The launch vehicle was thirty-three feet in diameter at the base and not much smaller at the top. From a distance the clustered thrust-engines—six of them—appeared diminutive, under the bulk of the vehicle. They were like bowl-shaped buttons sewn on—but up close he'd discovered that each was the size of an igloo. Saturn VI was a monster; Ivo had some inkling of the terrible power leashed within it, since it had to be enough to hurl the entire mass into space.

"This one's a one-stage booster. Nine million pounds of thrust, and it's the most versatile vehicle in the program," Groton said as they ascended in the elevator within the launcher-structure. "Used to take three stages to achieve orbit, but now it's mostly payload. These freighters are usually unmanned, so we'll be the only passengers aboard this time. Nothing to do but relax and enjoy the ride."

"Who touches the match to it?"

"Ignition is automatic."

"Suppose it fizzles?"

Groton did not reply. The lift stopped, and they traversed the high catwalk leading to the minuscule entrance-port near the top of the rocket.

Ivo looked down. The concrete launch-pad looked precariously small from this elevation, and the abutting structures were like so many white dominoes. The great torso of Saturn VI seemed to narrow at the base, with a tiny skirt at the ground.

Ivo found himself gripping the rail, afraid of the narrow height. Groton did not seem to notice.

"Where are you taking me?" Ivo inquired again as the automatic countdown commenced for takeoff. "Is Brad doing research at an orbiting station?"

"No."

"The moon?"

"No."

"Then where—?"

"The macroscope."

Of course! That was where Bradley Carpenter would be!

But the realization triggered another surge of nervousness. Brad would never have summoned him to such a place unless—

Ignition.

Ivo thought the rocket would shake itself apart. He thought his eardrums would implode. He thought he was a dry bean rattling loose in a tin can . . . in a tornado.

Gradually, through the blast of sound and vertigo, he became aware of the meaning and practice of multiple-gravity acceleration. Now his vision was of a medieval torture chamber: tremendous weights slowly crushing breath and life from the fettered victim. Had he undertaken such stress *voluntarily*?

Free-will, where is now thy—

But he knew that it only hit this level for a few seconds. He hoped he never had occasion to endure the same for minutes. His chest was aching as the load upon it reluctantly decreased; his fight for air had not been figurative.

Eventually there was free-fall. Then a bone-bruising jar as the lower segment of the rocket was jettisoned, and a resumption of acceleration, this time of bearable force.

"Hey!" Ivo gasped. "Didn't you say this was a one-stage item? What are we—"

"I said a one-stage *booster*. Not the most economical arrangement to achieve escape-velocity, but reliable. Government wanted to standardize on one model, and this was it. Actually, those discarded shells orbit for a considerable period; quite a few have become useful workshops in space, and eventually we'll run them all down and use the metal for another station. That should make a favorable impression on the taxpayer." Groton seemed to have no trouble talking against the acceleration.

How long would the journey take? He decided not to inquire. The macroscope station was known to be five or six light seconds away from Earth—say about a million miles.

Eventually the second drive terminated and permanent free-fall set in. Groton remained strapped to his couch and fell asleep. Ivo took this as a hint that the remainder of the flight would be long and tedious, since they had nothing to do but ride. He could not even appreciate the view; the single port overlooked nothing but emptiness. He tried to think of it as an evocative withdrawal from

Earth, the Ancestral Home, but his imagination failed him this time. He dozed.

He dreamed of childhood: ten years old in the great city of Macon, population three thousand, three hundred and twenty-three by the latest census, plus a couple thousand blacks. His brother Clifford was eight and baby Gertrude barely two, that summer of '52; he liked them both, but mostly he played Cotton Merchant with his friend Charley. They would set up as dealers, buying and selling, tunneling their warehouses from the rich red clay sides of the deep gully beside the highway. When the big slow wagons bound for the city passed, he and Charley would jump out and grab away handfuls of the cotton to store in the warehouses. If the slaves tending the wagons noticed, they never said anything, so long as the piracy was minimal.

Or picking up hickory nuts for pretend-money or jewelry; or searching for arrowheads, or simply fishing. It was fun out of doors. Nature was beautiful even in the winter, but this was summer.

Sometimes he would wander through the forest, playing his flute, and the neighbors would hear him and just shake their heads and smile, and the slaves would nod with the beat.

Ivo woke as they docked at the macroscope station. Actually, there had been several sleeps and two meals from tubes, but the unstructured time left nothing worth remembering. The free-fall state, too, had disoriented his perception of the passing hours. His life on Earth seemed at once hours and years distant, another plane of reality or memory.

Still there was no excitement. He knew that a complex chain of maneuvers had been accomplished, and that control had been duly shifted from Ground Control to Station Control, possibly with intermediate Controls between, as though the rocket were the baton in a relay race. But none of that had been evident to the passengers. Even the docking was tame; for all that was visible, they might have been stepping from the subway onto the platform back on Earth. Ivo was disappointed; like any tourist, he thought wryly.

A space officer wearing UN insignia was on hand to check them in and to supervise the unloading of supplies.

The lightness of Ivo's body attested to his off-planet location; the station's rotation provided "gravity" via centrifugal force, and this would be the inner ring, with the smallest actual velocity.

There was no physical inspection or other clearance; the over-thorough processes at Kennedy sufficed, apparently, as well they might. But where was he supposed to go now?

"Mr. Archer—report to compartment nineteen, starboard, G-norm shell," the officer said abruptly, making him feel as though he were being inducted into the navy.

"That's it," Groton said. "I'll drop you off—or would you rather find your own way?"

"I would rather find my own way."

Groton looked at him, surprised, but let him go. "G-norm is level eight," he said.

"Section eight. Right." But of course Groton didn't get it.

Ivo dutifully made the traverse, stepping into the lift for the descent to the specified level. The numbers indicating the shells blinked to life as he passed them, very much in the manner of the floors of an apartment building. He fancied that he could feel his weight increase, and that his feet were heavier than his head, specific gravity considered. Did the pull vary that sharply?

Level Eight ignited its bulb, and he hit the "Stasis" button. The panel slid aside to reveal a compartment even more like a subway stop. Two sets of tracks passed the central shaft, and beside them stood several four-wheeled carts. He determined from the placement of the sidings that the track on his right was for travel forward, in relation to his random orientation, and the one on his left was for motion in the opposite direction. Which was Compartment 19?

He didn't let it worry him. He climbed into a cart and secured himself in the sturdy seat, looking for the motor controls. There were none; it was an empty husk, as though it had been jettisoned in orbit. There was a simple mechanical brake set against one wheel.

Ivo shrugged and released the brake. The cart began to move, angling in to intercept the main track, and he realized that it was gravity-powered. Evidently the track tilted down, or outward, allowing the carts to roll until braked. Beautiful; what better mode of transportation, in a torus where power was probably expensive?

He saw the numbers now: 96, 95, 94, each no doubt representing an apartment or office. Those on the right were marked P, those on his left S. Port and Starboard, presumably. Starboard being right, he must be heading for the stern.

Of a *torus*? Exactly where were bow and stern in a hollow doughnut spinning in space? He must be halfway around it by now, but headed in the proper direction, since the numbers were decreasing.

Except that the levels were level, while the track was tilted. More precisely, the shells were curved to match the onionlike circumference of the station, while the track had a larger arc. An obtuse arc? Thus he was headed for the right number—but on the wrong level. Already he was halfway down to the ninth.

Well, one problem at a time. He had declined Groton's assistance, and now would muddle through in his own fashion, as was usually the case. One had to live with the liabilities of one's independence.

There was a vertical shaft between numbers seventeen and sixteen, and he guided the cart onto the siding by judicious manipulation of the brake. The track became elevated here, neatly slowing the vehicle so that only minimal braking was necessary.

He was on the eleventh shell. It occurred to him that what he had actually done was to drift from a tight orbit to a looser one, except that he had gained velocity instead of losing it. Or had he? At any rate, he now weighed a little more than normal, if his estimate could be relied upon.

The shaft was bipart: one side up, the other down. Probably the capsules were looped together, counterbalancing each other, in the interest of further economy of power. He ascended to the eighth level, then walked along the interior mall to apartment Nineteen Starboard.

The name on the door-panel was BRADLEY CARPENTER, as he had expected. No one else could have prepared the particular summons entrusted to Groton. He slid the section aside and stepped in.

A young man turned at the sound: tall, brown of hair

21

and eye, muscularly handsome. Sharp intelligence animated his features. "Ivo!"

"Brad!" They leaped to embrace each other, punching arms and tousling hair in a fury of reacquaintance, two subtly similar adolescents roughhousing companionably. Then both sobered into young adults.

"God, I'm glad you could make it," Brad said, hooking up a hammock and flopping into it. He indicated another for the guest. "Just seeing you brings back my boyhood."

"How could I help it? You sent your boar oinking after me," Ivo complained cheerfully. It was good to postpone the serious ramifications for a while. He set up the hammock and got the swing of it.

"All part of the trade, swine." Both laughed.

"But I have one crucially important question—"

"To wit: which way is Stern?"

Ivo nodded. "That is the question."

"I'm surprised at you, den brother. Haven't you learned yet that your stern is behind your stem?"

"My mind is insufficiently pornographic to make that association."

"Take your bow. It's inevitable."

Ivo smiled amiably, realizing that it was his turn to miss a pun of some sort. He would catch on in due course.

Brad bounced to his feet. "Come on—have to show you the femme. Business before pleasure."

"Femme?" Ivo followed him into the hall, somewhat bewildered still.

Brad halted him momentarily outside the girl's room. "She has a certified IQ of one fifty-five. I told her I was one sixty, okay?"

"Is that the proper mentality for liaison?"

"I'm infatuated with her. What do you expect me to do, humble clay that I am?"

Ivo shrugged. "Clay with the feet of a god."

Brad smiled knowingly and touched the bell. In a moment the panel slid aside, inviting entry.

Here the furnishings were distinctively feminine. Frilly curtains decorated the air-conditioning vents, and the walls were pastel pink. Brushes and creams lined the surface of the standard desk, and a mirror hung behind it to convert the whole into something like a vanity.

Here, Ivo thought, was the residence of someone who

wanted the entire station to know there was a Lady present. Someone who wasn't certain of herself, otherwise?

How many women were here aboard the macroscope station? What was their status, whatever their official capacity? There was something ambivalent about Brad's attitude toward this one.

She appeared from the adjoining compartment. She stood a trifle above medium height, slender of neck, waist, ankle; statuesque of hip and bosom. A starlet type, Ivo thought, embarrassed for Brad's superficiality. Her hair was shoulder-length and quite red, and her eyes as she looked up were contrastingly blue.

"Afra, this is Ivo Archer, my old friend from the neighboring project."

Ivo grinned, feeling awkward for no reason he could say. What was this piece, to him?

"Ivo, this is Afra Glynn Summerfield."

She smiled. Sunrise over the marsh.

Brad went on talking, but Ivo did not hear the words. In a single photographic flash the whole of her had been imprinted upon his ambition.

Afra Glynn Summerfield: prior impressions, prior liaisons—these were nothing. She wore a dress of slightly archaic flavor, with silvery highlights, and her shoes were white slippers.

The lines of her:

> Inward and outward to northward and southward the
> beach-lines linger and curl
> As a silver-wrought garment that clings to and follows the firm sweet limbs of a girl.

Afra: inward and outward, firm sweet limbs, hair the color of the Georgia sunset. Glynn: silver-wrought friend of his friend. Summerfield: his fancy lingered and curled.

Afra Glynn Summerfield: at this glance, beloved of Ivo.

He had thought himself practical about romance, with disciplined dreams. He had accepted the fact that love was not feasible for a person in his unique situation.

Feasibility had been preempted by reality.

"Hey, moonstruck—wake up!" Brad exclaimed cheerfully. "She hits everyone like that, the first time. Must be that polished-copper hair she flaunts." He turned to Afra. "I'd better get him out of here till he recovers. He gets tongue-tied around beautiful girls. See you in an hour, okay?"

She nodded and breathed him a kiss.

Ivo trailed him back into the hall, hardly aware. He *was* shy with girls, but this was of a different magnitude. Never before had he been so utterly devastated.

"Come on. The 'scope will settle your stomach."

Somehow they were already on the first level. They donned light pressure-suits and entered what Ivo took to be an airlock. It was a tall cylinder less than four feet in diameter set pointing toward the center of the doughnut, but at an angle, and it terminated in a bubblelike ceiling.

Brad touched buttons, and the air about them was drawn off and replaced by a yellowish fog. "Now stand firm and clench your gloves together, like this," Brad said, demonstrating. "Make sure your balance is good, and hold your elbows out, but tense, as though you expect to be hanging from them. Let out half your breath and hold it, and don't panic. Okay?" His voice was distorted by the sealed helmets.

Ivo obeyed, knowing that his friend never gave irrelevant instructions. Brad drew out a transparent tube with a filter on one end and poked a tiny spere into it. He screwed a springy bulb to the filter-end.

"Pea-shooter," he explained. "I am young at heart." He aimed the tube directly up and squeezed the bulb sharply.

Ivo saw the streak as the shot went up. Then he was launched into space, somersaulting uncontrollably. The giant torus of the station careened about him, a faceless mouth, the monster bands of its segment-junctures reminding him of the vertical cracks in parched, pursed lips.

A hand caught his foot and steadied him. "You didn't listen," Brad said reprovingly, straight-faced within the bubble-helmet. "I told you to watch your balance." His voice seemed to come from the depths, now conducted only via the physical contact between them.

"I didn't listen," Ivo agreed ruefully. He looked about and found that they were flying toward the center of the station: the fifty-foot metallic ball guyed by nylon wires extending to the inner rim of the torus. He and Brad were still rotating slowly, some of his motion having been imparted to his friend, but in free-fall this was inconvenient rather than distressing. He had to keep adjusting in order to keep his gaze on the destination.

"Don't tell me, let me guess," Ivo said when it was clear that Brad was not going to explain. "You popped a—a bubble, and the atmospheric pressure squirted us out. Since your airgun-spacelock is aimed at the center—"

"I see you have recovered a wit or two. Actually, I was showing off a little; that isn't exactly the approved technique. Wastes gas and is dangerous for the inexperienced, to name a couple of objections. We're supposed to wait for the catapult. Nobody does, of course. Even so, you're wrong about the aim. The tube is tilted to compensate for angular momentum; otherwise we'd miss the target every time because of the spin of the torus. Apart from all that, your guess was fair."

"Uh-huh."

"Now watch your footing as we land." Brad removed his hand, nudging the foot just enough to counter the remaining spin and send Ivo slightly ahead, and he fell upright toward the dark surface of the artificial planetoid.

He saw now that the guys were actually light chains. They merely anchored the mass in place, so that arrivals and departures such as theirs did not jog it out of alignment. Each hooked to a traveling roller magnetically attached, so that the rotation of the doughnut imparted no spin to the ball.

"This is the macroscope proper?" he inquired before remembering that his voice would not carry through the vacuum, now that contact was gone. Obviously it *was* the 'scope, painstakingly isolated from unwanted motions and intrusions. He had no doubt that their approach was being observed, or that it had been cleared well in advance.

The macroscope was the most expensive, important device ever put into space by man. The project had been financed and staffed internationally as research in the public interest: meaning that while no single government had cared to expend such considerable resources on such a farfetched speculation, none could afford to leave the potential benefits entirely to others.

Compromise had accomplished mighty things. The macroscope was functioning, and each participant was entitled to a share of its use proportionate to the investment, and a similar weighted share of all information obtained. That was most of what Ivo knew about it; exactly what hours fell to whom was classified information. Much of the result was general: details of astronomic research that had the astronomers gaping. The scope, it seemed, ground out exceeding fine pictures. Much was concealed from the common man, but the awe this instrument nevertheless inspired was universal.

He thought of it as basically nothing more than a gigantic nose, sniffing out the secrets of the galaxy. It still daunted him.

He landed at last, almost afraid his momentum would jar the machine out of line. Brad came down behind him, controlling his spin to land neatly on his feet. Ivo decided he would have to master that technique; his own touchdown had been awkward.

Brad took his hand so that they could communicate readily. "We'll have to wait for admittance. Could be several minutes if he's in a taping sequence. Just relax and admire the scenery."

Ivo did. He peeked cautiously toward the sunside, knowing that Sol was much fiercer here in space than to an observer sheathed in Earth's atmosphere.

A monster rocket floated there, similar to one he remembered.

"What's a Saturn VI doing *here*? A complete one, I mean. I thought the booster-stage never got out of orbit."

"Correct. This one's in orbit."

"*Earth* orbit, mister innocent. This is sun orbit, if I'm not totally confused."

"Oh, it can travel far—if refueled. That's Joseph, our emergency vehicle. Enough power there to blast us all to safety in a hurry—if ever necessary. Personally, I'd call space safer than tempestuous, seam-splitting Earth. Joseph is actually the tug that nudged the scope into this orbit. Now he's semiretired; no point in sending the old gent home empty."

"Must be quite a lot of oomph when you click your flint under his tail. No gravity—" The thrust, he knew, would not change; but here none of it would be counteracted by planetary drag, so the net effect had to be a much larger payload or higher velocity.

"To be sure. We've been tinkering with him on the QT. He still uses hydrogen as the working fluid, but stores it solid. But no ignition—combustion in a chemical engine is only a means, not an end. It is the velocity of the expelled propellant that counts, you know, rather than the per se heat of the engine, although—"

"Sorry, Brad. I *don't* know. If you *must* get technical—"

"I can make it simple for you, Ivo. I just can't resist bragging a little, because I was the lucky lad who happened to pick the key out of the scope."

"You're actually getting technology from—"

Brad moved a finger in their old-time code for caution. That implied that the question had awkward aspects that could only be cleared up more privately, which in turn implied that their present conversation might be overheard somehow. Perhaps through a pickup in the macroscope housing. And the implications of *that*—

Ivo shut up. Cloak and dagger did not thrill him; it brought back the restlessness in his stomach. Too much had happened in the past few hours.

"We've had the basic theory to adapt a gaseous-core atomic reaction to propulsion for years, but the thing is fraught with peril. We can mix the working fluid—that's the hydrogen we belch from the tail of the rocket to make it go—directly with the fissioning uranium in the chamber. That raises the gas to a temperature that makes possible a specific impulse ten times the best we can do with chemical combustion. But it's *too* hot. It melts any containing material we know of. What I discovered was a heat-shielding technique that—well, Joseph may look ordinary to you, but he's a Saturn VI in outline only. His engine produces a thrust you'd call over ten gravities—and he can keep it up for almost a week before he runs out of hydrogen. He never runs out of *heat*, of course. If you could only appreciate by what factor that outperforms the best Earth has known before—"

"Brad, I am appreciating with fervent fervor. But I'm still a layman. I never had technical training. I'll be happy to take your word it can do the job, whatever the job is."

Speech lapsed. Ivo knew that Brad's feelings were not hurt. They had merely taken the dialogue beyond the danger point—its relevance to the macroscope?—so that it was safe to drop it.

His attention had been on immediate things hitherto, but now he stared beyond the rim of the station, away from the uncomfortably brilliant sun, and saw the stars. He found to his surprise that they were familiar.

Ursa Major—the Big Dipper—was evident, with its dip pointing to Ursa Minor. And just who was Ursa? he always asked himself. That was no lady, that was the wife of a bear! he always replied. Draco the Dragon curled around the Little Dipper. Following the line the Big Dipper pointed on past the Pole star, he could travel at multiple-lightspeed all the way to Aquarius, perpetually chasing Capricornus. The runner was so close, but fated never to catch up. Somehow that saddened Ivo; there seemed to be a special, personal tragedy in it, though he could not determine why he felt that way.

The light he perceived at this instant had been generated by many of those stars over a century ago, or even much longer. Perhaps one of those brilliancies dated from the time he, as a lad of fourteen, had organized a company of some fifty youths like himself, to train with bows and arrows. Thus "Archer"—so fiercely patriotic, as the clouds of national dissension gathered, signifying the end of life as he had known it. Yet he might as readily have been named for the flute with which he used to serenade the young ladies. "Tutor," when he later taught at college, had indeed been corrupted to "tooter" by the students. Or "Plowman," because of the passages he liked to quote from *Piers Plowman*. . . .

He had been cultured then, polite, affable, dignified, replete with moral refinement. Not quite fifteen, he had entered Oglethorpe University at Midway, Georgia, parting his fair hair to the side and brushing it behind the ears. He wore good, but not ostentatious, apparel. Already a hint of a stoop to the shoulders, but brisk of gait. He had no taste for athletics.

There were fifty students at the college.

Music and books were his dearest companions—but those fair young ladies were never quite forgotten.

Once a student misunderstood him and denounced him as a liar. He struck that person immediately, though he was not himself strong. The student drew a knife and stabbed an inch deep into his left side, but he did not capitulate. Never was he known as a coward, then.

"What do you think of Afra?" Brad asked him.

That name brought him instantly back. What availed past courage, when the present battle was lost? "You're serious about her?"

"Who wouldn't be? You saw her."

"Brad, she's a hundred and two per cent cauc in the shade!"

"I'll say! Her DAR pedigree goes back to the Saxon conquest."

Ivo smiled dutifully. "The project—"

"The project's over. You know that. We're free citizens now."

"You can't erase the past. If she knew—"

Brad looked at him oddly. "I told her there were several projects, related but discrete. That I was a washout from the IQ set."

"A washout!"

"What would you call an intelligence quotient of one hundred and sixty, when the target was two hundred?"

"I see. And where did you tell her *I* was from?"

"Nothing but the truth, Ivo. That a private foundation gathered together selected stock from every corner of the sphere and—"

"And bred back to the multiracial ancestor they presumed mankind started from. So I'm Palaeolithic."

"Not exactly, Ivo. You see—"

They were interrupted by the lifting of a panel. Admittance was at hand.

The interior was a cramped mass of panels, but there was room for several people if they watched their elbows. A short tunnel beyond the airlock opened into a roughly spherical compartment. Ivo's first impression was of machinery; there were dials and levers everywhere, projecting from every side. He found it hard to orient because there was no gravity here and no visual "up." Wherever he planted his feet was ground; the slight magnetism that had held him to the outer hull remained effective.

The technician in charge was already getting into his suit. Brad spoke to him in a foreign language, received a curt reply, and said: "Ivo Archer—American." The man nodded politely.

"You see, it is all very carefully arranged," Brad said as they waited for the man to complete his suit-checkout.

"Thirty nations have put up the cash for this project, and each is allotted—but you must know that. We send in precise reports every day."

"This is the American Hour?"

"No. Personnel here don't bother with the official foolishness. This gentleman is not a gentleman—that is, not a Gentile. He's an Israeli geologist doing work for Indonesia. Their own geologist is busy on a private project."

"So somebody is paying off a favor?"

"Right. Indonesia will get the results, and the home state will never know the difference."

"How is it we can horn in, then?"

"I preempted the slot for more important work. He understands."

"Just to show me the macroscope? Brad, you can't—"

The Israeli held up his glove. "It is quite all right, Mr. Archer," he said. "We do not question Dr. Carpenter." He put on the helmet, pressured his suit, and mounted to the airlock. Ivo detected no shock of air puffing out; there were no games of that kind here. Probably the man was hauling himself along one of the guy-chains, not trusting himself to any drift through the vacuum. That was the kind of sensible procedure Ivo preferred.

Brad settled into a control seat of some kind and began making adjustments with sundry instruments. Ivo tried to make some sense out of the battery of dials and lights, but failed; it was far too complicated.

"Okay, friend, we're alone. No bugs here. I'm in a position to know."

Once more the nervousness came upon him. This was it. "Why did you summon me?"

"We need Schön."

Ivo met this with silence. He had known it.

"I don't like to do this to you, believe me," Brad said with genuine apology. "But this is crucial. We're in bad trouble here, Ivo."

"Naturally it wasn't my amiable half-witted companionship you missed. Not just to show off your fancy technology and your fancy girl."

Brad looked far more mature when serious, and he was far more serious now than the literal content of his speech indicated. "You know I like you, Ivo. You're a damned Puritan at heart, and you're afraid of anything that

30

smacks too much of pleasure and what you're doing here in the space age instead of the nineteenth-century Confederacy is beyond me to grasp. I *still* enjoy your company, more than that of Schön, and I wouldn't change one jot of your archaic and poetic fancies. But this is—well, it sounds cliché, but it *is* a matter of world security. It's frankly over my head. If your freak abilities were enough—"

"So playing a simple flute has become 'freak,' and—" But he knew what Brad meant, much as he didn't want to. "And who is an ignorant lad straining at one twenty-five to proffer advice to model one sixty? Particularly when he knows that's a lie for the only one in the project to be adjudged two hundred and—"

"Come off it, Ivo. You know better than anyone that those figures are meaningless. I tell you with all sincerity that the situation is *desperate*, and Schön is the only one I know with the potential to handle it. I have the privilege of calling him when I really need him. Well, it's been twenty years, and I *do* need him. *Earth* needs him. You have to do it."

"I'm not just thinking of myself. Brad, once you let the genie out of the bottle—you know what Schön is. Your work, your girl—"

"I may be giving up everything. I know that. I have no choice."

"Well, *I* have a choice. You'll darn well have to prove to me that the cure is not worse than the problem."

"That's why we're here. I'll have to acquaint you with the nature and function of the macroscope first, though, before I can make my point. Then—"

"Keep it simple, now. I can't even read your dials."

"Right. Basically the macroscope is a monstrous chunk of unique crystal that responds to an aspect of radiation unrelated to any man has been able to study before. This amounts to an extremely weak but phenomenally clear spatial signal. The built-in computer sifts out the noise and translates the essence into a coordinated image. The process is complex, but we wind up with better pictorial definition than is possible through any other medium, bar none. That was a major handicap at first."

"Superior definition is a *problem*?"

"I'll demonstrate." Brad applied himself to the ponderous apparatus, donned a helmetlike affair with opaque goggles, and cocked his head as though listening. Ivo felt another pang of nervousness, and realized that this stemmed from the superficial similarity between the goggles and the sunglasses he had bought when trying to avoid Harold Groton. That entire past episode embarrassed him in retrospect; he had acted foolishly. He threw off the memory and concentrated on Brad's motions.

The left hand hovered over a keyboard of buttons resembling those of a computer input. It probably *was* the computer input, Ivo reminded himself. There was a strap over the wrist to prevent the hand from drifting away in the absence of gravity; buttons could be awkward to depress without the anchorage of bodily weight. The right hand held a kind of ball mounted on a thin rod, rather like an old-fashioned automobile gearshift. As the left fingers moved, a large concave surface glowed over Brad's head.

"I'll cut in the main screen for you," Brad said. "Notice that my fingers control the computer settings; that covers direction, range and focus, none of it simple enough for human reflexes to handle. The vagaries of planetary motion alone, when that planet is not our own, are complicated to account for, particularly when we want to hold a specific focus on its surface."

"I'm aware of planetary motion." He remembered one of his old pet peeves. "I had to work it out when I wanted to criticize the concept of time travel. If a man were granted the miraculous ability to jump forward or backward in time, with no other travel, he'd arrive in midspace or deep underground; because the Earth is always moving. It would be like trying to jump off a moving rocket and jump on again."

"Nevertheless, we do travel in time, with the macroscope," Brad said, smiling.

"Oh, so you're going back to supervise your grandfather's conception?"

"Delicacy forbids." Brad's hands flexed. "I'll center on a precoded location: the planet Earth. The computer uses the ephemeris to spot all the planets and moons of the solar system exactly, and a good many of the asteroids and comets as well. The right-hand knob provides our personal tuning; once the difficult compensations have been made, we use this control to jog over several feet at a time, or to gain different angles of view. Right now we're orbiting the sun about nine hundred thousand miles from Earth—right next door, as interplanetary distances go. Just out far enough to reduce the perturbations of the moon. There."

The screen was a mass of dull red. "If that's Earth, the political situation has deteriorated since I left," Ivo observed.

"That *is* Earth—dead center. Per the coordinates."

"Center? Literally?"

"Definition, problem of, remember. Our corrected coordinates nail the heart of the body. The image is on a one-to-one ratio."

"Life size? It can—"

"The macroscope can penetrate matter, yes. As I told you, this isn't exactly light we're dealing with, though the time delay is similar. That's a representation of the incandescent core of our planet as it was five seconds ago, muted by automatic visual safeguards and filters, of course. We'll have to drift about four thousand miles off that point to hit the surface, which is what most people seem to assume is all the scope looks at. Right there, you can appreciate the implications for geology, mining, paleontology—"

"Paleontology?"

"Fossils, to you. We've already made some spectacular finds in the course of routine roving. Lifetime's work there, for somebody."

"Hold on! I ain't that ignorant, perfessor. I thought the bones were widely spaced, even in good fossiliferous sediments. How can you tell one, when you're in the middle of it, not looking down at it in a display case? You certainly couldn't *see* it as such."

"Trust me, junior. We do a high-speed canvass at a given level and record it on tape. The machine runs a continuous spectroscopic analysis and trips a signal when there's anything we might want. And that's only the beginning."

"A spectroscopic analysis? You said the macroscope didn't use light."

"*It* doesn't, exactly, but *we* do. We keyed it in on samples: every element on the periodic table. Thus we

33

are able to translate the incoming impulse into a visual representation, much as any television receiver does. The truth is, the macrons are far more specific than light, because they don't diffuse readily or suffer such embarrassments as red shift. Spectroscopy is really a superfluous step, but we do it because we're geared to record and analyze light, here. Once we retool to orient on the original impulse, our accuracy will multiply a hundredfold."

"It grinds that fine?"

"That fine, Ivo. We're just beginning to glimpse the potential of this technique. The macroscope is a larger step toward universal knowledge than ever atomics were toward universal power."

"So I have heard. But I'm sort of stupid, as you know. You were about to tell me what makes superior definition so difficult to adapt to, even with the computer guidance."

"So I were. Here is the surface of Earth, fifty feet above sea-level, looking down. Another keyed-in location."

The screen became a shifting band of color.

"Let me guess again. Your snoop is stationary, right? And the globe is turning at the equivalent of a thousand miles an hour. It's like flying a jet at low altitude near the equator and peering out through the bombsight."

"For a pacifist, you have violent imagery. But yes, just about. Sometimes over ocean, sometimes land, sometimes *under* mountains that rise above the pickup level. And if we move higher—" He adjusted the controls, and the scene jumped into focus.

"About a mile up," Ivo said. "Makes the scene clear, but too far for intimate inspection. Yes." He watched the land sliding by. "Why don't we just see a panel of air? What we have now is a *light* image, perspective and everything."

"What we see is the retranslation of the macronic image sponsored by visible radiation passing through that point in space. Maybe I'd better give you the technical data after all."

"Uh-*uh*. Just answer me this: if it's that sharp on planet Earth from five light-seconds, can it also handle other planets? Can it look at Jupiter from one mile up, or even Pluto? If it can—"

The headgear tilted as Brad nodded somberly. "You

begin to comprehend what a magnificent tool we have here. Yes, we can explore the other planets of our solar system, from one mile above ground level—those that have ground—or one inch or anywhere inside. We can also explore similarly the planets of other systems, with so little loss of definition that distance can be ignored."

"Other systems ..." This was distinctly more than he had anticipated. "How far—?"

"Almost anywhere in the galaxy. There is interference from overlapping images near the galactic center that complicates things tremendously, I admit, but the evidence is that there is more than enough of interest elsewhere to hold us for a few centuries of research."

Ivo shook his head. "I must be misunderstanding you. As I make it, our Milky Way galaxy is over a hundred and ten thousand light-years across, and we're about thirty-five thousand light-years from the center. Are you claiming that you can get a life-sized image from ground level of a planet orbiting a star, oh, fifty thousand light-years away?"

"Yes, theoretically."

"Then that's the key to interstellar exploration—without the need for physical travel. Why drive to the show when you can see it on TV?"

"Precisely. But we are hampered by those mundane practicalities just discussed. We can compensate to a considerable extent for rotary and orbital and stellar motions—but not every planet is the sitting duck Earth is." He twitched a finger and the fifty-foot elevation resumed, this time motionless. "Properly programmed, the computer can direct a traveling focus and follow the dizzy loops of a particular planetary locale, as it is doing now, and provide a steady image. It's a pretty fine adjustment, but that's what the machinery is for. At least we know the necessary compensations."

"And you don't know the motions of planets the regular telescopes can't pick up. But you should be able to figure them out soon enough from the—"

"We can't even *find* those planets, Ivo. It's the old needle-in-haystack problem. Do you have any proper idea how many stars and how much dust there is in the galaxy? We can't begin to use our vaunted definition until we know exactly where to focus it. It would take us years of educated searching to spot any significant proportion of the planets beyond our own system, and there's such a demand for time on this instrument that we can't afford to waste it that way."

"Um. I remember when I dropped a penny in an overgrown lot. I knew where it was, within ten feet, but I had to catch a bus in five minutes. Don't think I've ever been so mad and frustrated since!" His fingers felt the coin in his pocket again: he had missed the bus but found the penny, and he still had it.

"Make that penny a bee-bee shot, and that lot the Sahara desert, and instead of a bus, a jet-plane strafing you, and you have a suggestion of the picture."

"*Now* who's using violent imagery? I'll buy the bee-bee and the desert—but the jet fighter?"

"I'll get to that pretty soon. That's why we need Schön. Anyway, we'd need thousands of macroscopes to afford that type of exploration, and even this one is precariously funded. There's more important research afoot."

"More important than geology, when the Earth's resources are terminal? Than the secrets of the universe? Than questing into space in the hope that somewhere there is intelligent life: than the possible verification that we are not unique in the universe, not alone?" He paused, abruptly making a quite different connection. "Brad, you don't mean there's political interference?"

"There is, and it's serious, but I wasn't thinking of that. Sure, we can snoop out military secrets and get the dirt on public figures—but we don't. I admit I picked up a dandy shot of a starlet taking a shower once, and you'd be surprised what goes on in the average suburban family situation at the right hour. But aside from the ethics of it, this is picayune stuff. It would be ridiculous to try to spy on the antics of three billion people with this thing, for the same reason we can't try to map the planets of the galaxy. Be like using the H-bomb to drive out bedbugs. No, we're thinking big: interstellar communication."

Ivo felt a cold thrill. "You *have* made alien contact! How far away are they? What about the time delay? Do they—"

Brad's smile was bright under the goggles. "Ease off, lad. I didn't say we'd made contact, I said we were thinking of it, and we haven't forgotten the time-delay problem for a moment." His hands began to play upon the controls. "I have hinted at some of the problems of routine exploration and charting, but we do have techniques that are nonroutine. Time delay or no, we have a pretty good notion of the criteria of life as we know it, and—well, look."

The screen became a frame around an alien landscape. In the foreground rose a gnarled treelike trunk of yellow hue and grotesque convolution. Behind it were reddish shrubs whose stems resembled twisted noodles dipped in glue. The sky was light blue, with several fluffy white clouds, but Ivo was certain this was not Earth. There was an alienness about it that both fascinated him and grated upon his sensibilities, though he could not honestly identify anything extraordinary apart from the vegetation.

"All right," he said at last. "What is it?"

"Planet Johnson, ten light-minutes out from an F8 star about two thousand light-years from us."

"I mean, what is it that bothers me about it? I know it's alien, but I don't know how I know."

"Your eye is reacting to the proportions of the vegetation. This is a slightly larger world than ours, and the atmosphere is thicker, so the trunk and stems are braced against greater weight and heftier wind-pressure, and react differently than would an Earth-plant in a similar situation."

"So *that's* how I knew!" he laughed.

Brad manipulated the controls again and the scene switched. This was a higher view of a grassy plain, though it was odd grass, with stalagmites rising randomly from it. Low mountains showed in the hazy distance.

"Earth or alien?" Brad inquired, teasing him.

"Alien—but I can't tell a thing about the air or gravity, even unconsciously. What is it this time?"

"Those projections have two shadows."

Ivo made a gesture of knocking sawdust from his ear.

"This is Planet Holt. There are some fine specimens of pseudo-mammalian herbivores here, but I'd have to search for them and it isn't worth the effort right now. I'd probably lose the image entirely if I took it off automatic. This one circles a G3 star five thousand light-years away."

"So this picture is five thousand years old?"

"This scene is, yes, since it takes that long for the macronic impulse to reach us. I told you we traveled in time, here."

Brad returned to the controls, but Ivo stopped him. "Hold it, glibtongue! If this planet circles one, count it, *one* star—where does that second shadow come from?"

"Thought you'd never ask. There is a reflective cliff behind our pickup spot—another typical outcropping of Holt's crust."

"So my subconscious reasoning was spurious after all. How many of these things have you found?"

"Earthlike planets? Almost a thousand so far."

"You told me you couldn't locate planets—"

"Particular planets we can't. But with luck and sound analysis, we get a few. These are only a minuscule fraction of those available, and we've probably missed most of the closest ones, but chance plays a dictatorial part in such discoveries. Our thousand planets are merely a random selection of the billions we know are there."

"And they all have trees and animals?"

"Hardly. We only name the important ones. Less than two hundred have any life at all we can recognize, and only forty-one of *those* have land-based animals. Chief specialization seems to be size. I can show you monsters—"

"Maybe next time. I like monsters; I feel a personal affinity for them because they always get the negative characterizations in the science fiction reruns. I could romp with them for hours. But to the point: have you found *intelligence?*"

"Yes. Watch." Brad shifted scenes.

A tremendous hive appeared. Walls and tunnels were built upon themselves in a mountain, and fluid filled many wholly or in part. Strange squidlike creatures splashed and swam and climbed through the maze, disappearing and reappearing so thickly that Ivo could not tell whether he ever saw the same individual twice.

"This is Planet Sung, about ten thousand light-years distant. We have studied it with ferocious intensity the past few months, and we don't much like the implications. They are quite alarming, in fact."

The image was traveling over the planet, showing open water and desert land, with frequent warren-mountains inhabited tightly by the semi-aquatic creatures. Ivo was reminded of pictures he had seen of the beaches where walruses congregated; no vegetation showed at all. He wondered what the Sung denizens ate.

"This is intelligence? I haven't seen anything very alarming or even impressive, yet. Just a termite-society with very little pasture. Surely they aren't planning to loft a bomb at Earth?" But his scoffing covered what was beginning to be a discomforting degree of awe. This was a genuine extraterrestrial planetary species, and the very realization of its existence was nearly overwhelming.

"They hardly care about Earth. Remember, we were in our tedious prehistory at the time we see them now. I have no doubt that they are extinct at present."

The picture framed an individual burrow. Close up, the occupants seemed a lot less like seals or squids. Their bodies were fishlike but seemingly clumsy, with heavy fins or flippers at the sides and a trunklike tube behind. Two great frog-eyes were mounted on top, pointing mainly backward. The tube appeared to be prehensile, like the proboscis of an elephant.

"This is the closest you have found to civilization? Creatures who live in multiple-story beaver houses and splash in puddles?"

"Don't underestimate them, Ivo. They are technologically advanced. Ahead of us, actually. They've had the macroscope for a century."

Ivo looked harder, but saw only a small domicile with several fat fishlike creatures lolling listlessly in what he was sure was tepid water. Now and then one squirted a jet of liquid from its trunk and slid backward—or perhaps forward—from the reaction. "Maybe you'd better give me some more background. I'm missing something."

"I'll give you their edited paleontology. We've been into their libraries and museums as well as their bedrooms—yes, they have all three, though not like ours—and we have copied some of their animated texts. We haven't dubbed in any sound yet—this is still in progress—but I'll provide the running commentary." He switched from the live scene to film. "Behold: the species history of the proboscoids—'probs' for short—of Sung."

And Ivo was immersed in it, absorbing picture and commentary as one. He witnessed Sung as it had been millions of years in the past: mighty forests of ferns upon the land, and of sponges under the ocean. From that rich water came the lungfish types, gulping the moist dense atmosphere, and soon their soft egg-capsules hatched on land. Predators broke them open before the sun did, until survival dictated hatching within the body: live birth. Even then the tiny newborn were vulnerable, and natural selection brought forth at last the successful compromise: the placentile amphibian. This was the stem stock for the class of animal that was to dominate the planet. From its fifty-million-year radiation emerged its successor.

The primitive proboscoid was not an imposing order. Its families swam the shallow oceans by jetting water through their snouts, and climbed clumsily upon the shores with their flipper-fins. They were timid; their eyes were fixed upon the predators from whom they retreated, not upon their destinations. When they died, they died in flight, sometimes in panic, smashing into obstacles and killing themselves needlessly. Yet they were adept in motion; the funneled water could be aimed in any direction by a twist of the snout, and in some families it was impregnated with a foul-tasting substance that discouraged the pursuer. Their sense of smell sharpened; they were always alert to danger.

One genus retreated to the rocks of the treacherous surf, the area no other mobile creature desired for a habitat. The seas varied with the tide, and that tide of two near moons seemed to have a malignant passion. The great rounded rocks rolled about, crushing whatever lay beneath and wearing channels into the beach and ocean floor, then jumping into new territory as alternate currents converged and clashed. There was safety for neither land nor sea creature.

These probs became complete amphibians, their original breathing apparatus adaptable to either air or water and thriving on the combination. They developed the wit to read the shifting currents, to anticipate the tides, and to crawl from channel to channel when danger came. When large sea-predators ventured too far within the shoals, the probs arranged to divert certain currents and to isolate and perhaps strand the enemy. When land-dwellers set foot in the water, they too could be tempted into the traps of nature. Still timorous, the probs developed the taste for flesh.

Then the land uplifted and the shoals passed. It was the time of desperation for the probs, and few survived, for they could not compete with the established land and sea creatures in either complete habitat. One species, the cleverest, learned to make a home where nature provided none. Unable to run fleetly or swim swiftly or take to the air, it employed its still-generalized limbs to excavate trenches at the shoreline and to bring the water in. Labyrinths were formed, confusing to predators. Those who did enter found dead ends or narrow channels that inhibited progress, while stones were dumped upon them or shafts poked through cross-trenches.

Later those stones and shafts were adapted to construction, and the age of tools and weapons had come. The trunklike appendage, no longer required fully for locomotion, became refined for manipulation; the flippers lost what swimming facility they had had and became strong excavators. The brains increased in size. Communication of high order became essential. Air, vibrated through the snout, developed into a hornlike dialogue.

The labyrinth, in the course of a hundred thousand years, developed into something like a city.

Nature heaved again and the city was destroyed—but so were the habitats of many other creatures. The probs rebuilt; the less intelligent or adaptable animals perished. The probs lost much of their timidity, and their appetite for flesh increased.

Success brought population pressure, and the attendant demand for more food and more living space. In this manner the first colony was organized, instead of the prior lemminglike exoduses to relieve the situation. Perhaps the first successful colony was merely the last of the blind departures. It was not clear how individuals were selected to go or to stay, but a complete spectrum of builders, hunters and breeders were to be found in each party. The first colony settled several hundred miles away from the home grounds, upon another shoreline. The second went farther.

At last the shores of all the continents of the planet were riddled with maze-cities.

Now there was nothing shy about the probs. Large and sleek, they encroached upon the territories of ancient enemies. Organized and clever, they conquered. They

41

brought their habitat with them inland, developing methods of pumping and aerating and holding water above the level of the sea. Technology had come upon them.

Greater and greater ingenuity was required as the terrain became less habitable. Rain fell less frequently, and better pumps were developed; edible animal life diminished, and better breeds had to be fostered. The prob snout could now be reversed, to grip objects by its suction and move them about, but it was weak; it became easier to use this slight strength and great dexterity to build machines, and to let the machines accomplish the heavy labors.

With the conquest of the continents and the continued decimation of the vegetation, animals and minerals there, the probs next turned their technology toward really efficient food production. Sea-farms provided meat; hydroponics replaced the rest. Their science expanded to meet the new challenges, and reached into the very sky and on into space. Yet this required enormous power, and their world was already depleted by the wasteful ravagement of centuries past. They sought to colonize another world, just as they had the shores and continents of Sung, but could not afford the time and equipment for prolonged and inefficient interstellar travel.

Yet technology continued, though their world was starving. They developed the macroscope—and shied away from its revelations. Their land surface was a mass of watery warrens, their ocean a thoroughly parceled plantation. Those who could not afford to pay their debts were butchered; those who could not achieve sufficient success in life gained a few years of rich living by selling their bodies in advance for meat. It was a fashionable and comfortable mode of suicide, and at present some fifty percent of the individuals sublimated their lemming-instinct in this fashion. Yet the birthrate, fostered by competent medicine and the basic boredom of life, was such, and the average span of life before termination so long, that the population still nudged upward. The irreplacable resources of the planet plummeted.

"Why don't they control their population?" Ivo demanded. "They're breeding their way into extinction! Surely they can bring their birthrate down readily. They have the equipment for it."

"Why don't we human beings bring *ours* down?"

Ivo thought about that a moment and elected not to answer.

"I had a dream the other night," Brad said, still wearing the helmet and goggles though he obviously did not need to supervise the continuing image. It made him resemble some futuristic visitor from space, in contrast to his words. "I was standing on the top of a mountain, admiring the miracles my people had wrought upon the face of the Earth and on the structure of neighboring space, and I saw a live prob. It was a male proboscoid, very old and large and ugly, and it stood there upon a tremendous mountain of garbage and slag and bones and looked at me. Then it flopped down into the sludge of refuse and splashed it in my direction so that I flinched, and lifted its trunk and laughed. It laughed through its nose with the sound of a mellow horn, multiphonically, so that the melody seemed to come at me from all directions.

"At first I thought it was amused at my upright, stout-legged stance that we have always assumed was necessary for any truly competent creature. Then it seemed that the mirth was directed at my entire species, my world itself. The peals of it went on and on, and I realized that it was saying to me, in effect, 'We've been this route and now we're gone. It is your turn—and you are too foolish even to learn by our example, that we spread out so plainly for you!' And I tried to answer it, to refute it, to stand up for my people, but its humor overwhelmed me and I saw that it was already too late."

"Too late?"

"Look at the statistics, Ivo. There may have been a quarter of a billion people in the world at the time of the birth of Christ. Today there are that many in the United States alone, and it is sparsely populated compared to some. The population of the world is increasing at a record rate, and so are its concurrent ills: hunger, frustration, crime. If our projections are accurate—and they are probably conservative—we have barely one more generation to go before it starts. That means that you and I will be on hand for it—and at a vulnerable age."

"Before *what* starts? *What* will we be on hand for, apart from the affluence of the twenty-first century?"

"The inevitable. You saw it with the probs. And a few

43

glimpses at the ghettos of the world—and some entire nations are ghettos—through the macroscope ... I tell you, Ivo, things are going on right now that are horrifying. Remember Swift's *A Modest Proposal?*"

"Look, Brad, I'm *not* a professor. I don't know what you're getting at."

"Ivo, I'm not trying to tease you with my erudition. Some statements just aren't comfortable to make too baldly. Jonathan Swift wrote, facetiously, of a plan to use the surplus babies of Ireland for food. The irony was, he made a pretty good case for it—if you took him literally, as a certain type of person might. He suggested that 'a young healthy child well nursed is at a year old a most delicious, nourishing, and wholesome food, whether stewed, roasted, baked, or boiled ...' He attributed the information to an American, incidentally, and perhaps his tongue wasn't so firmly in his cheek as he would have us believe. He commented that such consumption would lessen the population—Ireland being severely crowded at the time—and give the poor tenants something of value to sell while lessening the expense of maintaining their families."

Ivo developed that unpleasantly familiar tingle in limbs and stomach. "Exactly what have you seen?"

"There is already a going business in the ghettos of certain populous countries. A bounty is paid on each head, depending on the size and health of the item. Certain organs are sold black market to hospitals—heart, kidneys, lungs and so on—who don't dare inquire too closely into the source. The blood is drained entirely and preserved for competitive bidding by institutions in need. The flesh is ground up as hamburger to conceal its origin, along with much of the—"

"Babies?"

"Human babies. Older bodies are more dangerous to procure, and suffer from too many deficiencies, though there is some limited traffic in merchandise of all ages. Most are stolen, but some actually are sold by desperate parents. It is cheaper than abortion. The going rate varies from a hundred to a thousand dollars, depending on the area. It really does seem to be a better thing for some families than trying to feed another mouth; their lives are such that existence is no blessing. But of course they get nothing when their children are stolen."

"I can't believe that, Brad. Not cannibalism."

"I have seen it, Ivo. On the macroscope. There was nothing I could do, since no government on Earth will admit the problem, and an accusation of this nature would backlash to suppress the use of the scope itself. People demand their right for self-delusion, particularly when the truth is ugly. But as I was saying, in another generation it will become a legal institution, as it did with the probs. A proposal no longer so modest."

Ivo kept his eyes on the screen. "I don't see that what happened to the probs *has* to happen to us. The danger exists, sure, okay, but inevitable? Just because *they* came to it?"

Brad's fingers moved over the controls. Ivo saw that the section for the macroscope-picture was comparatively simple; most of the massed equipment was probably for unrelated adjustments. The scene shifted.

"You're being subjective," Brad said. "Compare these."

And the screen showed an angelic humanoid face, feminine and altogether lovely. The eyes were great and golden, the mouth small and sweet. Above the still features flowed a coiffure of down, neither hair nor feathers, greenish but softly harmonious. Below the face a silken robe covered a slender body, but Ivo could tell from its configuration that the gentle curves of the torso were not precisely mammalian. It was as though a human woman had evolved into a more sublime personage, freed from the less esthetic biological functions.

It was a painting; as Brad decreased the magnification the frame came into view, then the columns and arches of an elegant setting. A museum, clean and somber, styled by a master architect.

"Intelligent, civilized, beautiful," Ivo murmured. "But where are the living ones?"

"There are no living creatures on Planet Mbsleuti. This is a royal tomb, as nearly as we can ascertain—one of the few to be buried deeply enough to endure."

"Endure *what?*"

Suddenly the scene was a heaving sea of sludge, breaking against a barren beach. Ivo could almost smell the contamination of the smoky atmosphere.

"Total pollution," Brad said. "Earth, air, water. We have analyzed the content and determined that all of it is artificial. They became dependent on their machines for their existence, and could not control the chemical and atomic waste products. Want to bet where they got their fresh meat, just before the end? But it only hastened their extinction as a species."

The picture of the royal woman was back, mercifully, but Ivo still saw her devastated world. "Because they overextended their resources?" he asked, requiring no answer. "Would not limit themselves until Nature had to do it for them?" He shook his head. "How long ago?"

"Fifteen thousand years."

"All right," Ivo said defensively. "That's two. Any other technological species on tap?"

"One more." Brad adjusted again, and a landscape of ruins came into view. After a time a grotesque four-legged creature shambled along a pathway between two overgrown mounds of rubble. Matted hair concealed its sensory organs, and it walked with its toes curled under—like a gorilla, Ivo thought. It looked sick and hungry.

"As we make it, civilization collapsed here less than five hundred years before this picture," Brad said. "Population reduced from about ten billion individuals to no more than a million, and is declining. There *still* isn't enough to eat, you see, and naturally no medicine. Most surviving plants are diseased themselves. . . ."

Ivo did not bother to inquire whether the hunched creature was a descendant of the dominant species. Obviously it had once been bipedal.

Of course three samples did not make a conclusive case. They could be three freaks. But, unwillingly, he was coming to accept the notion that Man might well be a fourth such freak. Overpopulation, pollution of environment, savagery—he refused to believe that it *had* to proceed to species extinction, but certainly it *could*.

Yet the sample *was* atypical, for there were no neolithic-era cultures. Chance would place many more species in this stage. . . .

"It was from the probs I got the heat-shielding technique," Brad said, allowing the subject to shift. He had brought the picture back to Sung, their planet. "We're still working on their books and equipment, and we're learning a great deal. And if we're lucky, one day we'll discover a *really* advanced civilization, one that has licked this problem of overbreed, and learn how to undo the damage we have done to our own planet. The macroscope has the potential to jump our science ahead more in days than it has progressed in centuries hitherto."

"I yield the point. This is major. But——"

"But why am I wasting time on you, instead of researching for the solutions to the problems of mankind? Because something has come up."

"I gathered as much," Ivo replied with gentle irony. *"What* has come up?"

"We're receiving what amount to commercial broadcasts."

Ivo choked over the letdown. "You can't even tune out local interference? I thought you operated on a different wavelength, or whatever."

"Alien broadcasts. Artificial signals in the prime macroscopic band."

Ivo digested this. "So you *have* made real contact."

"A one-way contact. We can't send, we can only receive. We know of no way to tame a macron, but obviously some species does."

"So some stellar civilization is sending out free entertainment?" His words sounded ridiculous as he said them, but he could think of no better immediate remark.

"It isn't entertainment. Instructional series. Coded information."

"And you can't decode it? That's why you need Schön?"

"We comprehend it. It is designed for ready assimilation, though not in quite the manner we anticipated."

"You mean, not a dit-dot building up from $2 \div 2$ or forming a picture of their stellar system? No, don't go into the specifics; it was rhetorical. Is it from a nearby planet? A surrender ultimatum?"

"It originates about fifteen thousand light-years away, from the direction of the constellation Scorpio. No invasion, no ultimatum."

"But we weren't civilized fifteen thousand years ago. How could they send us a message?"

"It is spherical radiation. That's another surprise. We assumed that any long-reaching artificial signal would be

47

focused, for economy of power. This has to be a Type II technology."

"I don't—"

"Type I would be equivalent to ours, or to the probs' level of power control. Type II means they can harness the entire radiation output of their star. Type III would match the luminous energy of an entire galaxy. The designations have been theoretical—until recently. Presumably this message is intended for all macroscope-developing cultures within its range."

"But—that's deliberate contact between intelligent species! A magnificent breakthrough! Isn't it?"

"Yes it is," Brad agreed morosely. On the screen, the hulking mound of indolent probs continued its futile activity. "Right when we stand most in need of advice from a higher civilization. You can see why all the other functions of the macroscope have become incidental. Why should we make a tedious search of space, when we have been presented with a programmed text from a culture centuries ahead of us?"

Ivo kept his eyes on the screen. "The probs had the macroscope, and this program should have been around for at least five thousand years then. Why didn't they use it? Or were they in the opposite direction, so it hadn't reached them yet?"

"They received the program. So did the humanoids, we believe. That was part of the trouble."

"You told me that they stopped using their macroscope, though. That strikes me as learning to read, then burning all your books. They should have used the alien instruction and benefited from it, as we should. The alternative—or are you saying that we'll wash out if we have to take advice from an elder civilization?"

"No, we're agreed here at the station that the benefits of a free education are worth the risks. Mankind isn't likely to get flabby that way. For one thing, we'd be pursuing all other avenues of knowledge at the same time, on our own."

"What's stopping you then?"

"The Greek element."

"The—?"

"Bearing gifts; beware of."

"You said the knowledge would not hurt us by itself—

and what kind of payment could they demand, after fifteen thousand years?"

"The ultimate. They can destroy us."

"Brad, I may be a hick, but—"

"Specifically, our best brains. We have already suffered casualties. That's the crisis."

Ivo finally turned away from the prob scene. "Same thing happen to them?"

"Yes. They never solved the problem."

"What is it—a death-beam that still has punch after ten or fifteen thousand years? Talk about comic books—"

"Yes and no. Our safeguards prevent the relay of any physically dangerous transmission—the computer is interposed, remember—but they can't protect our minds from dangerous information."

"I should hope not! The day we have thought control —"

"Forget the straw men, Ivo. We *do* have drug-induced thought control, and have for years. But this—five of the true geniuses of Earth are imbeciles, because of the macroscope. Something came through—some type of information—that destroyed their minds."

"You're sure it wasn't something internal? Overwork, nervous breakdown . . . ?"

"We are sure. The EEG's—I'd better explain that—"

"You simplified things for me with that pepped-up rocket you call Joseph. You simplified them again describing the macroscope. It's like income-tax forms: I don't think I can take another explanation."

"All right, Ivo. I'll leave the EEG's out of it. Just take my word that though we haven't performed any surgery, we know that this alien signal caused a mental degeneration involving physical damage to the brain. All this through concept alone. We know the hard way: there are certain thoughts an intelligent mind must not think."

"But you don't know the actual mechanism? Just that the beamed program—I mean, the radiated program— delivers stupefaction?"

"Roughly, yes. It is a progressive thing. You have to follow it step by step, like a lesson in calculus. Counting on fingers, arithmetic, general math, algebra, higher math, symbolic logic, and so on, in order. Otherwise you lose the thread. You have to assimilate the early portion of the

49

series before you can attempt the rest, which makes it resemble an intelligence test. But it's geared so that you can't skip the opening; it always hits you in the proper sequence, no matter when you look. It's a stiff examination; it seems to be beyond the range of anyone below what we term IQ one fifty, though we don't know yet how much could be accomplished by intensive review. A group of workmen viewed it and said they didn't go for such modernistic stuff. Our top men, on the other hand, were fascinated by it, and breezed through the entire sequence at a single sitting. Right up until the moment they—dropped off."

"They can't be cured?"

"We just don't know. The brain of an intelligent man does not necessarily have more cells than that of a moron, any more than the muscle of a circus strongman has more than the ninety-seven pound specimen. It all depends on the competence of the cells that are there. The cells of the genius have many more synapses—more connections *between* cells. This concept from space seems to have introduced a disruptive factor that acts on those extra synapses. That puts it beyond stereotaxic surgery—" Anticipating Ivo's renewed objection to the technical language, he broke off and came at it again. "Anyway, it is the expensive watch that gets hurt most by being dropped on concrete."

"Ah, this cheap watch begins to tick. I might look at it and yawn, but if *you*—"

"I don't think you'd better view it, Ivo."

"Anyway, I admit it's a pretty neat roadblock. If you're dumb, you lose; if you're smart, you become dumb."

"Yes. The question is, *what is it hiding?* We have to know. Now that we've felt its effect, we can't simply ignore it. If an elementary progression visually presented after being filtered through our own computer can do this, what other nasty surprises are in store? We can't be certain the danger is confined to the programmed broadcast. There may be worse traps lurking elsewhere. That may be why the probs lost their nerve."

"Worse than imposed idiocy?"

"Suppose someone came through it, but subtly warped—so that he felt the need to destroy the world. There are those at this station who very well might do it, given the proper imperative. Someone like Kovonov—he just may be more intelligent than I am, and he's a lot more experienced. The scope could provide him with exact information on military secrets, key personnel—or perhaps he could derive some incomprehensible weapon. . . ."

"I finally begin to see your need for Schön."

Brad removed the headpiece, blinked at Ivo, and nodded. "Will you——?"

"Sorry, no."

"You aren't convinced? I can document everything I've told you. We have to have access to the information available from space, from this Type II source. We fear that mankind will not bring down its birthrate or reduce its population in any other disciplined fashion, or even make sane use of the world's expiring resources. The problem is sociological, not physical, and no dictated solution we can presently conceive will overcome that barrier. We *must* go to the material and technology of the stars, before we begin—literally—eating ourselves. There *is* no salvation on Earth. The macroscope evidence—you've seen just some of it—is inarguable."

Ivo remained recalcitrant. "All right—all right! I accept that, for the moment. I'm just not sure yet that the situation requires this measure."

"I don't see how else I can put it, Ivo. Schön is the only one I believe has a chance to handle it. We don't dare tune in that band on the macroscope until we clear this up, and if any of it extends into the peripheral——"

"I didn't say no-final. I said no-presently. I don't have enough information, yet. I'd like to take a look at those casualties, for one thing. *And* the mind-blasting series. Then I'll think about it."

"The casualties, sure. The sequence, no."

"I have a notion, Brad. How about letting me work it out my own way?"

Brad sighed, covering his frustration with banter. "You always did, junior. Stubbornest mortal I know. If you weren't my only key to Schön——"

It was no insult. They both knew the reason for that stubbornness.

CHAPTER 2

Afra Summerfield was waiting for them at the torus airlock. She spoke to Brad as soon as his helmet came off: "Kovonov wants to see you right away."

Brad turned immediately to Ivo. "That Russian doesn't chat for the joy of it. There's trouble already, probably political, probably American, or he wouldn't ask for me. I have to run. You won't object if I dump you on Afra?" He was out of his suit and moving away as he spoke.

Who was this Kovonov who compelled such alacrity?

Ivo looked at Afra, and found her as stunning as before. She was in a blue coverall, with a matching ribbon tying back her hair, the whole almost matching her bright eyes. The astonishing revelations in connection with the macroscope had diverted his mind from her for an hour, but now he was smitten with renewed force.

"Take your time!" he yelled magnanimously, but Brad was already in the elevator. Afra smiled fleetingly, showing a dimple and striking another chord upon his fancy.

Ivo did not believe in love at first sight, ridiculous as it was to remind himself of that now. He did not believe in coveting one's neighbors things, either, but Afra overwhelmed him. It was a measure of Brad's confidence in

52

himself that he flaunted her so casually, heedless of her impact on other men.

"I suppose I'd better show you the common room," she said. "He'll look there first for us, when he's free."

The thought of accompanying her anywhere in any guise excited him. The imponderables of mankind's future receded into the background as Afra preempted the foreground. For the moment, her person and her attention belonged to him, however casual the connection might be. There was pleasure merely in walking with such a beautiful girl, and he hoped the tour would be a long one.

"Are you going to help us, Ivo?" she inquired, the implied intimacy of her use of his first name sending another irrational thrill through him. He felt adolescent.

"What did Brad tell you about me?" he countered. Her perfume, this close, was the delicate breath of a single opening rose.

She guided him to the elevator, now returned from Brad's hasty use. "Not very much, I must admit. Just that you were a friend from one of the projects, and he needed you to get in touch with another friend from another project. Shane."

He had not realized before how small these elevators were. She had to stand very close to him, so that her right breast nudged his arm. *It's only cloth touching cloth,* he thought, but couldn't believe it. "That's Schön, with the umlaut over the O. The German word for—"

"Why of course!" she exclaimed, delighted. Her intake of breath delighted him, too, but for an irrelevant reason. "That never occurred to me—and I have spoken German since I was a girl."

She was still a girl, as he was acutely aware. He felt the need to keep the conversation going. "Do you speak any other languages?" Adolescent? *Infantile!*

"Oh, yes, of course. Mostly the Indo-European family—Russian, Spanish, French, Persian—but I'm working on Arabic and Chinese, the written form of the latter for now, since it covers so many spoken forms. The Chinese symbols are based on meaning rather than phonetics, you know, and that presents a different set of problems. I feel so parochial when Brad teases me with Melanesian or Basque or an Algonquin dialect. I hope you're not another of those fluent linguists—"

"I flunked Latin in high school."

She laughed.

Ivo tried to untangle the physical reaction he experienced from the intellectual content of their conversation, afraid of a Freudian slip. "No, I mean it. 'Schön' is the only foreign word I know."

She studied him with perplexed concern. "Is it a— a mental block? You're good at some things, but not at—"

The elevator ride finally ended, and she disengaged her torso from his. They climbed into a cart. Now it was her thigh that distracted him, wedged against his. Could she be unaware of the havoc she wrought along his nerve connections—his synapses? "I guess Brad didn't tell you about that. I'm no genius. I *am* pretty good at certain types of reasoning, the way some feeble-minded people can do complex mathematical tricks in their heads or play championship chess—but apart from that I'm a pretty ordinary guy with ordinary values. I guess you thought I was like Brad, huh?" *Fat chance!*

She had the grace to blush. "I guess I did, Ivo. I'm sorry. I heard so much about Schön; then you came—"

"What *did* he tell you about Schön?"

"That would fill a small manual by itself. How did you come to meet him, Ivo?"

"Schön? I never did meet him, really."

"But—"

"You know about the projects? The one he—"

She looked away, and the loose ponytail flung out momentarily to brush his cheek. *Is she a conscious flirt?* No, she was being natural; *he* was the one reacting. "Yes," she said, "Brad told me about that too. How Schön was in the—free-love community. Only—"

"So you see, I did not actually share lodging with him."

"Yes, I was aware of that. But why are you the only one who knows where to find him?"

"I'm not. Brad knows. Other members of the project know, though they never talk about it."

This time her flush was frustration, and he felt the angry flexure in the muscle of her leg. *She doesn't like to be balked.*

"Brad told me you were the only one who could summon him!"

"It's an—arrangement we have."

"Brad knows where Schön is, but won't go for him himself? That doesn't sound like—"

The journey by rail was over, no tunnel of love. "Brad *can't* go for him himself. I guess you could call me an intermediary, or maybe a personal secretary. An answering service: that's closest. Schön simply won't come out for anyone unless I handle it. He doesn't involve himself with anything that isn't sufficiently challenging."

"An alien destroyer that has our whole exploratory thrust stymied—isn't that enough?"

So she knew what Brad had told him. "I'm not sure. Schön is a genius, you see."

"So Brad has informed me, many times. An IQ that can't be measured, and completely amoral. But surely *this* is cause!"

"That's what I'm here to decide."

They arrived at the common room: a large compartment of almost standard Earth-gravity, with easy chairs and several games tables. Ivo wondered what billiards or table-tennis would be like in partial gravity. Beside the entrance were several hanging frameworks: games ladders with removable panels. On each panel was a printed name.

"Who's Blank?" he asked, reading the top entry of the first.

"That's a real name," she said. "Fred Blank, one of the maintenance men. He's the table-tennis champion. I don't really think they should—I mean, this room is for the scientists, the PhD's. To relax in."

"The maintenance men aren't supposed to relax?"

She looked a little flustered. "There's Fred now, reading that magazine."

It was a Negro in overalls and unkempt hair. Beside him sat a Caucasian scientist, portly and cheerful. Both looked hot; evidently they had just finished playing a game. It seemed to Ivo that Afra was the only one disturbed, and that told him something about both her and the other personnel of this station. The scientists respected skill wherever they found it; Afra had other definitions. The portly white for the moment probably envied Blank his facility with the paddle, without being concerned with such irrelevancies as education.

In the center of the room stood a pedestal bearing a

shining statuette mounted at eye level. Ivo paused next to contemplate this honored edifice. It was a toy steam-shovel, of storybook design, with a handsome little scoop. The cab was shingled like the top of a country cottage, with a delicately sagging peaked roof and a bright half-moon on the door. Within the jawed shovel was a ball like a marble, and so fine was its artistry that he could see the accurate outline of the continent of North America etched upon the surface of that little globe.

The pedestal bore the ornate letters S D P S.

"What does it mean?"

Afra looked embarrassed again. "Brad calls it the 'Plat-inum Plated Privy,'" she murmured. quiet though no one else was close. "It really is. Platinum plated, I mean. He—designed it, and the shop produced it. The men seem to appreciate it."

"But those letters. S D P S. They can't stand for—"

She colored slightly, and he liked her for that, sensing a common conservatism though their viewpoints in other respects differed strongly. "You'll have to ask him." Then she shifted ground. "Here we are talking about unimpor-tant things and ignoring you. Where do you come from, Ivo? That is, where did you settle after you left your project?"

"I've been walking around the state of Georgia, mostly. All of us who participated in the project were provided with a guaranteed income, at least until we got estab-lished. It isn't much, but I don't need much."

"That's very interesting. I was born in Macon, you know. Georgia is my home state."

Macon! "I *didn't* know." But somehow he *had* known.

"But what interested you about that state? Do you know someone there?"

"Something like that." How could he explain ten years of seeming idleness, retracing the various routes of a native son?

She didn't press him. "I should show you the infirmary, too; Brad did mention that. I suppose he wants you to be able to describe it accurately to Schön."

They traveled on. Ivo wondered what was supposed to be so important about the infirmary, but was content to wait upon her explanation. He was learning more about

her every moment, and positive or negative, he was eager
for the information.

"One thing I don't understand," Afra fretted, "is why
Schön was in that other project. He should have been
with Brad."

"He was hiding. Do you know the parable about the
good fish?"

"The good fish?" Her brow furrowed prettily.

"The good fish that the fisherman caught in the net and
gathered into vessels, while the bad were cast away. Mat-
thew XIII:48."

"Oh. Yes, of course. What is the relevance?"

"If you were one of the fish in that lake, which kind
would you want to be?"

"A good one, naturally. The whole point of the parable
is that the good people shall find favor with God, while
the bad ones will perish."

"But what *happens*, literally, to the good fish?"

"Why, they are taken to the market and——" She paused.
"Well, at least they aren't wasted."

"While the bad fish continue to swim around the lake,
just as they always did, because no fisherman wants them.
I'd rather be one of them."

"I suppose so, if you take it that way. But what has that
to do with——" She broke off again. "What did they *do*
with the geniuses in Brad's project?"

"Well, I wasn't involved in that. But I would guess
Schön wanted to live his own life, unsupervised by the
experimenters. So he hid where they would never find
him. A bad fish."

"Brad had no trouble. I know he didn't fool them any
more than he fooled me. He's a lot more intelligent than
he says he is."

Ivo remembered that Brad had represented himself to
her as IQ 160. "That so? He always seemed pretty regular
to me."

"He's like that. He gets along with anybody, and you
really have to get to know him before you realize how
deep and clever he is. He was the big success of the
project—but of course you know that. Even if he does try
to claim he's stupid compared to Schön. I used to think
he made Schön up, just to amuse me; but since this
crisis—"

"Yeah. That's the way it was with me too, in a way. But now I sort of *have* to believe in Schön, much as I might prefer to forget all about him, or there isn't much point in hanging around."

She smiled. "I'd tell you not to feel sorry for yourself, if I didn't so often feel the same way. Nobody likes to feel stupid, but around Brad—"

"Yeah," he said again.

They entered the infirmary. It carried the usual aseptic odors, the normal aura of spotless depression. "These are the—five," she said, bringing him to a row of seated men. "Dr. Johnson, Dr. Smith, Dr. Sung, Dr. Mbsleuti and Mr. Holt. All most respected astronomers and cryptologists."

"Johnson? Holt? Sung? I've heard those names before."

"Yes, Brad would have mentioned them, if you weren't already familiar with their reputations. The significant planets they discovered were named after them. Did Brad explain—?"

"He showed me some planets. I didn't realize—well, never mind. I know now."

He looked at the seated men. Dr. Johnson was a saintly-looking man of perhaps sixty, with iron hair and brows and deep lines of character about the eyes. His gaze was direct and compelling, but fixed, as though he were concentrating on some transcendent intangible.

"Doctor," Ivo said, stepping close. "I admired your planet, with its noodle plants and yellow trees."

The serene gray eyes refocused. The firm jaw dropped; then, after a second or two, the lips parted. "Huh-huh-huh," Johnson said. A trace of spittle overlapped one corner of his mouth.

"Hello," Afra said distinctly. "Hel-lo."

Johnson smiled, not closing his mouth. A waft of ordure touched them.

"That's what he's trying to say," Afra explained. "Hello. He was always courteous." She sniffed. "Oh-oh. Nurse!"

A young man in white appeared, a male nurse. "I'll take care of it, Miss Summerfield," he said. "Perhaps you'd better leave now."

"Yes." She led the way out of the infirmary. "They don't have much control," she said. "We're trying to reeducate them, but there hasn't been enough time yet to

58

know how far they can recover. It's a terrible thing that happened to them, and we still don't—"

Brad was coming swiftly down the hall. "Crisis," he said, joining them. "There's an American senator coming, an ornery one. Someone leaked the mind-destroyer to him, and he means to investigate."

"Is that bad?" Ivo asked.

"Considering that we haven't released the information yet to anyone beyond the station, yes," Brad said. "Don't be fooled by our candor with you, Ivo. This is super-secret stuff. We've been fudging reports from all five victims, just to keep up appearances while we try to break this impasse. Until we crack it, no one leaves this station—no one who knows, I mean."

"What about that man who brought me? Groton?"

"He can keep his mouth shut. But all he knew, then, was that I needed you, where to find you, and what to say to you once he got you alone."

That explained the stalking. Groton hadn't wanted to make contact in the crowd, though he had finally had to.

"But don't misjudge him," Afra said. "Harold and Beatryx are very warm people."

Did that mean Groton was married? Ivo had not pictured that. It proved again how far off first impressions could be.

"Here's the situation," Brad said, bringing them to his room. "Senator Borland is on his way. He's class-A trouble. Borland is a first-termer, but he's on the make already for national publicity, and he's ruthless. He isn't stupid; in fact, there's a distinct possibility he's smart enough to get hooked by the destroyer sequence. It's certain he'll demand to see the show, and there will be merry hell if we try to fob off a substitute."

"But you can't show him the destroyer!" Afra exclaimed, alarmed.

"We can't hold it from him, if he's determined—and he is. He knows he's on to something big, and he means to make worldwide headlines before he finishes with us. Kovonov put it to me straight: Borland is American, so he's my baby. I have to neutralize him somehow until we can crack this thing open and get it under control, or the whole feculent mess will erupt."

"When's he due?" Ivo asked.

"Six hours from now. We only got the hint when he embarked, and it took until now to pin down his purpose. He's a real old-fashioned loudmouth, but he can keep a secret when it pays him to and he's no political amateur. He's obviously had this in mind for some time, and now he's coming to milk us for that vote-getting publicity."

"Why not tell him the truth, then? If he's that savvy, he should be willing to do something constructive for his votes, instead of—"

"The truth without the solution would wreck us—and put Borland on his party's next Presidential ticket. He isn't interested in *our* welfare, or in the future of space exploration. He'd be delighted to take credit for pulling America out of the macroscope."

"But the other countries of the world would keep it going, wouldn't they? Isn't it under nominal UN control?"

"More than nominal. They might indeed—in which case we'd become a has-been power in a hurry, as other breakthroughs like my heat-shield are achieved. America can't possibly match the alien science we know is there, once it becomes available. Or—the macroscope project might founder, frightened off by talk of a death-ray from space. The average populace has a profound distrust of advanced space science, perhaps because it doesn't match the old, space-opera conception. People might accept the notion of astronauts plunging into space fearlessly in rockets, but the ramifications of relativistic cosmology and quantum physics—"

"How about just giving the senator what he wants—a gander at the sequence, if it comes to that?"

"What would it settle? Either it would pass him by, in which case he'd have 'proof' that we were killing off world-famous scientists by less exotic means than claimed—an international conspiracy, naturally—or it would hit him. Then we'd have five scientists *and* a U.S. senator to explain."

Ivo shrugged. "I guess you're stuck, then."

"Our only chance is to crack the case before he gets here. For that we need Schön even more urgently."

"There isn't time to fetch him from Earth now," Afra pointed out.

Brad did not reply.

"I'm not sure Schön would help, anyway," Ivo said. "He might not care about America, or the macroscope."

"What *does* he care about?" Afra demanded.

Brad cut off any reply. "Let's take a break. We're acting as though no one else in the station is concerned."

Afra started to protest, but he put his finger to her lips and forced her to subside. Ivo could see that she accepted from Brad what she would have taken from no other person. On the face of it, her objection was reasonable. Brad had dropped a bomb in their laps with a six-hour fuse, then called intermission as though the matter was of indifferent concern. How could this spirited creature know that Brad had already done his utmost to summon the cavalry, or that the break he recommended was hardly the nonchalance it appeared? Yet she trusted him.

Oh, to have a girl like that . . .

The "break" was in the form of a rather elegant dinner with the Grotons. Ivo had assumed that Harold Groton was an ad hoc emissary, and had to revise his impression of the man once again. Brad's social taste was always good.

Beatryx, Harold's wife, was a plumpish, smiling woman somewhere in her forties, light-haired and light-eyed but probably never lovely in the physical sense. Their apartment was quite neat in an unobtrusive manner, as though the housekeeper cared more for convenience than for appearance, in contrast to the tale told by Afra's habitat. Ivo had the impression of stepping into an Earth-building, and thought he might glimpse a street or yard if he looked out a window. If he could find a window.

He found something better. The Grotons were situated at the edge of the torus, where the white-walls would be on a tire. The station was oriented broadside to the sun, so that one wall continuously faced the light and the other remained in shadow. This was the dark side. There was a large port looking directly out into the spatial night.

"It varies with the season." Brad said, noting the direction of his attention. "The station is a planet, technically, and does have an annual cycle. It rotates to provide weight for the personnel, and that rotation gives it gyroscopic stability. It maintains its orientation in an absolute sense while revolving about the sun, so its day becomes

61

sidereal. Three months from now that view will be twi-
light, and in six it will be full noon, and they'll have to
block it off with hefty filters."

Ivo looked out at the uncannily steady stars of this
arctic night. "They're moving!" he exclaimed, then felt
foolish. Of course they seemed to be moving; the torus
was spinning, so that the heaven as viewed from this
window rolled over in a complete circle every few minutes
as though tacked to a cosmic hub. They were the same
stars and constellations he had seen from the macroscope
housing, but this porthole vantage changed his perspective
entirely. It was, literally, a dizzying sight.

They all were smiling. "It's hard to believe they're
exploding outward, those stars," he said somewhat lamely.

"Most of the ones you see aren't," Afra said. "They're
members of our own Milky Way galaxy, a comparatively
steady unit. Even the other galaxies of our local group are
maintaining their positions pretty well."

Ivo realized that he had stepped from one inanity into a
worse one. But Beatryx, coincidentally, came to his rescue. "Oh," she inquired. "I thought every galaxy was flying
away from every other one at terrible speed. Because of
that big argument."

"The so-called big bang," Brad said, without smiling this
time. "You are right, Tryx. *Groups* of galaxies are moving
apart, or at least appear to be from our lookout. But this
should be a temporary state, and the reversal may already
be in process, since our universe is finite and falls within
the calculated gravitational radius. A few more years of
observation with the macroscope, and we'll have a better
idea. Assuming we can get around the galactic interference limitation."

"Reversal?" Beatryx was worried. "Do you mean everything will start flying *together?*"

"Afraid so. It will be quite crowded, by and by."

"Oh," she said, distressed.

"Yes, five or six billion years from now things may
really be hopping."

Brad was teasing her, a little cruelly Ivo thought, and it
was his own turn to come to the rescue. "What's this
galactic interference? You're not talking about the——"

"No, not about the destroyer. This is less blatant. Within the galaxy the scope of the macroscope is absolute——"

but we can't seem to get any meaningful images from other galaxies. No natural ones, that is. Nothing but a confused jumble that fades in and out. So our assorted telescopes are still superior for the million and billion light-year range."

"The Big Eye and the Big Ear are better for long distance than the Big Nose," Ivo observed.

"We're confident that advances in the state-of-the-art will bring the macroscope up to snuff, however."

"Meanwhile, I suppose you can make do with the local galaxy," Ivo said. "With a hundred billion or more stars to sniff in three or four dimensions."

"And every planet and speck of dust, given time," Brad agreed. "We can see them all, virtually—assuming we get the scopes and manpower to look."

"Four dimensions?" Beatryx again.

"Space-time continuum," Brad said. "Or, in human terms, our old problem of travel-time. The farther away the star we're looking at, the older it is, because of the time it takes our macrons to get here. This doesn't matter much when we snoop Earth, because the delay is only five seconds. The entire diameter of our solar system is only a matter of light-hours. But Alpha Centuri is four years away, and an intriguing monster like Betelgeuse—'Beetlejuice' to cognoscenti—is three hundred. That civilized species on Sung, the probs, that I showed Ivo today is ten thousand years away. So our galactic map, the moment we made it, would be out of date by a variable factor ranging up to seventy thousand years. Unless we recognize that added dimension of time, we're hopelessly fouled up."

"Oh."

"If we had some form of instantaneous travel—and that isn't in the cards, in this framework of reality—we'd still have the darndest time visiting that Sung civilization, presuming that it existed today," Brad continued. "We'd have to assume that our instant system was posted on universal rest, and that's trouble right there. Our galaxy is moving and spinning at a considerable rate. A star thirty thousand light-years distant would be nowhere near our mapped coordinates—even if they were entirely accurate by our present frame of reference."

"Why not orient on the galaxy, then?" Ivo asked. "The

stars are pretty stable relative to each other inside it, aren't they?"

"Too easy, Ivo. That implies that the galactic rotation can be ignored, and it can't. You jump thirty thousand light-years toward galactic center and you carry a sizable energy surplus with you. Angular momentum must be conserved. It's like the Coriolis force, or Ferrel's Law on Earth. You—"

"If I may," Harold Groton said, interrupting him politely. "I have been this route myself. Ivo, did you ever whirl a noisemaker at the end of a string?"

"No, but I know what you mean."

"And you know what happens when you pull it short?"

"Buzzes around twice as fast."

"That's what happens when you pull in toward the center of the whirling galaxy."

"*If* we had instantaneous transport," Brad said. "But the problem is academic, so I suppose it doesn't matter if our maps are outdated before we can make them up."

The meal was done, and Ivo realized that he had enjoyed it without paying any attention to what it was. Chocolate cake for dessert, and—

"Come on, Bradley," Groton said. "Relax your top-heavy mind with a sprout."

And light wine, and—

Brad laughed. "You never give up. Why don't you take on Ivo?"

Groton obligingly turned to Ivo. "Are you familiar with the game?"

"And mashed potatoes—" Ivo said, then blushed as they glanced at him in concert. He had to stop letting his thoughts run away with him! "Uh, the game. I guess not, since I don't know what you're talking about."

Afra was looking restless again, and now Ivo was also beginning to wonder. Brad *knew* he wasn't going to have Schön for the coming crisis with officialdom. Why did he persist in this party-game banter? It was costing crucial time. Brad should be setting things up to divert the senator and postpone disaster.

Still, what could any of them do, but play along? Brad's mind operated far more subtly than most people suspected, and he never gave up on a problem.

Groton brought out a sheet of paper and two pencils.

"Sprouts is an intellectual game that has had an underground popularity with scientists for a number of years. There are several variants, but we'll stick to the original one this time; it's still the best." He put three dots on the paper. "The rules are simple. All you do is connect the dots. Here, I'll take the first turn." He drew a line between two dots, then added a new dot in the center of that line. "One new spot each time, you see. Now you connect any two, or loop around and join one to itself, and add a spot to your line. You can't cross a line or a spot, or join a spot that already has three lines connected to it. The new ones formed on the lines actually have two connections already made, you see."

"Seems pretty simple to me. How is the winner determined?"

"The winner is the one who moves last, before the spots run out. Since two are used up and only one added, each turn, there is a definite limit."

Ivo studied the paper. "That's no game," he protested. "The first player has a forced win."

Brad and Afra laughed together. "Nabbed you that time, Harold, you old conniver," Brad said.

"I'll be happy to play second," Groton said mildly. "Suppose we start with a simple two-dot game, to get the feel of it?"

"That's a win for the second player."

Groton glanced at him speculatively. "You sure you never played this game before?"

"It's not a game. There's no element of chance or skill."

"Very well. You open a three-spot game, and I'll take my luck with that nonexistent chance or skill."

Ivo shrugged. He marked a triangle of dots

and drew a line between the top and the left, adding a spot to the center.

Groton connected the center spot to the isolated one.

Ivo made a loop over the top of the figure.

Groton shrugged and added to it.

Two more moves put an eye inside and a base below.

Ivo finished it off with an arc across the bottom, leaving Groton with two points but no way to connect them, since one was inside and the other outside.

"Now," Groton said, "how about trying it for higher stakes? Say, five or six spots?"

"Five is the first player's win, six—" he paused for a moment—"six is the second's. It's still no game."

"How can you know that?"

Brad broke in. "Ivo's special that way. He knows—and he can beat us all at sprouts, right now, I'm sure."

"Even Kovonov?"

"Could be."

Groton shook his head dubiously. "I'll believe that when I see it."

Ivo looked up and caught Afra looking at him intently.

"Sorry," he said awkwardly. "I thought I explained about that. It's nothing. Just a trick of reasoning. I've had it as long as I can remember."

"You interest me," Groton said. "Would you mind telling me when you were born?"

"Don't do it, Ivo!" Brad said. "You'll be giving away all your life secrets."

"He will *not!*" Afra cried. "Why be ridiculous?"

Ivo looked at each of them, trying not to linger too long on Afra's face, so lovely in its animation. "Have I missed something?" *Again?* he added internally.

"Harold is an astrologer," Brad explained. "Give him your birthday to the nearest minute and he will draw up a horoscope that really has your number."

Groton looked complacently pained. "Astrology *is* a hobby of mine. You may consider it a parlor game, but I'll stand by its validity when properly applied."

Ivo regretted his involvement in this dialogue, not because he was at all concerned with the subject but because he saw that he was being used to tease the man. He could not decide that he liked Groton, but cruelty, even this mild, was not in his nature. Brad sometimes seemed to be insensitive to the foibles of those less intelligent than he. "March 29th, 1955," he said.

Groton noted it on a little pad. "Do you happen to know the exact time?"

"Yes. I saw it on the record, once. 6:20 a.m."

Groton noted that too. "And I believe you mentioned that you were born in Philadelphia. Pennsylvania or Mississippi?"

Ivo tried to remember when he could have mentioned such a fact. "Pennsylvania. Does it make a difference?"

"Everything makes a difference. I could explain if you're interested."

"Let's not make this a classroom session," Afra said impatiently. Ivo could see that there were parameters of insensitivity about her, too; or perhaps it was merely impulsive emotion. She was like a race-horse, fretful, impatient to be moving, and unappreciative of the more devious concerns of others.

Why had Brad desired a race-horse?

Why did Ivo?

"Interesting figure of speech," Groton said, seemingly

unperturbed. "Astrology might well be taught in the class-room. I wish I had been exposed to it a dozen years earlier."

"I don't *understand*," Afra said with measured frustration, "how a competent engineer like you can take up with a common superstition like that. I mean, really—!"

"Didn't you teach in the classroom once, Harold?" Beatryx inquired, breaking in so gently that it took Ivo a moment to realize that she was intercepting a developing argument. Afra and Groton must have been through a similar dialogue before, and the good wife knew the signs. Ivo could read them himself: the stolid man replying seriously to facetious questions, never losing his temper, while the excitable girl worked herself into a frenzy. Perhaps Groton defended astrology merely because it was ludicrous, subtly or not-so-subtly baiting her.

Had he been sympathizing with the wrong person? Afra was beautiful and brilliant, but her temperament betrayed her. She might actually be at a disadvantage in this type of encounter.

No—Brad would have broken up any such contest.

Groton had said something, and Afra had pounced on it, while his mind drifted, and now somehow Groton was launched into a narration of his teaching experience. This had, it developed, predated his marriage to Beatryx. Ivo listened, finding to his surprise that he was interested. There was much more to Groton than he had thought.

". . . volunteered. I suppose quite a number of professional people were as naïve as I was. But the company I worked for then—remember, this was back in '67 or '68—had no sympathy with the striking teachers, and offered time off with full pay for any employee who was willing to give it a try. And of course the temporary salary from the school system was extra. So a number of us engineers set out to show the dissident teachers that *we* valued a functioning school system, even if *they* didn't, and that we were ready and able to preserve it, no matter how long they threw their collective tantrum. After all, we were as qualified as they were, since we all had BA's, MA's or doctorates in our field, and plenty of practical experience too. That's the way it looked to me at the age of twenty-seven, at any rate."

He paused, and Afra did not break in with any irate

remark this time. She was interested too. Beatryx had succeeded in pacifying things.

Twenty-seven. Two years older than Ivo was now. He could picture himself in that situation readily enough, however, assigned to fill in at a school where about half the regular teachers were out on their illegal strike. Technically, it was a mass resignation subject to withdrawal upon satisfaction . . . a transparent veil.

He dressed in a careful suit, trying to appear composed though his pulse raced with stage fright at the coming confrontation with a juvenile audience. Would he remember what to say? Would he be able to present clearly what was so well-defined in his own mind? It was so important that the material be properly covered.

This particular high school had not been able to keep all the classes going, and some of the lower grades were home, but there seemed to be kids everywhere. Boys were running down the halls and screaming, throwing books on the floor and collecting in noisy huddles; there seemed to be nobody with the authority to bring order. As Ivo waited with the other volunteers for briefing and specific assignments he observed some pretty heavy petting going on in a doorway, but the passing teachers ignored it. He had forgotten how mature, physically, sixteen- and seventeen-year-old girls were. Two boys broke out in a fight directly in sight of the principal's office; the harried executive simply stuck his head out, yelled "Break it up!" and glared until they ran off. The lovers were also startled out of their preoccupation, and sidled to a more distant doorway before resuming their courtship. Otherwise, chaos reigned.

His classroom was at the end of a wing, in the technical section. He was lucky, as it turned out: he was "in his field." Some of the engineers from his company found themselves trying to teach English or History, and one even wound up babysitting a Spanish class. The kids kept jabbering Spanish at him, and laughing, and he couldn't tell whether it was legitimate drill or dirty jokes at his expense. Ivo was to feel queasy, later, just thinking about that; it was like nakedness on a stage.

He stood before thirty-five senior engineering students. They were, in that quiet before the storm, reasonably

69

orderly, watching him intently. What should his first words be? How should he break the ice?

No problem: he called the roll. The principal had made that tediously clear. They could put up with a few fire-crackers and water balloons in the halls, but they could not omit that roll. It seemed that the state paid so much per head per day in class, and the school mustn't miss a head. Still, it did help control the situation. A kid running up and down the halls or necking in a corner did not get credit for attendance unless he got into his classroom in a hurry. So rollcall was not as stupid as it seemed at first.

Easier said than done. He did not know those boys by sight, and had to take their word when they answered to the names he laboriously pronounced. There was increasing merriment that he thought stemmed from his errors in pronunciation—until two answered at 'once on "Brown" and he realized that they were covering for an absent student.

He remembered, with relief, the seating chart. He could check them that way ... as soon as each boy was seated where he belonged. "All right, engineers—you know where you sit. Move. From now on, I want every one of you in the proper place."

"My place is home!" one quipped, and the rest joined in with a too-boisterous laughter.

His next task was to discover where they stood in engineering, so that he could start teaching meaningfully. It was a general course, mostly electronics, and the textbook was good except that it was sadly out of date. He would have to extrapolate from it, filling in the advances of the past decade, or the training would be almost useless.

One of the boys casually took out a cigarette and lit it.

Ivo snapped to classroom awareness. "Hey! You—" he looked at the seating chart—"Boonton. What are you doing?"

"Smoking," the boy replied, as though surprised at the challenge.

"Isn't there a school rule against student smoking?"

"It's permitted for seniors in the technical wing, sir."

Ivo looked about, suspecting that the boy was lying. Others in the class were covering smirks. They were trying the substitute out, as he had been warned they would.

This was the time for toughness. The principal had put it plainly to the group of volunteers: "Either the instructor rules the students or the students rule the instructor. If you're weak, they will know it. Put your foot down. The whole authority of the public school system stands behind you. Most of our kids are good kids, but they need to be governed firmly. Don't let the few bad apples take over."

Platitudes galore, he had thought at the time—was it only an hour ago?—but probably good advice. Now was the time to apply it. He affected a boldness he did not feel and laid down the local law.

"I don't care what the technical-wing rules are for what grades. I will not permit the fire hazard of smoking in my classroom. Put that weed away immediately."

Then they all were on him. "What do you mean?" "Mister Hoover lets us smoke!" "How do you expect us to concentrate?" "Cheeze!"

Ivo hesitated, suddenly unsure. He did not want to be a martinet. "All right, Boonton. You may smoke in class—" there was a spontaneous cheer—"*if* you can show me a note from the principal approving it."

Silence.

Then the boy jumped up. "I'll go see him right now! He'll tell you it's okay!"

Ivo let him go. He spent the rest of the period trying to pin down how much the boys knew about engineering of any type and how far into the text they had progressed. It was hard, taking over a functioning class from another teacher, and he could see that much effort would inevitably be wasted in the changeover, simply because of the differing styles of the two men.

Boonton never came back. Ivo didn't have time to be concerned with that. Probably the principal had been busy.

The bell rang for the end of the period, and he realized that he had really accomplished nothing. All he had done was call the roll and argue about smoking and try to find some place to start. As they cleared out and the next bunch came in, he remembered that he hadn't even given them a homework assignment. What a beginning!

The room was a mess. Balls of paper littered the floor, chairs were scattered, assorted slop was on the desks and strands of colored wire lay in odd places. And here he had to do it all over again with a new class!

Somehow he made it. But that afternoon he received a note from the principal, suggesting that he try to settle his problem in class instead of aggravating the students and involving the front office. That was how he learned that Boonton had simply gone home for the day with a story about being prejudicially kicked out of class by a temporary teacher. His mother had called the principal in a fury, and the reprimand was being duly relayed to the concerned teacher.

Ivo reread the note, appalled. No one had bothered to check his version of it. It appeared that any student could make any charge against any teacher—and be believed without question.

There were limits. He went to the principal's office at the beginning of his daily free-period, but the man was too busy to see him. Finally he settled down in the teachers' lounge and wrote a report covering the situation. That neatly used up the time he had planned to use for reviewing the lessons for the following day, but at least it would settle the matter.

"Ha!" Afra said.

Ivo was jolted back to reality: this was Harold Groton's experience, not his own.

"I was dead tired the end of that first day," Groton continued. "As nearly as I could tell, I had cleaned up enough debris and mispronounced enough names to last me for a normal year—but I hadn't taught anybody any engineering. And to top it all off, I received three calls at my home from irate parents complaining about my mistreatment of their hard-working angels. The last one was at one a.m. I think that was when I really began to understand what it meant to be a teacher.

"The next day was worse. The word was out that I could be taken. Everyone seemed to know that I'd had trouble with the office, and the students were determined to run me down. They talked out of turn, they slept in class, they looked at comic books; I couldn't make all of them pay attention all the time. I saw that few of them cared about the subject or had any real thought for the future, and the ones who needed instruction most were the ones who refused even to listen when it was offered. They drew pictures of girls and hotrods in their notebooks, and there was always some obscene word on one of the blackboards. I'd erase it, not making an issue of it—as I'd been advised—but another would be there again next period. There'd be an anonymous noise while I was talking—a clicking or a harmonica note or something similar—and it would stop the moment I did. I couldn't ignore it because every time it happened the whole class got out of control and became noisy, and I couldn't pin it down either. And the thing was, they knew as well as I did what would happen if I cracked down on anyone and sent him to the principal's office for discipline. *I'd* get spoken to, not the student, for letting things get out of control. It was *my* responsibility.

"Hell," Groton said, "is a roomful of rebellious juveniles—and a pusillanimous administration. I was committed, and I refused to quit—but I became obsessed with the progress of the negotiations between the state authority and the FEA."

"FEA?" Ivo asked.

"Florida Education Association. That was the teachers' group, and they still may be, for all I know. I really came to appreciate their stand. I never worked so hard in my life, in the face of such abuse. Oh, the newspapers were full of editorials! 'Wonderful Volunteers Filling In For Errant Teachers,' 'Nobody Cares About Our Innocent Children,' 'Governor Unavailable For Comment' and so on. But I was in a position, as I had not been before, to comprehend the truth. The boys were a lot less innocent than the editorialists! I was a scab—a strikebreaker—and while I think there may have been some better way to protest, the teachers certainly had compelling arguments on their side.

"The extra pay had seemed nice at first, like so much lagniappe. It enhanced my normal gross by a good fifty percent. But it wasn't worth it! For one thing, my time was never my own; I was grading papers every night and trying to do something about the ones with identical mistakes—pretty sure sign of cheating, but not *proof*—and preparing for the next day's sessions. I had trouble sleeping. I kept seeing those vulpine young faces peering at me, waiting for any slip, eager for my attention to wander so that they could sling another spitwad at the windowpane. And I realized that their regular teacher had to do this all the time—for no more pay than that fifty percent!

"But the worst shock came at the end. The teacher walkout collapsed after a couple of weeks, and most of them came back to fill their old places. I went back to my own job with voluminous relief. It was the weight of the world off my shoulders! But I paid one more visit to that school, after things were settled, because I wanted to meet the man I had replaced. I wanted to apologize to him for my ignorance and interference, and congratulate him for being a better man than I was. The education had been mine, really, and I had learned a lot of respect for him, knowing how good a job he had done under such conditions. I had seen his books and records, and knew he was a very fine engineer, too; *he* was right up to date, even if the texts he had to use weren't.

"But he wasn't there. His classes had been redistributed among other teachers. The school board had refused to hire him back. It turned out that he was an officer of the FEA, and one of the organizers of the walkout. So the board had its revenge on him and those like him, even though they were among the best teachers in the system. The mediocre teachers they kept; those were not 'troublemakers' who insisted on pushing for school improvements. I learned that this was happening all over the state, and I knew that the educational system there was never going to be the same again. They had brutally purged their most dedicated men and women, the ones who cared the most, rather than admit that the teachers' complaints were valid."

"Why didn't they pay their teachers more?" Ivo asked. "Buy better texts, and so on? Why did they let so many other states forge ahead where it counted?"

"The state was in a financial bind at the time. If they had allocated more for the teachers, they would have had to do the same for the other neglected professions—the police, the social workers, even migrant labor. That would have meant an increase in taxes—"

"Oh."

"Or a closing of tax loopholes," Brad added. "And that would have been even worse for the special interests in power at the time."

74

Ivo had a sudden vision of the proboscoids of planet Sung, abusing their resources into extinction. *This is how it happens,* he thought. Public apathy led to control by the special interests and unscrupulous individuals, and the trend was disastrous.

Had Brad known that the conversation would take this turn? Was this his way of showing Ivo that the tide had to be turned at this last frontier, the frontier of space? Senator Borland, representing the reactionary power of—

Groton smiled. "I'm sorry; I didn't mean to run on like that. I don't usually—"

"You never told me, dear," Beatryx said.

"Nobody likes to advertise his mistakes. That's why I tried to forget what my 'teaching' really was. It still gets to me, when I think about it—that hellish two weeks—it seemed like several months. It was a long time before I felt really settled again. Before I could forget that terrible insecurity of responsibility without authority, of degradation at the hands of the precious youth of our country, of the bitterness at unworkable and unfair policies and useless effort."

Yet he had not done anything *about* it himself, Ivo thought. How could mankind turn about, when even those who were shocked by the visible carnage merely retreated from it?

"At least I know better now," Groton said. "Now that I have Beatryx. And I stay out of 'causes.' Maybe I just had to get the mistaken idealism out of my system before settling down."

Oh.

Brad took Ivo to the confrontation. Afra was busy elsewhere, and he tried to keep his mind off her.

Senator Borland reminded him, shockingly, of the catatonic Dr. Johnson Afra had introduced him to in the infirmary. Borland's manner dissipated that initial impression in a hurry, however; he was younger and far more forceful than the scientist could ever have been. Ivo tried not to think of him automatically as the enemy. Borland had probably had nothing to do with the closing of schools and suppression of teachers.

It was amazing that one so young as Brad should be trusted to deal with such a man. But Brad was—Brad.

The Senator arrived with his personal secretary: a noisy young man who could only be properly described as a "flunky." The flunky did the talking, speaking of Borland always in the third person as though he were not present, while Borland himself looked alertly about as though not concerned with the dialogue.

"You!" the flunky cried imperiously, spying Brad. "You're American, right? The Senator wants to talk to you."

Brad approached slowly. Ivo could tell he was repressing irritation; he was hardly one to be ordered about abruptly.

The flunky consulted his clipboard. "You're Bradley Carpenter, right? Boy genius from Kennedy Tech, right? The Senator wants to know what you're pulling here."

"Astronomy," Brad said. There was a small stir among the assembled personnel of the station, and one big man with the Soviet insignia on his lapel smiled, not hesitant to show his contempt of the capitalist hierarchy. The West Europeans kept straight faces, though one had to cough. Borland had no power over them, but there were courtesies to maintain.

"Stargazing. Uh-huh," the flunky remarked. "The Senator means to put a stop to needless and wasteful expense. Do you have any idea how much of the taxpayer's hard-earned money you've squandered here in the past year?"

"Yes," Brad replied.

"The Senator means to get to the botton of this foolishness. This—" There was a doubletake. "What?"

"None."

"None what?"

"None squandered. You seem to assume that the purpose of research is the production of tangible commodities. The research is not in error; your definitions are."

Borland swung around to cover Brad. He touched one finger to his subordinate's arm and the youth froze. "Hold on there, lad. Suppose you prove that statement. What's so special about your telescope, makes it worth this many billion dollars? Just give me the tourist-class rundown, now."

"It isn't a telescope."

"The Senator didn't ask you what it *wasn't!*"

Ivo could tell by the silence that even the non-English-speaking personnel present were waiting to see the gadfly get swatted. Brad's obscure humor was not the only trait friends had come to appreciate.

They were disappointed this time. Brad *did* go into the elementary lecture reserved for visiting dignitaries. After a moment Ivo realized why: Brad was swatting for the gad, not the gadfly.

"According to Newton's theory of gravitation, every object in the universe attracts every other object with a force directly proportional to their masses and inversely proportional to the square of the distance between them. Currently we prefer to think of gravity as the physical manifestation of the curvature of space in the presence of matter. That is—"

"What about the *telescope?*" the flunky demanded. "The Senator doesn't have the time for irrelevant—"

Borland touched him on the arm again. It was like lifting the needle from a record.

"That is," Brad continued, having taken advantage of the break to move to one of the blackboards, and now erasing the complex "sprouts" diagram there, "we might visualize space as a taut elastic fabric, and the masses in our universe as assorted objects resting upon it. The heavier objects naturally depress the surface more."

He drew a sagging line with a circle in its center, then added a smaller circle. Ivo tried to imagine how a sprouts game might achieve such a configuration, but his talent did not help him there.

"This is the way the depression of space in the vicinity of our sun might affect the Earth, making due allowances for the two-dimensionality of our representation," Brad said. "As you can see, the small object will have a tendency to roll in toward the large, unless it should spin around it fast enough for centrifugal force to counteract the effect. But of course the Earth creates its own depression, and objects near it will be similarly attracted unless they establish orbits.

"The universe as a whole, therefore, is both curved and immensely complicated, since there are no real limits to any depression, large or small. No actual 'force' is necessary to explain the effects we experience in the presence of matter, apart from the basic nature of the situation. The gravitic interactions are everywhere, however, ripple upon ripple, and with constantly changing values. Any question so far?"

"GTR," Borland said.

"General Theory of Relativity, yes. Our concern is with these interactions." Brad marked a place on the diagram, between the sun and Earth, but nearer the latter so that it crested the wave. "We find that the peculiar stress of overlapping depressions—fields of gravity, if you will—creates a faint but unique turbulence, particularly at points in space where two or more fields are of equivalent potency. You might liken it to the sonic boom, where a physical object impinges the domain of sound, or Cerenkov radiation. It is, like the Cerenkov, a form of light—or rather, a subtle harmonic imprinted upon light passing through the turbulence. This aspect of light was not understood or even measurable until very recently; our technology was not sophisticated enough to detect such perturbations, let alone analyze their nature."

Borland held up his hand as though in a classroom, reminding Ivo again of Groton's experience. Now the spitwads were political. "*Now* a question, if you please. You tell me a beam of light passes through this gravity turbulence between two objects in space, and gets kinked a bit. But the way I figure it, there's hardly a cubbyhole in the cosmos that doesn't have gravitational equivalence of some sort; there are just too many stars, too many specks of dust, all with their little fields crossing into infinity. Your beam of light should have a thousand kinks, and kinks on kinks, if it travels any distance. So how do you figure which is which? Seems to me you're better off just taking your light as is, through a regular telescope; that's uncluttered, at least."

It occurred to Ivo with a little shock that a very sharp mind lurked behind the senatorial façade.

"This is true, ordinarily," Brad admitted carefully. "The 'kinks' our instrument detects are crowded. But while raw light is superior both for short work and long range, definition suffers in the intermediate range of say, one light-minute to a hundred thousand light-years. The macronic imposition, in contrast, is, for reasons we have yet to understand, more durable. We find the macrons in a beam emanating from a thousand light-years away to be almost as distinct as those from our own sun's field. The same is true for virtually any galactic distance. As our range increases—"

"I'm with you. You can shout down the hall, but you need a phone for the next city, even if it sounds tinny, and it works the same for the next continent. Now that term you used—macron—that sounds like a thing, not a quality."

"Yes. Our nomenclature is vague because our comprehension is vague. We appear to be dealing also with the particle aspect of light, more than with the wave, and perhaps with particles of gravitation. That may be the reason the effect appears to be independent of the square-cube law."

"Mate a photon to a gravitron and breed a macron," Borland remarked. "Damn interesting. I can see the implications of such interaction between light and gravity, untrained as I am in quantum mechanics."

Untrained but hardly ignorant, Ivo thought.

"So you either get *all* your macron, or none of it," the Senator continued after a pause. "But how can you get pictures of objects on or inside a planet, where there is no light?"

"The turbulence is removed from the source of the field, since it is equivalence that counts. Even an object *in* a planet has mass of its own, and its field interacts with that of the planet and of neighboring objects. At some point there will be an interaction that occurs in light—and some of the resultant macrons will reach us, however far away we are. It is only necessary for our receiver and equipment to be sufficiently sensitive. A computer stage is required for the initial rectification, and another to sort out and classify the myriad fragmentary images obtained. It is not a simple process. But once complete—"

"You are able, with your macroscope, to inspect any point in space—or on Earth?"

Brad nodded.

"I observed your emblem."

"We do not use it that way," Brad said shortly.

Ivo realized that they were talking about the platinum-plated shovel: the S D P S. Who could fathom its meaning by guesswork? Evidently the Senator understood the initials well enough. Perhaps he had prior information? He sounded less and less amateurish to Ivo. Had Brad met his match?

"Naturally not," Borland was saying. "Certain persons might not take kindly to such observation. Some might even feel so strong a need to protect their privacy that they would institute stringent measures. Do you follow me?"

"Yes," Brad said, his tone showing his disgust. The gad had not been swatted yet, though the gadfly had merged with the background.

"No you don't. Have you ever lived in one of facing tenements? Your window opening to a courtyard of windows?"

"No."

"You missed a good education, lad." Borland looked around. "Anybody else?"

The scientists of the station stood awkwardly.

"In a tenement," he repeated softly. "Anybody."

A brown hand went up from the doorway. It was Fred Blank, of the maintenance department, also table-tennis champion. His signal was tentative, as though he didn't like calling attention to himself at such a gathering.

Borland faced him. "Ever use the glasses?"

Blank looked sullen.

"Or maybe a cheap telescope?" Borland persisted. "Yeah, you know what I mean. Ten, twenty, maybe a hundred windows, depending on your location, and maybe half with no shades. Who wastes dough on shades, on nigger wages? Some girls don't know they're putting on a show. Some don't care. Some figure it's good for business. Same for some men. And family fights are fair game for capacity audience." He returned to Brad. "You know how you cure a scoper?"

"I'd call the police."

Borland wheeled to point at Blank. "That right, soul brother?"

Blank shook his head no. He was, reluctantly, smiling now.

"Yeah, you know." Borland had assumed complete control of the dialogue. "You was there, Kilroy. You had the education. Calling cop ain't in the book."

The scientists of the station stood mute, except for those translating for their companions. Borland was showing them all up for impractical theoreticians.

"Now you begin to follow, maybe. To put it in highbrow for you: mass voyeurism is a typical consequence of the cybernetic revolution, and you aren't going to curb it by invoking prerevolution methods. Back in the old days when we were nomads scrunching in tents, anybody poke his snoot in your door uninvited, you bash it in with your horny fist. The agricultural revolution changed all that, made cities possible—and cities are by definition crowded. The industrial revolution, maybe five thousand years later, made it ten times worse, because then every Joe had the wherewithal to poke into his neighbor's business with impunity. The cybernetic revolution really tied it, because then that average Joe had the wherewithal *and* the time to pry—and nobody pays for a canned show when there's a live one free.

"Now we've got the superscope, and we can diddle in our stellar neighbor's business, as though our own weren't enough. Now how do you figure a smart ET who likes his privacy is going to stop you from peeking—when there's maybe a fifteen-thousand-year time-delay?"

The station personnel looked at each other in dismay. Obvious—yet none of them had thought of it! A mind-destroying logic-chain that wiped out the peeping tom, wherever and *when*ever he might be. The most direct and realistic answer to snooping.

Borland waited for the babel of translation and discussion to die away. The men who had studied him with veiled contempt showed respect now, and the Russian had stopped smiling. "Now, comrades, suppose we forget about preconceptions and tackle the main problem. I know most of your governments better than you do—yes, even yours, Ivan—because that is my profession. Politics. I also know something of human nature—the reality, not the theory—and thereby it figures I know something too of *alien* nature. You're in trouble here, and so am I in certain respects you wouldn't care about. Why don't we forget our differences, pool our resources, and find out

81

what we can come up with? Maybe we can help each other a little."

Men looked at each other over the renewed murmur of the translations. Tentative smiles broke out. "Maybe we can, Senator," Brad allowed.

Borland spoke to his helper. "Go hold a preliminary press conference, kid. Tell 'em what the Senator means to do—but stay well clear of the facts. Irritate 'em if they get nosy. You know the routine."

The flunky left without a word.

"Li'l wonder, ain't he?" Borland remarked. "Took me years to find a foil like that. Now where's this tape?"

"Tape?"

"Lad, my reconnaissance is not *that* clumsy. The recording you have of the destroyer. The one that clouds men's minds, ha-ha-ha. The Shadow knows."

"It isn't a tape, or even a recording," Brad said. "We can't record it—at least, what we take down doesn't have the effect. The—meaning doesn't register."

"But you *can* pipe it in here live, right? No sense inspecting a dead virus. We want to know what makes it kick. It only comes in on one station, right? And it's continuous; you can tune it in any time?"

"One segment of the macroscopic band, yes. The center segment, where reception is strongest. The one we could use most effectively—if we could only tune the destroyer *out*."

Brad showed the Senator to a smaller projection room. Most of the scientists and personnel dispersed, satisfied that the situation was coming under control. Afra appeared in blouse and skirt, making even plain clothing look elegant. Ivo tagged along, forgotten for the moment.

"This is where we set it up," Brad explained tersely. "It amounts to a computer output, with the main signal processed at the receiver. There are electronic safeguards to guarantee that none of the effects penetrate beyond this room. This device is dangerous."

"A program," Borland said musingly. "A mousetrap in a harem. But why make up a show like that, instead of simply lobbing a detonator into the sun?"

"Evidently the originator isn't against *all* life," Brad said. "This is selective. It only hits the space-traveling, macroscope-building species like ourselves. The snoopers.

So long as we keep our development below a certain level, we're safe."

"My sentiments too. That the kind of safety you care for?"

"No."

"Let's run it through again. I put out a theory, just to show you how it could be, but I'm not putting my money on it yet. GIGO, you know. Garbage In, Garbage Out. Maybe my notion is the right one, but let's eliminate the others first. Like that song: 'Oh why don't I work like other men do? How the hell can I work when the skies are so blue? Hallelujah, I'm a bum!' Feed that to a minister and he'll tell you it's profane. Should be 'how the heck,' the church-approved euphemism. Try it on a professor and he'll tell you it's agrammatical: should be *as* other men do.' But a worker will tell you the whole thing's been censored. Should be 'how the hell can I work when there's no work to do!' Us lowbrows get to the root, sometimes. Not always. You figure they're afraid of the competition from some smart-aleck new species?"

"Fifteen thousand years late? And if we had a light-speed drive, which we never will, it would still take us another fifteen millennia to reach them. We can't even reply to their 'message' sooner than that. So it's really a delay of thirty thousand years. And I don't see how they could be sure we'd be ready to receive or reply in that time."

"Could be a long-term broadcast. For all we know, it's been going on a million years," Borland said. "Just waiting for us to catch up. Maybe time is slower for them? Like fifteen thousand years being a week or so, their way?"

"Not when the boradcast is on *our* time scheme. We haven't had to adjust to it at all. If they lived that slowly, we'd have a cycle running a thousand years, instead of a few minutes."

"Maybe. You figure they're crazy with hate for any intelligent race, any time?"

"Xenophobia? It's possible. But again, that time-delay makes it doubtful. How can you hate something that won't exist for tens of millennia?"

"An alien might. His mind—if he has one—might work in a different way than mine."

"Still, there are conceded to be certain criteria for intelligence. It isn't reasonable—"

"Stop being reasonable. That's a mistake. Try being philosophical."

Brad looked at him. "What philosophy do you have in mind, Senator?"

"I mean philosophy in its practical sense, of course. You can be reasonable as hell and still be a damned fool, and that's your problem. You figure your Scientific Method is the best technique you have for working things out, right? I tell you no."

"Observe the facts, set up a hypothesis that accounts for them all, use it to predict other facts, check them out, and revise or scrap the original hypothesis if the new evidence doesn't fit properly. I find it workable. Do Aristotle, Kant or Marx have a better overall system?"

"Yes. The primary concern of philosophy is not truth. It is meaning. The destroyer is not a truth-crisis, it is a meaning-crisis. You don't begin with assumptions and piece them together according to the rules of mathematics; you question their implications, and you question your questions, until nothing at all is certain. Then, maybe, you are getting close to meaning."

Brad frowned. "That make sense to you two?"

"No," Afra said.

"Yes," Ivo said.

"It doesn't *have* to make sense to you, so long as it opens your mind. This isn't any game of chess we're playing; we don't even know the rules. All we know for sure is that we're losing—and maybe we'd better start by questioning that. So this thing wipes out intelligence. Is that bad?"

"Cosmologically speaking, perhaps not," Brad said. "But the local effect is uncomfortable. It would be easier to live with it if it erased our *least* intelligent, rather than—"

Borland frowned. "You're talking about IQ type brains? 'Intelligence Quotient defined as Mental Age divided by Chronological Age times 100'?"

"We think so. Of course we can't be certain that a numerical IQ score reflects anything more than the subject's ability to score on IQ tests, so we may be misinterpreting the nature of the destroyer's thrust. A numerical score omits what may be the more important factors of

84

personality, originality and character, and even when detail scores are identical—"

"It is no sure sign that the capabilities or performance of the *people* are identical," Borland finished. "I know the book, and I am aware of the shortcomings of the system. I remember the flap fifteen or twenty years ago about 'creativity,' and I remember the vogue for joining high-IQ clubs. When I want a good man, I stay well clear of the self-professed egghead. I can tell just by looking at faces who's a sucker for the club syndrome."

Borland peered at faces. He pointed a gnarled finger at Afra. *"You!"*

She jumped guiltily. "You belong, right?" he said. Without waiting for her startled nod of agreement he moved on. "You—no," he said to Brad. "That big Russky who just left—no." He looked at Ivo. "They wouldn't let you in." He returned to Brad. "But IQ *is* the only practical guide we have to the generalized potential of large numbers of people, so we have to use it until we have something better. Let's just define it as the ability to learn, and say that a person with IQ one twenty is probably smarter overall than his brother with IQ one hundred. It's only a convenience so we can get down to the important stuff. OK?"

Brad laughed. "Oll Korrect, Senator. Apply your philosophy."

"Now you tell me this signal is nonlinguistic, so anybody can follow it, but it has a cutoff point. You have to be pretty smart, by one definition or another, for it to hit you. Does it hit the smarty sooner than the marginal one, or is it like the macrons: you get it or you don't?"

"It seems to hit the brighter minds sooner. Intelligence is such an elusive quality that we can't be sure, but—"

"Right. So let's run this through in some kind of order. You have an IQ of two fifteen—"

"What?" Afra demanded, shocked.

"That isn't—"

"I know. I know, I know," Borland said. "Figures don't mean anything, but if they did they still wouldn't apply to you, because you're smarter than the Joe who tries to test you. But remember we're talking convenience, not fact. No, I haven't seen your data-sheet; I do my own interpolation. If the figures *did* register for you, that's about the way it would read, right?"

Brad did not deny it, and Afra did not look at him. Ivo knew what she was thinking. She had supposed he might be 175 or 180, still somewhere within range of her own score. Scores would be very important to her. Suddenly she knew he was as far above her as she was above the average person—and the average, to her, was almost unbearably dull.

"So chances are that of this group, you would be the first to be hit by it," Borland said. "So let's put you at the head of the table. Now I'm comparatively stupid—at least, about fifty points below your figure, and that's a military secret, by the way, 'cause brains are a nonsurvival trait in the Senate—and your girl here runs about ten points below that. This lad—"

"About one twenty-five," Ivo said. "But it's unbalanced. I have—"

"There went another military secret," Brad muttered. "I don't think Mr. Archer should—"

"I insist on taking my place in your theoretic lineup," Ivo said seriously.

"Good. You're here, and it's a nice gradient, so might as well use you," Borland said. "Now let's bring in someone who sits at one hundred even to round it out."

"There's nobody on the station—" Afra began.

"Ask Beatryx," Brad murmured.

"Ask—!"

"It is no insult to be average, intellectually," Brad told her gently. "The rest of us are freaks, statistically." Afra flushed and went out.

"High-tempered filly there," Borland observed. "Technical secretary?"

"More—until two minutes ago."

"Let's get with it. You can activate that relay right now, right?"

"You seem to be assuming that we're really going to watch it."

"Lose your nerve, son? You knew it was coming. Step outside and leave me with it."

"Senator, there's no way to demonstrate the destroyer to you without destroying *you*. You'd be committing mental suicide."

Borland squinted at him. "Say I see it and survive it. Say I assimilate what the aliens are trying to hide. Where would that put me, locally?"

"Either stupid enough for a chairmanship, or—"

Ivo understood the pause. The Senator was hardly stupid. If he should survive the destroyer with a whole mind, he might have at his command the secrets of the universe, literally. He could become the most powerful man on Earth. He was the type of individual willing to gamble total loss against the prospect of total victory.

He was serious. This was what he had come for. He would view the destroyer. And Brad could not allow him to make that gamble alone. The Senator's victory might well be more costly to Earth than his defeat—unless Brad could solve the destroyer first.

Borland's gaze was fierce. "You want it the hard way, junior?"

"Congressional subpoena?" Brad shrugged. "No, we'll undertake this suicide pact now, together."

"Go it, lad."

Brad glanced at Ivo, saw that he wasn't leaving, and slapped a button under the table. The television screen that filled the far wall burst into color. All three rotated to face it.

Ivo, astonished at the suddenness of the decision and action, realized then how neatly they had done it. The three of them constituted a bracket, to honor that pretext, and Brad would not have wanted either woman to take the risk. Afra would never have excluded herself voluntarily, had she known what was brewing.

Shape appeared, subtle, twisting, tortuous, changing. A large sphere of red—he could tell by the shading that it represented a sphere, in spite of the two-dimensionality of the image—and a small blue dot. The dot expanded into a sphere in its own right, lighter blue, and overlapped the other. The segment of impingement took on a purple compromise.

Ivo's intuition caught on. His freak ability attuned to this display as readily as it had to the game of sprouts. This was an animated introduction to sets, leading into Boolean Algebra, with color as an additional tool. Through set theory it was possible to introduce a beginner to mathematics, logic, electronics and all other fields of

87

knowledge—without the intervention of a specific language. Language itself could be effectively analyzed by this means. One riddle solved; the aliens had the means to communicate.

The colors flexed, expanded, overlapped, changed shapes and intensities and number and patterns in a fashion that to an ordinary person might seem random ... but was not. There was logic in that patterning, above and beyond the logic of the medium. It was an alien logic, but absolutely rational once its terms were accepted. Rapidly, inevitably, the postulates integrated into an astonishingly meaningful whole. The very significance of existence was—

Ivo's intuition leaped ahead, anticipating the denouement. The meaning was coming at him, striking with transcendent force.

He knew immediately that the sequence should be stopped. He tried to stand, to cry out, but his motor reflexes were paralyzed. He could not even close his eyes.

He did the next best thing: he threw them out of focus. The writhing image lost definition and its hold upon him weakened. Gradually his eyelids muscled down; then he was able to turn his head away.

His entire upper torso dropped on the table. He was too weak to act.

The program ground to its inevitable conclusion. He was aware of it, though he did not watch. There was no sound in the room.

The door burst open. "Brad!" Afra cried, distracted. "You didn't wait!"

Ivo was jarred out of his trance. Strength returned. He lurched to his feet, finding his balance. He lumbered along the table, reaching for the button Brad had touched. He scratched under the surface, his fingers uncoordinated, trying to make it work, and finally the image cut off.

Afra unfroze in stages. She had been hooked already by the destroyer, just entering its second cycle, but had not been exposed to more than a few seconds of it. There had not been time for her mind to go.

Others were crowding into the room, intent on the seated men. Now Ivo allowed himself to look at his friend.

Bradley Carpenter sat silently, oblivious to Afra's fevered ministrations. His eyes gazed without animation and his jaw was slack and moist. Already the station doctor was shaking his head negatively.

The Senator was slumped farther down the table. The doctor went to him next and performed an intimate check.

"He's dead," he said.

CHAPTER 3

A persistent rapping at the door brought Ivo out of an uncomfortable sleep. He was not used to the hammock, and the shock of what had happened was too fresh and raw. He had not forgotten that he occupied the apartment of a man whose mind was virtually dead; he felt like an intruder.

He righted himself and stumbled across the compartment. He crashed open the sliding door, rubbing his eyes.

Afra stood there, lovely in bathrobe and slippers. Her sunburst hair was tied under a nebulous kerchief, up and back in the manner of a busy housewife, and she wore no makeup, but to Ivo she was dazzling.

Her blue gaze smote him. "Special delivery," she said without humor. "Telegram." She held out an envelope.

Ivo accepted it, then became abruptly aware of his condition. He was standing before this beautiful girl in sleep-rumpled jockey shorts. "I—thanks. Must change."

She put her hand against the door, preventing closure. "*Is* it yours?"

He looked at the address. It was a stylized representation of an arrow. Nothing else.

"Now that just might signify entropy," she said, stepping forward and so forcing him to jump back. "Time's

Arrow, as it were. But I remembered that your first name, Ivo, is a variant of the Teutonic Ivon, meaning a military archer. And your last name—"

"Yeah, I guess so," he said, ill at ease. If only he had something *on!*

"The feminine form would be Yvonne," she continued blithely, pushing him back another step. "Names always derive from something interesting. Mine means 'A greeter of people'—Teutonic, again."

He looked at her more carefully, suspicious of this brightness. Neither her voice nor her expression betrayed it at this moment, but he knew she was crazy with grief for Brad. Her eyes were shadowed and there was a mild odor of perspiration about her. Was she afraid to be alone, or did Brad's room have a perverse attraction for her?

"But I suppose you'd better read it, just to be sure," she said. "I found it beside the teletyper. The operator was asleep—very bad form, you know—so I took it. . . ."

She was disturbed, all right. She must have been pacing from area to area, talking with anyone, grasping at any pretext to distract her attention from the horror in her memory. She cared nothing about Ivo Archer or his clothing; for the narrow present, the telegram was necessarily tantalizing.

He opened it while she whirled about the room, touching her hands to Brad's things but not moving them. She glanced eagerly toward the message.

One word jumped out at him. Ivo crumpled the paper angrily.

"What are you doing! We're not even sure it's yours!"

"It's mine."

"What does it *say?* You can't just—"

"I don't know what it says. Just that it means trouble."

"At least let me—"

"Sure," he said, too curtly, and flipped the ball of paper at her. "I have to dress."

She was oblivious to the hint. She spread out the sheet and concentrated on it while he turned his back and climbed hastily into trousers and shirt.

"Why—this is polyglot!" she exclaimed. "I thought you said you couldn't—"

"I can't."

She glided to the little table and set down the message. "Who would send you a note like this? It's fascinating!"

"It's trouble," he repeated. He came over to look at it again, actually only wanting to be near her.

The printing was plain enough: SURULLINEN XPACT SCHÖN AG I ENCAJE.

There was no signature.

"What a mishmash!" she said, producing a pencil. "I'm not sure I can put it all together, but I know it means something. If only Brad—"

She dropped her head, realizing, and he saw the dry sobs shake her shoulders. Then she lifted her face determinedly and refocused on the message. Ivo stood by, doing nothing, longing for the right only to touch her in comfort—and feeling guilty for that desire. What a girl she was!

"Schön—that's German, of course. It—" She stopped again. "Schön! Brad's friend from the project! You were supposed to take this to Brad for translation."

"Could be." He wondered whether he should have destroyed the note instead of letting her have it. She didn't come close to Brad in intelligence, but she was not exactly slow.

"Schön—he's the one who—if anybody can—"

Ivo grimaced behind his face, knowing that she was grasping at straws and would soon realize it. Even Schön could hardly regenerate his friend's damaged brain tissue. That had to be accomplished internally, and such healing did not take place in the higher animals.

"I must know what it says. Then we can answer it. . . ." She bent to the task with renewed vigor. The kerchief bobbed as her head nodded. "That last word—ENCAJE— that's Spanish for 'lace.' And the next to last —I—could be English. It would be just like Brad to slip in a 'straight' term, and I understand Schön is even worse that way." She filled in the English equivalents beneath the printed terms while Ivo watched, intrigued in spite of himself. He had never envied the geniuses their polylingual facility, but working on the message vicariously through Afra's ability he could imagine himself caught up in the excitement of the chase. A search for a word could be as exciting as a manhunt, in the proper circumstance, he decided.

Even though he already knew the outcome.

"xpact—that's no Romance-language word, or Germanic," she murmured. "Or Finno-Ugric ... of course! It's in the Slavic group. Russian ... no—well, it's related. Let's see." She rewrote the word in more exotic script.

She looked up, her blue eyes startlingly intense. Ivo wondered how it was that he had never appreciated the luster of such color before he had met her. "Acorn, I make it. Does that make sense?"

Ivo shrugged.

"And surullinen—that's Finnish for 'sad.' One word left ... I think it's Turkish ... 'mesh,' perhaps." She sat back and read it off: "Sad acorns, beautiful mesh I lace.' "

Ivo chuckled, and she made a fleeting smile. "But that 'lace' is a noun," she said, "so we don't have it yet. No verb in it—it can't be a sentence—not as we think of it. And that 'I' doesn't really fit—aha! That could be the Polish 'and.' 'Beautiful mesh and lace' contrasted with the miserable acorns." She worried it some more, tongue appearing and disappearing between even white teeth.

What if she solved it? he wondered. Should he tell her the truth now, try to explain? That didn't seem wise.

He saw her enthusiasm for the problem and decided to leave it with her a little longer.

"Gloomy oak, lovely plait and lace," she said at last. "Something in that vein. I can't take the words any farther, and I don't know where to begin interpretation. God, I'm tired! Why would he go to the trouble of sending such a message to you?"

"Glooms of the live-oaks, beautiful-braided and woven," Ivo said.

She was on it immediately. "It *does* mean something to you. A line of poetry?"

"Yes." She was too sharp; he had said too much.

"A work you're both familiar with? Something you can quote from? Something that suggests the course you should follow?"

"Yes." He knew she was about to ask *which* poet or which poem, and he was not ready to tell. She would identify it anyway, or . . . or what kind of persuasion would she turn on him?

"Now I can rest," she said. She shuffled to the hammock and flopped upon it, her knees brought up to one side, letting her slippers droop and fall to the floor.

She had forgotten where she was—or didn't care. Perhaps, he thought with unreasonable jealousy, she was *used* to sleeping here. In Brad's room.

He looked at her, at the soft hair breaking free of the twisted kerchief, at the slender arm falling over the edge of the hammock and swaying as it rocked; at the embraceable shape of her curled body, the smooth white knees exposed, the firm round ankles and small feet. He felt ashamed for his yearnings.

Afra was the epitome of the feminine adorable, by Ivo's present definition. It did not matter that the definition followed the fact, rather than the other way around. He had schooled himself not to resent more alert intelligence than his own, but also not to expect it in the girl he might marry. Not to require supreme beauty, not to dwell on small character defects . . . a hundred little cautions, in the interests of probability and practicality. He was not an extraordinary man, apart from that one unique aspect that negated any purpose he might have had in life, and it was not to be anticipated that he would win an extraordinary woman. *Any* woman, really.

He knew now that he had disastrously underrated his susceptibility to sheer physical beauty. He had loved Afra the moment he saw her, before he knew anything fundamental about her. Vanquished, he could only hope for compassionate terms.

"I thought nothing could hurt me again," she murmured sleepily into the small pillow-cushion, "after I lost my father. But now Brad—almost the same way, really. . . ."

Ivo did not speak, knowing that no reply was wanted. She was oblivious to him, her mind encapsulated within an isolated episode juggled to the surface by misery. The news surprised him, however; there had been no prior hint of tragedy in her background. Her father must have died, or lost his sanity suddenly, so that she spoke of him only under extreme stress. Now it had happened to Brad. He made a mental note never to mention the subject of parents to her.

"And he told me how to—I can't remember—something else about Schön. . . ."

Suddenly it had become relevant to himself. "He" had to mean Brad. What had Brad told her about Schön? Ivo listened tensely, but she had drifted into silence. Her eyes were closed, tears on the lashes.

Brad's girl. . . .

Ivo let himself out, leaving because it hurt him to watch her. He grieved for Brad too, but it was not the same.

He made his way to the infirmary.

Six figures occupied the chairs. It was as though they never moved from them, for this was station night.

"Hello, Dr. Johnson," he murmured as he passed. The patriarch stared past him. "Hello, Dr. Smith. Dr. Sung. Mr. Holt. Dr. Carpenter."

The male nurse appeared, yawning. "What do you want?"

Ivo continued to watch Bradley Carpenter, mercifully asleep. Merciful for the observer, for his friend no longer had the intellect to care what had happened to him.

Why had Brad done it, knowing the penalty he would pay? It had been an act of suicide; he could have fended off the Senator's demand, had he chosen to. A subpoena would have entailed substantial publicity, but would still have been a far smaller evil. This death was more horrible because it was partial. The mind was gone, lobotomized, while the flaccid body remained, a lifetime burden to society and torment to those who had known and loved Brad in his entirety.

"Oh—you were his Earthside friend," the nurse said, recognizing him. "Too bad."

Brad woke. The lax features quivered; the eyes fought into focus. The lips pursed loosely. Almost, some animation came into the face.

"Sh-sh-sh . . ." Brad said.

The nurse placed a reassuring hand upon his shoulder. "It's all right, Dr. Carpenter. All right. Relax. Relax." Aside, to Ivo: "It isn't good to work them up. They may be capable of some regeneration of personality, if the condition isn't aggravated. We just don't know yet, and can't take any chances. You understand. You'd better go."

Brad's eyes fixed with difficulty on Ivo. "Sh-sh—"

"Schön," Ivo said.

The straining body relaxed.

The nurse's brow wrinkled. "What did you say?"

"It's German," Ivo explained unhelpfully.

"He was trying to—that's astonishing! It's only been a few hours since—"

"It meant a lot to him."

Brad was asleep again, his ultimate accomplished. "The others couldn't even try for several days," the nurse said. "He can't have been hit as bad. Maybe he'll recover!"

"Maybe." Ivo walked away, sure that the hope was futile. Only a transcendent effort, perhaps the only one he would ever be capable of, had brought forth that word, or that attempt at the word. It was clear now, in awful retrospect: Brad had sacrificed himself in an effort to force the summoning of Schön. He had been that certain that only Schön could nullify the destroyer and handle the problem of the macroscope.

It had been for nothing. How could he introduce Schön to this tremendous source of knowledge and power—knowing how much worse the world would be, if Schön's amoral omnipotence replaced the Senator's ambition? He could not do it.

He met Groton in the hallway near the common room. "Ivo," the man said, stopping him. "I know this is a bad time for you, but there is some information I need."

"No worse than any other time." The truth was that he was relieved for some pretext to take his mind off the present disaster. He knew now that Groton was not an obtuse engineer; the man had important feelings about important things, as the school-teaching narration had shown. It was always dangerous to be guided by prejudice, as he saw himself to have been guided at his first meeting with Groton. "What kind of information? I don't know much."

"I've been working on your horoscope—couldn't sleep right now—and, well, it would help if you could describe certain crises in your life."

So Groton, too, felt it. Every person had his own ways of reacting to stress. No doubt astrology was as good a diversion as any.

"Like *this* crisis? I'm not objective yet." Did he really want to contribute further to this exercise? Still, what he had just reminded himself about prejudice should hold for this too. The fact that Ivo Archer found astrology unworthy of serious consideration did not mean that discourtesy was justified; Harold Groton obviously was sincere. There were stranger hobbies.

"I was thinking of your past experience. Perhaps during your childhood something happened that changed your life—"

"I thought your charts told you all that, from the birth date." Or was that an unkind remark?

"Not exactly. It is better to obtain corroborative experience. Then we can understand the signals more precisely. Astrology is a highly confirmatory science. We apply the scientific method, really."

"And some philosophy?" Ivo inquired, thinking of the Senator's remarks in that connection.

"Of course. So if you—"

They entered Groton's apartment. Ivo could smell breakfast cooking and knew that Beatryx was at work. It made him feel obscurely homesick; nobody ever took institutionalized food if they could help it, though that served in the station was exceptionally good.

"I had no childhood," he said.

"You mean the project. A controlled situation, certainly, and perhaps undistinctive. But after you left—"

Ivo remembered the turning point. Perhaps it had begun, if it could be said to have had a beginning, the day he was twenty-three. February third, 1865. The day he admitted to himself that he had consumption.

Point Lookout, Maryland—as horrible a place as any he could imagine. Surely this was Hell, and Major Brady the devil. Twenty acres of barren land surrounded by palisades. The prisoners were Southern White; many of the guards were Black. The Negroes took pleasure insulting and torturing any people they chose, but the cold of winter was worse yet. There was not enough food, clothing or sanitation, and no medical facilities for the prisoners. The water was foul. The only shelter was the collection of A-tents and Bell-tents. They slept on the bare, damp ground, denied both planks and straw for bedding, and no wood was permitted inside the compound for any fire. Objection of any nature to these conditions brought infamous retaliatory measures and further reduction of the scant rations.

He shared a tent with a dozen men. While the crowding provided a certain blessed amount of bodily warmth, it

97

also spread disease at a savage rate. Diarrhea, dysentery, typhoid fever, scurvy and the itch ... fifteen to twenty men died every day. And now he could no longer deny the tubercular coughing and the wastage of his own body. He realized he was dying.

Had it been only four years ago that the great state of Georgia voted secession from the Union? He had not at first been a secessionist, but the vote had been held at Milledgeville, only two miles from where he eked out his living by tutoring. The sentiment, like disease, had been highly contagious; even the clergy were belligerently patriotic. *The afflatus of war was breathed upon them all.* Somehow he had become convinced of his ability to whip at least five Yankees, singlehanded; indeed, any stalwart Georgian could!

Now he looked about him at the human desolation of Point Lookout. "What fools we were!" he whispered. The conceit of an individual was ridiculous because it was powerless, but the conceit of a whole people was a terrible thing.

Flushed with patriotic illusion, he had volunteered to fight. He, whose only skill was musical!

It had not all been hard. He remembered fondly the time he, a bedraggled soldier, had passed beneath the windows where a local Philharmonic Club was rehearsing. He had taken out his flute and played there in the street—and the orchestra ceased rehearsal, listened, and arranged to grant him honorary freedom of the town!

During furlough there had been concerts with friends, and of course the ladies! He was always in love, and never ashamed to win fair hearts by the music of his flute.

He had smuggled that flute into the prison camp, and its music now was one of the few comforts he had. It had been the one thing he refused to part with. when the *Lucy* was captured in the Gulf Stream, running the Yankee blockade. He, as Signal Officer, had refused to declare himself to be an Englishman, preferring capture to a dishonorable escape.

Today he was dying of that decision, as his nation was dying of the Union armies. Somehow, until today, he had had hope. Was not God just?

Harold Groton was waiting for his answer. What could he tell the man?

"It's very hard to define. I came near death when I was twenty-three. Is that what you want?"

"If it affected you deeply, yes. Some people nearly die and are hardly concerned, while others are profoundly moved by an innocent remark. It isn't the event so much as its personal importance to you."

"It is important to me. I was sick and in—prison. Some friends—put up bail. On the ship home—"

"You weren't in America?"

"Not exactly. The ship I was on was frozen in the ice for three days on the way to City Port, Virginia."

Groton refrained from commenting.

Was it worth the effort to make the man understand? For the sake of accurate data for the pseudo-science of astrology? Ivo remained distracted by his grief, and could not bring himself to care.

Three days icebound, early March, 1865. He and the other repatriated prisoners huddled in the hull, shuddering with the cold. The end for him was very near.

Another prisoner practiced on the flute. A little girl, daughter of a passenger above, heard it and marveled at the melody. "If you think *I'm* good, you should hear that other fellow play!" the man told her. "But he's not going to last long, in this cold."

She reported the episode to her mother. "I know only one person that skilled with the flute," the woman said. "An old friend of mine. Surely he could not be *here!*"

But she investigated, nagged by the possibility—and found him there in the hold, wrapped in an old soiled quilt, eyes staring, wasted body subject to spasms of pain. She knew her friend.

It was so crowded in the hold that they had to pass him over the heads of the other prisoners to get him out. She plied him with brandy, but he was too far gone to swallow.

She warmed him and ministered to him, she and her little girl. By midnight he revived somewhat. She presented him with his flute—the best medicine!—and weakly he began to play.

The prisoners below yelled for joy as they heard the sound of it. He was going to recover!

"That act of friendship—I think that was the turning point," Ivo said. "I surely would have died, otherwise."

99

Groton shook his head. "It is a strange story you tell, Ivo. But as I said, its validity lies chiefly in its importance to you, not in the overt details. I'll apply it to my researches."

Ivo, nervous again, declined to share breakfast with the Grotons and found his way to the mess hall. He was not very hungry.

It was still early, by the station's day, when he finished, and he continued to be restless. Was Afra still sleeping in his—Brad's—room? Should he go back yet?

He stopped off at the latrine—and realized suddenly that every toilet faced in the same direction. The arrangement was such that when a person sat, he had to face the "forward" orientation of the torus.

"When you take your inevitable bow, your stern is sternward." he said aloud, finally appreciating Brad's pun—a pun inflicted upon the nomenclature of the entire station.

He blinked, feeling his eyes moisten with the pathos. Bradley Carpenter, PhD in assorted space technologies at age twenty-two—straining with all that remained of his mind at twenty-five to utter one German word. . . .

Brad—pride of the nameless project the participants had mischievously dubbed "The Pecker Experiment." It had been patterned after, or at least inspired by, a much better known effort antedating it by twenty years: The Peckham Experiment. But if the good doctors of Peckham had suspected what sinister offshoots their well-meant research would spawn, they might have had severe misgivings.

A certain British medical group, as Ivo understood it, had set out in the nineteen thirties to ascertain the nature of health. It had seemed to them that the medical profession's attention to illness was mistaken; how much better it would be to take the steps necessary to preserve *health*, so that tedious and only partially effective remedial measures became unnecessary. A regular, complete physical checkup for everyone, the basic unit of attention being not the individual but the family. But would the average family respond favorably to such a service?

The center established in Peckham in 1935 soon demonstrated that they would. For several years many of the families within a radius of a mile had participated, enjoying a sensation of well-being they had never known before. Astonishingly, the records showed that ninety percent of the participants—presumed to be a representative cross-section of the nation—were not in good health at the time of application. The "normal" person was an ill person.

What might group life be like if ninety percent were *healthy?* The Peckham Experiment had offered only tantalizing glimpses. The Second World War, that trauma of the sick society, had cut it short. A postwar reorganization had expired for lack of financial backing, and the bold experiment was over.

But not forgotten. It was a topic for informed conjecture for many years thereafter. Certain persons studied the implications of the experiment and drew forth an intriguing supposition. If the average person were sick, and "normal" were in fact subnormal, so that he never comprehended his true physical potential—what of his *mental* potential? Could it be that health and proper upbringing might convert the average into superior, and the superior into genius?

What benefits might derive from genius cultured artificially? What would industry pay for employees of guaranteed IQ? How might the nation benefit? Just how high was the limit?

Certain private interests decided to speculate. Money appeared, and preliminary researches commenced. What might be the elements of a suitable upbringing for genius-on-tap? What was the best stock for production? As beef, not contented cows, was the object of ranching, so IQ, not conventionality, was to be the object of this project.

Studies performed in the interim since Peckham suggested astonishing facts. Heredity was vital, yes—but so was environment, in ways more devious and wonderful than suspected before. Health was essential—but so was education. The basic theory and practice of conventional schooling was long overdue for revolution.

Item: The expectation of the supervisor affected the performance of the subject. Thus American "self-fulfilling prophecies" resulted in lower grades for Negro and Indian schoolchildren, higher grades for Whites of prominent families—*regardless of merit by objective standards.*

Item: There was no correlation between school performance and life achievement. There was no practical advantage in additional years of schooling or the possession of diplomas *apart from the self-fulfilling prophecy of society.*

Item: Whatever was useful in the current eight-year introductory scholastic curriculum could be effectively mastered by a normal twelve-year-old child in four months —who would pick up most of it *without formal instruction.*

Item: The true "creative" child tended to be skeptical, independent, assertive, and had a wide range of interests: a natural maker of waves. He was, by normal definition, *not a "good" student.*

Item: In the human child, the brain achieved eighty percent of its adult weight by the age of three years, compared to a body weight of twenty percent. *Any retardation occurring in this period became permanent.*

Item: Creatures—of any species—raised in the dark developed no rods and cones in the eyes, and thus were blind for life. Creatures—of any species—raised in a restrictive, nonstimulating environment never developed their full "normal" mental or emotional capacities, and thus were dull for life. Physical infection, malnutrition, and sensory and cultural deprivation *actually created inferior specimens.*

Item: It was theoretically possible to raise the IQ of the average child by thirty points or more—merely by providing suitable equipment and information and permitting free rein for normal initiative. The child, thus encouraged, would fulfill a greater proportion of his natural potential— *a fulfillment denied to his contemporaries.*

Thus the project. All over the world, money was spent lavishly to locate potential genius stock and fatten it into complete health and vigor, that it might produce outstanding offspring. The offcolor nickname stemmed from conjecture how this had been accomplished. Virile, intelligent men of every race mated to women not their spouses, women at the peak of health, both parties paid liberally for their service. Tour of duty perhaps two years; illness, hunger or reproductive laxity frowned upon.

The babies had never known their biological parents. They had been removed from their various locales of production and committed to the maximum-security grounds of the project, there to be subjected to the most healthful and stimulating environment envisioned by man. Their individual families were replaced by something better: the group family. The adult staff, male and female, was trained to withhold nothing from any child except freedom to leave the project, and never to interfere needlessly in juvenile matters.

The results, as the years progressed, were generally disappointing. After phenomenal early growth, the average project child settled into bright but not exceptional mentality, and became, relative to expectations, moderately talented. It was as though this vast effort had succeeded largely in accelerating the rate of growth, but not the ultimate achievement. The children spread out in the normal bell-shaped curve, centered on IQ 125—a result that would have been predicated on heredity alone, without the benefit of the improved environment. Only one true genius showed up on the tests, though there were a number of very intelligent children too—and as many who were average (IQ 100) or slightly below.

Officially, then, the project was a failure. Something evidently had been overlooked. There would be no assembly-line genius to market. The financial backing dwindled. After fifteen years it had to be disbanded and the subjects set free.

The officials had not known about Schön.

A group of men were seated in the common room, silent and somber. They looked up as he approached, their faces impassive.

"Please—a private meeting," one said.

"Sorry." Ivo passed quickly to the far door, not wanting to intrude. The "night" shift was barely over; why had they gathered at this time, almost surreptitiously? What were they doing, so privately? None of his business.

Harold Groton was coming down the hall from the other direction, full from his own breakfast. "There's some kind of meeting," Ivo advised him. "Exclusive. I ran afoul of it already, in the common room."

"I know. I was just—" Groton paused, catching at Ivo's arm. "By God! I just realized—you saw the destroyer and survived!"

"I fell below its critical limit, it would seem."

103

"Afra says you know someone important—someone who can untangle this mess."

"Afra says too much." Ivo jerked his arm away, fed up with irrelevancies.

"That trick with the game—the intuitive calculation. Was Brad serious? Can you win every time?"

"Yes, if it's the right type, and if I have the choice of openings." What was he getting at? A Senator was dead, six other minds had been blasted by an alien destruction signal, and organizational chaos was incipient. Yet Groton, who had seemed yesterday to have some depth of feeling, concerned himself first with astrology and then with a superficial game!

"Come on—I'll yield my slot to you."

"What are you talking about?"

"No time to explain. We're late already." Groton pulled him back toward the common room.

Ivo shrugged and went along.

The still figures looked up again as they entered. Some were women, he saw now; he had not looked carefully before. "This is Ivo," Groton said. "He was Dr. Carpenter's friend. Therefore he has the privilege, and I am giving him my seat in the tourney."

Tourney?

The others exchanged glances and shrugs. They did not appear pleased, but Groton evidently had the right of it.

"I can't stay," Groton said to him. "There's no kibitzing. Play seriously. Good luck." He was gone.

Ivo looked about. There were eight men and two women, of divers nationalities. He recognized among them the big Russian who had smiled disdainfully at the Senator, and Fred Blank, ubiquitous maintenance man. This was not, then, an astronomy discussion, though the ranking scientists of the station appeared to be represented.

Three tables had been set end to end to form one long narrow panel. Upon it was a collection of colored crayons.

They arranged themselves at this counter, five on a side, facing each other in pairs. There was no chair for Ivo.

He stood there awkwardly, until one man rose and guided him to a separate table placed against the wall. It was the Russian who evidently recognized him, too. He planted Ivo before a chair facing toward the wall.

The meaning of two firmly spoken directives in Russian was clear. Ivo sat down and kept quiet.

The Russian nodded and returned to the main table.

There was a rustle of movement, then silence. Ivo stared at the wall—which was, he realized with a shock, covered with graffiti in many languages—and waited.

His imagination began percolating.

This? Having failed at science, the leaders of this space-borne project were turning to magic. They were a cabal holding a seance, a black mass, a conjuration . . . and all they had lacked, until this moment, was an innocent lamb for the blood sacrifice. The nether god had to be propitiated. First the secret rites had to be performed, the voodoo chanting, the knife ritually honed. . . .

A few minutes passed. A stir commenced. Chairs shifted. Ivo's back prickled. *The sacrificial blade—*

Someone approached his table.

—lifted high by the muscular priest—

And touched his shoulder.

Ivo stood up, and the man took his place.

The others had resettled themselves. One seat was now empty. Ivo marched over and took it.

Opposite him was the older of the two women, and between them were red and blue crayons. That was all.

Down the length of the table the four other pairs sat, each with similar apparatus. In uncanny silence, hands selected crayons, made obscure markings on the glossy surface of the table.

The woman facing him picked up the blue crayon and carefully printed eight dots on the counter in a rough heart-outline:

Ivo glanced at this in perplexity, not knowing what was expected of him. He looked sidelong at the couple's paper to the left—and caught on.

They were playing sprouts!

He had, with typical perspicacity, missed the obvious. Groton had even mentioned the game as he dragged him to the common room.

He reached for the other crayon, but the woman set her hand on his, preventing him from lifting it. Apparently she had selected the color as well as the number of dots. He let go, and she handed him the blue.

It was his opening move, then. He had to play the eight-spot game of sprouts with this woman—was she South American? He'd know if she spoke—and defeat her. Groton said so.

He concentrated, trying to figure the forced win, but could not be certain. There were too many complex interrelationships, and too much depended upon the confluence of opposing lines of strategy.

He decided to keep it simple until the outcome was fathomable. The probability was that he would see the correct strategy before she could. He connected the southward-pointing dots, bisecting the heart, and placed the new spot in the center.

She recovered the crayon and made a butterfly-shape looping from the top, encircling the two highest dots. She placed the new one in the crevice.

Idle play, or artistry? Did it matter? Ivo decided that it did not, and proceeded with an asymmetric offshoot.

The woman continued without objection, and he knew that it was all right. These games were not being judged on esthetics. Soon he was able to determine the win, and played through to it without difficulty.

The others finished about the time he did, and again there was the shuffle as all stood up, wiped away the evidence, and moved one step around the table. The travel was clockwise; the woman he had defeated went out to the supernumerary chair and sat there, while the spare man came to occupy Ivo's last seat. Now this was clear, too: with five facing five and one to carry, each rotation brought about new combinations that would not repeat until each person had played every other.

It was indeed a tourney.

His next opponent was a venerable gentleman bearing the emblem of Nove-Congo. Ivo judged him to be of Bantu stock with a strong Alphine admixture; the skin was an intermediate brown, the body stocky but lacking the Caucasoid hairiness. The turbulent history of his country was reflected in his genetic heritage, and Ivo felt sympathy. Ivo was himself a controlled conglomeration of Mongoloid, Negroid and Caucasoid, as had been every member of the project, and he felt that the purebreds were lacking in something. But he had obtained his chromosomes the easy way, and had lived protected and pampered. This man could have been conceived only in misfortune, amidst violent antipathies against miscegenation; perhaps he was the child of rape. Yet he had won his way to the foremost circle of modern technology, and that too spoke eloquently about him.

The NoCon picked up the blue crayon and planted nine dots upon the board—and to Ivo it seemed as though they formed a crude map of his nation. Conscious, unconscious, or strictly in the eye of the beholder?

Irrelevant. Ivo played, this time observing that the players on the opposite side of the table invariably selected color and dot-pattern. Those on his side had choice of moves—and sometimes declined to make the opening one. As in football: one side chose the field, the other had the initiative. He would get to set up the spots once he progressed to the proper side.

He noted also that no game began with less than six spots; these people were aware of the extent of the advantage accruing to the person with the choice of moves, in the lower ranges. In the higher numbers, skill really did become the dominant factor, since nobody could anticipate or execute the forced win.

He won again without undue difficulty. These people, skilled as they might be in other types of endeavor, and practiced as they might be at sprouts, nevertheless lacked his own intuitive analytic faculty. Probably any of them could outperform him in almost any field—except this one. A billiards tournament, or table-tennis ... but this happened to be sprouts, a game of semimathematical analysis. He was able to determine the winning strategy several moves before they could, and to have the victory in hand before they were aware. The real test of his skill was in determining the win, rather than in the play.

Groton had known of his power in this respect; that he had, in effect, an unfair advantage. Why had Groton chosen to send him into this contest? What was there to be won, that had to be won this way?

Should he arrange to lose?

No. It was not in him to throw a contest, any contest, for any reason. He could decline the prize, but he had to do his best in the competition.

The third encounter was with the Russian. The man picked up the red crayon and made seven dots.

Ivo strained, but could not quite pin down the automatic win. Seven was just beyond his intuitive competence. The opening move seemed wrong, however, so he declined it, brushing away the proffered crayon as though it were a tip refused.

The Russian nodded and accepted the onus. They played, and very shortly Ivo lined it up and established his winning mode.

The Russian paused instead of playing, after the key move, hairy brow wrinkled. "Misère?" he inquired. It was the first word spoken since the games had begun.

Ivo shrugged, wondering why the man did not make his play. Was he conceding already?

The Russian touched the shoulder of the woman next to him. She was, Ivo perceived, a younger person, perhaps no more than thirty-five, and the pride of her femininity was still about her. She was classic Mongoloid: stocky, flattish face, almond eyes, coarse straight hair and very small hands. She probably had come from Fringe-China, and was in her way as definitive a specimen as Afra was in hers. He was as closely related to this woman as to Afra: about one-third overlap of race.

The Russian asked Ivo something, when the woman's attention had been gained. Then, again: "Misère."

"He inquires whether you understand that it is misère," she said softly to Ivo. "The red—to avoid the last move."

To play to lose! That was the significance of the color. Red, naturally, for the deficit game. He had missed—yet again!—the obvious, while concentrating upon the subtle. And he had already forced the win—for the Russian, unless the man should make a mistake. That, in view of this interchange, seemed unlikely.

He had made an error—in not acquainting himself with the complete rules of play. He should have questioned the purpose of the second color. It was as valid a mistake as a misplay on the board.

"I understand," he said.

That was it. They finished the play, and he lost.

Fred Blank was next, also picking up the red crayon. Ivo defeated him.

No one kept official score. Apparently it was up to the individual. By the time Ivo completed the circuit, he had nine victories, one defeat.

The group dispersed, the entertainment over. There was no celebration, no awarding of any prize. He could not believe that what he observed was all of it, but hoped to learn the truth from Groton very shortly.

Ivo headed for the door, wondering whether Afra could still be sleeping—there. This entire "night" had a surrealistic flavor; nothing was quite as he expected, though he had thought he had no expectations.

Once more there was a hand at his shoulder. He paused to look down at the woman who had translated for him. "You—you are one loss only," she said.

He nodded.

"And so with Dr. Kovonov." She gestured, and he observed the Russian still seated at the table. Everyone else was gone.

"A playoff? What's the prize?"

She left without answering, and there was nothing to do but rejoin Dr. Kovonov. Now, at last, it came to him: this was the man behind the scene, mentioned so often. The important Russian who compelled even Brad's intellectual respect.

Did this weird tourney connect with Brad's rush meeting with this man, yesterday? Had they agreed then that Brad should watch the destroyer with Senator Borland? Did Kovonov know Ivo's own secret, the power he had over Schön? He doubted that last; he just couldn't imagine that Brad would have told anyone that. Unless Afra—no! Still, this man appeared to be the most tangible source of information about Brad's action. And he spoke no English!

Kovonov picked up the red crayon and made seven dots, just as he had before. Ivo smiled; the good doctor really wanted to win this one!

This time, familiar with the rules, Ivo played flawlessly and had the victory, misère.

109

The Russian did not move or change expression. Ivo erased the design and picked up the blue marker, looking askance. A nod. He set down fifteen spots.

Kovonov smiled and took the crayon. The play was on.

The strategy was fiendishly complex, and his opponent dwelt a long time on each move. Ivo felt the strain as his peculiar talent wrestled with the problem and was baffled. He realized that Kovonov's greater experience was telling. Having plunged in well over the level of the sure guide of his instinct, Ivo knew that he was not a good player at all. If Kovonov fathomed the game before he did, his talent in the later stage would not avail him; it would only inform him when to concede. The situation was so complex that he might find himself in the losing position even if he did fathom it first; the proper strategy could guide the Russian to victory without complete analysis.

Twenty minutes passed. Kovonov's broad forehead was damp and his dark hair seemed to erect itself stiffly. Ivo was nervous, too, having no idea where he stood in the game, or whether he really wanted to win. Something very serious was at stake; something Kovonov might well be more competent to possess. The prize might not be a physical one at all.

Why should he let victory or loss concern him? Groton wanted him to win—but Groton hardly knew the truth. There were so many far more important matters to worry about, yet he was taking this foolish tournament as seriously as he ever had taken anything. What did the sprouts championship of this station matter, when his closest friend was a vegetable? So victory would place his name at the top of the sprout-ladder; would that make everything worthwhile?

Then the state of the game clarified: he saw that he could win. Three moves later the Russian reluctantly conceded, and it was over.

Kovonov stood up and walked regretfully over to the statuette ensconced in the middle of the room. Two out of three was it, Ivo decided. Carefully the man lifted the gilded steam-shovel from its pedestal—Ivo could see that it was very heavy, for its size—and brought it to the table.

This was the prize? "What does it mean?" he asked, pointing to the letters on the pedestal, S D P S. He could think of no other comment to make.

He had not expected an answer, in the circumstances, but he received one. "Sooper Dooper Pooper Scooper," Kovonov said with Russian accent, and smiled evilly. Then he, too, left, and Ivo remained to stare at this final evidence of Brad's subterranean humor.

A platinum-plated steam-shovel, including the crescent moon symbol, with a world in its mouth. Exactly the type of image Brad would fashion. A friendly insult to the station with the day's most powerful nose.

So they had had a tourney in Brad's memory, and the winner inherited the icon. Its value was undoubtedly very high, monetarily and symbolically—but did he really want it?

Ivo tucked it under his arm somewhat awkwardly—it *was* heavy—and marched back to his room. He was afraid the gesture might be misunderstood, if he returned it to its pedestal.

Afra woke as he entered, instantly alert. "What are you doing with that?" she demanded. She was, of course, still in night clothing, and she had forgotten to replace her slippers. It was quite a contrast to her usual precision of dress, but her beauty powered through all obstacles.

"I guess I won it."

"You *guess* you won it!" There was pink polish on her toenails.

"I entered this contest, and it was the prize. Should I put it back?"

"Shut up and let me think." She recovered her slippers, dusted off her feet, jammed on the footwear. She paced around the room as a man would pace, taking wide strides and swinging into the turns abruptly. The motions, however, did unmanly things to her body.

Ivo watched, still supporting the S D P S. He discovered that he liked Afra angry, too. She had torn off the kerchief, and her bright hair swirled as she spun. Absolutely refined Caucasian, Northwest European, no admixtures ... her torso a marvelous sight as thighs braked, arms accelerated, midriff flexed to avoid some structure. Definitely not for the polyglot creature that was what she would perceive him to be. Georgia born ...

She halted, hair, breasts and slippers stabilizing in unison. "All right. It's *not* all right, but all right! We'll have to make the best of it. Go fetch Harold—he put you up to this, I'm sure of it—and bring him to my room pronto. No, leave that thing here. Go—on."

Ivo set down the statuette and retreated before her urgency. He had intended to consult with Groton first; what had brought him back here with the S D P S?

Whom was he fooling? He *knew* what had brought him back.

"You did it!" Groton exclaimed when Ivo told him. "You took the Scooper!"

"I did it, yes. Now Afra's furious. She wants to see you in her room. Pronto, she says."

"Right. Smart girl, that. We're going to be busy as hell." Ivo had not heard Groton speak that colloquially before, and he took it as another indication of strain. *The afflatus of war*, he thought ironically, *was breathed upon them all*. History repeated itself, as ever. The Senator, in death, had destroyed the macroscope, and all that it might accomplish for the benefit of mankind.

Groton raised his voice. "Beatryx!"

"Yes, dear," came the quick answer.

"Get into your suit and stand by the tube; we'll be ferrying some stuff out in a hurry." Without waiting for her acknowledgment, he drew Ivo back into the hall. "God, I'm glad you did it," he said. "They have the screws into us, and this is the only way."

"You've left me behind. What are you talking about?"

"No time," Groton said.

Ivo shrugged once more and followed.

Afra was already in her own suit, the transparent helmet flopping at her back. "Change, Ivo," she snapped. "Better stick with him, Harold; he's slow on the uptake."

"I ask again: what is this all about?" Ivo said as Groton hurried him into his space suit. "Why did you have me enter that tourney, and why is Afra so upset about it? Has the whole station lost its mind?" *The afflatus of—*

"It's that dead senator," Groton said, as though that clarified everything. "Borland is very important in politics, and we're taking the rap for assassinating him. That flunky of his got on the teletype before we knew it and screamed murder—exactly that. That wipes us out."

"Well, of course there would be an investigation. But he demanded to see the destroyer, and he had been warned. The evidence should be clear enough."

Groton stopped for a moment. "You are out of touch! Don't you know the situation here?"

"Just that the macroscope is under nominal UN auspices, as are all the projects beyond Earth-orbit. Brad told me about the formula for time and financing—" Actually, he could understand why a thing like the destroyer could result in the dismantling of the macroscope, particularly when scandal of this nature developed. But he wanted to hear Groton's explanation, because that might finally clarify this other business with the tourney and the S D P S.

Groton finished dressing Ivo, then turned to his own suit. In succinct bursts between motions he delivered the political reality, as seen by one who had not talked with the Senator directly. Ivo found this parallel viewpoint intriguing.

Senator Borland (Groton said) was no ordinary man. His connections were potent, not so much in America as in the UN. There were many influential personages behind him, and not a small amount of cash. His boast that he knew the governments of the station's member-countries (that remark had orbited the personnel rapidly!) better than did their own nationals had not been empty; he was a sophisticated parlayer of influence on an international scale. He would do such-and-such, if in such-and-such a position, and the figures behind the thrones and presidencies knew what and how. It was to China's interest that he achieve greater influence in the American farming scheme, for the potential of trading in grain remained; it was to Russia's interest that he make the automotive-exports standards committee, for it regulated other machinery than cars, ranging from precision ball-bearings to theodolites; to South Africa's interest that he establish private liaison with BlaPow, Inc.

Borland was all things to all peoples—but he was good at it. A promoter could accomplish a great deal, if sophisticated enough. He had already shown that he could and would deliver the goods while making political hay doing it. He had the connections, he had the charisma; somehow private meetings with him made public converts.

Ivo, remembering the Borland-Carpenter dialogue, understood that. Ivo himself was such a convert.

The death of such a man (Groton continued) was bound to mean real trouble, whatever the circumstances.

113

Too many projects were balancing in the air, and the demise of the juggler meant that many would crash. Pledges could no longer be honored, repercussions no longer stymied.

The macroscope was the major UN effort. More international interests were crucially involved there than in any other area. Borland surely had seen its potential, and had acted to make it his own. It represented a ready way to make good on all his commitments, while benefiting the world as a whole. And perhaps he had intended to do just that, for altruistic reasons. (Ivo had not expected this tack.) Perhaps his ambition had gone beyond power, since he was in a position to appreciate how desperately the world needed help. Perhaps the answer to the ruin forecast by the Sung planet's example had been Borland: someone to organize a more practical application of the immense knowledge available. Who could say for sure, now?

But Borland had died, and in the worst possible manner. He had not trusted hearsay evidence; he had not really believed that the destroyer could bring him down. So he had called its bluff—and lost. The UN would believe that the station personnel had murdered him, perhaps by tricking him into confrontation with that killer from space.

Trouble? As the international eggs began to fall and splatter, the need would grow very strong for an international scapegoat. The seeming cause of crisis: the macroscope.

Now they were both suited and Ivo had still not discovered what they were going about so urgently.

Afra was at the storeroom, moving things about with apparent abandon in the fractional gravity. Ivo spied crates of drugs, spices, grains, bandages and cheese, as well as cylinders of oxygen and liquid nutrient. "What's your blood type?" she demanded of him.

"O-positive." What could he do, but answer?

She selected a canister and dumped it near the door. Ivo looked at it: CONDENSED BLOOD O-POSITIVE. There was more technical description, but he averted his eyes, feeling unpleasantly giddy. Presumably there were ways to adjust for the myriad other factors involved in the matching of blood safely. *What made her think he would need this?*

The storeroom supervisor sat at his desk, head drooping forward as though he were asleep. "Shouldn't he be checking this stuff out?" Ivo inquired.

"I fed him a mickey," Afra said. "Or were you being facetious?"

Ivo did not know how to answer that, so didn't try. There was so much he didn't know about this situation!

Afra turned to Groton. "I'll shape this up here and move it with the powercart. You get the personal junk assembled. Better make it one box each, limit."

"What do you need?" Groton asked Ivo.

So many unanswered questions, but *he* had to do the answering! "If you mean what do I take with me when I leave this place, nothing. I have my flute with me."

"I fogot—you're already suited," Afra said. "I'll select some clothing for you; more efficient that way." She turned to Groton. "Better fetch Joseph."

Ivo started. "Joseph! Isn't that the souped-up rocket?"

"Right," Groton agreed. "Come on."

He and Ivo jetted across to the huge rocket much as Brad had demonstrated the first trip to the macroscope proper, except for the necessary change in course this time. Spurts from a cylinder of hydrogen peroxide took care of the propulsion.

Joseph's hull was like a planetoid, seeming much vaster than it was, since there were no nearby objects to contrast for size. Ivo managed to land on his feet, having gained from his prior experience, and the magnetic shoe-bands took hold so that he could walk. They marched to the control compartment airlock and knocked.

The interior was larger than that of the shuttle. Joseph had been gutted and rebuilt, so that the layout was like nothing Ivo had seen in space. Evidently the atomic equipment occupied less volume than had the chemical fuel before it, so that one of the monster internal tanks could be used for living space. He could almost imagine that he was in a futuristic submarine.

In a manner of thinking, this *was* a futuristic sub.

"Course correction," Groton said to the attendant. "Can you hitch this baby up to the scope?"

"Sure, in a couple of days," the man said amicably.

"This is an emergency. Two hours."

115

"I can move it there, but I can't hitch it up in that time. Take a trained crew of twenty men to do that."

Groton rolled his eyes. "Ouch! Well, you move it over and I'll do what I can. Ivo, better jet back to the scope and tell Afra, while I check with Kovonov. This is going to be sticky."

The attendant held up a hand. "I don't know what you're talking about, naturally—but don't you think *you'd* better see Miss Summerfield?"

"No. Ivo doesn't—" Groton stopped. "Damn, yes. It has to be that way. Ivo, go tell Kovonov what we need. Then join us there. Don't waste any time."

Ivo hung on to his patience. "Exactly what are you doing? Why do you want to hitch Joseph to the macroscope?"

"To correct the scope's course, as I explained."

"What's the matter with its present course? It's attached to the station, after all."

"We think it is about to fall into the sun."

"That's ridiculous! It's in orbit! And the station—"

The attendant smiled. "It might as well fall. The UN will destroy it anyway."

"So you see, we need that crew immediately. Tell Kovonov."

Ivo saw that they weren't going to give him a legitimate explanation. Angrily, he snapped his helmet to and left the compartment.

Kovonov's office was a niche in a heavy-gravity shell. It struck Ivo that this was an effective way to keep visits brief; anyone who stayed too long would fatigue rapidly. Momentary weight-increase could be put up with, but a steady diet of it was distinctly unpleasant. He wondered how the host endured it.

Kovonov looked up from a book set in what Ivo assumed to be Russian type. He did not speak.

The language barrier! "Groton says we need a crew of twenty men to stop the macroscope from falling into the sun," Ivo said, knowing that the Russian could not understand a word.

Kovonov listened gravely, then touched two switches. Ivo heard his own words played back: they had been recorded. Another voice rattled off incomprehensible syllables: the translation.

116

Kovonov nodded.

"Can you tell me what this is all about? I don't—"

The hand came up to silence him. Kovonov switched off the machine without obtaining the translation and brought out a small blackboard and two colored pieces of chalk. He made three blue dots.

What was this fascination with sprouts? The scientists of this station acted as though a simple game were more important than life or death. Did Kovonov seriously mean to ignore his question and rechallenge for the championship?

But it was not a contest this time. Kovonov filled in the connections himself without offering the chalk to Ivo. He was setting up a three-spot demonstration game of no particular complexity. The series went seven moves:

The result reminded Ivo of a shovel. "But it isn't finished," he said. "There's a free spot at either end."

Kovonov turned the panel over without erasing it and set up three dots more nearly in line, this time in red. He played through in the same fashion as before. This game, when halted, looked more like a telescope.

He handed the board to Ivo.

Obviously the designs were significant, rather than the games from which they were derived. The shovel on one side, telescope on the other. They were topologically

117

equivalent, Ivo's talent informed him; one could be distorted into the other without the erasure or crossing of any of the lines. They were, in fact, the same game, played in the same fashion. A three-spot sprout effort brought to one step from conclusion.

Kovonov was trying to tell him something.

Then he had it. The shovel, the scope—the same, linked by the sprouts. By extension, the steam-shovel and the macroscope. He had entered the sprouts tourney—

And won the macroscope!

Senator Borland's death spelled the end of the project, by whatever line of reasoning one approached it. This was a culmination none of the participating scientists or other personnel desired. There was no internal rivalry in this connection; nationality had been superseded by a higher calling. There appeared to be no way to reverse the ponderous, political, UN decision.

Unless someone took away the macroscope, and thus preserved it from harm. Kovonov had obviously intended to win this privilege—until Ivo had defeated him in the runoff. Now the onus was his own.

It would mean banishment from Earth, of course. Such a colossal theft—

Ivo knew he was going to do it. They were right: the macroscope was far too valuable to abolish, or even to entrust to political whim. The presence of the destroyer, far from arguing against the macroscope, pointed up the extreme necessity of further study. Mankind could not turn isolationist; that was the way of the proboscoids.

The knowledge of the universe (the galaxy, at least) lay within man's reach, if not his grasp. It was a knowledge man had to have, however shortsighted the local politicians. Ivo had the ability to use the macroscope, since he had demonstrated his ability to survive the destroyer. He did not have to fear ambush and mindlessness in the main band. He also had contact—potential contact—with the person who could make the most of that knowledge: Schön. Perhaps this was the real reason Brad had summoned him. Not to crack the destroyer; to make use of the knowledge behind it, once cracked.

Except that he did not intend to involve Schön. This was something he would undertake by himself—no matter how lonely a task it was. He had won the right. At least he would have the macroscope for company, and would be able to watch the events of Earth. If the political situation changed, he would know it, and could bring home the instrument.

Kovonov was waiting patiently for his chain of thought to finish. Ivo erased the blackboard, both sides, and set it down. He stood up and gravely offered his hand to the Russian. Perhaps, of the two of them, the Russian had the more difficult task, for the UN investigation would not be kind. Heads, figuratively and possibly literally, would roll.

In a gesture as grave as Ivo's, Kovonov took that hand.

CHAPTER 4

The crew was already at work; Kovonov's terse instruction had evidently been sufficient. It was amazing how much could be accomplished on an unofficial basis. Nobody had to admit to complicity in the theft, and he was sure the UN would have an impossibly difficult time making a case against anyone staying behind. How would they, for example, prove that the storeroom attendant had knowingly accepted Afra's doped offering?

On the other hand, that same theft might solve the UN problem. If they intended to close down the macroscope—well, that had already been accomplished for them. There could be a great public hue, but minor private sorrow.

How extravagantly his conjecture fluctuated! One moment he was sure disaster stalked the station personnel; the next, that all was well. But he would not need to conjecture. He could watch the whole show on the macroscope!

The rocket's snout fitted into a matching cavity in the bottom of the scope's housing, so that docking was possible without fouling the guy lines. He was sure that depression had not been there before; the crew must have removed the covering plates. Probably it was crowded inside, too, with that metal intruding, but it was a neat travel arrangement.

The assembled package resembled a massive mushroom, with stubby rootlets and a relatively small spherical head. The fifty-foot diameter of the macroscope housing bulged beyond the thirty-three-foot-thick rocket, but was smaller in overall volume. Even so, it hardly seemed large enough to hold the complex equipment necessary—but of course the computers were miniaturized, using laser memory and other remarkable techniques. Presumably the unit would take off at right angles to the doughnut, breaking the ties, then maneuver to head in the right direction.

What *was* the right direction? He had no idea. Space was vast ... yet where could Joseph go, where could he hide, where the telescopes of Earth could not locate him, the missiles seek him out? The immense honor of the task seemed to have less desirable ramifications.

Ivo drifted across to the scene of activity. Men were still busy, but the task appeared to be virtually complete. No one paid attention to him—a deliberate and necessary slight, he realized. He could anticipate the coming dialogue:

UN: What happened to the macroscope?

PERSONNEL: We didn't see anything. Must've been that new fellow, the one Dr. Carpenter brought in. We were just shaping it up for a shift in orbit—

And Dr. Carpenter would not be in condition to answer questions.

As a matter of fact, their investigation into the circumstances surrounding Senator Borland's demise would run into the same blank end. Only two people had shared the experience that killed him; one was absent in mind, the other would be absent in body. Perhaps the alien signal was to blame for both? Kovonov would remark upon the strangeness of the thief's prior actions: barging into an innocent recreational session, removing the station emblem from its pedestal, poking around the premises. There would be the recording of his voice, as he intruded into the Russian's study: expressing confusion. Obviously that terrible session with the destroyer had killed one, stupefied the second, and thrown the third into a borderline aberration that prompted him to abscond with the scope.

121

It was not the place in history Ivo would have selected for himself, but it was necessary. The macroscope had to be saved from the UN repercussion, and it was better that a person like Ivo Archer bear the onus than one like Dr. Kovonov. Even through the language barrier, Ivo had come to appreciate the qualities of the man.

He landed on the head of the mushroom and made his way to the lock. No workmen, coincidentally, were facing in his direction. The coincidence held for the several minutes it took him to reach the lock and figure out its mode of operation. It seemed it *could* be opened from the outside, with the proper tool—and such a tool had been forgotten nearby. It was stuck to the metal hull, held there by its magnetism. An insertion, a twist; the mechanism clicked over, and the lock came open with no wasteful outrush of air. He climbed inside and shut himself in.

Groton was waiting for him. "Everything clear? We want to be ready to move as soon as the crew finishes. I don't know how rapidly the UN ship will get here."

"They seem to be finished outside, if that's what you mean."

Groton put on earphones. "Ivo's here," he said into the intercom. "Give us two minutes to strap down, then cut loose, girls."

Ivo could not hear the reply, but he had been reassured of one thing: Afra was coming along. He had known she had to come, yet doubted it too. To go to space with her

. . .

They tied down on either side of the mighty nose cone that transfixed the center compartment. There was a port set in its side for direct admission to Joseph, but this remained sealed.

The framework shuddered; then they were smitten by the power of the atomic rocket. At triple-gravity acceleration, the macroscope tore free of its moorings.

Five grueling minutes later the drive cut off and they were in blessed free-fall again. "We're on our way," Groton said soberly. "Let's confer with the pilot." He unstrapped and jostled around to the hatch in the nose of Joseph.

It opened, and a helmeted figure emerged, clumsy and drifting upward (according to Ivo's orientation) in the confined absence of gravity. Groton held on to the deck with his toes hooked into a handhold and offered a steadying arm. It was Beatryx.

A second figure floated through: Afra. "I think we'd better put him in here," she said. "He doesn't need to move about. . . ."

"Him?" Ivo asked.

She trained those beautiful eyes upon him: "Brad. I couldn't leave him behind, of course."

Paradise lost! Yet with the keen disappointment came the relief of something else as well: guilt. The dead man was here to look after his own.

And Brad had been Ivo's friend, too.

They got the limp body set up in a nook formed by outthrusts of inscrutable equipment. Ivo, entering Joseph, found stacked, tied crates: the plentiful supplies whose lading Afra had supervised. They seemed to have planned this theft carefully.

The immediate chores accomplished, they clung to handholds (the magnetic shoes had been discarded with the suits) and stared at each other. Carefully planned? It seemed that no one had looked beyond this point. The break had been made, almost incredibly; what next?

Afra stepped into the breach. "Obviously we have two objectives: keep clear of the UN, and pick up Schön. We should be able to do the first as long as we keep moving away from Earth—but we can't accomplish the second without coming in *close* to Earth. That's our problem."

"That's assuming Schön is on Earth," Groton said.

Afra closed on Ivo. "*Is* Schön on Earth?"

"No."

"Wonderful! We'll have much less trouble reaching him in space, though it won't be easy even so. The moon station wouldn't really be much of an improvement, but one of the asteroid units . . . Where is he?"

"I am not free to tell you."

Afra's mercurial temper showed. "Now look, Ivo. We have gone to a good deal of trouble, not to mention banishment, to make it possible for you to summon Schön and bring him to the macroscope. You can't simply—"

"Excuse me," Groton said. "We know Ivo isn't trying to be obstructive. Let's give him a chance to explain what he means."

Ivo found this approach no more acceptable than the other. "I can't explain. Schön isn't—well, I'm just not certain yet that we need him."

Afra became deadly quiet. "You mean you *won't* bring him?"

"I guess that's what I mean."

Her righteous wrath magnified. "And all by yourself you're going to hide Joseph and operate the macroscope and get medical help for—"

This time it was Beatryx who broke in. "I think I have a letter for someone," she said. "I found it in the chute, but everything was in such a hurry—"

Groton took it from her. "Could be an unofficial farewell from someone." He looked at the address. "An arrow?"

"An arrow!" Afra was suddenly interested. "That's from Schön!"

Ivo took it and opened it, not happily. It was obvious that Schön was at least partially aware of recent events, and that surely meant trouble.

The paper within contained no words, just a diagram. The others clustered around to look at it.

"A pitchfork," Beatryx said, concerned because she had delivered the message. "What does it mean?"

"I hesitate to point this out—" Groton began.

"Let me think!" Afra said. "I've been through this before. Schön doesn't like to communicate directly for some reason, but what he has to say is bound to be important." She took the paper and floated off by herself, concentrating.

Groton produced his notebook and wrote something down. "Schön must know where we are and what we're doing," he said. "Could this be a hint where to find him?"

"It isn't that easy," Ivo said.

"Neptune!" Afra exclaimed. "That's the symbol for Neptune!"

"God of the sea—and more," Groton said, holding out his paper. Upon it, Ivo saw now, was the word NEPTUNE. Groton had known, waiting only for Afra's confirmation.

124

"The *planet*," she said. "That's the trident. All the planets have their symbols. Mars is the spear and shield of the god of war; Venus is the goddess's hand-mirror. So this is Neptune."

"Your interpretation is interesting," Groton said, privately amused about something. "But remember, those symbols do have other connotations."

"Male and female, of course," Afra said. "But Neptune is unmistakable."

Groton did not push the matter, but Ivo was sure he had been driving at something else.

"Even Earth?" Beatryx inquired, catching up to an earlier comment.

"That's an upside-down Venus symbol. I don't remember them all, but I am sure of Neptune."

Groton was still entertained. "I agree. It is Neptune. But I repeat: is this to be taken as an indication of location, or is it something more subtle?"

"Isn't Neptune very far away?" Beatryx asked.

"Ridiculous!" Afra said hotly, ignoring the other woman. "No ship has gone there yet."

"Not to mention the problem of delivering the letter here," Groton added.

"Something is wrong. We have misread the signal."

"I wonder," Groton said. "What was that earlier contact you mentioned that you had with Schön? Was it like this?"

"No. It—" She turned abruptly to Ivo. *"What* poem? *Which* poet?"

Thus, in delayed fashion, she had come at it. He had foolishly told her that the earlier message represented a line of poetry with which he was familiar, and she had not forgotten. Could he stave off her assault?

"American. It was just Schön's way of telling me that he knew what was up. Of telling *you* actually, since I couldn't read it."

"That much was obvious. Name the poet and piece."

"I don't see that that is relevant to—"

"An American poet, you said. Prominent?"

"Yes, but—"

"Born what century? Seventeenth?"

"No. Why do you—"

"Eighteenth?"

"No." She would not be denied.

"Nineteenth?"

"Yes, but—"

"Whitman?"

"No."

"Frost? Sandburg?"

"No."

"But male?"

"Yes."

"Eliot? Pound? Archibald MacLeish?"

"No." He remained helpless before her intensity.

"Ransom? Wallace Stevens? Cummings? Hart Crane?"

"I hate to break in," Groton said, "but we do have more pressing—"

She pointed her manicured finger at Ivo. "Vachel Lindsay!"

"The UN may be on our tail," Groton said. "If we don't make our decision soon, we could lose it by default."

"All right!" she snapped, returning to him. "First, reconnaissance. We have to know whether there is pursuit yet, and of what type, so we can take evasive action. Once we're safe, we can start running down Schön. I'm convinced our sprout-winner here is hiding something important. Once we get that, we'll have a better notion what Schön is doing, and where."

"I appreciate your ruthlessness," Groton said dryly. "Where do we go from here?"

Ivo was immensely relieved to have the subject change. Afra was correct: he was hiding something important. "How will we know where the UN is? Don't we have to keep radio silence, or something?"

She only glanced disparagingly at him. How else, he realized then, but with the macroscope itself?

"Trying to run down a single ship with this equipment is like aiming the atomic cannon at no-see-em gnats," Groton observed.

"The torus will know," Afra said. "We'll have to watch it—the teletype, maybe, to monitor incoming messages. Or we can simply blast off now in any direction and outrun whatever pursuit forms."

"Not," Groton said succinctly, "a robot."

She straightened, startled. "All right. I'll get on the scope. We'd better know the worst."

"Can you stay off the haunted frequency?"

"Calculated risk. With practice—"

"With practice like that, we'll have *two* casualties aboard to clean up."

Ivo recalled the loss of intestinal control of the victims and realized how hard such a notion would strike a finicky girl like Afra. "I seem to be immune," he said. "At least, I can avoid it successfully. And I did win the privilege. If you will show me how to operate the controls—"

This time Afra seemed relieved. "I'll instruct you. I'll have to operate blind, but it should work. Here, I'll turn off the main screen; you use the helmet."

And she set him up in the control chair and fastened the equipment upon him, placing the heavy goggles over his eyes. Ivo wished there were more than sheer practicality in the operation, but knew there was not; it was more efficient for her to do these things for him than to direct him through it, this first time.

"Your left hand controls the computer directives. Here, I'll put you on the ten-key complex." Her hand took his and carried it to a buttoned surface like that of an adding machine. This was not the same control he had seen Brad employ, he was sure. Alternate inputs? A junior set for the novice? The goggles cut off all outside vision, so he, not she, was "blind."

"We have a number of important locations precoded," she continued. "You should memorize them, if you're going to do this regularly, but right now I'll give them to you. These will place you on Earth, the Luna bases, any of the artificial satellites or the macroscope station—the torus." She spieled off numbers, and he obediently pressed the buttons. Twice he miskeyed and had to start over; the third time she placed her hand over his and depressed his fingers for him in the proper order and places. Her digits were soft and cool and firm—as he imagined the rest of her body to be.

Light flared into his eyes. He was a hundred yards from the torus, looking down at it from sunside, blinded by the reflection from its metal plates.

"The next coding is for semimanual control," she said. "You can't possibly keep the celestial motions aligned, but

127

you can override portions of the computer's automatic correction and drift a little." She directed him through the necessary numeric instruction. "Now you can apply your right hand. Drive it as you would a car—but remember it is three-dimensional." He felt the mounted ball, its surface actually sandpaper-rough for perfect traction. "Tilt for direction of motion, twist for orientation. Be careful—this is where the destroyer sometimes intrudes. You have to stick to fringe reception—which is more than adequate, at this range. Now set your drift toward the torus; don't worry, you'll pass right through the walls. You'll have to practice a bit to get it down. . . ."

Ivo tilted and twisted—and was rewarded by a dizzying tailspin in which the intolerable blaze of Sol scorched across his eyeballs every three seconds.

"Not so much!" she cautioned after the fact. It was a lesson that would not have to be repeated.

He reduced his efforts and began to slide toward the station, twitching the direction of his gaze to cover it properly. The computer, he thought, must perform a tremendous task, for surely a completely different flow of macrons would be required for each change in direction—yet the transition was smooth. Probably at distances of many light-years such versatility diminished, until a view from the far side of the galaxy would be one direction only, take it or leave it.

It was beginning to work for him, and it gave him a feeling of power.

There was an odor.

"No, that's my job," Afra said, calling out to someone else. "You keep practicing, Ivo; I think you have the general idea. Try to work your way inside. I'll be back in a moment."

The smell and the sound told him: nature had summoned Brad, and Afra had a job of cleaning up and changing to do. He had to admit she had grit.

He thought of the right-hand control as a flute, and though there was no particular resemblance, control was suddenly easier. Now he could draw on his other talent, that peculiar digital dexterity and sense of tone musicians possessed. He shot through the wall of the torus, schooling himself not to wince, and stopped within the first hall. He reoriented, and was sure he was maintaining spatial stabil-

ity, but the hall was tilting over steadily. He corrected—
and lost it again.

Then he realized: the station was spinning, of course!
He had to compensate not only for its motions in space,
but for its internal rotation. He had to perform, in effect,
a continuing spiral, matching velocities with whatever portion of the station he chose to view. An intricate adjustment, indeed!

He mastered it, driving his viewpoint around as though
it were a racing car upon a treacherous track. Then he
oriented for a "walk" along the hall. A twist superimposed
upon the other adjustments, and he was facing the way he
wanted; a tilt, and he was trotting down the hall toward
Kovonov's office.

The Russian was playing solitary sprouts. "If only I
could talk to you, Kov!" Ivo exclaimed. "Just to ask you
where that UN ship is, if there is one. . . ."

"In Russian?" He jumped, but of course Kovonov had
not spoken. Afra was back, her tone deceptively sweet.

Ivo felt the slow flush move up his face to the goggles
and knew she was seeing it also, but he kept a steady
image of the office. There had to be some way to make
contact, and he was sure Kovonov was the key. The man
had been too knowledgeable, too familiar with the necessary problems—perhaps because he had rehearsed this
voyage himself. If anyone could communicate, across this
barrier so much greater than that of language—

He concentrated on the board before the Russian. A
vital message had been communicated through this board
not so long ago, and perhaps another waited. Meanwhile,
this was practice of another sort, since he had discovered
in the course of his adjustments that size, too, could be
directly controlled. Such adaptations would necessarily become more and more precise as the range increased, in
future forays, and he felt he ought to have it down pat.
This fine-tuning became an art; it was hardly accident that
his musical ability was telling.

"What are you doing?" Afra demanded.

Ivo stifled an irritable reply. Surely she realized how
delicate—

"Reexamining the portents, you might say," Groton
said, and Ivo realized with relief that Afra's question had
been directed at the older man.

"Your damned astrology tomes!" she exclaimed. "Your wife brought texts on art and music, but *you* had to bring—"

"Better than the pretty clothing *you* packed," Groton replied, his tone showing his unperturbed smile. But the argument was on. Tension had to seek its sublimations.

And control came. Smoothly Ivo brought the focus down upon the sprouts-board, keeping it clear, magnifying the picture, until the dotted lines and loops loomed enormously across his field of vision. He centered on a single dot, making it swell up as though it were a planet. The illusion captured him, as illusions did; he was coming in for a landing, spaceship balanced. Time for the braking rockets. . . .

"Doesn't it seem just the merest trifle ridiculous to twiddle with squiggles on paper while there is so much of importance going on?" Afra inquired, and again Ivo had to confine a guilty start.

"I would prefer to call it the interpretation of the nuances of a horoscope," Groton said calmly. He was better equipped, temperamentally, to fence with her than Ivo was. Beatryx must have gone back to the supply compartment. since she was not present to break this up. "I hardly consider it ridiculous to explore our situation and resources with the best instruments available. There is, as you point out, much of importance going on."

"Are you seriously trying to equate the use of the macroscope with your occult hobby?"

"I do not consider astrology to be in any sense 'occult,' if by that term you mean to imply anything fantastic or magical or unscientific. In the sense that both are tools of immense complexity and potency, yes, I would equate astrology with the macroscope."

"Let me get this quite straight. You make a representation of the constellations—only those within the narrow belt of the zodiac, ignoring the rest of the sky—and planets—those of Sol's system exclusively—as they appear in Earth's sky at the moment of a person's birth . . . and from that mishmash you claim to be able to predict his entire life including accidents and acts of God, so that you can tell him—for a suitable fee—to watch out for trouble on a given day or to invest in a certain stock—and yet you claim there is nothing supernatural or at least unethical about this procedure?"

"What you describe is undoubtedly supernatural and possibly of dubious ethics, but it *isn't* astrology. You are attributing erroneous claims to this science, then blaming it because it does not and can not make good on them."

"Exactly what is your definition of astrology, then?"

"I can hardly define it in a sentence, Afra."

"Try." Did she think she had him?

"The doctrine of Microcosm and Macrocosm—that is, the concept of the individual as the cosmos in miniature, while the greater universe is total man in his real being."

The dot-planet broke up into swirls and blobs. He was too close; the resolution of the chalk was not that fine. Soon he would have to center on one section of it, then on a subsection, and so on into the microcosm. . . .

Doctrine of microcosm. . . .

"A microscope!" he said, finding it excruciatingly funny. For the macroscope *was*, in this case, a microscope. An astonishingly versatile instrument. Could it be that each dot in a game of sprouts had its own gravitic aura that set up macronic ripples for him to pick up? Talk of sensitivity!

"What?" Afra sounded angry.

Oops. "Nothing." Carefully, he reversed the action, and the scattered chalk coalesced. Now he was taking off from the planet, watching it reform into a distant dot that became a mere point of light against the black background of space. The other lines appeared, marking constellations of the night sky. Could Groton analyze them astrologically?

"All right," Afra said. "Score one for you. You put me off again. But this time I'm not going to let you slip out of an honest discussion. I want to have your specific rationale for this foolishness."

Nothing like handing him loaded dice, Ivo thought wryly—but he, too, was curious.

"Well, it is evident that there are certain objects in the universe," Groton said gamely, "and that they are in constant motion, relative to Earth and to each other. That's one reason we require the assistance of a computer to orient the macroscope. These masses, and their respective movements, interrelate considerably. That is, the sun carries its family of planets along with it and forces them into particular orbits, while the planets affect their satellites and even distort the orbits of other planets."

"That is not precisely the way modern theory describes the situation, but for the sake of argument we'll accept it. So granted. The Solar system interacts." She sounded impatient, eager for the kill.

"Similarly, there are a number of human beings and other creatures on the Earth, and they relate to each other and interact in an almost impenetrably complex pattern. We merely draw a parallel to the apparent motions of the—"

"Now we come to it. Mars makes men warlike?"

"No! There is no causal connection. In astrology the Earth is considered to be the center of the universe, and the individual's place of birth is the center of his chart. This is not at all contrary to astronomy, incidentally; it is just a modification of viewpoint, for our convenience."

Just as, Ivo thought, he was now performing all kinds of clever manipulations to make his macroscopic viewpoint stable. It would be impossible to accomplish anything if he tried to orient on galactic or even Solar "rest." The center of the universe had to be where the observer was.

He was now paying more attention to the dialogue than to the semiautomatic refinements of macroscopic control, but was jolted back to business. His image was gone! Had he lost touch?

No—Kovonov had merely removed the board. How easy to forget reality, to become involved, to begin to believe in one's fancies, and to see the monster hand of the image as the hand of God, drawing away the firmament. He had to guard against personification; it could unhinge him.

He adjusted the image so as to watch Kovonov, life-sized. The man looked about almost furtively, then drew from his desk drawer a card. He set this on the table.

There was print on it. Skillfully now, Ivo centered on that print, clarified it, read it. It was not Russian!

S D P S

A message for him! Kovonov *was* trying to communicate!

After a minute the Russian put the card away and replaced the board. He resumed his sprouts doodling.

Could that be all? Where was the rest of it?

"So you claim the positions of the planets in the sky at the moment of my birth determine my fate, despite anything I might have to say about it."

"By no means. I merely want you to concede the possibility of a relation between the configuration of the heavens at any particular moment and that of human affairs. It doesn't have to be a *causal* relation, or even a consistent one. Just a relation."

"You bastard," she said without rancor, "you've got me halfway into your camp already."

Bastard? Ivo thought. Was this the innocent girl who had blushed so delicately at the very mention of S D P S? He certainly was seeing another side of her now.

"Of *course* there's a relation!" she continued irately. "There's a relation between a grain of sand at the bottom of the Indian Ocean and my grandfather's gold tooth. But it is hardly significant—and if it were, what proof do you have that your astrology can clarify it, when science can not?"

"Astrology *is* a science. It is built upon the scientific method and endures by it. The discipline is as rigorous as any you can name."

"Geometry."

"All right. How do you 'prove' the basic theorems of geometry?"

"Such as A = ½ BH, for a triangle? You're the engineer. There must be a dozen ways to—"

"One will suffice. You're thinking of making constructs and demonstrating that your One-times-Base-times-Height figure is the sum of congruent pairs of right-angle triangles, or something like that, correct? But how do you prove congruence? Don't tell me angle-side-angle or side-side-side; I want to know how, in the ultimate definition, you prove your proofs. What is your true basis?"

"Well, you can't have a strictly geometrical proof for the initial theorem, of course. You have to start with one assumption, then build logically from that. So we assume that if one angle between two measured sides is fixed, the entire triangle is fixed. It works perfectly consistently."

"But what if it's wrong?"

"It *isn't* wrong. You can measure triangles full-time for a lifetime, and you'll never find an exception."

"Suppose I transfer side-angle-side from a flat surface to a torus?"

She almost spluttered. "You have to match surfaces. You know that."

It seemed to Ivo that Groton had just scored another point, but for some reason the man didn't follow it up. "So experience is your guideline, then," Groton said.

"Yes."

"That's the basis for astrology, too."

"Experience? That the position of Mars determines man's fate?"

"That the zodiacal configuration at a person's birth indicates certain things about his circumstance and personality. Astrologers have been making observations and refining their techniques for many centuries—it *is* one of the most ancient of disciplines—until today the science is as close to accuracy as it has ever been. There is still much to learn, just as there is about geometry, but it is experience and not guesswork that modifies our application. I do not claim that the stars or planets determine your fate; I do suggest that your life is circumscribed by complex factors and influences, in much the same way as the motions of the planets and stars are circumscribed, and that the complex of your life and the complex of the universe may run in a parallel course. Astrology attempts to draw useful parallels between these two admittedly diverse areas, since what is obscure in one realm may be apparent in the other. In this way it may be possible to clarify aspects of your life that may not otherwise be properly understood. The one correspondence we can fix with any degree of certainty is the moment of birth, so we must use that as the starting point for the individual—but that is all it is. A starting point, just as your side-angle-side measurement is a possible starting point for the entire science of geometry. The difference is that astrology does not attempt to determine facts, since these are things you may ascertain for yourself. It reveals nothing that is hidden. Instead it facilitates the measure and judgment of what is actually encountered in experience."

Ivo remembered the Senator's distinction between truth and meaning in philosophy.

"That sounds closer to psychology than astronomy," Afra said.

"It should. The relation between astronomy and astrology is entirely superficial. We depend upon the astronomers for measurements of planetary motions and such, but after that we part company. The metaphysical opinions of astronomers have no bearing on astrology; these gentlemen are simply not competent in that area, however competent they may be in their own field, that I admit they have mastered with a skill they have not even thought of applying to astrology. A good astrologer doesn't need a telescope; he does need a sound grasp of practical psychology."

Ivo had been watching Kovonov all this time, but there had been no other sign. It was time to get advice. "I hate to interrupt," he said, "but I seem to be stalled."

Afra came over. "I'm sorry. I let fantasy distract me and forgot all about you. What is it?"

Ivo described what had taken place in the torus.

"Obviously he is referring to the statuette," she said.

It was amazing how stupid she could make him feel, how quickly. He dollied the image through the wall and down the hall to the common room.

The S D P S was gone, of course, but the pedestal remained. Upon it was a sheet of paper. An anonymous message, he realized, that could implicate no one. It was printed in teletype caps:

CRAFT ALERTED. PROCEEDING FROM MOONBASE THIS DATE 1300 TORUS TIME. ARMED. ACCELERATE WHEN ADVISED. URGENT.

"Oh, God, they *are* on our tail!" Afra snapped. "And here I've been wasting precious time on—"

"Armed?"

"That means a ship-mounted laser. Supposed to be top secret, but we all knew about it."

"So there *has* been some poop-scooping."

"In self-defense. Space is supposed to be free of weapons, and the UN enforces that—but Brad was suspicious of a UN-sponsored industrial complex on the moon. Ruinously inefficient location, with all supplies ferried up from Earth. So we peeked. Presumably it's for good use—to *keep* the peace—but the UN is building a fleet that is very like an incipient armada. That space-borne

135

laser is dangerous at indefinite range—as we may discover first-hand if we don't behave."

"Why don't they burn us now, then? They must have us spotted."

"Because they want to preserve the macroscope. You can be sure that if they officially dismantle it, there will be an unofficial remantling. An insidious group has obtained control of the UN space arm, or *will* obtain it; again, we only know because we . . . scooped. A fleet of ships and the macroscope—that's about as real as power gets. That could have been what Borland was really investigating. He had the nose for that sort of thing."

"And they would want to keep their laser secret," Groton put in. "If they use it, everyone will know, and that will be sticky."

"*And* because the only equipment precise enough to aim a beam that narrow accurately for that range is right here with us," Afra said. "They'll have to get pretty close before they can be sure of us with one-burst, particularly if we're maneuvering."

Ivo was fazed by such political reality. "Why don't they just broadcast an ultimatum to us?"

"And admit to the world that somebody has snitched the macroscope from under their nose? They can certainly keep *that* secret if we can. Can you maintain contact with the station under acceleration?"

"You mean, if we take off and . . . if there's a computer setting for it," Ivo said. "Doesn't it keep track of any changes in our location, and compensate?"

"Naturally. It's been doing it right along while you practiced. Otherwise every one of the coded locations would be off by the distance we are from the torus. But under actual acceleration there would be drift because of the change in our orientation. Is your hand steady enough to compensate?"

"I can try," Ivo said.

She strapped him down while he held the focus. "We'll have to employ intermittent bursts, and change our own orientation erratically," she said. "That way they won't ever be quite sure where we're going."

"Where *are* we going?" Groton inquired.

"Neptune," Ivo said, but it wasn't funny.

"What's two billion, eight hundred million miles among

136

friends?" Afra said, and that wasn't funny either. Ivo was sure it would be years before they could get to such a planet on an economy orbit. The 1977 probe of the four gas giants, after all, was still less than halfway out.

"We may be able to fool them for a little while—a few hours, say—but will it change the end?" Ivo asked her.

"No. Unless we undertake sustained acceleration, the advantage is with them. They have to catch up eventually."

Ivo still had the focus on the printed warning in the station common room. "Oh-oh," he said. "Somebody is changing the sign."

A technician, seeming to move carelessly, picked up the first sheet with a gloved hand and deposited another. Ivo read it off:

ROBOT BEING FITTED. ACCELERATE IMMEDIATELY. URGENT.

"I'll get on it," Groton said. "One G until we think of something better." Ivo heard him scrambling through the lock.

"Why can't we set course for—well, Neptune, since it's vacant and far out—and keep clear of them that way? It might take a little time, but at least we'd be safe until we could figure out something better."

"You're right," Afra said sourly. "At a million miles per hour, direct route, we could make it within four months. At a steady one-gravity acceleration we could achieve that velocity in, oh, half a day. We have supplies for the five of us for a good year."

Weight hit them as Groton cut in the drive. They were on their way—somewhere.

Ivo, still on the scope, lost the focus, but was able to bring it back by diligent corrective twists. The computer was on the job, holding to the coded location, but it didn't care what way up the picture was, and it was evident that the loaded weight of the ship threw the calculations off a trifle. The computer was not using the macroscope; it was judging by thrust and vector to estimate the changes and corroborating by telescopic observations. Trace corrections were necessary.

"What's wrong with that idea, then?" he asked, trying not to sound plaintive.

"First, that robot can take more acceleration than we

can, since it has no fallible human flesh to hinder it. It would catch us enroute if the regular ship didn't. Second, we might get a little hungry, if we *did* get away, after that year."

"Oh." That stupid feeling was threatening to become chronic. "Couldn't we, er, grow some more food? Refine natural resources or sprout whole grain—I saw bags of—"

"On *Neptune?*"

He didn't press the point. "We could come back within the year. The situation could change in that time. Politically."

"I suppose it could, and we could. That leaves only the problem of outrunning the robot ship."

"Oh." He kept forgetting that. "Wait a minute! I thought Joseph was a special vehicle. An atomic heatshield, or something. Brad told me—"

"We are traveling in verbal circles," she said. "Joseph can probably deliver enough thrust to fire us off, even burdened with the weight of the macroscope housing, at a sustained ten gravities. No problem there. The robot would run out of chemical fuel in a hurry trying to match that."

"How long would it take to reach Neptune at ten G's?"

She was silent a moment, and he knew she was working it out with a slide rule. This, at least, was one problem she couldn't do quickly in her head or answer from memory, and he refrained from reminding her that *he* could.

"Assuming turnover at mid-point for deceleration, with constant impetus, top velocity of thirteen thousand, two hundred miles per second—ouch! That's one fourteenth light-speed!—we could make the trip in just five days."

"Why not?" he asked, satisfied.

"No reason worthy of mention. Of course, we'd all be dead long before we arrived, if that's any disadvantage."

"Dead?"

"Did you fancy surviving at a sustained ten G's?"

Ivo thought about weighing over three quarters of a ton for five days without letup. Power, he decided, was not everything. And of course he should have known that; she had already stated that problem, though it hadn't sunk in before. He'd been thinking minutes, not days, for that acceleration.

"You have too many nays for my yeas," he told her.

"Suppose we take off at a steady one G in the general direction of Neptune. How long will it take that UN cruiser to catch us?"

"That depends. The manned one is our immediate problem. If it orients immediately and projects for interception, it could rendezvous within two days. If it takes a more conservative approach, to economize on fuel and allow for our possible maneuvering, it would take longer. Since they'll know fuel is not a problem for us, the latter course is more likely. They wouldn't want to damage the macroscope. They would try to keep us occupied until the robot was functional, which might be several more days."

"How would they know about our drive? I thought that was Brad's private project."

"Nothing is *that* private—not from the organization footing the bill. But spectroscopic analysis of our drive emission would remove any doubts they might harbor. That would make them more cautious about closing with us, but it wouldn't stall them very long. They'd be even more determined to capture us intact, for the sake of that heat-shield." She paused. "We might bluff them a while, though. We'll be heading into the sun, and if we threatened to lock suicidally on that—"

"But Neptune is farther out than we are. We'd be headed *away* from the sun."

"Not when Neptune's in conjunction."

"Conjunction?"

"The opposite side of the sun from Earth."

"I thought that was opposition."

"Brother!" she said in exasperation. Then: "Exactly what, if anything, were you thinking of using those two or more days of freedom for?"

He refrained from making a cute answer. "The macroscope."

"I had the distinct impression you were already occupied in some such capacity. One does live and learn."

"I meant the programmed aspect."

"Oh." It was her turn to feel stupid. It set her back only momentarily. "It seems to me that our problem is fairly well defined. We can't expect to outmaneuver or outrun the UN pair of ships, nor are we in a position to build any fancy equipment to discommode them. Surely you don't expect to adapt the mind-destroyer impulse as a personal weapon?"

"No. But I'm convinced there is galactic information on that channel, if only we could get past the barrier. No one has ever looked *beyond* that opening sequence." Was there anything beyond, he wondered abruptly, or did it merely repeat endlessly?

"No," she said, her voice subdued. He knew she was thinking of Brad again. "Ivo—do you really think you should—touch *that?*"

It was the first genuinely personal concern she had shown for him, and he valued it immensely. "It doesn't hurt me. We already know that."

"It *hasn't* hurt you—yet. What possible thing could you learn worth the risk?"

"I don't know." That was the irony of it. He had no evidence there was anything to find. "But if there *is* any help for us, that's where it has to be. They—the galactics, whatever they are—must be hiding something. Otherwise why have such a program at all? They can't really be trying to destroy us, because this is a self-damping thing. I mean, a little of it warns you off, just as it did for the probs. But the discouragement would really be more effective if there were no signal at all. The signal itself is proof there is something to look for. It is tantalizing. It's as though—well, interference." He hoped.

"Interference!" she said, seeing it. "To prevent someone else's program from getting through!"

"That's the way I figure it. Must be something pretty valuable, to warrant all that trouble."

"Yes. But it could be something philosophic or long-range. We need an immediate remedy. Something impossible, like an inertial nullifier or instantaneous transport—and that simply isn't going to happen."

"I thought I'd give it a try."

Thus they oriented on Neptune, economy route. It was as good a long-range destination as any. As the vessel turned and began its steady drive toward the sun—actually a cometlike ellipse that would carry it within the orbit of Mercury and out again into space—Ivo gave it his try. He did not need to be concerned about the irregular shifts and pauses in acceleration (designed to confuse the pursuit) because the destroyer was everywhere, always in focus.

No, the alien signal was not difficult to locate. He knew its frequency—or, more aptly, its quality—and it was easier to drift into it than to avoid it. But he felt the perspiration on his body as he aligned the great receptor and allowed the pattern to develop. It was death he was toying with: the potential death of his mind, and perhaps with it, his body.

. It came: the same devastating series whose terminus abolished intellect. The pictures built rapidly into symbolic concepts, the concepts into meaning. . . .

Why did it always hit in sequence? Even if it were a recorded, endlessly repeating program, one would expect to pick it up randomly, beginning in the middle or at the end as often as at the introduction. How could it act on the recipient in the ordered manner it did, no matter when he peeked?

He broke the contact with a convulsion of the fingers that threw him far into the static of fringe reception and waited a few seconds. Then he approached again.

The sequence picked up at the beginning, but not as it had been before. This was even faster, spinning through constructions at the maximum rate he could assimilate them. It was as though it were a review of familiar material—as indeed it was.

Startled, he broke again, glad that at least his prior experience had given him the strength to cut it off in mid-showing. Could it be adjusted to him, personally? A signal fifteen thousand years in the transition? The notion was ridiculous!

He reconnected—and the review was so swift as to be perfunctory. Then, as he reached the point at which he had cut it off the first time, it slowed, and a more sedate series resumed. This was, however, still faster than the version he had seen at the station.

Once more he broke, alarmed by the implication as much as by the deadly series. This was not, could not be a recording in any normal sense. It was more like a—a programmed text. A series of lessons embodying their own feedback so that the pupil could constantly check himself and rethink his errors. Inanimate, yet governed by the capability of the student. Such a text was the closest approach of the printed word to an animate teacher, just as a programmed machine-instructor approached sentience without consciousness. It was the *student's* burgeoning comprehension of the material that animated the machine or text and gave the illusion of awareness.

Strange that this had not occurred to him before! Yet it was implicit in the groundwork for the program. One had to comprehend the distinction between—

What a mind-expanding thing this was! Already the concepts of the program were spilling over into his human framework. The concepts were real, they were relevant, to himself and to the universe. Philosophy, psychology—even astrology were assuming new significance for him, as he fitted their postulates into his increasing comprehension.

"Afra," he said, closing his eyes to the fascinating sequence.

She was there. "Yes, Ivo."

"Is it possible to—to say something in such a way that it—that all possible—"

"That it applies to many situations?" she suggested, trying to help him.

"No. To *all* situations. I mean, so it is true no matter how you use it. True for a person, true for a rock, true for a smell, true for an idea—"

"Figuratively, perhaps. 'Good' might apply to all of these, or 'unusual.' But those are subjective values—"

"Yes! Involving the student. But objective too, so that everyone agrees. Everyone who understands."

"I'm not sure I follow you, Ivo. It is impossible to have complete agreement while retaining individuality. The two are contradictory."

"Not—personality. In learning framework. In comprehension. So anyone who understands—this—can understand anything. By applying the guidelines. A—a programmed mind, I think."

"That almost sounds like the Unified Field Theory extended to cover psychology."

"I don't know. What does—"

"Albert Einstein's lifework. He spent his last twenty-five years trying to reduce the physical laws of the universe to a unified formulation. In this way gravity, magnetism and atomic interactions could all be derived as special cases of the basic statement. The practical applications of such a system would be immense."

"So that the theorems of one could be adapted to any other?"

"I believe so, if you thought of it that way."

"Like adapting astronomy to human psychology? And to music and art and love?"

"I really don't—" Once more the pause that portended trouble. "Are you taking up Harold's line?"

"I don't know. Whatever it is, the macroscope has it."

"The Unified Field? Are you sure?"

"The whole thing. The set of concepts that apply to our entire experience, whoever or whatever we are."

She pondered before answering. "That might be the key to the universe, Ivo."

"No. It's the mind-destroyer concept. I don't quite follow it all yet, but a few more runthroughs—"

"Stop!" she cried. "Stay away from that!"

Was the anguish in her voice for him, or for the fate of the macroscope if he should fail? "I don't mean that I'll ride it to the . . . end. Just far enough to—"

"Just far enough to get hooked. Find some other way. Circle around it. Leapfrog it."

"I can't. I have to comprehend before I can go on. Otherwise I won't be able to apply those advanced concepts."

"Advanced con— Mindlessness!"

"I see it now. Things our species has never dreamed of. Concepts that supersede our realities. But I have to nullify this—this destructive aspect first, or I can never move on."

"Ivo, you can't control a fire by cooking yourself in it. You have to handle it remotely, never actually touching. The—the others tried to bathe in it—"

"I don't think the information *has* to destroy. It's many-faceted. If I can come at the right angle—"

"Ivo," she said persuasively, and her voice gave him adolescent shivers. "Ivo, did you have to comprehend the mathematical theory of the sprouts game before you could win the tournament?"

"No. That's—I just see the right course a step at a time, like a road through a forest, and I win. I don't know anything about the math, really."

143

"Then why do you feel you have to comprehend the destroyer? Isn't it enough to know what to avoid and to pass it by, a step at a time? Think of it as a bad move, Ivo. A tantalizing but losing strategy. Skip it and go on to the next."

He thought about it. "I suppose I could do that."

"Just hold off the comprehension. Blind yourself to the fire. Shield your mind so that you can get beyond it."

"Yes, I think I can. But everything I pick up on that basis—it will be like wiring a radio together from a diagram, without knowing anything about its principle of operation. Connect Lead A to Terminal B. It isn't true knowledge."

"Not many of us have true knowledge, Ivo. One of the things about civilization is that it is far too complex for every person to master every trade. We must skim the surface of things, we must turn dials, we must memorize procedures without thinking—we exist upon derivatives, yet it is enough. We have to accept the fact that none of us will ever or can ever grasp more than a tiny fraction of the knowledge and nature of our culture. It isn't *necessary* to comprehend—just to accept."

Again he marveled. Was this the sharp-tongued woman who had so recently bickered sarcastically with Groton? Which facet reflected the essence of her?

But all he said was: "Schön could comprehend."

"You resent him, I know—just as I sometimes resented Brad. But such feelings are pointless. Each of us has to accept his place in the scheme of life, or the entire structure will collapse. Each of us has to be like Sandburg's nail."

"Whose nail?"

"The great nail that holds the skyscraper together. It seems a lowly task, but it is just as important as that of the pinnacle."

"So I'm as important as Schön?"

"Of course, Ivo."

"Even though Schön might bring Brad back, while I certainly can't?"

There was no sound from her, and he was immediately sorry he had said it.

After what seemed like a very long time she spoke.

"I'm sorry. I was mouthing platitudes. I'm not as objective as my preachments."

He had liked the platitude better than the fact. "I'll—I think I can get some of the information. Whatever it is. Without understanding it. I'll try, anyway."

"Thank you, Ivo."

But she made him take a break then, while she saw about changing Brad's soiled clothing again and feeding him: with a spoon, as with a baby. "I can do that," Beatryx offered, but Afra would not give up the task.

Then the four of them ate: cold concentrates from the supplies. It was a somber occasion, since no one expected any real breakthrough via the macroscope and Brad's presence morbidly illustrated the danger in trying. The flight from the torus had been a spectacular gesture, but unrealistic. How could they physically escape from physical pursuit, however much theory they might attain? Their equipment could do it, but not their frail bodies.

Ivo, rested, took up the goggles and controls once more. He knew he had some exceedingly intricate maneuvering to do, because the mind-destroyer was a monstrous sun drawing him into its inferno. He had to approach it, and skirt it, and travel beyond—without getting burned.

In much the same fashion, the group of them had to approach and skirt the sun, on the way to Neptune, while avoiding the opposite menace of the UN pursuit. Another common denominator.

The symbolic patterns formed, leaping through the deadly sequence. Now if only he could follow their import without committing himself to the full denouement—

If he could only, somehow, find a way to survive a sustained ten gravities acceleration, so that they could outrun the robot—

To obtain the answer without absorbing the meaning. To use the voltage without being electrocuted. To remain selectively ignorant. To draw the honey without getting stung.

Again and again he broke the contact, feeling too great a comprehension. The progression was so logical! Every step widened his horizons, prepared him for the one ahead, and induced a savage taste for completion. It was a siren call, luring him in though he knew it was disaster. Yet he was gaining on it, developing, if not an immunity,

145

a resistive callus in his brain. Each approach brought him farther without plumbing the uncontrolled depths. The trick was to keep control of his own reception, to keep it braked, not let the alien program take over entirely. He was becoming automatically blind to key portions, building a barrier—

And it had him. The immense gravity of that conceptual body caught him before he could break again and drew him into itself irresistibly. He knew too much! He had skirted too close, become too familiar, so that his slower intelligence had overcome the cognitive inhibition. He could not draw back from the pyre of that denouement.

Down, unable anymore to resist . . .

And the universe exploded.

That act of friendship had been enough: he survived, when he would have died. It was as though he had passed through purgatory and been exonerated after almost succumbing; his vision of Hell was behind him.

Though not at all well, he left the ship and set off for home on foot. It was a long walk from the Virginia coast to Macon, Georgia. He arrived March 15, 1865, to spend three months convalescing from St. Anthony's Fire.

And in that time of personal recovery from the physical misery of headaches, vomiting, chills and fever, his emotions suffered blows as well. Macon fell to the Union army under General Wilson on April 20, and too soon thereafter President Jefferson Davis himself was taken in the same vicinity. Hope dwindled and expired; the war was lost.

Gussie Lamar, the girl he loved, married a wealthy older man. True, Ginna Hankins remained, but somehow his passion for her had abated. The seemingly carefree days of youth were gone; the war had done for youth.

He wrote poetry through the pain in his joints, and knew even as he applied it tediously to paper that it was not good to express his distress in such fashion. Poetry, like music, reflected beauty, and with his hot reddened skin and swollen and blistered flesh he could feel little affinity for beauty. Unable to work constructively, he boarded for a time at Wesleyan College.

He recovered—but not completely. The consumption had taken hold upon his lung and ravaged it, never to let go entirely. It tightened its cruel grip when he attempted to tutor again, forcing him to give that up also, though he was desperately in need of the money. At last he joined his brother as bookkeeper at the Exchange Hotel, and gained a satisfactory if mundane livelihood.

Reconstruction was upon the land. Unjust laws and corrupt government fomented civic stagnation. Law had largely broken down. The phenomenal expectations of a nation had degenerated into apathy and despair.

Yet gradually his personal fortune improved. The New York literary weekly, *Round Table*, printed some of his poetry and encouraged him, giving him literary success of a sort. And in the spring of 1867 the Rev. R. J. Scott, editor of *Scott's Monthly,* checked into the hotel. This was an opportunity not to be allowed to pass unchallenged.

Scott liked the manuscript.

Yet it was his brother Clifford who actually succeeded as a novelist. The publisher that rejected his own novel brought out Clifford's *Thorn Fruit* in 1867. That was a wonderful thing, and he was glad for his brother—but how he longed for some similar success!

He refused, as ever, to give up. Despite his health, he journeyed to New York, where a wealthy cousin provided help. He searched the city for a publisher.

His novel reflected his burning desire to say it *all,* to convey the whole of his mind and ideal to the reader. It was a kind of spiritual autobiography . . . and no one was interested.

Finally he subsidized its publication himself, though he could ill afford the expense. It was the only way.

He met another long-time friend, Mary Day, and that which had not bloomed before did so now.

On December 19, 1867, they were married.

CHAPTER 5

Gentle hands steadied his head and wiped his face with a wonderfully cool sponge. A woman's touch, and it was good; he could imagine nothing so sure, so comforting.

For a moment he savored the attention, dreaming of recovery from devastation, of marriage. Then he opened his eyes.

It was Beatryx. "He's awake," she murmured.

The others seemed to materialize as she spoke. He saw Harold Groton's anxious, homely face, and Afra's careful glance of assessment.

"No, I'm not brain-burned," he said.

"Thank God!" Afra said.

"What happened?" Groton asked at the same time.

"Now don't go jumping on him like that," Beatryx chided them. "He needs a chance to rest. His forehead is hot." And she brushed his face expertly with the sponge again.

Her analysis might be simplistic, he thought, but his forehead *was* hot, and he was tired with a fatigue that extended deep into the psyche. Gratefully, he fell asleep.

Hours later he was ready to talk to them. "How close is the UN ship?"

"The optic spots the manned one about a day behind

us," Groton said. "We don't have more than twenty-five hours before it comes within effective laser range."

Ivo remembered. The laser itself could reach them anywhere in near-space, but could not be properly aimed unless coordinated by an instrument as precise as the macroscope. So it became essentially a short-range weapon, against a maneuvering target, good only for a few thousand miles. "Good. I mean, I think that gives us enough time."

"You—you have the solution?" The dawning of hope on Afra's face was a blessed thing to watch.

"Solution?" he repeated, finding it unreasonably funny. "Yes. Something very like it. But first I'll have to explain what happened."

"Ivo, I don't want to rush you," Groton said, "but if we don't get away from that UN ship soon—"

"I'm sorry, but I do have to explain first. There is some danger, and if I—well, one of you would have to take over the scope."

"Suddenly I get your message," Groton said. "What *did* happen? Afra came screaming to us about the mind-destroyer, and we were afraid—anyway, I'm certainly glad it wasn't so. But you certainly were out of it for a while."

"No—I was *in* it. I was fighting to protect myself against the destroyer by—well, no need to go into that just now. I almost had it, but I—slipped, mentally, and got drawn in too close. I thought that was the end, and I couldn't even resist, but I was lucky. I still had orbital velocity, and it spun me through the corona and out the other side."

"I don't see—"

"*I* do, Harold," Afra said. "Think of it as an analogy. A planetoid plunging into the sun. The important thing is that he skirted the destroyer and only got stunned for a while."

"Yes, physically. Not mentally, if that makes sense. And beyond it—I guess you'd call it the galactic society."

"You saw who sent the killer signal?" Groton.

"No. That's a separate channel, if that's the word. It's all done in concept, but one is superimposed upon another, and you have to learn to separate them. Once you isolate the destroyer, the rest is all there for the taking."

"Other concepts?" Afra.

"Other programs. They're like radio stations, only all on the same band, and all using similar symbolic languages. You have to fasten on a particular trademark, otherwise only the strongest comes through, and that's the destroyer."

"I follow." Groton. "It's like five people all talking at once, and it's all a jumble except for the loudest voice, unless you pay attention to just one. Then the others seem to tune out, though you can still hear them."

"That's it. Only there are more than five, and you really have to concentrate. But you can pick up any one you want, once you get the feel for it."

"How many are there?" Afra.

"I don't know. I think it's several thousand. It's hard to judge."

They looked at him.

"One for each civilized species, you see."

"Several *thousand* stations?" Afra, still hardly crediting it. "Whatever do they broadcast?"

"Information. Science, philosophy, economics, art—anything they can put into the universal symbology. Everything anybody knows—it's all there for the taking. An educational library."

"But *why*?" Afra. "What do they get out of it, when nobody can pick it up?"

"I'm not clear yet on the dating system, but my impression is that most of these predate the destroyer. At least, they don't mention it, and they're from very far away. The other side of the galaxy. So if it took fifteen thousand years for the destroyer to reach us, these others are taking twenty thousand, or fifty thousand. Maybe the local ones shut down when the destroyer started up, but we won't know for thousands of years."

"That bothers me too." Afra. "Thousands of years before any other species receives their broadcasts, even if the destroyer is not considered. Far too long for any meaningful exchange between cultures."

"Even *millions* of years." Ivo. He was still organizing the enormous amount of information he had acquired. "They're all carefully identified. As I said, I don't follow the time/place coordinates exactly, though I think I'll nail that down next time; but the framework is such that some

150

have to be that far. One, anyway; I discovered it because it was different from the others. Smoother—I don't know how to put it, but there was something impressive about it. Like caviar in the middle of fish eggs—"

"Millions of years!" Afra, still balking at the notion. "That would have to be an extragalactic source, and the macroscope doesn't reach—"

Ivo shrugged. "Maybe the rules are different, for broadcasts. As I make it, that's one of the most important stations, for our purposes anyway, and it is about three million light-years away. That's the main one I listened to. It—but I guess I said that."

"I removed the helmet and goggles the moment you passed out," Afra said as though debating with him. "How much did you have *time* for?"

"Time isn't a factor. Not in reception, anyway. Not for survey. It's—relative. Like light, only—"

"Ah," Groton said, not appalled at the concepts as Afra seemed to be. "The analogy I used earlier. Light approaches the observer at the same velocity by his observation, no matter how fast or in what direction he is moving relative to the light source. Michelson-Morely—"

"Something like that. I absorbed a lot in one jolt, then had to sort it out afterwards. I'll have to go in again to get the details, but at least I know what I'm looking for."

"What *are* you looking for?" Afra asked. "*Is* there something that will help us right now?"

"Yes. Apparently it's a common problem. Surviving strong acceleration, I mean. This extragalactic station has it all spelled out, but it's pretty complicated."

"I still don't see *why*," Afra said petulantly. She was less impressive when frustrated, becoming almost childlike. "It doesn't make sense to send out a program when you know you'll be dead long before it can be answered. Three million years! The entire culture, even the memory of the species must be gone by now!"

"*That's* why," Ivo said. "The memory *isn't* gone, because everyone who picks up the program will know immediately how great that species was. It's like publishing a book—even paying for it yourself, vanity publishing. If it's a good book, if the author really has something to say, people will read it and like it and remember him for years after he is dead."

"Or making a popular record," Groton agreed. *"When it is recorded is much less important than how much it moves the listener."*

"But there'll never be any feedback!" Afra protested.

"It isn't *for* feedback. Not that kind. These civilizations are publishing for posterity. They don't need to worry about greatness in their own time or stellar system; they know what they have. But greatness for the *ages,* measured against the competition of the universe—that's something that only the broadcasting can achieve for them. It's their way of proving that they have not evolved in vain. They have left the universe richer than they found it."

"I suppose that's possible," she said dubiously.

"Maybe you have to be an artist at heart to feel it," Ivo said. "I'd like nothing better than to leave a monument like that after me. Knowledge—what better way can you imagine than that?"

"I'm no artist," Groton said, "but I feel it. Sometimes I am sick at heart, to think that when I pass from this existence no one besides my immediate acquaintances will miss me. That I will die without having made my mark."

Ivo nodded agreement.

"Whatever for?" Beatryx asked, sounding a little like Afra. "There is nothing wrong with your life, and you don't need friends after you're gone."

"Must be a sexual difference, too," Groton remarked, not put out. "Every so often my wife pops up with something I never suspected she'd say. I wonder, in this case, whether it is because men are generally the active ones, while women are passive? A woman doesn't feel the need to *do* anything."

Both women glared at him.

"Whatever it is, it extends to culture too," Ivo said. The joint distaff gaze turned on him. "The *space*-cultures," he explained quickly. "At least, the ones that advertise. It's as impressive a display as I have ever dreamed of."

"But can it get us away from that UN laser?" Afra's mind never seemed to stray far from practicalities.

"Yes. Several stations carry high-acceleration adaptors. But the intergalactic program has the only one we can use now. We don't have facilities for the others."

"One is enough," Afra said.

"But it's rough. It's biological."

"Suspended animation? I suppose if we were frozen or immersed in protective fluid—"

"We don't have a proper freezer, or refrigerated storage tanks," Groton said. "We can't just hand bodies out the airlock for presto stasis. And who would bring us all out of it, when the time came? Though I suppose I could adapt a timer, or set the computer to tap the first shoulder."

"No freezing, no tanks," Ivo said. "No fancy equipment. All it takes is a little time and a clean basin."

Afra looked at him suspiciously, but did not comment.

"What are you going to do—melt us down?" Groton.

"Yes."

"That was intended to be humorous, son."

"It's still the truth. We'll all have to melt down into protoplasm. In that state we can survive about as much acceleration as Joseph can deliver, for as long as we need. You see, the trouble with our present bodies is that we have a skeletal structure, and functioning organs, and all kinds of processes that can be fouled up by a simple gravitic overload. In a stable situation there is no substitute for our present form, of course: I'm not denigrating it. But as protoplasm we are almost invulnerable, because there isn't any substantial structure beyond the molecular, or at least beyond the cellular. Liquid can take almost anything."

"Except pouring or splashing or boiling or polluting," Afra said distastefully.

"Methinks the cure is worse than the UN," Groton mumbled. "I don't frankly fancy myself as a bowl of cream or soft pudding."

"I said it was rough. But the technique is guaranteed."

"By a culture three million years defunct?" Afra asked.

"I'm not sure it's dead, or that far away. It might be one million—or six."

"That makes me feel ever so much better!"

"Well, I guess it's take it or leave it," Ivo said. "I'll have to show it to you in the macroscope, then you can decide. That's the only way you can be keyed in to the technique. I can't explain it."

"Now we have to brave the destroyer too," Afra said. "All in a day's work, I suppose."

"Hold on here," Groton said. "Are you serious? About us dissolving into jelly? I just can't quite buy that, fogyish as I may be."

"I'm serious. Its advantage over the other processes is that it eliminates complicated equipment. Any creature can do it, once shown how, and guided by the program. All you need is a secure container for the fluid, so it doesn't leak away or get contaminated, as Afra pointed out. Otherwise, it's completely biologic."

"Very neat, I admit," Afra said tightly. "How about a demonstration?"

"I'll be happy to run through it for you. But I think you should learn the tuning-in technique first, just in case. I mean, how to find the station and avoid the destroyer."

"If it doesn't work, we hardly need the information!" Afra pointed out.

"Exactly how are we going to get around the destroyer impulse," Groton asked. "Individually or en masse?"

"I—know the route, now. I can lead you to the station one at a time, and bypass the destroyer, if you let me—do the driving. I can't explain how, but I know I can do it."

Groton and Afra both shook their heads, not trusting it. They might differ on astrology, but they had lived with the knowledge of the destroyer longer than he had, and shared a deep distrust of it.

"I will go with you," Beatryx said suddenly. "I know you can do it, Ivo."

"No!" Groton exclaimed immediately.

Beatryx looked at him, unfazed. "But I'm not in danger from it, am I? If I get caught it won't touch me; and if I don't, it will prove Ivo knows the way."

Groton and Afra exchanged helpless glances. She was right, and showed a common sense that shamed them both—but a surprising courage underlay it.

Brad had said something about a normal IQ being no dishonor. Brad had known.

Groton looked tense and uncomfortable as Beatryx donned a duplicate helmet and set of goggles, but he didn't interfere. It was evident to Ivo that mild as Beatryx was, when she put her foot down, it was down to stay.

He took her in, sliding delicately around the destroyer with less of the prior horror and finishing at the surface of the galactic stream of communications.

"Oh, Ivo," she exclaimed, her voice passing back into the physical world and making a V-turn to reach him down his azimuth. "I see it, I see it! Like a giant rainbow stretching across all the stars. What a wonderful thing!"

And he guided her down, seeking the particular perfume, the essential music, on through the splendor of meaning/color, to the series of concepts that spoke of the very substance of life.

The patterns of import opened up, similar at first to those of the destroyer, but subtly divergent and far more sophisticated. Instead of reaching into a hammer-force totality, these delved into a specific refinement of knowledge—a subsection of the tremendous display of information available through this single broadcast. Ivo knew the way, and he took her in as though walking hand in hand down the hall of a mighty university, selecting that lone aspect of education that offered immediate physical salvation.

"But the other doors!" she cried, near/distant. "So many marvelous—"

He too regretted that they could not spend an eternity within this macronic citadel of information. This might be merely one of a hundred thousand broadcasts available—the number began to suggest itself as he grasped more nearly the scope of the broadcast range—yet it might have in itself another hundred thousand subchambers of learning. University? It was an intergalactic educational complex of almost incomprehensible vastness. Yet they, in their grossly material imperatives, had to restrict themselves to the tiniest fragment, ignoring all the rest. They were hardly worthy.

The microcosm of biophysical chemistry: and it was as though they stood within a vat of protoplasm, able to experience its qualities while remaining apart from its reality. Vaguely spherical, it pulsed with its multiple internal processes, held together by a sandwichlike plasma membrane. It seemed at first to be a simple bag of proteins, carbohydrates, lipids and metal ions, the whole with a neutral pH. But it was more than that, and more than physical.

"What *is* it?" she asked, bewildered.

"Model of a single cell," he said. "We have to become acquainted with this basic unit of life, because—"

But she retreated in confusion, unable to follow the technical explanation. He was hardly able to provide it, anyway, ignorant as he knew himself to be in the face of the immense store assembled. "See, there's the nucleus," he said instead.

That seemed to satisfy her. She contemplated the semisolid mass of it, this major organelle floating and pulsing in the center of the cell. It was as though it were the brain of the organism, containing as it did the vital chromosomes embedded in a cushiony protective matrix. From the nuclear wall depended the endoplasmic reticulum—a vast complex of membranes extending throughout the cell. This could be likened to the skeleton and nervous system of an animal, providing some support and compartmentation of the whole and transmitting nervous impulses from the nucleus. Tiny ribosomes studding its walls labored to synthesize the proteins essential to the organism's well-being.

"It's—alive," she said, coming at it in simpler terms.

It was alive. It had an apparatus called the Golgi complex that produced specialized secretions needed by the cell and synthesized large carbohydrates. It breathed by means of the mitochondrion organelle. It fought disease by using circulating lysosomes—balls of digestive enzymes that attacked and broke down invaders. Every function necessary for survival was manifested within this living entity.

"This is what we have to preserve," Ivo explained. "The body as we think of it can disappear, but the functioning cells—of which this is typical—must remain. They must not die; their chromosomes must not be damaged."

"Yes," she agreed, understanding the essence if not the detail. "I will remember."

Carefully, then, they withdrew from the model. Back they went, up out of the broadcast, the university, holding these concepts like a double handful of champagne, inhaling them, recalling them, back to mundane existence.

They removed the receptors and looked about. Afra and Groton were standing there anxiously.

"There's so much to know!" Beatryx informed them happily.

The rest was comparatively routine. He took Groton, then Afra, and finally even Brad. Mind was not actually necessary for this familiarization, and could even be a liability because of the lurking menace of the destroyer. Brad, at least, had no more to fear from that.

"It is a kind of mutual contract," Ivo explained at some point. "It isn't just a matter of you seeing it; *it* has to see *you*. Not the cell-model; that's only a visual aid. The *program*. So it is able to key in on your cells, your body and your mind for the—transformation, once you understand and agree. You have to agree; you have to want it, or at least be acquiescent. So it can set up an individual program. This is like a delicate surgical operation, and it is the surgeon." It occurred to him that he was using a lot of simile in his discussion of the macroscosm—but there were no direct terms for it. As the universe was greater than the solar system, so the universal knowledge was greater than man's terminology.

"Three million years old," Afra said. "I can imagine a human doctor, or an alien one, or even a robot. But a beam of pseudo-light . . . !"

"Do any of you think you can maneuver around the destroyer now? This familiarization has to be done within a few hours of the process, each time."

"No," Afra returned bluntly. "I am afraid of that thing. It—had me when it—got Brad. I can't fight it because it appeals to my intelligence. With you, just now, I closed my eyes, figuratively, until we reached the—cell. I refused to comprehend, and I don't know the route."

Which was, evidently, the way it had to be, for her. She could comprehend the destroyer, so was vulnerable to it.

"I felt the danger," Groton said, "but I didn't grasp it fully. It was like standing at the brink of a waterfall a thousand feet high, feeling the spume and hearing the thunder and smelling the smashing water, but not touching the falls itself. I suppose I am safely below the limit. I believe I could find the way around it, now that you have shown me—if I had to. I would much rather not *have* to, though."

So Groton too had to resort to simile.

"It was beautiful," Beatryx said. "Like poetry and music—but I could never go there by myself. All those rainbow threads—"

And Beatryx.

"One is enough." Afra asserted herself again. "Next

157

problem: do we trust the procedure? How can we be sure it won't dissolve us and leave us puddled forever? I appreciate the experience and the review of cellular structure, but I'd like to see a complete cycle before I entrust my tender flesh to it."

"It *could* be a more subtle version of the destroyer," Groton said. "Second-line defense."

"I don't believe it. This predates the destroyer. All those programs do, but this is so far ahead that—well, *three million years*. And everything I've seen has been positive, not negative." Ivo had a sudden thought. "I wonder whether the destroyer-species is trying to make its mark by undoing the work of all the others? It can't compete positively, so it—"

"Dog in the manger?" Afra said. "Maybe. Maybe not. Evil I could easily believe, but that would simply be nasty."

Groton was using the optical system again. "I have a metallic reflection. That UN ship is right on course. We'd better act soon or resign ourselves to capture. How long does a melting cycle take?"

"Not long for the breakdown, as I understand it," Ivo said. "But the reconstitution—several hours, at least, and it can't start for at least a day, for some reason. So it could be a couple of days for the complete cycle."

"There goes our margin," Afra said. "If we test it and it works, it will be loo late for anyone else to use it. If we *don't* test, we may be committing a particularly grisly form of suicide."

"We could start someone on the cycle," Groton said. "If it means death, that should be apparent very soon. The smell—"

"All *right*!" Afra.

"But if everything appears to be in order—"

"All right. A test-cycle, halfway. *Who*?"

"I said I was willing to—" Ivo began.

"Better you go last," she said. "It's your show. If it bombs out, you should take the consequences."

"Afra, that isn't very kind," Beatryx objected. The negative comment was obviously an effort for her.

"We're not in a kind situation, dearie."

Groton left the telescope assembly and faced Afra. "I'm

glad you see it that way. We do have the obvious choice for the testing cycle."

She understood him immediately. "No! Not Brad!"

"If the process works, he must undertake it sooner or later unless we leave him behind. If it doesn't, what kind of a life does he have to lose? It is not, as you pointed out, a kind situation."

Afra looked at Brad. He was sitting up with his hair boyishly tousled, a day's shadow on his face, and saliva dribbling down his chin. His trousers were dark where he had wet them again. He was watching something, half-smiling, but his eyes did not move about.

"Let me handle it," Afra said soberly. "No one else. I'll—tell you how it comes out."

Ivo explained in detail what would be necessary. Groton retired to the underbody of Joseph for some work with the power saw, and brought forth the required basin. They set everything up and left her with Brad. The three of them retreated again into Joseph. No one spoke.

There was a short silence. Then Afra screamed—but as Groton went to look, she cried out to be left alone, and he yielded. Faintly they could hear her sobbing, but nothing else.

No one dared conjecture. Ivo pictured Brad slumping down into an amorphous puddle, first the feet, then the legs, then the torso and finally the handsome head. Had she screamed when the face submerged? Tense and silent, they waited.

Half an hour later she summoned them. She was pale and her eyes were open too wide, but her voice was desperately calm. "It works," she said.

Brad's clothing was folded neatly on his former chair. Near it was a covered coffinlike container. There was no other sign of what had passed.

But Afra was very uneasy. "Let's assume it works—the complete cycle. That we come through it and emerge exactly as we are now, to all appearances. I still can't accept it intellectually—no, I mean *emotionally*. How do we *know* we have survived it? That the same person comes out of it that goes in?"

"I'll know if *I'm* the same," Ivo said defensively.

"But will you, Ivo? You may look the same, sound the

same—but how do we *know* you are the same? Not another person of identical configuration?"

Ivo shrugged. "*I'd* know it. I'd know if anything were different."

She concentrated on him with that disarming intensity. She was loveliest when expressing emotion. "*Would* you? Or would you only *think* you hadn't changed? How could you be sure you weren't an impostor, using Ivo's body and mind and experience?"

"What else is there? If I have Ivo's physique and personality, I'm Ivo, aren't I?"

"No! You could be an identical twin—a congruent copy—a different individual. A different self."

"What's different about it?"

"What's different about *any* two people, or any two apples or pencils or planets? If they coexist, they're discrete individuals."

"But I'm not coexisting with anybody else. Any other *me,* I mean. How can I be different?"

"Your soul could be different!"

"Oh-oh," Groton said.

"How else can you term it?" Afra flared at him. "I'm not trying to bring religion into it—though that might not be a bad idea—I'm just asking how we can verify the price we pay for this wonder from a foreign galaxy. How can we measure self, when physique and mind are suspect? I don't want to be replaced by a twin that looks and thinks like me; I don't care how good the facsimile is, if it isn't *me.*"

Ivo wondered more urgently just what she had seen happen to Brad. She had been profoundly shaken, and now was clutching at theoretical, philosophical objections.

"It happens I've thought along similar lines," Groton said. "I used to question whether the person who woke up in the morning was the same as the one who had gone to bed at night. Whether the identity changed a little with each change in composition—each new bite of food, each act of elimination. I finally concluded that people *do* change, all the time—and that it doesn't matter."

"Doesn't matter!"

"The important thing is that we perform our functions while we exist," he said. "That we live each day as it comes, and don't regret it. If a new person lives the next day, *he* is responsible. He is guided by his configurations, and his successors after him, and it is not right or wrong so much as predestined."

"Astrology again?" she inquired disdainfully.

"One day you may come to have a better opinion of it, Afra," he said mildly.

She sniffed, astonishing Ivo—he had not thought the mannerism could be executed naturally.

He also wondered whether the fervor of her reactions against Groton's ideas indicated a lurking suspicion that there might be something to them after all.

"At any rate," Groton continued, "it seems we must either undertake this process, or submit to the approaching UN party. Perhaps the question is whether we prefer to escape in alternate guise, or to surrender in our own."

"You," Afra said, "are a fourteen-carat casuist."

"What are we going to do?" Ivo asked.

"All right. Since I object the most, I'll go first. But I want some subjective reassurance. I've *seen* it; you haven't. Once you witness it, you'll know what I'm talking about. I don't care *what's* foreordained; I want to believe I'm me."

Groton kept a straight face. "No one else can do it for you."

"Yes they can. I want someone *else* to believe I'm me, too."

"Does it matter what *we* think?"

"It does."

"Feedback," Ivo said.

Unexpectedly, she flashed him a smile. Then she unbuttoned her blouse.

The three watched, hesitating to comment. Afra stripped methodically, completely, and without affectation. She stood before them, a splendid figure of a woman in her prime. "I want—to be handled."

"Confirmation by tactile perception—very important," Groton said, not mocking her; but he did not move.

"I don't understand," Beatryx said, seemingly more put out by this display than the men were.

"I want you—all of you—to handle me," Afra explained as though she were giving instructions in storing groceries. Her voice was normal but a flush was developing upon cheek and neck and spreading attractively downward. "So that afterwards you will know me as well as you can, not just by sight or sound." She smiled fleetingly. "Or temper. So that you can tell whether it is the same girl, outside. When you watch me melt down, you'll never believe I'm whole again, unless you prove it with all your senses. And if *you* don't believe, how can *I?*"

"I couldn't tell one girl from another, by touch," Ivo objected, feeling his own face heating.

"Do it," Groton muttered.

"Me?"

Groton nodded.

Ivo stood up, far more embarrassed than Afra appeared to be. He walked jerkily toward her. He raised one hand and stopped, overcome by uncertainty. Almost, he wished the drive would fail; anything to break this up.

"Pretend you're a doctor," Beatryx suggested sympathetically—but there was an overtone that hinted at hysteria. This must go, he thought, entirely against her grain.

And what of his own grain? Brad had called him prudish. Brad, again, had known.

"No!" Afra said in reply to Beatryx. "No impersonal examination. That's pointless. Do whatever you have to do to *know* who I am."

"I already have some idea." Ivo was aware that he was now blushing visibly—a phenomenon that very seldom appeared in him, since his complexion was dark. Before he met Afra, he corrected himself. The suffusion of his features fed upon itself, summoning more blood; this, too, was feedback. He was embarrassed *because* he was embarrassed. Could Afra have any inkling how he felt about her?

"This is as hard for me as for you," she said. "I *don't* like acting like a whore. I just don't see any other practical way. Here." She caught his hand and jammed it against her midriff.

Ivo remained frozen, shocked as much by her words as her action. It had been, by his dubious reckoning, less than forty-eight hours since their first meeting, and hardly more than that since this entire adventure had dropped on him. His hand, half-closed, rested against her warm, smooth, gently-heaving abdomen.

"She is trying to preserve her identity," Groton said

helpfully. "But it isn't an entirely physical thing. She requires an *experience*—emotional, sexual, spiritual—the words are hardly important."

"Sexual?" The inane query was out before he could halt it.

"Not stimulation in the erotic sense," Groton replied carefully. "It is possible to copulate without any genuine involvement, after all. Rather, a shared sensation. Your actions and reactions are an important part of it, for they deepen its relevance. When you interact with intimacy, you accomplish something meaningful. She does not exist alone; she needs an audience. Otherwise, like the unread book or the unheard symphony, she is unrealized. Move her, be moved by her; make an experience whose significance will not easily fade. *React!"*

Afra nodded quickly, and the motion sent a tremor through her flesh and his. "Yes, yes—I think you understand it better than I do," she said, speaking to Groton.

"Merely your way of publishing for posterity," he said. "I knew male and female weren't *that* different."

Surprised, she nodded again, and Ivo felt her diaphragm tighten. Still he stood there, unable to initiate this high-minded inspection, averting his eyes uncomfortably. His hand, so dark in contrast to her pale flesh, felt dead, encysted in plastic, immovable and incredibly clumsy.

"Ivo," she said, "It's my *life*, my *self*. I am afraid—I admit it, I announce it, I brag of it. I need this reassurance, and I think you will need it too, once we get into this, this cycle. So humor me, but *do* it. You don't have to like it."

"I'm afraid I *would* like it," he blurted.

There was something more fundamental than vanity involved. Ivo grasped that now, but it did not help him. *He* did not imagine security in handling, and he doubted Groton did, for all his explanations. Women, more than men, were made for such caresses. Publishing a book made sense; this—

"Where are you afraid to touch me?" Afra demanded, nervous and impatient. "The UN won't hold off forever." She grabbed at his hand again and lifted it in both of hers forcing his fingers to uncurl. "Here?" She plastered his right palm against her left breast.

He had been wrong about the insensitivity of that extrem-

163

ity. Hot/cold shocks ran up his arm and exploded in his consciousness, making him dizzy. React? How could he help it!

"Here?" she demanded again, and rubbed his fingers against the firm lower crease of her left buttock... Ivo snatched his hand away. His entire body was shaking. He felt ridiculous, yet excited.

"Praise God for naïveté," Afra remarked, not unkindly. "I'm not making passes at you, Ivo. I just have to prove to you that I mean it. There can't be any prudery for this. Now go ahead, please. There isn't much time."

She had accomplished her purpose. After the intimacy of the contacts she had forced upon him, hesitancy was ridiculous. He started at her head, running his fingers over her forehead, her cheeks, her nose, her closed eyelids, stroking her delicate lips, cupping her chin. There were two faint freckles on her neck near the right ear. He combed through her loose hair with splayed fingers, getting the texture of it, finding it more substantial than he had anticipated, more resilient. He circled her sleek white neck and pinched her earlobes gently between thumb and forefinger.

"Bite it, taste it," she said quietly.

He brushed his lips to her ear. He knew her and loved her—guiltily.

He closed his eyes and ran his hands down one arm and then the other, feeling the smooth outlines of bone and flesh and sinew and skin, while she stood submissively. It was like a dream—more than a dream, for she was fair in every part and in every physical respect. The tonus of her moderate musculature was good; the curves and planes were without tactile blemish. Her fingers were slender and finely molded; the hollows around her collarbones perfectly sculptured. Only in her armpits was there roughness: the stubble of hair shaved clean a few days before, growing back already. This reminder that she was not an animated statue shook him again; *he was handling her.*

Her breasts were heavy but not as large as they had seemed by eye, nor did the nipples project so much—until he touched them. Internal texture of the breast was not consistent; pressure showed up the clumped masses of the mammary glands beneath. Men, he thought, had been so fascinated with this distinguishing mark of the female

164

that they had identified the species through it: mammalian. Yet the feature typical of it—not the species, he remembered now, the *class*—the most typical feature was hair. The mammals were hairy-bodied. Even whales had some pubic hair. . . .

Eyes still closed, he brought his errant mind back to business. To the sides the breasts faded into lightly covered ribs, that in turn dropped off into a much wider space above the hips than he had suspected. Her back was almost flat, mounded by the shoulder blades on either side, ridged by the backbone down the center. The ribs angled up in front to disappear somewhere near the solar plexus.

Her buttocks as his hands experienced them were astonishingly generous, the soft flesh overlapping onto hip and thigh. In front, the stomach and abdomen were rounded, projecting more than he expected, and the hips were so wide he had to open his eyes to verify his location.

Afra's eyes were closed; she was not watching him or reacting to his increasingly personal explorations in any overt way. He did not know whether that pleased him or disturbed him.

Her hips and buttocks were normal, considering the sex and general health of the subject. He had been judging by his own anatomy, and his slowly traveling hands had magnified her dimensions unrealistically. He closed his eyes again, kneeled and continued.

He touched her pubic hair and passed over it lightly, finding no more reason to probe within it than he had to feel the insides of her ears, nose or mouth. Her legs were braced somewhat apart; he ran his hands down the insides of her thighs, up again and around to the projections of the glutei maximi behind. Then down over the large muscles of the legs, under greater tension than those of the arms or rear, and to the knees, far more esthetic than his own.

The calves were tighter yet, and as he squeezed them he could feel their shifting as trace corrections of balance were made. The ankles were narrow, the tendons flexing through them and over the tops of the feet. Her arches were good, the toes small but strong. As he traversed this final portion of her, one great toe flexed upward, a parting

165

salute—and abruptly his diminishing embarrassment resurged.

He had indeed been handling a live woman.

"Do you know me now?" she inquired, eyes open.

Do I know a goddess? "Yes," he said, uncertain whether it was truth or untruth.

Dazed, Ivo returned to his place and watched Groton go over her in much the same fashion. He felt like a voyeur and suppressed it; he felt a crude jealousy and suppressed *that*. Afra belonged to neither man, and this experience meant nothing, except in whatever intangible way she chose to take it.

Then Beatryx reviewed her, and this embarrassed him once more. For a man to handle a woman—that was provocative but in the natural course. For a woman to handle a woman—

He was still reacting foolishly. He would have to learn to divorce his instincts from current necessities, as the others had. Perhaps the time would come when he could clap his hand upon Afra's cleft without . . .

He was glad no one was watching him, for he was sure he was reddening brilliantly.

Afra's inspection was over. She, still naked, glanced inquiringly at Beatryx. Was the other woman going to undertake a similar ordeal?

Beatryx looked calmly at her husband.

Groton smiled. "With all due respect for these proceedings," he said, "I believe I will know my wife in whatever guise she may manifest herself. Trust her to me."

Beatryx returned the smile. "I should hope so, dear."

Ivo was glad Beatryx had not undertaken similar handling. He imagined himself passing his hands over her body as he had for Afra, and recoiled. She was older, and she was married, and this did seem to make a difference. A married woman should not be touched by other men.

He tried to turn it off, but his mind proceeded against his will, fascinated by the morbid. He saw his fingers touch the flesh of the older woman, finding it flabby and rough in comparison, unattractive. How was a woman of that age to compete with such as Afra? Age, intelligence, appearance—as washerwoman to a princess. The exploration of Afra was the guilt of forbidden fruit; of Beatryx, merely aversion.

Yet this was a dire wrong to Beatryx, even in fancy, for he knew already that she had qualities of compassion and courage that Afra lacked. He was judging by sex appeal—his own possibly juvenile standards, too—and that negated the evidence of experience and intellect.

How much better to feel guilt for lusting after a woman than to feel it for failing to lust!

He came alert with a start. The preliminaries were over and they were ready for the supreme commitment.

Afra lay within her basin, and the others stood by while Ivo positioned the projector directly overhead. This was nothing more than the large macroscope screen; once a person had been primed—that is, introduced to the broadcast—the existence of a certain situation and frame of mind triggered a beam of light originating within the alien channel. This bypassed the computer; it was direct contact with intergalactic science.

Groton had somehow produced five man-sized containers. Ivo suspected that they were pirated chemical tanks sliced lengthwise. Afra, in hers, was lying in several inches of clear sterile water, spread out so that the beam could catch an entire side at once. That was all they had to do.

Was it a horrible demolition he aimed at her? How could he be sure that this was not after all another destroyer, as Groton had suggested; more subtle than the first, set to catch the few who circumvented the first?

Afra looked up at him. "You believed in it before."

So he had. Why was it suddenly so chancy when she was the one? Because he loved her and would survive to witness his mistake?

"It takes a couple of minutes to warm up," Afra said. "Stand back."

Numbly, Ivo obeyed. He wished he could think of some appropriate remark to make, but he had never felt so stupid. He was afraid, too, as he had not been before.

Inevitably the seconds passed. He could not stop them. "Joseph!" he exclaimed. "Who will pilot it, while—?"

"Eight hours from now the macroscope computer will jump the engine to a full ten G's acceleration and modify our course accordingly," Groton said. "We have taken care of the programming. What did you think we were doing while you slept?"

So the others had committed themselves to Neptune even before he—

A flash; the projector came on. A thin yellow light bathed Afra's body, making it oddly sharp; the flesh tones stood out deeper than in life, the hair brighter, the irises, as the eyes dropped closed, a clearer blue. It was as though some famous painter had enhanced the predominant hues.

He knew that this was only the surface manifestation. It was the cell that counted, that the beam was seeking out and rendering individualistic. The bulk of the radiation was invisible, acting within her substance, setting up unusual relations, breaking down lifelong bonds. A change was beginning—one unlike any experienced by the human form before.

Except for Brad . . .

The epidermis—the outermost layer of the skin—dissolved. The reddish tones of the dermis intensified as subcutaneous fat departed, and out of the flowing protoplasm rose the intricate venous network, all over her body. Arms, legs, torso—it was a though she had donned a loosely knit blue leotard that was now falling apart.

Ivo looked at Afra's face, but saw it relaxed. She was unconscious, and had probably been knocked out by the first impact of the radiation. He was glad of that.

The skin was melting from her head, too. Body hair had gone immediately, leaving her nude and bald. Now there was a great blue branching tube descending from her forehead. It hooked into the streaming eye, crossed the cheek, and finally disappeared under the jaw muscle on its way to the throat. Whitish nerves splayed across the side of her face from the region of the ear, weaving between and through brownish muscles, and almost under the earhole was a tapioca mass of something he couldn't identify. Into his mind came the word "parotid," but it meant nothing to him. Upon the dome of the skull bright arteries interwove with veins and nerves, making a tripartite river gathering toward the ear.

Already these superficial networks were eroding under the beam from space, merging with the runoff from the liquefying muscular structures. The cartilage of the nose was coming into sight and, gruesomely, the naked eyeballs. Ivo turned his gaze aside, afraid of being sick, and concentrated on the legs and feet.

These were hardly more comforting. Skin, surface nerves and veins had gone together with much of the avoirdupois, but tendons and arteries remained, and the bulk of the great limb muscles. Slowly these diminished, and in the front of the lower leg the bone appeared, a lighter-colored island rising from the runoff. Above it the patella—the kneecap—already floated free, and it fell with a slow splash into the burgeoning fluid in the trough. Below, the incredibly long, thin foot-bones showed, loosening as the connecting ligaments yielded.

Individually, the phalanges folded and toppled, toe-bones no more, and lay scattered in the rising sea of protoplasm. The original water Afra had lain in was no longer visible at all; the meltoff covered it. The little bones were slow to dissolve completely, and he wondered whether the process would ever finish. Perhaps the action would continue after the beam desisted, the liquid eating away at the pockets of resistance for hours and even days. That would be one compelling reason for the minimum time limit; the reconstitution could not safely proceed until all components had been processed and made available to the organism.

At last the skeletal outline lay bare, half-submerged in brown liquor.

Now Ivo half-understood Afra's need for tactile confirmation. She had watched this process, had seen the complete demolition of physique. He had to agree: after such an experience, nothing less than extreme evidence would convince him that Afra had survived such demolition. It had become an emotional, rather than intellectual, matter.

Even if he manipulated every portion of her anatomy, he would retain the mind's-eye image of—this.

Yet he would have to survive it himself, before he could verify it in anyone else. Would a pseudo-Ivo pass approval on a pseudo-Afra, both agreeing that all five red eyes were exactly as they had been before, and then the entire party settling down to a wholesome meal of astrology-on-rye?

He looked about, feeling as though an enormous period had elapsed but knowing it to have been a few minutes only. Groton and Beatryx were watching too, neither seeming particularly robust. They, like him, had become morbidly impressed with the significance of this process, and neither reacted to his movement.

This was like the destroyer, he thought. It was repulsive, yet the eye riveted to it.

Ivo followed the direction of Groton's absorption and discovered that it was the head, or perhaps the throat or thorax. The progression here had continued alarmingly. The skull was bare of flesh and vein, the ears and nose were gone; eye-sockets were empty; teeth bulged loosely from bare jawbones, gaunt in the absence of cheek or gums. If the brain itself had been affected yet, this was not apparent behind the enclosure of the fissured skull.

But it was the neck that appalled. Here the dissolution had been more selective. It was the first evidence he had that this was not merely a melting of flesh as the conveniences of surface and hardness dictated. Fat and muscle and tendon were largely absent, but the internal jugular vein remained beside the large red carotid, servicing the brain. The small offshoots of both had been sealed over, so that they were now direct tubes. What modification of the alien program had dictated this astonishing precaution?

Either the distant civilization had anticipated human physique and function to an impossible extent, or the program was of such versatility and sophistication that it automatically adapted to *any* living system. Already it had reduced the solid portion of Afra's bodily mass by half, without killing her. This was surgery beyond man's capacity, performed without physical contact—yet it was only an incidental portion of galactic or intergalactic knowledge.

Ivo had not allowed himself to realize how complex an organism the human body was in detail. He had thought of it melting as an ingot of steel might melt in a blast-furnace; as ice cream might dissolve in sunlight; as a bar of soap might liquefy in a basin of warm water. Ridiculous! He understood now that long before the bones of the legs surrendered their calcium, the brain would die—unless precisely protected. The velocity and order of the process were critical, if life as it had been were to be preserved.

The great spiral-banded trachea also remained intact, and air continued to pass through it. The pipe terminated at what had been the larynx, now a funnel opening upward. His gaze followed it back down to the thoracic cavity, still enclosed by the circling ribs. Though Afra's breasts were long since gone along with all other superficial processes, the important muscles of her chest were present and functioning, maintaining the circulation of air within. He could tell by the pulsing of the adjacent arteries that the heart continued its operations, too.

The melting seemed to have halted at this stage, in this region, and he did not see how it could resume safely. The hands, arms and shoulders were deteriorating bones, all flesh taken; the head and neck had been stripped of expendable appurtenances. If the chest muscle went, the lungs would stop and the brain would drown, deprived of its oxygen; if the brain went, the remainder of the body would cease to function and would suffer damage before the slow melting could complete the job. The system had to function as a unit until there was no unit to function—a paradox.

Beatryx was staring at the abdomen, her hand unconsciously clutching at her own. Ivo looked there—and regretted it.

The reproductive system, like the sensory organs, had been among the earliest to go. The abdominal cavity was open, pelvic musculature absent, the guts exposed. Ivo could not have told from what he saw to which sex the carcass belonged. Above the bleakly jutting hip-bones the action was well advanced: bladder and uterus melted, large and small intestine puddled along with the digestive refuse within them. Only the two large kidneys remained, and their arterial and venous connectors, their wastes evidently dissolving as they formed. Stomach, liver, spleen, pancreas, duodenum—all of it flowed away into the common sewer, leaving the vertebrae bare.

Had these remains ever been a person? This mass of eroding bones immersed in a deepening pond of sludge?

It was not over. Unsupported, the skull canted, causing all three observers to jump, and from its hollow earhole and empty lower eye-socket the gray-white fluid trickled heavily. Ivo realized that the optic nerves had left their tunnels through the solid bone, and now the brain itself was dissolving. First the frontal lobes? Or one hemisphere only?

Simultaneously there was a breakthrough in the chest

cavity. The membranes lining the ribcage on the right had let go and run off; the lung collapsed, so that there was air under the bones. The muscles on that side melted, showing those ribs, and underneath them the hollow section remaining. Within this beat the heart, centered rather than situated to the left as he had thought, still pumping the red blood up the huge aortic artery toward brain and kidneys, and the blue blood up the pulmonary artery to the lungs for oxygenation. Similarly massive veins brought it back from its travels, now considerably circumscribed. Lymph nodes dotted the area, and tiny vessels enclosed the heart itself, and the nerve trunk remained leading into the skull. That, apart from the bones and minimal tissue, was all.

Had this been the splendid body he had explored with his two quivering hands, so long ago? Was this the physical object whose makeup compelled his fascination?

The kidneys went; the second lung collapsed; the heart beat momentarily longer, then ceased. If death were the destined conclusion of this chain, it had come at last.

Yet the process continued. The last muscles fell, the heart sagged and opened, the blood ran out as protoplasm. The skeleton lay amidst its liquid flesh, defunct.

The beam from the projector shut off.

Ivo looked at the other two. They looked at him. No one spoke.

Again the common thought: had they conspired unwittingly to commit a gruesome murder, and had they now accomplished it?

Fifteen minutes passed, and the slow action did not halt. The ridged vertebrae hung loose within their settings; the ribs sagged. Wherever the dull fluid touched, it dissolved, though it would be long before the skull and hip-bones finally disappeared.

As the fluid became still, light from the chamber struck the surface and refracted through the forming layers, some of it reflecting back eerily. It was as though a ghost flickered where the girl had been.

Groton stood up unsteadily. He walked to the long basin, bent over, and placed its cover upon it, cutting off the reflection-spirit. Carefully he pulled it over to the side, set it beside the prior melt, and anchored it securely to the deck. He had removed it only a few feet, since the

172

compartment was small, but it seemed to Ivo like a tremendous distance. It was amazing how far one could adapt to the space available, so that cubic yards became as great, subjectively, as cubic rods.

Groton drew the second—actually, third—basin into position. Silently he undressed, casting his clothing absently on the pile left by Afra. He lay down.

Beatryx turned away.

This time Ivo timed it by his watch: twenty-four minutes until the beam desisted. Another skeleton lay within its vat. Beatryx had not looked at all.

Again they waited. Two murders?

Ivo moved the remains, discovering that the container slid readily. He was irrationally fearful of slopping some of the juice over the side. He sighed in silent relief as he set the cover, though it was light and did not actually seal the basin. Air had to enter, or it would quickly become a coffin. He found the snaps Groton had fashioned to connect to the floor-plugs. This was the kind of detail an engineer would think of; Ivo certainly had not. Of course, free-fall or jerky acceleration would throw the protoplasm out to splatter over the equipment—but Afra and Groton would have anticipated this also, and accounted for it in the programming. Probably the engines would never cut off at all; Joseph would perform a turnabout under 10-G acceleration and commence 10-G deceleration without affecting its contents enough for any slopping.

Ivo positioned the next basin.

"No!" Beatryx cried, near hysteria. She had seemed calm, but obviously this type of experience had brought her to her breaking point. He could not blame her.

He waited, and after a few minutes she spoke again, still facing away. "I'm afraid."

"So am I." It was the total truth.

That seemed to encourage her. "I have to go next. I didn't know it would be like this. I wouldn't be able to do it myself. And I have to."

"Yes." What else could he say?

"He has his charts," she said, meaning her husband. "When he gets bothered, he just settles down for a few hours with his diagrams and figures and houses and planets, and he works it all out and finally he's satisfied. But I never understood all that. I don't have anything."

173

Now he did not dare even to agree with her.

"He told me," she said quickly, "I don't know what it means but I remember it—he told me that when I was thirty-seven my progressed midheaven would square with Neptune."

"Neptune!"

"And he said my progressed ascendant would be opposite Neptune, and my progressed Mercury opposite Neptune. And he said Neptune was the planet of obligation—I think that's what it was. And—"

"And we're going to Neptune," Ivo finished for her. "I don't know what all those terms mean either, but it sounds as though you have to—progress to Neptune." *Could* it mean anything, or was it sheer coincidence?

"I'm thirty-seven now," she said.

Ivo had an inspiration. "It must mean you'll get there safely!"

Still she didn't move.

Finally Ivo, sensing what was needed, went and led her to the basin and carefully removed the clothing she had so carefully preserved until this moment, while she stood listlessly. He could never, prior to the past few hours, have conceived of himself performing such an action. Undressing an older woman! What secrets remained for her to hide?

He steadied her as she got down, then he stood up to move away.

"Hold my hand, Ivo."

He knelt just beyond the field of the beam and took her hand, trusting that its melting could catch up later.

The beam came on. She relaxed, unconscious, but he stayed where he was. The skin melted away from her arm up to just beyond the elbow; forearm, wrist and the hand he held remained whole.

Suddenly it came to him that the hand could die, stripped of its supplying mechanisms. He had to return it to the field before he disrupted everything.

His own hand lost sensation as it entered the field, and hers slipped down. He withdrew hastily, alarmed. A film of slick moisture already covered the exposed portion, and feeling did not return. Stupid! Did he think he was playing a game of tag with the alien signal?

He went to sit upon the edge of the last basin, holding

the hand above it so that any moisture that dropped would fall inside. The nerves were out for the duration, that was evident; but there did not appear to be any further erosion. He had lost hair follicles and a scraping of skin: not serious.

What *would* happen if a person were only partially exposed? Could a limb be painlessly amputated and preserved in such fashion, in case of injury? He was sure it could. This, perhaps, had been the original purpose of the technique. There might even be instructions somewhere concerning the regeneration of such a limb. How little he knew about the process he had invoked!

Morbidly he watched Beatryx's intestines come exposed. The light seemed to eat through the packed convolutions while it worried at the muscular bladder below them. What, indeed—what possible secrets could a woman have to hide, after the literal depth of her had been thus probed and vanquished? What physical act could approach the devastating intimacy of this association? There was her uterus, there the open channel of her vagina, there her anus and colon, seen from the inside in surgical cutaway. How was she different from Afra now?

How was *anyone* different from anyone else, in this ultimate reckoning?

And he had been embarrassed to touch Afra's body! He was glad now that at least one woman had insisted on it. The memory of the feel of that firm whole flesh was about the only comfort he had now, knowing that that flesh was whole no more.

God! (both prayer and expletive)—was the salvation offered by the macroscope worth it?

The beam ceased, startling him. Beatryx was done.

He realized that he was alone. He had only to wait a few more hours, and the UN ship would fetch him in, and the adventure would be over. He would not have to take the terrible risk the others had taken; he could be sure, at least, of life.

He was not honestly tempted. The others had not yielded to their fears; indeed, they had trusted him so far as to undertake this bizarre transformation before him, risking horrible extinction for the sake of the mission. *His* mission. That was the stuff of heroes. That was the stuff he

175

meant to prove to himself. He, Ivo—not the grandiose
Schön he had been summoned to summon.

And it was, he realized now, the only way he could
follow Afra. If the UN caught them now, the macroscope
would be taken away, and the vats of protoplasm would,
in the course of months, gradually deteriorate. A year was
about the limit, for shelf-life, as he understood it. After
that, reconstitution could become ugly.

He stripped awkwardly, because of his unconscious
hand. He moved Beatryx beside her husband and covered
her and tied her down. He positioned his own bath and
climbed in.

Then he climbed out quickly, remembering something.
The clothing of four people lay scattered recklessly. It
could be dangerous when the rocket maneuvered. He
bundled it all together, separating out coins and pens and
wallets and keys and pins and women's purses and placing
them in separate storage bins.

He looked at the worn old penny he had saved so long,
memento of a foolishly missed bus. He also still had the
unused bus token. Suppose one of those were to drift loose
during maneuvers, and drop into someone's vat of jelly?
Ouch!

He climbed in a second time. He would remain beneath
the beam, of course, and it would come on again at any
time after the minimum period had elapsed, provided that
conditions were appropriate. That meant, in this case,
normal gravity.

How could it tell what 1-G was, Earth definition? Too
late to worry about that now!

Ready or not, he thought, not even frightened any
more. Ready or not, here I—

Could experience be inherited? Lysenko, the Russian
scientist of yore, had argued that it could. His theory of
environment above heredity had seemingly been discred-
ited by his own malfeasance and the winds of political
change—but later researches had thrown the issue open
again.

The alien beam melted down functional flesh and reduced it to quiescent cells that required little nourishment,
surviving during their estivation largely upon their internal
nutrient resources. The reconstitution would re-create the

original individual—*along with all his memories.* All of it had to be in the cell—the lifetime of experience as well as the physical form. Only if that experience, right down to the most evanescent flicker of thought, were recorded in the chromosomes, the genes, or somewhere in the nucleus, of every tiny cell of the body—only thus could the complete physique and personality be restored.

The alien presentation said it could be done. The alien intellect was in a position to know.

Unless the flesh of Earthly creatures were not quite typical of that of the rest of the planetary species in the universe. . . .

"Put up or shut up!" Ivo thought somewhere—before, after, during?—and waited for his answer.

What a joke if the alien were mistaken!

Here I—
Swimming through a thick warm sea, an ocean of blood, smooth, delicious, eternal.
Here—
Climbing on the cruel heavy land, a continent of bone, hot, chill, transient.
How to speak without a lung? To think, without a brain?
A jumble of sensation: curiosity, terror, hunger, passion, satiation, lethargy.
An eon passing.
" . . . come." Ivo opened his eyes.

He was lying in the container, uncovered, bathed in lukewarm water. He felt fine. Even his hand was whole again.

He sat up, shook himself dry, and donned his clothing. Then he brought over the next coffin, able to tell by its weight and his own that gravity was 1-G, and removed the cover.

Inside was an attractive, vaguely layered semifluid. No bones showed. He withdrew.

The beam came on, illuminating the jellylike substance. The protoplasm quivered, but nothing obvious happened at first.

Patience, he told himself. *It worked before.*

Gradually a speck developed within its translucent upper layer; a mote, a tiny eye, a nucleus. It drifted about; it expanded into a marble, a golf-ball. It opened into a flexing cup that sucked in liquid and spewed it out through the same opening, propelling it cautiously through the medium. The walls of it became muscular, until it resembled an animate womb perpetually searching for an occupant. Then the spout folded over, sealed across the center, and became two: an intake and an outgo. The fluid funneled through more efficiently, and the creature grew.

It lengthened, and ridges along its side developed into fins, and one hole gravitated to the nether area. Patches manifested near the front and became true eyes, and it was a fish.

The fins thickened; the body became stout, less streamlined. The fish gulped air through an ugly, horrendously-toothed mouth and heaved its snout momentarily out of the fluid, taking in a bubble of air. It continued to grow, and its head came into the air to stay. Its near eye fixed on Ivo disconcertingly. Now it was almost reptilian, with a substantial fleshy tail in place of the flukes, and claws on well-articulated feet. The mouth opened to show the teeth again, fewer than before, but still too many. It was large; its mass took up half the fluid at this stage.

Then it shrank to the size of a rodent, casting off flesh in a quick reliquefication. Hair sprouted where scales had been, and the teeth became differentiated. Ratlike, it peered at him, switching its thin tail.

It grew again, as though a suppressant had been eliminated. It developed powerful limbs, heavy fur, a large head. The snout receded, the eyes came forward, the ears flattened onto the sides of the head. The limbs lengthened and began to shed their hair; the tail shriveled; the forehead swelled.

It was beginning to resemble a man.

Rather, a woman: multiple teats assembled into two, traveling up along the belly to the chest. The hairy face became clear, the muscular limbs slim. The pelvis broadened, the midsection shrank. The hair of the head reached down; the breasts swelled invitingly.

Goddess of fertility, she lay upon her back and contemplated him through half-lidded eyes.

Age set in. Her middle plumpened; her fine mammaries lost their resiliency; her face became round.

The beam cut off.

"Is it over, Ivo?"

He started, ashamed to be caught staring. "Yes."

He turned his back upon Beatryx so that she could dress in privacy. The reconstitution had not been as alarming as the dissolution, but it had had its moments. Worst was his impression of awareness throughout. The entire evolution of the species recapitulated in—

He checked the time.

—four hours. It had seemed like four minutes.

"I will fix lunch," she said. That was how he knew that she did not want to watch any other reconstitutions.

Groton revived next, and this time Ivo knew it was four hours. Finally Afra, and it seemed like eight.

"Check me," she said immediately. She had not forgotten.

The two men handled her in turn, hardly embarrassed this time around, and pronounced her real. "Yes," she said. "I was sure I was." The transformation was a subjective success.

Nothing was said about Brad. By mutual unspoken consent they let him remain as he was, in suspended animation or storage. What point reviving him now?

CHAPTER 6

They sped toward Neptune, a scant two million miles distant. Ivo needed no instrument to contemplate its grandeur. From this point in space the planet had an apparent diameter twice that of Luna as seen from Earth, or a full degree. It was a great-banded disk of green speckled with dots and slashes, as though a godlike entity had played a careless game of sprouts upon its surface.

They were in free-fall, with Brad's container sealed and aerated by an electric pump.

"Dull," Afra murmured facetiously. "Just a minor gas-giant nobody would miss."

Dull? Ivo appreciated the irony, for he had never seen a more impressive object. As he concentrated he was able to discern more detail: the comparatively bright, yellowish equatorial belt, blue-gray bands enclosing it above and below, mottled green "temperate" sections merging into the black poles—a rather attractive effect. Earth, compared to this, was a bleak white nonentity. Neptune's spots were concentrated in the central zone and were mostly dark brown or black, and he almost thought they moved, though he had no objective evidence. A single dark blue oval showed near the horizon in what he thought of as the northern hemisphere. The planet was not visibly oblate, yet his eye filled in what he thought was there. He imagined a celestial pair of hands compressing the planet so that its midriff bulged, the belt taut.

Now he studied the surrounding "sky." It was seemingly sunless, with fiercely bright and crowded stars. The largest object, apart from Neptune itself, was a disk several diameters to the left.

"Triton," Afra said, observing the direction of his glance. "Neptune's major moon. There's a smaller one, Nereid, that's farther out than we are now. Nereid's orbit is cometlike; very unusual for a planetary satellite. Of course, there may be other moons we haven't discovered yet; new ones keep popping up around the major planets."

"This is all very interesting," Beatryx said, obviously only marginally interested. Ivo suspected that she still suffered from the shock of the melting procedure, but tended to internalize it. "But now that we're here, what do we *do?*"

No one answered. Neptune loomed larger already, green monarch of the sea of space around them.

"It looks so big," Beatryx said. "And—wild. Are you sure it's safe?"

Groton smiled. "Neptune is seventeen or eighteen times as massive as Earth, but it is a lot less dense. What we see is not really the surface of the planet—it is the cloud cover. So it *is* large and wild, but don't worry—we won't try to land on it. We'll take up orbit around it."

"We'll just *love* a year of free-fall," Afra said.

Ivo watched the crumbs of their meal floating elusively in the currents of the forced-air circulation and knew what she meant. Free-fall was fun to visit, but not to stay. The space was too confined for long-term residence of four people, and muscles would atrophy in weightlessness if the body didn't malfunction in other ways first. And keeping Brad aerated yet contained would be tedious, perhaps dangerous. The melting was supposed to be a high-gravity alleviant, and might be vulnerable to prolonged weightlessness.

No—an orbit around Neptune was no answer.

"How about Triton?" Groton said. "It's about the size and mass of Mercury, I understand. Surface gravity should be about a quarter Earth-normal, and there might even be a little atmosphere. We'll need a base of operations, if only to process hydrogen for the tanks. And it would be fairly simple to intercept Triton at this angle, since we're coming up behind it."

"That does sound very nice," Beatryx said.

Groton was just warming up. "Now as I see it, our original purpose was to rescue the macroscope from deactivation or worse by the UN. To accomplish this it was necessary to remove the instrument from the immediate vicinity of Earth in a hurry. This much has been accomplished. Our main responsibility now is to keep ourselves advised of the situation at home, and to be ready to return the scope when the time is appropriate. Meanwhile, we can utilize the scope for reconnaissance."

Ivo smiled. "You mean Super-Duper Poo—"

Afra quashed him with a glance. Oh, well. Call it reconnaissance or call it poop scooping, there was no sense going back blind.

"What's this?" Afra demanded. They looked at her, startled. She had apparently been reorganizing her purse during the preceding dialogue, and now was looking at a page of a little stenographer's notebook.

Ivo saw strange squiggles on the sheet.

"It's in stenotype—a script version," Afra said. "I never heard of such a thing! I use Gregg."

"Oh, shorthand," Groton said. "Can you make it out?"

Afra concentrated on the half-familiar symbols. "It doesn't make much sense. It says 'My pawn is pinned.' "

"Another message from Schön!" Beatryx exclaimed.

"He must have planted notes all over the station," Groton said. "That polyglot, then the Neptune-symbol, and now this. He could have written them all at once and distributed them for us to find randomly—"

"But why didn't he come to us directly?" Beatryx wanted to know. "If he was close enough to get into Afra's purse—"

"Schön is devious," Ivo said. But the explanation sounded insufficient, even to him. What other little surprises did the genius have in store for them?

Neptune had grown monstrously by the time the ship braked down to something resembling orbital velocity. The planet's disk was fifteen times the apparent diameter of Luna from Earth, and its roiling atmospheric layers were horrendously evident. The great bands of color hardly showed now; instead there was a three-dimensional melange of cloud and gas and turbulence suggesting a photograph of a complex of hurricanes. The spectators were still too far removed to perceive the actual motion, and could contemplate at leisure the awesome extent of the frozen detail.

Ivo felt as though he were peering into a cauldron of layered oils recently disturbed by heating. He had a vision of Brad's basin perched on a furnace—and suppressed it, shocked at himself. Gray-blue bubbles a thousand miles across seemed to rise through the pooled, heavy gases, while slipstreams of turbulence trailed at the edges. In one place the recent passage of a bubble had left a beautifully defined cutaway section of gaseous strata, yellow layered on green on pink and black. In another, masses of whitish substance—hydrogen snow—were depressing the seeming ocean beneath, ballooning downward in a ponderous inversion. He was reminded of hot wax flowing into cool water.

No, there would be no landing in that.

Afra had retreated to the bowels of Joseph to supervise the maneuvering. They had cut inside Triton's retrograde orbit and were overhauling the moon at a rate that was rapid in miles per hour but seemed slow because of the immensity of the scale. The thirty-one-thousand-mile disk of Neptune dwarfed everything, and its rainbow hues rendered its satellite drab.

Yet baby Triton had its share of intrigue. Only a tenth the diameter of Neptune, it was still one and a half times the span of Luna, and three and a half times Luna's mass. Triton, mass considered, was the true giant of the moons of the Solar system, though there were others with a larger diameter. It expanded until its disk was the size of that of the mighty Neptune, then larger, and it was as though the two were sister planets. But where Neptune was stormy and bright, Triton was still and dark, from this angle. Its surface was timelessly rigid.

"Rigid ridges," Ivo murmured, half expecting Afra to say "What?" But she was not at hand.

There were craters: mighty broken rings of rock, shadowed in the middle, some pocked by smaller craters within. There were mountains: overlapping wrinkles across the surface. There was a brief atmosphere hazing the planetary outlines. And there were oceans.

"Must be some compound of oxygen and nitrogen," Groton said. "Water is out of the question." Intrigued, he had Ivo focus the macroscope on it and code in a spectroscopic analysis. "Atmosphere is mostly neon and nitrogen," Groton said as he studied the result. "With a little oxygen and trace argon. The ocean is a liquefied compound of—"

Then they spied the object in space.

"Alert!" Groton snapped into the intercom. "We're overhauling something, and I don't mean Triton."

"A ship?" Afra's voice came back. "Schön?"

Ivo centered the small finder-telescope upon it. The thing leaped into focus: a fragment of matter about forty miles in diameter. "Too big," he announced. "It's rock or another solid—and it's irregular." He checked the specific indications, since they were passing it rapidly enough to measure parallax. "About fifty miles long, thirty-five wide at the thickest point."

"I see it!" Afra cried. "We have it on Joseph's screen now. We—*that thing is in orbit!*"

"Not around Neptune," Groton protested. "It's heading in toward the planet. Couldn't—" He paused to take in his breath. "A moon of a *moon?* I don't believe it."

But it had to be believed. Due observation and analysis showed that it was a satellite of Triton, orbiting at about ten thousand miles distance with its broad side facing its primary. Its direction was "normal"—opposite to that of retrograde Triton. Its composition: H_2O.

It was a solid mass of ice, so cold that its surface would be harder than steel—and at the edges it was translucent. The light of stars shone through it, separating into prismatic (though very faint) flashes of color, a constant peripheral display.

"What a beauty!" Afra exclaimed. "Whatever shall we name it?"

"Schön," Groton said succinctly.

Ivo waited for Afra to object, but there was no reply from the intercom. Presumably she was waiting for *him* to object. The implications—

"This," said Groton, "is a break. We won't have to set up an orbit; one is waiting here for us."

"But we *have* to land on Triton," Ivo protested. "Schön couldn't possibly provide the gravity we need. Schön-*moon*, I mean." He had been made edgily aware of the unsatisfied curiosity about Schön-*person* that continued to nag at the others' minds.

"No question there. But we can't simply settle down with the macroscope on Joseph's nose. We're geared for space; a landing would crush us."

"But if the ship stood up under ten G's, and this is only a quarter G—"

"Sorry, it doesn't work that way. The ten G's were steady and uniform; the drop would be another matter. The effect of it would be many times ten G."

"Oh." At least Groton wasn't superior about his knowledge. "But if the ship can't land, and *we* can't stay in free-fall—"

"Planetary module. We'll get down all right. It will actually be easier to shuttle back and forth, and we won't have to risk the macroscope on land. Just so long as we don't lose Joseph in the sky after we desert him. But with an object as big and bright as Schön to zero in on, we won't have a problem. We'll be able to spot that in the sky without a telescope, any time."

The reasoning evidently appealed to Afra, because they were already phasing in on Schön. The block of ice seemed to drift closer, and the pits and bumps of its frigid surface magnified. The moonlet filled the screen, until it seemed as though they were coming in for a landing on a snowbound arctic plane—except that there was no discernible gravity.

Gently Afra closed with it, guiding the ship in by means of the tiny chemical stabilizer jets set in the sides. Ivo wondered what would happen when they came to rest, since the macroscope housing bulged well beyond the girth of Joseph—then remembered that with so little attraction there would be no particular stress. Actually, they were closer to synchronous orbit than to a "landing," and it would be wise to tie the ship down.

At fifty miles an hour, relative velocity, they approached, coming up underneath the moonlet; then twenty, and down to five. Schön seemed near enough to touch and the sense of being underneath it had dissolved; it was now like drifting *down* in a blimp. Finally, at barely one mile an hour, they covered the last few feet and jolted into contact. They were down.

"Let's stretch our legs," Groton suggested as the two women came forward. "The recondensing water vapor will anchor the ship as it cools, and that won't be long at all. We have no responsibilities, for the moment."

They went out upon the surface, and it was like flying. It was a vacation from reality. The trace vapors generated by the leaking warmth of their suits buoyed them up, away from the cold surface, and they had to use their gas jets to control their motion. A single push, and Ivo sailed along at a ten-foot elevation, feeling both powerful and insecure. To have a physical landscape so close, yet not to be bound by it . . .

Schön, like Triton, was locked to its primary. They had landed upon the "downward" face, and this accentuated the wrongness. Triton was too big, too close; when they looked at it they seemed to be above it, and when they drifted too high it was like falling, except that they fell, instead, *up* toward Schön. Was it the stuff of dreams—or of nightmares?

Ivo approached the horizon, and it did not recede from him. He drifted over the edge and had to correct as the "ground" dropped away from him, a new horizon a mile ahead. This really was a flat world; it *was* possible to fall off the edge, though the fall would be away rather than down. He navigated the intervening mile and found a third horizon, half a mile distant. One more, he thought; one more, then quiet. This experience was tiring.

But, fascinated, he traversed two more—and there was Neptune.

He knew that the ruling planet was no larger than it had appeared from the ship. He reminded himself of that. But then he had been closed in, protected; here he was exposed, and seemingly ready to plunge directly into it. The gaping face of it appalled him, so close, so fierce—the aspect of a physical destroyer. God of the sea—terror of man.

Ivo fired his jet and retreated hastily.

They had to take the ship into space again—a mile or so—to effect the separation of the module; then Afra piloted the chemical craft while Groton brought Joseph back to Schön. Ivo and Beatryx watched the entire maneuver from the landed macroscope housing, and he was not certain which of them was more nervous. An accident, even a slight mishap—and they could be stranded where they were for the duration. Until death did them part—shortly.

There was no accident. They loaded minimum supplies into the module and set off as a group for Triton. Not until the rough landing was over did Ivo allow his mind to function normally again. The experience had frankly terrified him, and he knew that Beatryx had reacted similarly.

Here at last there was gravity. Suited again, they stepped upon their new moon-planet home and looked about.

They were in a valley formed by the curving walls of adjacent craters that were now great mountain ranges jutting to either side. Other ranges were visible in the distance. Not far from their landing spot was an immense crevasse: a geologic fault running between the craters, V-cleft, and filled at the bottom with liquid. The ground surface was packed with dust, somewhat like solid snow, with rocks nudging through it irregularly. Mighty Neptune provided a dim illumination; there was nothing like Earth's sunlight out here.

"Well, we have our world," Beatryx said dubiously, after they had returned to the module. "Now what do we do with it?"

"We'll have to camp in the module until we can construct permanent quarters here," said Groton thoughtfully. "But before we do that, we'd better survey the area for good locations."

Afra had stripped off her suit in the pressurized cabin and was wiping the perspiration from her body with an absorbent cloth. Ivo realized that she was nude from the waist up—and further realized that their situation had intensified group interaction to such an extent that he hadn't even noticed her action until this moment. He suspected that it would be a long time before there was room again for modesty, when cubic yards were all the space available for the four, here. The macroscope had been roomy, compared to the module.

"I'd like first to know how long we're going to stay,"

187

she said. "Is Schön-person somehow going to find us here, and if so, how soon? No sense building anything fancy if it's only for a few days." She had not interrupted her clean-up.

Ivo remembered the breastless carcass he had watched melting, and was tempted to reach out and verify again that what he saw here was real. He refrained.

"Ivo?" Beatryx prompted.

He jumped. "I don't think Schön is coming. Anything we do, we'll have to do on our own."

"Can you find him or can't you?" Afra demanded, peeling down the nether portion of her suit. "Or contact him. You've been more and more mysterious, and there's still that business about that poet—"

Beatryx interrupted what was threatening to become a tirade. "Afra!"

"But he's refusing to cooperate! We can't put up with—"

It was Harold's turn to interrupt. "If the rest of you will leave off, I will address myself to the problem of Schön. I'll make a report when I have something to report. Meanwhile, there's nothing to stop us from setting things up. We'll need a base of operations regardless of the company. Let's just do things in an orderly manner and see what develops."

Afra did not seem fully satisfied, but she shrugged into shorts and a fresh blouse. She didn't bother with a brassiere in quarter-gravity. "Assuming that we find a suitable location, exactly how do you propose to construct 'permanent quarters'? The only abundant building materials we have are plain rock and cold dust, and those have certain limitations."

"I am aware of the limitations. But I figure Ivo can take another peek through the scope and come up with some galactic blueprints for us. This must be a fairly common situation, galactically speaking, and there must be survivors' handbooks. Why not use them?"

"I can try. Tell me what kind of information you seek, and I'll look for it. I can't use the computer's automatic search pattern, since this is intellectual, but—"

"Fine. I'll work out a schedule and talk to you again, and we'll ferry you up to the scope in a few days. I suppose we'd better set a limit on free-fall time, though—

say, no more than one day in three. That sound reasonable?"

Afra and Ivo nodded. Whatever leadership existed here seemed to be gravitating steadily to Groton, perhaps because their immediate problems had become ones of engineering—or perhaps, Ivo thought, just because of his level-headed calm.

"Should he be alone?" Beatryx inquired.

"Um, that too," Groton agreed. "Maybe we'd better make another rule that nobody be alone. That macroscope is dangerous, as we know—but so is Triton. We'll have to watch each other all the time, because we may not be able to survive as a group if even one of us goes."

"Should we make sure each of us can do each task?" Afra asked next. "Right now, Ivo's the only one competent on the scope. Harold and I can pilot—"

"If we can't get along without all of us," Ivo pointed out, "it doesn't really matter what any one of us knows. We function as a group or not at all."

"There is a macabre sense in that," Groton agreed, "if we ignore the possibility of someone's temporary incapacity. Let's assign tasks, then, and let people train for others as circumstance dictates. Ivo, you're the scoper, of course; Afra, you're the pilot, because I'll be the construction engineer. Beatryx—"

"Cooking and laundry," she said, and they laughed.

It was Beatryx who stood watch with him his first day on scope duty. Afra had piloted them off Triton and ensconced them safely in the macroscope, then dropped back to keep Groton company and help him survey for his construction. He had remained below in his suit, no one thinking to invoke the never-alone rule against him this time. Ivo had a carefully rehearsed headful of specifications, and his job now was to locate some galactic station that had the products required. He hardly comprehended the electronic terms, but he hoped that he could at least match bid to asked.

The first assignment was rough: a survey of galactic physical technology. But Beatryx was there when he emerged from the awesome visions of the cosmos, and she was cheerful and unassuming, encouraging and sympathetic. Ivo could appreciate the reason Groton, no intellectual

189

slouch himself, had passed over the female engineers he might have had and chosen a woman like this. It was the feeling of familiarity, of home, that he needed most when the revelations of the ages shook his fundamental assumptions, and she carried about her a pleasing aura of homebody Earth.

Again he remembered Brad's remark about normality being no insult, and again he appreciated it intensely. Intelligence might be defined as facility at solving problems—but it was only one talent among many required for existence. What about the problem of being fit to live with? By *that* definition, Beatryx was the smartest among them.

"Now I know what Lanier meant by the relation of music to poetry," he said as he removed helmet and goggles, his head revolving with the music of the spheres and the meter of communication. "The rules are identical—there."

"Lanier?" she inquired. "Sidney Lanier who wrote about the marshes?"

He looked at her, realizing his slip. "You know of him?"

"Only a little. I never understood the interpretations they taught me in school, but I did like some of the verse. I suppose I liked the American poets because they seemed closer. I remember how sad it made me when I learned about Annabel Lee."

"Annabel who?"

"She was by Mr. Poe. I always used to think he was Italian, because of the river. I mean, he wrote about her. I memorized it because it made me cry."

Ivo looked at her, seeing a woman of 37 who only once in the brief period he had known her had shown a sign of unhappiness. "Do you remember it now?"

"I don't think I do, Ivo. It was a long time ago. Let me see." She concentrated. " '*She* was a child and *I* was a child. In this kingdom by the sea; But we loved with a love that was more than love—I and my Annabel Lee.' " She shook her head. "She died—it was a wind blowing out of a cloud—but he loved her forever anyway."

"I didn't realize you liked poetry," he said. "What's your favorite poem of all time?"

"Oh, I remember that one," she said, her face animated. Ivo had judged her to be forty or more the first time he met her, then had learned her true age; now she seemed to have lopped half a dozen more years off that. People became so much much more *alive* when occupied in something really interesting to them. "It was so sad, but it seemed so true. I mean, I don't know it any more, but it was my favorite. It was about Jesus Christ and how they slew Him, when He came out of the woods. Oh, I wish I could remember how it went—"

" 'Into the woods my Master went/Clean forspent, forspent./Into the woods my Master came/Forspent with love and shame.' "

"That's it! Oh, Ivo, that's it! How did you know?"

"A Ballad of Trees and the Master," he said, "by Lanier."

"Yes, yes, I had forgotten, yes that was his! But how did you know it?"

"I know—quite a bit of his work. I—well, it's a long story, and I don't suppose it matters now."

"Oh yes it does, Ivo! He's such a good poet—I know he is—you must tell me! I remember it, I think. He came out of the woods— 'When Death and Shame would woo Him last,'—"

" 'From under the trees they drew Him last;/'Twas on a tree they slew Him—last/When out of the woods He came.' "

There were tears in her eyes that would not fall in the trace gravity. "He found peace among the trees—and then they crucified Him on a tree. Wood, anyway. Such an awful thing." She reflected on it for a moment. "But you didn't tell me how you know about Sidney Lanier."

Ivo was touched by her genuine appreciation and interest. "It was a kind of game we played. You see, none of us knew who our real parents were—"

"You didn't *know?* Ivo, where *were* you?"

"In a—project. They took people of all races and—mixed them together for a couple of generations and got children who were a combination of everything. The idea was to breed back to the basic stock of man, or at least obtain something equivalent to what he would have been if he hadn't split into so many races. To see if he was any better than the—well, the whites and the yellows and the browns and the blacks. They wanted to reduce cultural

191

influences and make it all the same, so we had no parents. Just supervisors."

"How horrible, Ivo! I didn't know."

"It wasn't so bad. Matter of fact, we had quite a time. We were never hungry or cold or neglected, and had all the best of everything. It was quite stimulating, as it was meant to be. There were several hundred of us, all the same age and—race. I didn't really realize until I got out of the project that I was not a normal American."

"*Not* a—"

"We're considered nonwhite."

"But that shouldn't make any difference, Ivo. Not in America."

He did not pursue that aspect farther. "Anyway, since we had no parents or relatives, some of us invented them. It got to be quite a serious thing. We'd pick figures from history and trace the lineage and work out a line of descent for ourselves. We had the whole world to choose from, of course—all times and all races. We'd show how these ancestors resembled us in some way, or vice versa. Anyway, my white ancestor was Sidney Lanier."

"I think that's very sweet, Ivo. But what made you decide he was the one?"

"I suppose it was the flute playing. Lanier was a fine flutist, you know—perhaps the finest in the world at that time. He earned his living for several years as first flutist for a prominent orchestra, even though he had tuberculosis, before he got more serious as a poet."

She frowned. "The flute? I don't see— Ivo! You play the flute!"

He nodded.

"Did you bring it with you? You must be a very good musician!"

"Yes, I brought it with me—the only thing I *did* bring. That's the way Lanier would have done it. I guess music *is* my strong point. A single talent, like my math-logic talent. I never really worked at it, but I could play the flute better than any of the others."

After another session with the macroscope, he yielded to her importunings, assembled his flute and played for her. The notes were oddly distorted in the confined space and trace-gravity air, but she listened raptly.

For her? He was playing for himself, too, for he loved

the flute. He caressed the instrument, letting the music flow through his being as though they were merely two stops between composer and audience. He lived each note, feeling his soul expand and renew, animated by the melody. This was the theme that brought him closer to his ancestor.

After that it became a regular routine between them, for he felt comfortable while playing and her pleasure was genuine. He played the cold out of the bleak Schönmoonlet landscape; he played mighty Neptune up over the Triton horizon (Triton never turned a new face to Neptune, but Schön's revolution about it caused a regular eclipse of impressive dimension); he played the spirit of Earth into their exile.

Sometimes, too, he took time off from the galactic bands to survey Earth and pick up the headlines from a New York newspaper, because Beatryx liked to know what was going on locally. In many respects, these sessions with her were as comfortable as anything he had known.

Meanwhile, below, developments were impressive. If flute-playing was Ivo's genius, machinery was Groton's.

"The problem is this," Groton had explained. "Information does *not* equal gadgetry. The amount of detail work required to build even a crude shelter at a place like this, with temperature, gravity and atmosphere problems, is appalling. Cutting, fitting, finishing, sealing, installing, testing—many thousands of man-hours, not to mention the equipment! So I need to know how a party our size, with a macroscope and an atomic engine and a planetary module and a few hand tools can terraform a world like Triton within, oh, six months. There must be a program for it somewhere. Find me that program!"

Ivo found it. One of the far galactic stations had a complete A-to-Z presentation beginning with a way to tie down a Type I technology rocket so that the heat and power of the blasting motor could be utilized planetside, and ending with the proper etiquette for the housewarming party.

Groton spent a tedious month fashioning the first crude semielectronic prerobotic tool: a type of waldo adapted to respond to a galactic instruction-beam. This device greatly facilitated the detail work for other machines, and progress multiplied.

An alien factory melted the rock of Triton, mixed it with chemical elements extracted from the ocean and produced a fine, strong, airtight nonconductive material that bonded to itself in a matter of hours upon contact, regardless of ambient temperature. Other units carried huge blocks of this "galactite," light in the quarter-gravity but still heavy as inertial mass, to the lakeside site Groton had selected for the human enclave. Soon there was a pyramid of dominoes fifty feet on a side, completely sealed. The airlocks were more complicated, but a week of signal-directed labor sufficed. This castle was pressurized and heated and lighted, and the human party was able to move in and reside in suitless comfort.

Meanwhile, Afra took her turn to babysit. Beatryx had the first several sessions, but the group felt that rotation was best, in the long run. Ivo was at this point transcribing the horrendously complicated data the early machines required. He hardly understood the terms or concepts, and had to consult with Groton frequently for lessons in elementary electronics. He did not dare augment his very limited comprehension through the program itself, because that might also let in the destroyer. He was forced to perform in ignorance, and it was hellishly fatiguing.

It was not easy to be alone with Afra, however. She was too bright, too beautiful, too bitter. Ivo could hardly blame her, yet it was hard to accept her subtle coldness with equanimity.

"You never knew your parents?" she inquired during one of the breaks.

"None of us did." Evidently Beatryx had been talking to the others. Well, he hadn't asked her not to.

"How many of you were there?"

"Three hundred and thirty. Of course, there may have been other groups, for other ages; we were all within a year of each other. A few months, actually." Why had she grown so curious about his background? Or was it merely a ploy to fill time?

"So you and Brad and Schön are the same age?"

"Yes." As he said it, he realized the trap. Brad had told her that the groups were separate, and he had just admitted that they were not.

She was silent for so long he felt moved to break the mood. "The idea was to combine—"

"I know!" Then, guilty at her own ferocity. "It is just so hard to believe that Brad could have been colored. I never suspected it."

This vestigial bigotry in Afra, though he had suspected its existence, came as a nasty shock to Ivo. "We varied in appearance, but the ratios were similar. Brad happened to be very light-skinned, while some were considerably darker than me. Does it matter?" Foolish question.

"Yes. Yes it does, Ivo." She turned away and looked out over the ice. "Oh, I know I'm supposed to say I'm a Georgia girl brought up in the twentieth century without prejudice. I *know* what a person *is* is what matters, not his lineage, and everyone is equal in our society. That the seeming inferiority of the nonwhite population stems from cultural and economic disadvantage and has no genetic basis. I understand that when Black Power burns its ghettos and pillages stores it's only the frustration speaking that the complacent white majority has fostered for a century. That all we need to do is work together, all races and all subcultures, to build a better society and negate the evils of the past. But—but I wanted to *marry* him!"

She spun about to face him, gripping the handrail. "It just isn't in me to love a Negro. I don't even know why. All my experience—"

She let go and floated, both hands covering her face. "Oh, Brad, Brad, I *do* love you—"

Damned either way. Ivo kept his mouth shut, remembering the thousand little ways he had been advised of his own inferiority, once he left the project. The liberals liked to claim that discrimination was a thing of the past, but few of them were to be found residing near Negro families. Official segregation no longer existed, but he had discovered how unpleasant it could get, how rapidly, when the powerful unofficial guidelines were ignored. He had heard from others how suddenly positions advertised as "equal opportunity" became "filled" when a nonwhite applied—and reopened for subsequent whites. Brad had chosen to "pass" —and had risen too high, too fast for reprisal when the truth leaked out. And evidently the truth had not reached Afra's ears, at the station. Ivo had chosen not to pass—and had paid the penalty. He was not one-third Caucasian, one-third Mongoloid; he was one-third *Negroid,* and that meant he was black. $\frac{1}{3}C + \frac{1}{3}M + \frac{1}{3}N$ $= N$. He was less intelligent than a purebred white, despite the white tests that said otherwise; he was less wholesome, though he washed as often and brushed his teeth with a popular white dentifrice; he was indefinably but definitely unequal and everybody in America knew it, whatever they might utter for public consumption. Whether it was "Get out of here, Nigger!" as it had been in 1960, or the rigid courtesy he had experienced in 1970, or selective blindness in 1980, he was an intruder upon society.

It had been impossible not to react. Hatred bred hatred, and the ghostly white skin of a stranger had come to make him tense up momentarily and think "White!" however objective he tried to keep himself. Yet he had been pitched calamitously into love at sight of the whitest skin of all. . . .

Afra had come out of it. "I am wrong. I know it. But I can't just change it, presto. I can call myself a white bigot and feel guilty, but that's still my nature." She looked at him in a way that hurt him. "You and Brad and Schön— all together?"

"Yes."

"The color and the IQ and the sex—all at once?"

"Yes."

"Why did he lie to me!" she cried in anguish.

That required no answer.

"And you, Ivo—you're lying to me too!"

"Yes." A half-truth was also a half-lie.

"You were in this free-love thing too. You've had more experience—"

"The project broke up when we were fifteen."

"Stop it! I can read you, Ivo. Tell me the truth. Tell me about you and Brad and Schön."

"It isn't—" He stopped. What she was after, she would get, however much he might temporize. "There were a hundred and seventy boys and a hundred and sixty girls. We were raised together from infancy—one big dormitory, no segregation between sexes. We chose our own rooms and roommates and there were no hours."

"A commune," she said tersely.

"A commune. But the adults always appeared when there was real trouble, so everyone knew we were watched all the time. It didn't matter. Most of the kids were pretty smart."

"They were selected for that," Afra said. "The complete man was supposed to be a genius."

"Genetics and environment and statistics indicated that there would be something like genius somewhere within that group, yes. Every day there was education, starting as soon as a child could react to stimulation. Maybe before that—I don't remember. We were fed high-potency diets and protected against every disease known to man and given constant physical and intellectual stimulation. I think there were as many adult supervisors as children, but they only showed up for the teaching. Almost everyone could speak and read by the age of three, even the slow ones."

"Group dynamics," she said. "It was competitive."

"I guess so. But they were always snooping—the adults, I mean. That was another game—to fool them. Rigging the scores, faking sleep, that sort of thing. They were so gullible. Maybe it was because they were all so educated. They had too much faith in their tests and their bugs and their bell-shaped curves."

"I can imagine. What about the girls?"

He did not pretend to misunderstand her. "They knew they were female. A number of the kids were precocious that way too. But children four years old don't see sex the same way as adults do. The anal element—"

"And Schön? That's where he got his name, isn't it?"

"I guess so. We named ourselves; we were just numbers to the adults. To keep it impartial, I suppose. That's why my name is a pun. Schön—he got interested in language early—"

"*How* early?"

"Nobody knows. It just seemed he learned six or seven languages at once, along with English, and I understand he could write them too. I didn't know him then—or ever, for that matter. I think he knew a dozen by the time he was three."

Afra digested this in silence.

"And he was very pretty. So he roomed with lots of kids, and they all liked him at first. So he was *sehr schön*. I think the *sehr* means—"

"I see. Just how far can four-year-olds go?"

"Sexually? As far as anybody, the motions. I think. At

197

least, Schön could, and the ... girls. But he got bored with it pretty soon."

"You're still lying by indirection, but I can't pin it down. How did Brad fit into this?"

"He was Schön's best friend. His only friend at the end, perhaps. Schön didn't really need anybody. I guess it was because they were the two smartest, though Schön was really in a class by himself."

She was silent again, and he knew she was thinking of Brad's 215 IQ. "They were—roommates."

"Yes." Then he grasped the direction of her thinking. "You have to understand—there weren't any social conventions from outside. No restrictions." But it bothered him as sharply as it bothered her; he was defending it from necessity. "It was all play—homo or hetero or group—"

"Group!"

Ivo shrugged. "What's wrong with it, objectively?"

"I seem to have more prejudices than I thought."

Ivo was discovering how much more reasonable a shared prejudice seemed. "But there wasn't any challenge to that. It didn't mean anything. So most of our energies were concentrated on learning, and outwitting the fumbling adults."

"How intelligent *was* the average child, if the supervisers didn't know?"

"I don't know either. But I'd guess the adults thought it was one twenty-five, while actually it was 25 or 30 points above that."

She became thoughtful once more, perhaps pondering existence in a group where she would have been barely average. But her next words proved otherwise: "Your 'experts' didn't do their homework well enough. Didn't they know what happens to children deprived of their family life?"

"It wasn't possible to have—"

"Yes it was, if they'd really wanted to take the trouble. They could have placed each child in an adoptive home, or at least foster care, with the formal training and stimulation and what-have-you provided centrally. Similar in that respect to the way the Peckham Experiment functioned."

Ivo tried to conceal his surprise at her reference. She

was better educated than he had thought, despite what he already knew of her abilities. "They weren't trying for family harmony. They wanted brains."

"So they defeated themselves by precipitating an unrestrained peer-group. When parental guidance is absent, the standards of the peer-group take over early—and they aren't always 'nice' standards. If the average American child is perverted to some extent by the increasing preoccupation, neglect and absence of his parents, and by the violence of TV and news headlines, and the viciousness of deprived peers that are his chief contact with the world, think how much worse it would be for the children who never had families at all! No incentive to excel at useful tasks, no development of conscience. You need a father in the house for that, or a good strong father-substitute. And the notion that only persons with masters degrees in education are qualified to raise children—no wonder they came up with someone like Schön!"

Ivo hadn't seen it that way before, but it made sense to him now. What he was experiencing here, with Harold and Beatryx and Afra herself, was actually a family situation. Already it had stimulated him to performance far beyond anything he had approached before. And—he liked it. Argument, danger, gueling work and continued friction there might be—but they were all pulling together, and it was better than the life he had known on Earth.

"Didn't that adult-baiting game bore Schön pretty soon too? What did he do about it?"

Back to specifics. "He left."

"From a monitored dormitory? An enclosed camp? Where did he go?"

"Nobody knew, exactly. He was just gone."

"You're lying again. Brad knew."

"I guess so."

"And *you*—you knew. You still know! Even Brad couldn't fetch him, but *you* could—except you wouldn't!"

Ivo did not answer.

"And it's all tied in somehow with that poem of yours, and the planet Neptune, and that damned pinned pawn."

Had she assembled the puzzle? Schön evidently wanted her to. Did she know how readily she could summon the genie, knew she but its abode? Could she suspect the consequence of too rash a conjuration?

199

The pyramid—actually a tetrahedron—became a splendid center under the patter of little metal feet supervised by instructions from space. One face was flush with the ground, and a triangle of triangles pointed at Neptune. Dull, impervious blocks on the outside gave way to twenty-first century comfort on the inside. Each person had a room—Groton and Beatryx an apartment, with electric accommodations and sophisticated plumbing. Spongy warm rugs lined the floors, and the walls were painted attractively.

With power and a machine shop, and the incoming galactic program, Groton directed an irregular stream of wonders. He produced a device that converted Tritonian soil into protein, and another that generated a field of force that would enclose a larger area outside the tetrahedron and retain an Earthlike atmosphere. Yet another served to focus gravity and bring their weight, in this limited area of the planet, up to Earth-normal.

Matter-conversion, force-field, gravity control—these things staggered Ivo's imagination. They had assumed that galactic technology would exceed that of Earth, but the fact was somewhat overwhelming. How many decades—how many *centuries*—would be required for Earth to develop such things on its own? The proboscoids of Sung had never achieved this level. They, of course, had not been able to penetrate the destroyer and receive the programs beyond it. Otherwise, many of their problems could have been materially alleviated.

The recurring question: why, then, did the destroyer exist? And the recurring answer: data insufficient.

Ivo tried to compliment Groton on his achievements. "I'm just an engineer following instructions," the man said blithely. It was to a considerable extent the truth, since his position had become analogous to that of a child turning on a television set and sitting back to watch experts at work. But however detailed the program, Groton deserved credit for making it applicable to their situation. It was his heyday.

No longer were they required to walk the barren surface in space suits. An artificial sun replaced the minuscule original star in the sky, and light and heat blazed down upon the landscape twelve hours of each twenty-four, riding the fringe of the force-field. Beatryx planted beans from the ship's food supplies, and they sprouted in a garden stocked with the protein soil-mockup beside a reservoir of H_2O—i.e., a genuine crescent-lake.

Ivo, for his contribution to the good life, arranged to photograph images on the main screen of the macroscope, and made regular prints of Earth newspapers, magazines and books. These the others could read without danger of encroachment by the destroyer, since only its "live" image killed. Far from being a lonely, frozen exile, their stay on Triton had become, in a few active months, an independent vacation.

Groton finally took his turn with Ivo at the macroscope, refusing to claim indefinitely the privilege of moonside duty that his continuing performance had warranted. "Do the machines good to have time off," he remarked. "I told 'em to be back on the job 8 a.m. Monday and sober." For the first time since the onset of this adventure, the two men were together privately when there was time to converse.

Ivo suspected there was a reason for it, since Groton still had important other chores to do and had already proven himself to be an indefatigable worker. Afra had been overshadowed and relegated to the role of technical assistant, and of course Beatryx had been the chief baby-sitter. Had Groton made time now for a reason?

He had. "You remember I'm interested in astrology," he said.

That was not the subject Ivo had anticipated. "Yes, you took my birth date and a significant experience." So long ago, it seemed! Back the other side of the melting—a whole separate existence, receding into memory. And did it make a difference, for the astrological discipline, that the childhood Ivo had made his own was that of Sidney Lanier? He felt a twinge of guilt, but was afraid that an explanation at this point would be awkward. "I also overheard you discussing it with Afra, way back when."

"Yes. Brilliant girl, but her mind is resistant to certain concepts." Ivo had become aware of that, too. "Doesn't matter. I don't require that anyone else accept my values, and I am confident that astrology can stand on its own merits. But I have been casting horoscopes for each of the members of this party, and there is a certain mystery about you."

Ivo wondered when the man had found time for this, in the face of the colossal job he had been doing on Triton. Here he shared Afra's perplexity: how was it that such a competent and realistic engineer was able to take a pseudo-science seriously? Groton did not seem to differentiate between the real and the unreal, yet his approach to all things seemed to be totally practical.

"If you don't mind," Groton said after an interval, "I'd like to discuss this with you."

"Why not? I can't say I believe in astrology any more than Afra does, but I don't mind questions."

"Can you say you know enough about astrology to believe or disbelieve intelligently?"

Ivo smiled. "No. So I guess I'm neutral."

"It is surprising how certain most people are about what they like or don't like, or believe or don't believe, when their information is really too scanty for any meaningful decision. If I had chosen before the fact to disbelieve in the possibility of a signal from space that could build advanced machinery, our residence on Triton would be less comfortable than it is. Prejudice is often expensive."

It occurred to Ivo that he had just had another lesson in open-mindedness. He had objected to Afra's views on race, but his own mind had been as one-sided in the matter of astrology. And, like Afra, he *still* couldn't reverse his standing attitudes; astrology, to him, was essentially fakery. He was as prejudiced as she.

"Still, that's irrelevant," Groton said. "What I want to do is give you portions of two descriptions, and have you judge which one fits you best. It's a kind of psychological exercise—but don't misunderstand. I'm not trying to psychoanalyze you. This may help me to clear up my problem, and perhaps show you a little of what astrology is in practice."

"Fire at will."

"Odd you should choose that wording." Groton paused to collect his thoughts. "Here is the first description: This person is determined to get on the inside of things and to control the machinery of life. This position always encourages a conscious response to the undercurrents of the moment. At his best he is able to recognize the basic unity of experience, or to bring unsuspected and helpful relations into play; at his worst he is apt to cultivate suspicion or encourage half-baked effort. Life for him must be exciting, and he must be self-reliant. He is essentially fearless, and likes to move quickly and positively, taking the full consequence of whatever he does. He does not care much for abstract considerations, and gives little thought to other people."

Groton paused. "Now here is the second one: This person is determined to test the mettle of reality in every possible sort of hard effort. He desires to bring everything down to a utilitarian basis. At his best he is able to organize or redirect the energies of himself and others to an increased advantage; at his worst he is apt to become wholly malcontent and unsocial. Life for him must be purposeful; he is readily stimulated. He is high-visioned, optimistic, gregarious to a fault and often gullible. He must be challenged to do his best, or he becomes dogmatic and jealous. He is a realist in minor things, a do-or-die idealist otherwise."

Ivo thought about it. "They're both so general, and I'm not sure I like either one too much. But the second seems closer. I do like to help people, but too often it doesn't work out. And I'd much rather earn my way by hard work than do something dramatic. I'm certainly not fearless."

"This is my impression. Human traits are not portioned off precisely, and we all have a little of everything, so character summations are necessarily vague in spots. But the first hardly describes you. It is Aries the Ram in the twelfth house. Aries is part of the fire element—that's why I commented on your figure of speech."

"My—?"

"You said 'fire at will. ''

"Oh."

"The second is Aquarius the Water Carrier in the sixth house—air element. I could go on with the other planets—this was the sun, of course—but this differentiation is typical. You appear to fit Aquarius, not Aries."

"And my birth date?"

"Aries."

"So I'm a misfit. Don't know where I belong. Whose birthday is Aquarius?"

"I played a hunch from something my wife mentioned. Sidney Lanier."

Ivo felt a nasty emotional shock. Pseudo-science or not, this was striking pretty close. "So you say I should be fire when I seem to be air. Could you have miscalculated?"

"No. That's the mystery. I rechecked very carefully and it stands. Your personality is entirely different from the one indicated by your horoscope, and your personal episode only corroborates that difference. I could be mistaken in detail, but hardly to this extent. So: assuming my tenets to be valid, either your birth date is not the one you gave me, or—"

"Or—?"

"Do you play chess?"

"No." Ivo did not challenge the abrupt change of subject.

"It happens that I do. I'm not very good at it, but I used to play quite a bit, before I found more important uses for my time. So I believe I know what that message means."

"Message?"

"Schön's last. You remember: 'My pawn is pinned.' That's a chess expression."

"I wouldn't know."

"I think you would, Ivo, but I'll explain. Each piece in chess has a different motion and a different value. A pawn is a minor piece reckoned at one point and it moves straight ahead, one step at a time. The knight and the bishop are worth three points each, and their motions are correspondingly more intricate and far-ranging. The castle is worth five, and the queen nine or ten, so you see she is a very powerful piece. The pointages are only general guides to strategic value; no numerical score is kept, of course. The queen moves as far as she wants in any direction; it is her mobility that gives her strength, and her presence changes the entire complexion of the game."

"I don't entirely follow the explanation, but I'll take your word for it."

"Doesn't matter. The point is, you dare not ignore the queen. She can strike from any distance, while a pawn is severely limited. So the queen can check and even mate the king without danger to herself, but the pawn has to be guarded."

"Mate? Guard?"

Groton sighed. "You really *don't* know chess, do you! Here." He brought out a blackboard and made a checkerboard on it in chalk. Blackboards seemed to be popular among engineers. "The squares are black and white, but forget that for now." He added some letters. "Here's the black queen—she's circled. It could be a black bishop, of course; principle's the same. She's on king's-rook-eight, while all the whites are set up on the seventh and eight ranks, so." He ignored Ivo's confusion. "Now white's pawn is about to be queened, but can't because it is pinned. *That's* what Schön is talking about."

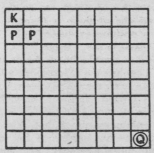

Ivo contemplated the illustration. "I'm glad it makes sense to you."

Groton pursued his logic relentlessly. "The king is the game, you see. You can't allow him to move into check. Your opponent will call you down for incorrect play if you do; there are no pitfalls of that nature in chess. Look—pawn moves up like this, next it's black's move and queen checks king. So pawn *can't* move, not while it's pinned. It has to protect the king."

"That much I follow. I think. The pawn is like a bodyguard—if it steps out, assassination."

"Close enough. But here is the rest of it: the pawn is a special piece, especially in this position, because if it gets to the back row it changes into a queen, or any other piece it chooses to. That can change the whole course of the game, because an extra queen in the end-game is a terror."

205

"It does look pretty bad for that king, bottled in the corner like that."

"White pawn promotes into a *white* queen; that's good for this king. Matter of fact, it means white can win the game—if that pawn can only move up. That's why the pin has to be broken; it is the crux of the game."

"We're white?"

"Right. And black is some alien intelligence fifteen thousand light-years deep in the galaxy."

"The destroyer?"

"That's what I mean. Somebody set up that alien queen, and she has our king threatened, all the way across the board. And all we have are pawns to hold her off."

"And we've lost six pawns already."

"Right. Our seventh and eighth are on the board at the seventh rank. And one of them is pinned—the important one. The one in a position to queen."

"Which one is that—in life, I mean."

"*That* one." Groton aimed a heavy finger at Ivo.

"Me? Because I can use the macroscope a little?"

"Because you can fetch the white queen. Schön."

"But how am I pinned?" Groton, now that he was on the trail, was as persistent as Afra.

"I have been wondering about that. You are obviously Schön's pawn, and he has confirmed his involvement by sending us cryptic little messages. My guess is that he would come to us if he could. He told us why he can't, if we can only make sense of it." Groton looked at his diagram. "Now that pawn is pinned by the queen, so that's you pinned by the destroyer. If that pawn could move even one step, it would be another queen. So it is in effect a queen that is pinned, in the guise of a pawn. They are the same; the one is inherent in the other."

"I suppose so, but—"

"And that explains several things, such as the dichotomy in my charts. So it must be right."

"So *what* must be right?"

"That you are Schön. The fire element."

"Sure. And the pin?" Careless words—but the game was over.

"You sat through the sequence that put away Brad and killed the senator. You survived it, probably because you came below its critical limit. But Schön is buried in your mind, unconscious or penned in somewhere. He doesn't get burned because your mind takes the brunt, and you're just a pawn. But the moment he comes out—when you turn queen—that memory is there, waiting to blast him. And he knows it. So he *can't* come out; his pawn is pinned."

Ivo nodded. "You take your time, but you do get there."

"So you were aware of it? I thought it might be hidden from you." Groton glanced out the port at the frigid plateau, not seeming gratified at his success. "Your horoscope pointed the way, of course. There had to be an explanation for the chart's failure to match observation, and as is so often the case, the error was *in the observation*. So now the question is, how do we remove the pin? We can't get at the queen and we don't have many pieces on our board. Of course it's not so simple as I have it—this illustration has loopholes even taken purely as chess—but I could set up a sounder analogy if it were worth the trouble. It seems that the four of us will have to do it if it's going to be done at all. Do you agree?"

"I think so. But how do you wipe out a memory? And even if you could, Schön probably couldn't use the macroscope himself. Not with that signal still there."

"I don't know. That falls beyond the province of engineering, I fear. But we might hold a meeting on it, let Afra take a crack at it. But one other consideration—"

"I know. What happens when Schön comes. To me."

"Right."

"I'm gone. The truth is, I only exist in Schön's imagination."

"This, again, is what your horoscope suggested. It spelled out, in the sometimes perplexing way they do, Schön rather than Ivo. Nevertheless you seem pretty real to me."

"I'm not. When Schön got fed up and decided to leave—which happened when he was about five years old—he did it by inventing an innocuous personality and setting it loose. Someone not too bright, so that the project supervisors wouldn't be attracted, but not suspiciously stupid either. Someone more or less colorless, but again, not suspiciously. Someone average in his exceptionality, if you see what I mean. So he worked it out and set it up in one aspect of his mind, and went to sleep. I am what remains—a genuine programmed personality. Somehow he cleared it with all the kids who knew him, and they forgot what he had been like and thought I had always been there. Except for Brad, of course. He sort of watched over me. But I was born full-blown at the age of five and never had a project childhood."

"Most people would consider ages five to ten the flower of childhood."

"Not at 330 Pecker Place! It was all over when I got there. That's what I meant when I told you before that I had no childhood episode for you. Everything was—set."

Groton let that sidelight drop. "And Schön never came back?"

"Well, he has to be summoned. That's my job—to judge when the time is right. But he had no reason to return. Ordinary life is unbearably tedious to him, so he leaves the mundane maintenance to me."

"He left just because of tedium? But that isn't very likely, is it? Why would things *have* to be tedious for Schön? And why would he make his return involuntary— on his part, I mean? I'd be inclined to suspect some more urgent reason for that setup."

"What else could there be?" Ivo asked uneasily. His own understanding of the conditions of his existence was beginning to seem insufficient to him.

Groton plainly was not satisfied. "I may take a more careful look at the chart."

"Best luck. Meanwhile, I'll just muddle along as well as I can."

"Muddle? I'd call it a mature adjustment to reality on your part."

"That's the nicest description for desperation I've heard today! When he wakes—and he'll have to wake, if the time comes—I'll be reintegrated into his total personality, and all my memories and aspirations with me, and I'll be gone. It's like a planetoid falling into the sun."

"I was afraid of that. When the pawn queens, it isn't a pawn any more, not even in part. I can see why you never were anxious to invoke Schön."

"I'm selfish, yes. Now that I'm here, I want to live. I want to prove myself. I don't like Schön."

208

"I believe I would feel the same way." Groton thought for a moment more. "That trick with the sprouts—"

"That's one of the few talents Schön bequeathed me in the name of not being a complete nonentity. That, and the flute playing. The supervisors had a ball analyzing the reasons I was so advanced in those areas and so retarded in others. I think they developed a whole new theory of child-potential, deciding that in a normal family situation both talents would have been suppressed. I don't really know. Anyway, that's where you see Schön's full power—except that he's like that in just about *every* area."

"And you wiped out the sprouts champion of the station, after one practice game, without even sweating."

"I wouldn't say that. There *are* limits, and sprouts gets pretty complicated."

"Uh-huh. And my wife says you play the flute better than any person she's heard. And she has heard the masters; she's a classical music nut."

"She never told me that."

"She wouldn't."

"Well, I didn't expect to keep the secret forever."

"One by one we pry into your qualities. The Triton situation is too intimate for proper privacy."

"That's the way Purgatory is, I guess."

"No. That's the way friendship is. A great sharing, a good sharing." He paused again, troubled. "Look, Ivo, despite all that, I don't much like this particular turn of the wheel. Maybe I prefer Aquarius to Aries. Afra will catch on soon enough anyway. What say we let it ride for a while, see what develops?"

Gratefully, Ivo nodded.

Base operations continued apace, until the physical plant was complete. Then, with the urgency gone, the isolation pressed in again. Triton was not Earth, no matter how luxurious it became, and all of them were increasingly aware of it. The news from Earthside was depressing; hope faded that any return was politically feasible within a span of years.

Ivo spent his allotted time at the macroscope, transcribing processes for which they had only theoretical use. There were truly potent force-fields capable of compressing solid rock into a state of degenerate matter; there

209

were heavy-duty robotoids capable of constructing duplicate macroscopes. For what purpose, such miracles? They already had everything they needed except home.

Groton enlarged the atmospheric screen and made other nominal improvements. Beatryx cooked and did their laundry by hand (though they easily could have had food and clothing that needed neither treatment) and cultivated and weeded her garden, while the galactic devices for such tasks stood idle.

Afra reacted most strenuously. She set up a formidable laboratory and buried herself in it for many hours at a time. She demanded a search for specialized galactic medical techniques, and pored over what Ivo obligingly produced until her eyes were sunken and staring. She insisted on an extension of the macroscope screen for her lab, though they all knew it would have been suicidal for her to watch it. The great glass vat in which she had arranged to store Brad's protoplasm (bubbling eerily because of the aeration) rested upon a shelf, morbidly overlooking her efforts.

"I don't like this," Groton said privately to the others. "She *can't* be thinking of reconstituting Brad and operating on him herself. But I'm afraid she is."

"Does she have surgical training?" Ivo asked.

"No. She's trying to learn it all now, on her own. She'll kill him."

"What is she going to do?" Beatryx asked, worried.

"As I make it, she means to remove his damaged nervous tissue and grow it back or replace it with galactic substitutes. As though she were grafting an artificial hand."

"But it's his *brain* that's burned. . . ." Beatryx said.

Ivo mulled the point. How could it be possible to replace any portion of the brain, without drastically changing the personality? Even if Afra were to accomplish it, the result would not be the Brad she had known. And the civilization that set up the destroyer would surely have known about feasible corrective techniques, and arranged to make them useless, lest its barricade be breached. Salvation could not lie in that direction.

Or was he rationalizing, jealous of the possible return of a rival? Had there not been something about becoming

210

dogmatic and jealous, in that Aquarius portrait Groton had provided?

"She can't reconstitute him unless I tune in the station," Ivo remarked.

"Are you sure? Don't forget, she supervised his melting. She insisted on having a macroscope-screen extension. And that reconstitution signal tunes in itself, as it has to to revive a melt when nobody's around to supervise. I'd say she can do it—and *will*."

"I don't know. I'd hate to risk it."

This, too, had to ride. They were pinned. Any interference was as likely to provoke calamity as to alleviate it.

Afra's preparations neared completion. They could tell by the way she hummed in her laboratory, by her air of expectancy, though she turned aside all questions.

When the tension became unbearable, Groton went to reason with her—but she had locked them out. "Could get around that soon enough," he muttered, since he had directed the building of room, door and lock, and still had functioning mechanicals available. "But what's the point? She means to see it through, and she's an imperious lass. All fire and earth."

Ivo was beginning to recognize astrological allusions. Fire burned and earth endured—or something like that. "Should we let her do it?"

"All in favor of stopping her by sheer physical force," Groton said, and shrugged. Neither Ivo nor Beatryx cared to register a vote.

"But we should watch her," Ivo said. "We know it's disaster, but we don't know exactly what kind. There will be pieces to pick up."

"Literally," Groton agreed. "Ours, if we break in."

"I was thinking of the macroscope."

Groton's eyes widened. "Let's go!" he cried. "Beatryx, you stay here—but don't go in after her, no matter what you hear. Unless she calls for help."

Frightened, she nodded. She looked, in that moment, haggard; she had lost sleep and weight. Ivo had not realized until this glance how deeply involved in this crisis Beatryx, the only other woman on Triton, felt herself to be. Why did he so often forget that other people had emotions as pressing as his own?

The two men scrambled into their suits, checked each

211

other hastily, and ran heavily into the domed garden. Tall wheat and barley waved in the intermittent artificial breeze (Beatryx insisted that it seemed just like a *real* breeze to her, but it derived from machinery and not meteorology), and green potato plants clustered near the exit. The heart-shaped, orange-tinted foliage of a sweet-potato vine angled toward the floating sun. Controlled mutation was theoretically available through galactic programming, but Beatryx would have none of it; she wanted only the plants of Earth that could be enticed to germinate from the stores.

They charged down the garden path (gravel, with invaluable weeds arranged adjacently) and plunged through the atmospheric force-screen in a shower of crystals: the air carried across with them dropped almost instantly to a temperature that made its survival as gas impossible, and its water vapor solidified and shattered. Inside the dome of enclosure, behind them, the momentary backlash froze the nearest plants and created a localized snow flurry.

Beyond the transparent shield the surface of Triton remained as before, a barren waste a hundred and eighty degrees below zero centigrade. The sea of cold oxygen-nitrogen picked up where the lake of warm oxygen-hydrogen left off, the field insulating the one from the other all the way to the bottom.

The planetary module stood in isolation two miles distant. They ran toward it clumsily, still within the area of 1-G. A hundred yards beyond the dome this eased to slightly below Triton-normal. The gravity-focuser concentrated the attraction of an area a hundred miles square into a circle a few hundred yards square, taxing the major area for the benefit of the minor. It was not possible for this equipment to remove *all* gravity from any section, nor to magnify it without limit; this was a channelizer rather than a shield or amplifier. Much more powerful processes were available, but as Groton pointed out during one of their technical discussions, extremes were not advisable. A strong imbalance could destroy the atmosphere and much of the surface of Triton, and even jog the moon from its present orbit. Why risk it?

The men made long bounds, keeping them shallow for speed, and moved rapidly through ¼-G toward the module. Through they had been waiting almost idly for weeks,

Ivo felt now as though a single wasted minute could make them too late. He reached the module first, ascended the ladder by bounds, and entered the airlock. It seemed so clumsy, after the sophistication of the force-field! They had been benefiting from the gimmicks of Type II technologies, and now were thrown back to their own Type I.

He pressured the lock and went on into the interior, clearing the chamber for Groton's entry. He activated the internal heating mechanism, not for the occupants' sake but to insure proper functioning of the equipment. This machinery was suppose to operate at "comfortable" temperatures—say, within fifty degrees of freezing.

Ivo now knew how to use the module, though he was not a sure pilot. The controls were deliberately simple, and the frequent trips to the Schön base had educated him rapidly in the subject of Type I space jockeying. Takeoff was routine.

Finally they floated into the macroscope housing. This was maintained at a constant temperature and pressure because of the intricate sensory apparatus and the connected computer. They stripped to light clothing and settled down to work. Neither was concerned about the destroyer, since Ivo knew how to shield his mind from its influence and Groton had long since experimented under controlled conditions and verified that he was not affected unless he really concentrated.

Groton had also tried to use the scope himself, in order to facilitate early construction, but had found that the same limit that protected him from mind-ravaging prevented him from assimilating the alien signals beyond. The typical mind was receptive to both or to neither. Ivo was a fluke—perhaps because he was not a complete person.

It had been a long time since he practiced at such close range, though he knew that theoretically the macroscope could pick up anything, even its own functioning apparatus, if the proper adjustments were made. Definition in such cases was poor, however; too strong a signal was worse than too weak. He set the range for minimal and concentrated on the moon below.

A section of the interior of Triton appeared: blank rock. Then, as he found his level, the surface showed, slightly fuzzy but readable. He shot across craters and clefts and oceans, guiding the pickup toward the dome while Groton watched. This type of exploration Groton could have handled, since it was of the basic nonintellectual level. But practice had given Ivo far greater skill, and they were in a hurry.

"Coasting on ninety-five," Groton remarked. Ivo realized that the man had never had occasion to watch this particular maneuver before.

"We're not exactly coasting. Faster this way than computing the exact coordinates of the camp. I wouldn't try it on a distant target, though." Something nagged him about Groton's remark, but he was too preoccupied to place it.

Then they were in the dome. He slowed, feeling his way into the pyramid, and on toward the laboratory. There was a flash of Beatryx sitting nervously in the kitchen, and Groton grunted. *He does love her,* Ivo thought, finding that a revelation though he knew it had always been obvious.

At last he closed on Afra's laboratory and brought the entire room into reasonably clear perspective. She was there, lying on a bunk; she had not yet started her ... project. "We're in time," he said. "I don't know whether that's good or bad."

"Good I can appreciate. Why bad?"

"Because we're too far away to do anything if there's trouble—and I guess there will be. All we can do from here is watch."

Groton nodded thoughtfully. "You're in love with her."

The observation did not seem impertinent or out of place, now. "Since I saw her first. Brad introduced her— 'Afra Glynn Summerfield'—and I was—well, that was it."

"Why would Brad do that?"

"Do what? It was our first meeting."

"Make up a name. Didn't you know?"

"You mean her name isn't Afra? Or Summerfield? I don't understand."

"Isn't *Glynn*. I don't know what her middle name is, but it isn't that. I believe it is a family designation, Jones or Smith or something."

Ivo sat stricken. "Brad! He did it on purpose!"

"Did what?"

"The name, don't you see? He set it up for me."

"You've lost me, Ivo. You didn't fall in love with a name, did you?"

Ivo's gaze was anchored to Afra where she lay. He remembered the time she had lain in his hammock, tormented and lovely, so soon after the destroyer disaster. "You didn't hear about me and Sidney Lanier? I told Beatryx, and you made that horoscope—"

"My wife is circumspect about personal information. She must have felt that the details were confidential. All she mentioned was that you admired Lanier's poetry. Unfortunately I'm not familiar with his actual writings."

"Oh. Well, I have this thing about the poet. I've studied his life and works, and anything that relates to him, and I react automatically to any reference—"

"Oh-oh. That key sentence I fed you, back at the dawn of time. That was—"

"A quotation from Lanier's *The Symphony*—perhaps his greatest piece. The moment I heard that, I knew Brad wanted me, and that he was serious. There's a special kind of—uh, brotherhood, between members of the project— peer-group compulsion, it's called. It's extremely strong, irresistible, maybe. I couldn't question such a call."

"Oh, yes—the children of the kibbutzim have that, too. And that name, what was it—?"

"Glynn. From another major poem, *The Marshes of Glynn*."

Groton strained to remember. "Didn't we drive by—"

"The marshes of Glynn. In Georgia. Yes. The same ones Lanier drew his inspiration from. His poem was published anonymously at first, but it received such acclaim—anyway, that's why I was in the area, instead of looking for some high-paying Northern position, the way many of the others did. I spent years running down his historic travels."

"Like that, eh?"

"Like that, yeh. And Brad understood that perfectly."

"So he wasn't just playing a game with names. He wanted you to fix on Afra. She's even Georgian, like your marshes."

"*Lanier* was Georgian. He fought in the War of the Rebellion—civil war, to you—Confederate."

"I don't understand Brad's motivation. Afra says she and Brad were engaged to be married. Why would he want to stir up trouble like that?"

"Maybe because he wanted Schön that bad. He knew I

215

wouldn't walk out while Afra was around, and *she* wouldn't walk out while *he* was around. He even—he even threw us together, just to make sure the virus took hold. Having her show me around the station ... It doesn't take much, with a girl like her. And I never caught on!"

"Love is blind."

"Good and blind. It was all so obvious. Insurance, in case he lost out to the destroyer. Ivo pinned to Afra's sleeve—and the only way I could get off it was to turn Schön loose."

"You *can* call up Schön? When you decide?"

"I *can*. But I can't put him down again, once I do."

"And Schön wouldn't give a damn about Afra?"

"Not a damn. Schön might be intrigued by someone on his own level, but Afra—"

"A moron. I can see why he got bored at the age of five. No one in the world he could—say! 'My pawn is pinned!'—could that have meant you and Afra? You can't let go because then you'd lose her?"

Ivo thought about it. "It could. But I think that's incidental. Love is nothing to Schön."

"And not much to Brad, methinks. That's as sinister a piece of handiwork as I've come across. Using his own fiancée—"

"That wasn't the way *he* described their relation," Ivo said dryly. "Still, that's another reason I hesitate to uncork Schön. He's totally unscrupulous. He could probably solve our problem with the alien signal, but—"

"But you can't be sure which color the queen might see herself? I appreciate your caution more and more."

Ivo appreciated the appreciation, after having kept his secret so long. His initial impression of Groton had been so negative—and so wrong. He had seen a fat white slob, when he should have seen his own prejudice. Now the man—not fat at all!—was his closest ally. In similar fashion he had come to appreciate the individual qualities of Beatryx, who demonstrated so plainly and in such contrast to Afra that there were other things besides intelligence and beauty. Afra—

Afra still slept or rested, her breathing even. "I guess it wasn't as late as we thought. Maybe we should take turns watching, until something happens."

"Good idea. I'll snooze for a couple hours, then you

216

can." And Groton pushed off and floated in the air as though it were a mattress, utterly relaxed.

Ivo watched the laboratory. He felt a twinge of guilt for his snooping, but he was afraid to do otherwise. He did not want anything to happen to her. Brad's trick had been obvious—in retrospect—but devastatingly effective. Afra had indeed captured Ivo's imagination, and he felt a thrill every time he looked at her or thought about her. She *was* an impressive woman and she *was* from Georgia, whatever her faults might be. Call it foolishness, call it prejudice: he was committed for the duration.

Had Brad really been in love with her, or even, as he had put it, infatuated? Ivo doubted it now. He had allowed himself to forget how cynical Brad could be about human relations. Many of those raised in the project were like that. They tended to be strong on capability and weak on conscience, especially when dealing with the outside world, with Schön the logical extreme. They were independent, morally as well as intellectually and financially. To Brad the challenge had always been more important than the individual. Afra might simply have been the handiest entertainment available for off-hours at the station, intriguing as a classic WASP—and useful for special purposes, such as the tethering of Schön's pawn. A Georgia girl for the Georgia historian.

If she should succeed in reviving Brad as the man she had known, that in itself might represent disaster. No doubt her current fever of activity had been brought about by guilt over her own prejudice. Brad was like Ivo: tainted. He had Negroid blood in his veins, melanin in his skin. If she lost him, she would convince herself that it was due to her rejection of his racial makeup.

Yet—bless her for that sensation of guilt! Was not that in essence conscience? Normal persons were held in bounds by limitations of pride and guilt; abnormal ones were defective in these qualities, and were thus dangerous to society. Even the subtle racism of the educated Southern white had its rules and restrictions; it was not inherently evil.

Schön, on the other hand, had neither intellectual nor ethical limitations. He had no guilt, no shame. He would be a terror.

Afra stirred. She stretched in a manner she would not

217

have essayed in public and walked to the adjacent bathroom. This was not in the field of vision, and Ivo did not follow her. He was not, thanks to *his* guilt, a voyeur.

In a few minutes she emerged and walked to the counter. Electronic equipment was set up above it, and he saw that she had adjusted her extension-screen to aim straight down from head-height. She contemplated the transparent vat for ninety seconds, then stooped to manhandle out the basin from a lower compartment.

No doubt now: it was about to begin.

"Harold."

Groton woke, windmilling his arms for a moment before adjusting to the free-fall state. They watched.

Afra opened the valve and let the thick liquid flow into the basin. She stood back, watching it. Ivo tried to imagine her thoughts, and could not. It was Bradley Carpenter that swirled into the container: her beloved.

"I don't see any instruments," Groton said. "If it's surgery she has in mind—"

True. There was no special equipment in evidence. But if she had given up on that, what did she plan? Certainly she did not intend to nurse him indefinitely.

The protoplasm, freed from confinement and placed in a suitable environment, seemed to respond. It rippled and sparkled. Afra flushed the glass container out with water and allowed the rinse to pour into the basin too. And—the beam came on.

Here they were, using the macroscope to spy on her— yet the alien signal was able to transmit itself through the system simultaneously. This was a property Ivo had not known it had.

Once more the eye formed, the jellyfish, the pumping tunicate, the evolving vertebrate.

"You know," Groton said, "there's such a simple answer—if it works. What would happen if the process could be stopped a moment early? Just a tiny fraction of a lifetime—"

"So the destroyer never happened?" It *was* simple ... too simple. Why hadn't the galactic manual recommended it?

"She could be running him through once or twice, just to isolate the spot. To zero in on it. When she locates it—well, she must have something ready. He might be

218

short some recent memories, but she could fill them in easily enough."

The form continued to develop, achieving the air-breathing stage.

"Or," Groton conjectured, "she might experiment with changes in the mixture. If it were possible to isolate the damaged cells in the fluid state and substitute healthy protoplasm—"

"But it would be protoplasm with some other lineup of chromosomes!" Ivo said. "And where would she get it?"

Neither man cared to conjecture.

Afra trotted out a machine with pronged electrodes. Ivo remembered fetching the specifications for it from the macroscope, but had no comprehension of its purpose. Evidently Afra had studied its application more carefully. He saw now that the basin she was employing was metal, not plastic; it would conduct electric current.

"A jolt just before the destroyer," Groton said. "To freeze the process right there—"

"But the melting occurred *after* the destroyer," Ivo said, still namelessly disturbed. "The way the process works, every experience is part of the plasma. You can't take it away by timing—not without shaking up the entire system, and that's dangerous. I wouldn't—"

"We're about to find out," Groton said. "Watch."

Somehow the four hours of the reconstitution had elapsed already. Helplessly, Ivo watched. Afra placed one electrode upon the rim of the basin and fastened it there; she laid the other, a disk, upon the metamorphosing head. Timing it apparently by intuition, she touched the power switch.

There was current. Ivo saw the figure in the vat stiffen.

"Shock therapy?" Groton murmured. "That makes no sense to me."

Afra cut off the power and removed the disk. She stepped back.

The figure, now recognizably Brad, ceased its evolution. The eyelids wavered, the chest expanded.

"Can she have done it?" Groton said disbelievingly.

"She's done *something*. But I'm still afraid that destroyer experience is in him somewhere, waiting to take effect. Maybe after he's been around a few hours or days—"

Or was it his jealous hopes speaking?

"Oh-oh."

There was certainly trouble. The shape in the basin, instead of coming fully alert, was changing again. "It's regressing!" Ivo cried. "She didn't stop it, she reversed it!"

"Then it should melt, shouldn't it?"

"It isn't melting!"

Whatever was happening, it was no part of the cycle they had seen before. The beam remained on, and Afra watched, hand to her mouth, helpless. The change accelerated.

The head swelled grotesquely, the legs shrank. The body drew into itself. Hands and feet became shapeless, then withdrew into mere points. The figure began to resemble a giant starfish, complete with suckers upon the lower surfaces of the projections.

And there it stopped, absolutely unhuman.

Afra screamed. Ivo could see her mouth open, lips pulled back harshly over the even white teeth, tongue elevated. He saw her chest pumping again and again, and could almost hear her desperate, ghastly sounds. She screamed until the spittle became pink.

In the basin, the star-shaped thing struggled and heaved. It raised a tentacle as if searching for something, then dropped it loosely over the edge. The beam was off now, further evidence that this was the end. For a moment the creature convulsed, almost raising its body from the bottom; then it shuddered into relaxation and the five limbs uncurled.

Slowly it changed color, becoming gray. It was dead.

CHAPTER 7

Beatryx was weeding the garden: some shoots of wheat were coming up beside the tomato plants, and she was carefully extracting them without damage to either type of plant. The tediously preserved shoots would shortly be transplanted to the south forty—forty square feet of verdant field.

Ivo squatted down beside her but did not offer to help. This was her self-appointed task, and his unsolicited participation would constitute interference. Meaningful tasks were valuable. He noted that she had continued to shed weight; the round-faced matron was disconcertingly gone, replaced by the hollow-faced one. Material comfort did not automatically bring health and happiness, unfortunately.

"You know she's taking it hard," he said after a suitable delay.

"What can we do, Ivo? I hate to see it, but I just can't think of any way to help."

"As I make it, she's having the reaction she suppressed when Brad lost out to the destroyer. She knew he was gone, then, but she refused to admit it. Now—"

"Now we have to take turns standing watch over her, treating her like a criminal. I don't like it, Ivo."

An understatement. Her whole body reflected her concern. Beatryx, physically, was in worse shape than Afra. "None of us do. But we don't dare leave her alone."

She lifted a blade of green and placed it tenderly in her basin of moist sand. "It's terrible."

"I wondered whether—" He paused, disturbed by the audacity of his idea. "Well, we *are*, as you say, already treating her like a criminal."

"We have to do *something*," she said.

"Maybe this is all wrong. That's why I wanted to talk it over. I thought, well, if she feels guilty, we might give her a trial. Sort of bring out the evidence, one way or the other, and all take a look at it, and decide who was how guilty of what. Then it would be—decided."

"Who would decide, Ivo? *I* couldn't."

"I don't think I could, either. I'm not objective. But—you know him better than I do—I thought your husband might—"

"He's fond of her, Ivo. He wouldn't want to pass judgment on her." There was no sign of jealousy in her manner, and Ivo knew she was not the type to conceal what she felt, in such an area. It told him something about her, something nice; but it told more about Groton.

"He'd have to agree, of course. But if it seemed a real trial would clear the air—make things all right again—"

Beatryx stiffened. "Look, Ivo! Look!"

Alarmed, suspecting mayhem or calamity, he followed her gaze. There was nothing.

"On that tomato leaf!" she whispered, trembling with excitement.

He looked, relieved that it was nothing important. "Looks perfectly healthy to me. But you'll have to spray—"

Then he brought up short. "A bug!"

"A bug!" she repeated.

"It must have been a worm in the tomato," he said. "I thought everything was sterilized."

"Maybe we'll have lots of bugs," she said, excited. "Triton bugs. And flies and spiders and worms. Maybe they'll get in the house and we'll have to put up screens!"

It had been so long since they had seen any creature apart from the four members of the party that this was a signal discovery. "We are not alone," he said. "It's a good omen."

"Do you think it's warm enough here for it?" she inquired anxiously. "Should I bring it some food? What do they eat?"

Ivo smiled. "Nature knows best. I'm sure it's sitting on its supper right now. If we leave it alone it will probably raise a family soon. But I'll photograph a bug-book for you from the macroscope, so you can identify it."

"Oh thank you!" she said sincerely.

He left her kneeling beside the plant. If there *were* such things as omens, this was surely a sign that the nadir for the Triton party had passed.

"A trial." Groton considered it. "There may be something in that. Certainly something needs to be done. That girl is very near the edge." If Beatryx had changed because of the stress of recent months, Groton had not. He seemed to have the most stable personality among them.

"I got the idea from something I remembered. A bit on animal psychology. A dog had strayed or got lost somehow—I don't know the details—but after a few days his master got him back. The master was very glad to have him safe, but the dog just moped around the house, hardly eating or resting. Finally the man asked a veterinarian about the problem. The man said to roll up a newspaper and give the animal a good swat on the rear."

"That wasn't very helpful."

"It cured the dog. It seemed the dog expected to be punished for getting lost, and couldn't revert to normal until that punishment was over. He was just waiting for it, brooding, knowing things weren't right until it came. One token swat, and that dog almost tore the house apart for joy. The slate was clean again, you see."

"You suggest that a swat on the rear will cure Afra?"

"I don't know. It can't bring Brad back, of course, but the guilt—"

Groton sat down. "You know, you're right about the guilt. It has no outlet—we don't *blame* her, really. But a trial? Well, hard to say what would do the job of expunging guilt. . . ."

"You would have to make the decision. On her guilt, I mean. Weigh the evidence, institute appropriate punishment—"

"Yes, I suppose I would." Ivo could appreciate Groton's

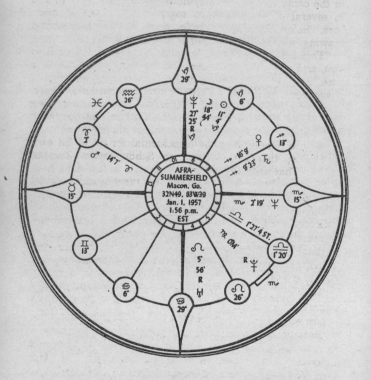

AFRA-
SUMMERFIELD
Macon, Ga.
32N49, 83W39
Jan. 1, 1957
1:56 p.m.
EST

unease. They were *all* guilty, by their prior inaction, as much as Afra by her action. Who were they to pass judgment upon her?

Groton opened the roll-top desk he had built for his study and drew out a sheet of paper. It was a circular chart divided into twelve pie-sections, with a smaller circle in the center. There were symbols all around the edge and in several of the segments, together with assorted numbers. Below the large circle were several geometrical drawings identified by further symbols.

"This is her horoscope. Suppose I explain some of it to you, and you tell me whether this thing we contemplate is wise."

Ivo doubted that this particular tack would help, but he was becoming accustomed to Groton's method of getting at a problem. If the astrological chart helped him to make up his mind (as Beatryx had once hinted), more power to it. He also remembered the coincidental insight of his own horoscope, that had pointed to Schön rather than to himself. That had been uncanny.

"Do you know what I mean by the houses, cardinal signs, alchemy of the elements, portmanteau analysis—"

"Say again, quarterspeed?"

Groton smiled. "Just testing. I didn't want to insult you by oversimplifying. I'll stick as much as I can to layman's language—but I want you to understand that this *is* simplified, to the point where what I tell you is only approximately true."

"Why can't you just give me the summaries, as you did before?" Ivo did not want to say that a detailed technical lecture was something other than he had bargained for.

"Because that would be too much of *me* speaking. I need to show you enough of the principles so that you understand the essence of what the chart says, on your own. You may have a different opinion from mine, and your interpretation could help me to reach my own decision."

Groton's manner reminded him of Afra's when she had insisted on the handling. The full meaning and validity of her request had not been clear to him until later; then he realized that her instinct had been sure. Groton evidently had reservations about this procedure, but was overruling them for some good reason. It would be wise to oblige. More and more, he was being made aware that his own views of things were often based on pitifully inadequate information.

"All right. One opinion on tap, for what it's worth."

Groton pointed to the chart. "Notice that this is in twelve segments. Actually, it is twenty-four segments: twelve superimposed on the other twelve, but for convenience we employ a single diagram. I have placed the identifiers around the rim, you see."

"I recognize the numbers one through twelve; that's about all." He continued to study the obscure markings, however. "And Neptune! I couldn't forget *that* symbol. There in the six-box."

"That's enough for a start. Let's call that the top disk: the twelve houses, numbered counterclockwise. The houses, roughly, represent circumstance: the situation, the potentiality the individual has to work with. That's not good or bad in itself; he may exploit it or not. But it's there, much as the chessmen we discussed before are there, ready for the game."

"Twelve different circumstances?"

"Yes. The first house represents identity, the second possessions, the third environment, and so on. That's really an oversimplification—"

"You explained. Ballpark estimates."

"Yes. Now the planets move through these houses, that are really segments of the celestial equator. Three-dimensional segments, to be sure, like those of an orange—but twelve of them make up the heavens about Earth."

Ivo looked at the chart again. "So the center circle is Earth, and the outer one is the rest of the universe, carved up into twelve big houses, and we're looking down at an orange sliced in half. Yes."

"Close enough. The planets represent the particular ways in which the individual asserts himself. The sun in the first house means—"

"The sun? I thought you said planets."

"We consider the sun and moon to be planets. It is best to set aside what you know about astronomy, for this; it has almost no genuine relation to astrology."

"I begin to appreciate your sincerity. So the sun is a planet."

"Viewed from Earth, they are all moving bodies, Sol and Luna no less than Venus or Pluto. They all have changing positions in the sky. We're not revising astronomy; we are merely arranging our terms to suit our convenience. Technically, it is *astronomy* that did the revising; it was originally a subdivision of astrology, and all the early astronomers were primarily astrologers. There is no conflict."

"I follow."

"The sun indicates purpose, the moon feeling, Mars initiative, and so on. There are tables in the books that give all this, if you find it helps. So the sun in the first house puts the planet of purpose in the house of identity. A person with this configuration, according to one description, is determined to exalt his ego one way or another, and tries to dominate his immediate situation. That doesn't mean he succeeds; this is merely his impulse. He may be bombastic rather than great."

"You sound as if you have a reservation. Are there other descriptions for what sun-in-first means?"

"There are always differences in interpretation. But my reservation stems from the oversimplification. The whole chart must be considered, not just the sun, or unfortunate mistakes can be made. You see, one of our group has this particular placement."

"Afra!"

"That's what I mean. It *isn't* Afra, as you can see by her chart; the first house is empty. It's Beatryx."

"I think I'm catching on. If a person is born when the sun is in one of these segments, that tells something about his personality—but only something, not everything. And I guess the sun *has* to be somewhere. What is the second house?"

"Possessions, among other things. Here, I'll make out a list; that's easiest, I think."

"Oh yes. So the sun in the second house puts purpose in possessions. That man will be out to make money."

"Or to achieve personal advantage some other way," Groton said, not pausing in his listing. "You have the general idea. Again, there is no guarantee he'll make a fortune—but he'll probably try."

"Where is the sun in my—in Schön's horoscope?"

"The twelfth house. That's confinement."

"Purpose in confinement." Ivo thought that over. "This begins to grow on me, I must admit."

"Just remember that the sun, important as it is, can be outweighed by an opposing configuration elsewhere. And of course the entire horoscope represents probability, not certainty. Heredity is obviously a major influence. Leo is the sign of the lion, but a mouse born into Leo is still a mouse."

"I'll remember," Ivo agreed, smiling. "A leonine Mickey."

"Notice the position of the sun in Afra's horoscope."

Ivo studied the chart once more, finding it less confusing. "Is that the little circle with the dot inside? That's in the ninth house. But that's not the only thing there."

"It certainly isn't alone, and in certain respects this is a remarkable chart. But let's ignore the others for the moment. The sun symbol goes near the rim, you see, followed by the ecliptic position in degrees and minutes, and on the inside is the zodiacal sign, which we'll go into in a moment."

"What does the ninth house stand for?"

"Understanding, consciousness, knowledge."

"So Afra has purpose in understanding. That means she wants to know things—and if her heredity gives her high intelligence, she'll come to know a great deal."

"The text says: 'The sun in the ninth house places the practical focus of life in a determination to exalt the ego through high standards and broadened interests. This position always encourages a conscious lean towards an intellectual understanding or a religious orientation. At his best the native is able to bring effective insights or genuine wisdom to every situation, and at his worst he is apt to meet all reality with a complacent intolerance or bigotry.' "

"That sounds close enough. But it is really so general it could apply to almost anyone."

"We'll try to get more specific—one planet at a time. You can't divide all humanity into twelve basic groupings without being general. By the time we check ten planets against twelve houses and twelve signs and verify with the symbols of the ascendants and overall patterns, we begin to have definition resembling that of the macroscope. Now where do you see the moon?"

"Right beside the sun. Same house."

"The moon represents feeling."

"So that's feeling in understanding. To know her is to love her?" He said it lightly, but knew it had happened to him.

"No, that's an outside impression, not controlled by her horoscope. It's what *she* feels and understands that's important here. Specifically: 'The moon in the ninth house centers all personal experience in issues of morality, elevating ends and reasons above practical needs. This position exaggerates every concern over ideas and motives. The native at his best is able to approach reality with an understanding support for every human capacity, and at his worst he is apt to worry over abstractions and dissipate every impulse to action.' Do you recognize Afra there?"

"Yes, in a way. You know, this is—well, isn't it really pretty private? I have the feeling I'm prying into things that aren't my business." He saw that he was tacitly admitting an acceptance of astrology, but didn't care. "Nudity of the body is one thing, but—"

"Good point. I consider a person's detailed horoscope to be very like the privileged information given to a lawyer, or perhaps a priest. Or medical or financial statements. This is one reason I hesitated to show you her chart before. But if we are to pass a judgment on her that may affect her entire life—"

Ivo saw the point. "I'll—keep all this confidential. Even if she doesn't believe in astrology, or *I* don't, it's still—"

Groton went on to another section. "The signs of the ecliptic define character. There are twelve of them, spaced similarly to the houses, but they are not identical to the houses. That's why we have to mark their symbols; the indications around the edge are only approximate, since the signs are not geometrically defined in the manner of the houses. Where do you spot the sun this time?"

"The sign is a cross between a square-root symbol and a hunchbacked musical note."

"That's Capricorn—the Goat. This is—"

Ivo interrupted him to run down a nagging connection. "What did you say Schön was?"

"Aries—the Ram. You can recognize his symbol by the spreading horns, situated in this case at the cusp of the twelfth house."

"I see it. The circle with the antlers."

"No, not that one; that's Taurus the Bull. Next above it."

Ivo located the correct symbol. "So that's how you separate the sheep from the goats! But what's Aries doing on the Goat's chart? I thought—"

"All houses and all signs appear on all charts. There's a little of everything in every person's makeup. But the positions of the planets show the emphasis for any one person. Schön's sun is in Aries, while Afra's Mars is in Aries; an entirely different matter, I assure you."

"The sun is more important?"

"That depends on the configuration. Generally, it is; that's why the popularized horoscopes use it, though that's like saying that your brain is more important than your heart. Aries rules the brain, coincidentally. But you can't get along without either one. In Afra's case Mars does have great weight, and perhaps makes her as much a fire person as is Schön. But the combination of sun, moon and Mercury in Capricorn puts enormous stress on earth— well, I don't want to get off into subjective interpretation. This is a BUCKET pattern, and the handle-planet, Mars, reveals a special capacity or important direction of interest. So this aspect of her chart indicates initiative and extreme self-containment."

Ivo was beginning to get lost, much as he had when Brad attempted a "simplified" explanation. He did see the bucket-shape, however, with the handle toward the left and a semicircle of filled slices to the right. "So the way Afra just went ahead on her own to revive Brad, without worrying about the risk or what she would do afterward— that was spelled out the moment she was born? Because Mars happened to be in Aries? And you could have predicted—"

"It's hardly that simple, Ivo. There are so many other factors, and she could have reacted in some entirely different fashion. Hindsight is no justification. But I did foresee some kind of crisis. There is an activation of Saturn at about this time in her life, following the emphasis of Mars that seemed to account for her prior problem with Brad. When he became destroyed. In another year there is a predomination of Uranus. That's three crises in fairly rapid order, for her—but the timing can vary by a year or more either way, and I simply cannot pin any of these down precisely."

"But the odds are she'll have a third crisis as bad as the first two, within a year?"

"In your terms, that about sums it up. Remember, I make no claim to—"

"I remember. Is it possible for me to read this chart and look up the descriptions myself? You said you wanted to get an independent opinion—"

"I don't think you'd find it very instructive, Ivo. It takes years to—"

"I'll bet the chart on me says somewhere that I like to do things for myself."

"Not exactly." Then Groton paused, catching the hint. "As you wish. Here are the texts. Here are the listings of symbols I wrote out, and you already have the chart. There are things I haven't explained yet, such as the grand trine in fire, and—"

"I think I have enough to go on. Suppose you leave me to it for an hour or so? I may misread terribly, but I'll try to come up with a notion where I stand. Then we can decide about the trial. And I think I'd better have the other charts, too, for comparison."

"It's in the stars," Groton said, yielding with good grace, and left him to it.

Ivo began by checking Beatryx's chart. It was a twelve-slice disk like the first, but the markings differed. In the center it gave her date and place of birth: February 20, 1943, 6:23 CST a.m., Dallas, Texas, 33N 97W. Geographic coordinates, he decided. Below were several mathematical notes and the word SEE-SAW. He ignored these and concentrated on the symbols.

He found the sun in the first house, just as Groton had said. "Purpose in identity," he murmured, and leafed through the nearest text until he came to a section titled "The Planets in the Twelve Houses." A glance at the description assured him that he had researched correctly.

With more confidence he located the moon in the seventh house. "Feeling in partnership," he said, checking his lists. He found the place and read: ". . . at his best is able

231

to find common elements in his associations with any other individuals, and at his worst he is apt to make things unnecessarily hard for himself." He recollected the interests she shared with him, poetic and musical, that had only appeared when there was need for conversation and companionship, and nodded. He also recalled her intensely personal reaction to Afra's folly.

He tried next for the signs. Her sun was in Pisces: purpose in sympathy. The first volume was open at the houses and he wanted to keep his place, so he opened the second. It was an old, weathered tome.

"Pisces produces a very sensitive nature. . . ." he read. "Longing to understand and forgive his fellow men, to feel himself one with them and above all to succor those who are ill-treated by the world . . . vaguely sad idealism . . . often somewhat of a Cinderella in practical life. . . ."

He paused to think about that, too. It was as apt a description of Beatryx as he could imagine. It was almost as though the passage had been written with her in mind.

He flipped back to the title page: *Astrology and Its Practical Application*, by E. Parker. Translated from the Dutch. Published in 1927.

Fifteen years or more before Beatryx had been born.

He checked her chart again and located the moon in Virgo. "Feeling in Assimilation," he thought. The book said: "There is much love for the fine arts, especially for literature. Works of art are often inwardly enjoyed without its being much shown. . . ."

Excited, now, he went to the other text—one copyrighted 1945 by one Marc Edmund Jones—and looked up moon-in-Virgo for confirmation. "Reacts to others with a deep hunger for common experience. . . ."

Be objective, he told himself. *You're only reacting to what matches.*

But still he wondered. . . .

He drew forth Afra's chart and began looking up its elements and making notes. Even so, he quickly lost track of the multiple factors, and found some conflicts between texts. Finally he decided to handle it in businesslike fashion: he made a table of the abbreviated elements, so that he could consider it as a unit:

232

Planet	House	Sign	Description
Sun	9th	Cap.	purpose X understanding, discrimination
Moon	9th	Cap.	feeling X understanding, discrimination
Mars	12th	Aries	initiative X confinement, aspiration
Venus	8th	Sag.	acquisitiveness X regeneration, administration
Merc.	9th	Cap.	mentality X understanding, discrimination
Jup.	6th	Libra	enthusiasm X duty, equivalence
Sat.	7th	Sag.	sensitiveness X partnership, administration
Ur.	4th	Leo	independence X home, assurance
Nep.	6th	Scorp.	obligation X duty, creativity
Plu.	5th	Virgo	obsession X offspring, assimilation

Ivo contemplated his production with a certain frustrated pride. He had made an unintelligible horoscope intelligible; he had reduced voluminous verbiage to its essence. Chaos to order, as it were—and he still didn't know what to make of it. There was a lot of discrimination, tied in with purpose, feeling and mentality, and this certainly seemed to reflect Afra's drives. But understanding tied in with the same three qualities. Then there was enthusiasm for duty and equivalence; obligation for duty and creativity; obsession for offspring and assimilation?

What did all this say about her probable reaction to a Tritonian trial? Would it help her, or would it drive her to suicide? Or would she see through it all and laugh?

Afra was a *person*, not a chart or a table.

He should have left the astrology to Groton.

Ivo shook his bursting head as though to rattle loose a productive notion and put the papers aside. He went to his own apartment and picked up the box that held his useless artifacts of Earth. He had never returned them to his clothing after the melting. The penny should still be there, amidst the junk . . . yes, his questing fingers found the disk. He fished it out without looking, flipped it into the air, caught it and slapped it against his wrist. "Heads we try her, tails we forget it," he said aloud. Then he looked.

It was the bus token, possessing neither head nor tail.

Groton rapped for attention. "We do not need to be unduly formal. Ivo, you've been assigned to prosecute. Please make your case."

Ivo rose, feeling for a moment as though he were actually in a formal courtroom, addressing a jury of twelve. "Harold, it is my purpose to demonstrate beyond reasonable doubt that Afra Summerfield did willfully and with malice aforethought murder Bradley Carpenter. She —"

Afra jumped to her feet in a fury. "What a thing to say! Of all the ridiculous, unwarranted, slanderous—"

She broke off, seeing the other three silent and solemn.

Groton turned slowly to address her. "You are of course entitled to express yourself, Afra. But it would be better if you let Breatryx speak in your defense. We do need to ascertain the truth of this matter, if we are to exist in harmony here."

She subsided, pitiful in her misery and sudden uncertainty. "Yes, of course, Harold. I understand."

"Proceed, Ivo, if you please."

"We have here a pampered and arrogant young woman of the upper middle class. She was raised to believe herself superior to the common folk, by reason of the purity of her breeding, the finances of her family and the quality of her education. She possesses an alert mind and tends to deem those of more leisurely intellect to be inferior for that reason, too. At the same time, she resents those of demonstrably greater intelligence than hers, since such people appear by her definition to occupy a higher niche in the hierarchy. They are, in a word, superior."

Afra watched him, appalled. "Is that what you really believe? That I—" But she halted again, seeing his impassive demeanor. "I'm sorry. I won't interrupt again."

"Now picture the situation that obtained when she became employed within the orbiting Macroscope Project as a high-powered secretary. Many—perhaps most—of the trained personnel there exceeded both her education and her natural ability. Compared to them she was both ignorant and stupid. Surely this fostered in her a state of continuing resentment. No one likes to believe himself to be inferior, or to have others believe it, whatever the actual case may be."

Ivo had intended to overstate the case, not really believing it himself, but he found himself responding to his own rhetoric. In accusing her, he was voicing some of his own attitudes. *He* felt inferior, and he had never liked it. And Afra *was* an intellectual snob.

"In addition, these personnel were multiracial. Negroes, Mongolians and halfbreeds were ranked above her, inherently and socially. Even certain members of the maintenance crew were able to earn privileges she was denied. Remember, she is Georgia-born. To her, such persons are niggers, chinks and spics, tolerable so long as they 'keep their place' but never to be acknowledged as equals, let alone betters. These were also of foreign nationalities and foreign ideologies: to wit, socialist, communist and fascist. To her, a belch after a meal is uncouth and a cheek-to-cheek greeting between members of the same sex disgusting."

He was going too far, bringing in irrelevancies, but could not seem to stop. His resentments were coming out, and she personified them. He was angry at her because he loved her.

"But one thing kept her there, despite her obvious unsuitability for the position. She met an attractive young American scientist only slightly more intelligent than she who was willing to fraternize. She—became infatuated with him." Translation: Ivo was angry because Afra loved Brad. . . .

A crease appeared in Afra's brow and her color heightened, but she did not move or speak.

"But it turned out, after a brief but intimate liaison, that this American had deceived her. He was far more able intellectually than she, having falsified his status in that respect. He had far more education, and regarded what she had taken to be a commitment for marriage as no more than a temporary entertainment. Further, he proposed to reassign her favors to an acquaintance. She thus found herself reduced to the lowest status imaginable to her: so-called white slavery."

Beatryx gestured in distress. "Ivo, that's horrible. You have no right to accuse her of—"

He felt cold now, no longer angry. "Of *de facto* prostitution? I was not doing so. I was making the point that Bradley Carpenter treated her as a diversion. His real purpose—"

"You're overdoing it," Groton cautioned him. "Brad isn't on trial."

Ivo was glad to let that aspect drop. Brad had, after all, been his friend. He had known for twenty years what Brad was like: a polite, cautious, dull Schön. If Brad used people ruthlessly, what would Schön do?

"It subsequently turned out that her supposed fiancé was himself of mixed blood: by her definition, a mulatto or worse. And he had been raised in a free-love colony where morality in the conventional sense was unknown. Thus she learned that she had not been the first to share intimacies with him; rather, she was the last in a very long line, and followed after girls—and boys—of all the races of the world."

Some condemnation! Ivo himself was as conservative as Afra, and as biased, despite what he knew of his origin. Yet he had shared much of the life of the project until its breakup. When, thereafter, he had encountered individual girls from it, he had indulged in the usual amenities. Outsiders would have considered this to be flagrant promiscuity. Yet the project bond was special; its members shared a heritage, and there were no reservations between them. What was more natural than a sharing of intellect and experience, in this way recapturing a fragment of that larger camaraderie?

Ivo had been shocked by Afra's nudity and actions at the time of the handling—but that was because she was a nonproject girl. Had he been properly objective, he would have had no problem. She had been true to her viewpoint, then and in her relation to Brad, while he was a thorough hypocrite. *He* should be on trial, not she. . . .

Time to wrap it up, before he got carried away again. He gestured at Afra. "It is not for us, as it was not for her, to judge the morality of Bradley Carpenter. He is dead by this woman's hand. It is for us to determine whether the defendant had motivation for murder—and surely, by her bigoted definitions, she had. Her act must be interpreted in this light. There can be no verdict but guilty."

He had spoken well, but he felt tight and sick. This trial had shown him unwelcome things in himself.

Beatryx, assigned counsel for the defense, took the floor. She was gaunt now, and troubled, but her voice was strong. "Harold, this is all wrong. Ivo has put things all out of proportion. There's hardly anybody who couldn't be condemned by that sort of reasoning. Afra was trying to bring back the man she loved, and she tried very hard, but it didn't work. Nobody else did anything. The rest of us would have let him fade away, there in his tank. If she had known what would happen, she never would have—"

"No," Afra said. "I couldn't stand to have him remain as jelly, or as an idiot. Better to have him dead, than that."

Ivo froze. Beatryx was making a good case—and Afra had just undermined it.

"That isn't true!" Beatryx told her. "You just think because he died, you have to take the blame. But he did it himself—he watched the destroyer on purpose."

Afra stared straight ahead. Beatryx was right. Afra hadn't tried to kill Brad. She had taken a wild gamble in an effort to bring him back—from the dead, in effect. Her failure did not imply malice.

"Do you have any statement to make on your own behalf?" Groton asked Afra after a moment.

There was no response.

"In that case, having heard the presentation and being already familiar with the background of this case, it behooves me to render an impartial decision."

Groton was going through with it, but it seemed to Ivo that this "trial" was in a shambles. Afra had not fought back properly, and so had not been officially vindicated. They had accomplished nothing.

"I find the defendant guilty of conduct prejudicial to the well-being of the decedent, Bradley Carpenter. Motivation for overt, premeditated murder, however, has by no means been shown, and more than a single interpretation may be placed on the defendant's physical actions. At worst, they were reckless. The actual instrument of demise appears to have been the phenomenon we term the destroyer, combined with an incompletely understood function of the melting cycle. Rehabilitation of the defendant therefore seems feasible."

Brother! Would Afra swallow this?

"Are you saying it was an accident?" Beatryx asked. "But she still has to pay for it?"

"Just about," Groton conceded. "Recklessness, though, has been well established in my judgment."

"I suppose that's all right, then."

Ivo nodded aquiescence.

"I therefore sentence you, Afra Summerfield of Georgia, to exile from the equal society of man until such time as the neutralization of the said destroyer seems feasible, so that no other person need ever be similarly afflicted. This will be considered penance by corrective endeavor. Further: because to a considerable extent your personal pride was at fault, this sentence includes a period of confinement at onerous labor. You shall assume the gardening and cooking and laundry chores for the Triton encampment and shall not leave the garden-kitchen-laundry areas except to make beds and to perform such other menial tasks as may be required of you by the other members of this encampment. This labor shall terminate only upon the group's departure from the present locale, at which time you shall be permitted to petition the group for readmittance to its society on a probationary basis.

"Until that point you shall not again be addressed by name, nor shall you address any member of the group by name."

And Afra, amazingly, nodded. She *wanted* to be punished!

"This sentence," Groton said after a pause, "is suspended, owing to—"

"No!" Afra said dully. "It's a fair sentence."

So Groton had intended only a token reprimand. Afra, anticipating this, had insisted that it be real. Her privilege, of course—but were they helping her to recover, or merely catering to her masochism?

"Girl," Ivo snapped into the intercom.

After a few seconds Afra's voice came back. "Sir?"

"Report to the drawing room for conference."

She appeared duly, clad in a simple black skirt falling

below the knees, with a long-sleeved blouse overset by a loose housecoat. A drab kerchief bound her hair, giving her something of the aspect of a nun.

She stood silently, waiting for him to speak.

"Sit down."

"Sir?"

"Down. I have somethng to show you."

She settled on the least comfortable perch available.

Ivo took his stance before the blackboard he had set up. "A conception of cosmology," he said, assuming the manner of a lecturer. "The evidence available indicates that our universe is in a state of continual expansion. Calculations suggest that there is a finite limit to such expansion, governed by variables too complex to discuss at this time. For convenience we shall think of the present universe as that four-dimensional volume beyond which our three-dimensional physical space and matter cannot expand: the cosmic limitation. We shall further consider these four dimensions to be spatial in nature, though in fact the universe is a complex of n dimensions, few of which are spatial and many of which interact with spatial planes deviously. Do you understand?"

"Which other dimensions are you thinking of?"

"Time, mass, intensity, probability—any measurable or theoretically measurable quality." She nodded, and he saw that he had her interest. There was nothing like a few weeks of household drudgery to make the stellar reaches more exciting. "Now assume that the 3-space cosmos we perceive can be represented by a derivative: a one-dimensional line." He drew a line on the board. "If you prefer, you may think of this line as a cord or section of pipe, in itself embracing three dimensions, but finite and flexible." He amplified his drawing:

"Quite clear," she said. "A pipe of macroscopic diameter represented by a line."

"Our fourth spatial dimension is now illustrated by a two-space figure: a circle." He erased the pipe-section and

239

drew a circle on the board. "Within this circle is our line. Let's say it extends from point A to point B on the perimeter." He set it up:

"The ends of the universe," she agreed.

"Call this 3-space line within this 4-space circle the universe at, or soon after, its inception."

"The fabled big bang."

"Yes. Now in what manner would our fixed circle accommodate our variable line—if that line lengthened? Say the line AB expanded to a length of 2 AB?"

"It would have to wrinkle," she said immediately.

"Precisely." He erased his figure and drew another with a bending line:

"Now our universe has been expanding for some time," he continued. "How would you represent a hundredfold extension?"

She stood up, came to the board, accepted the chalk from him, and drew a more involved figure in place of his last:

"Very good," he said. "Now how about a thousandfold? A millionfold?"

240

"The convolutions would develop convolutions," she said, "assuming that your line is infinitely flexible. May I draw a detail subsection?"

"You may."

Carefully she rendered it:

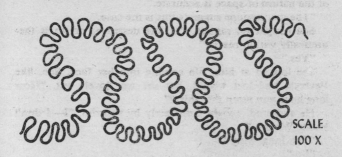

SCALE 100 X

"This would be shaped into larger loops," she explained, "and the small ones could be subdivided similarly, until your circle is an impacted mass of threads. The diameter and flexibility of your line would be the only limitation of the process."

"Excellent," he said. "Sit down."

She bristled momentarily, then remembered her place. She sat.

"Now assuming that this is an accurate cosmology," he lectured, "note certain features." He pointed with the chalk. "Our line touches itself at many points, both in the small loops and large ones. Suppose it were possible to pass across those connections, instead of traveling down the length of our line in normal fashion?"

"Down the line being traveled from one area to another in space? As from Earth to Neptune?" He nodded. "Why —" She hesitated, seeing the possibilities. "If Earth and Neptune happened to be in adjacent loops, you might jump from one to the other in—well, virtually, *no* time."

"Let's say that this is the case, and that those adjacent subloops are here." He pointed to the top of the first major loop. "Assume that arrangements and preparations make the effective duration of any single jump a matter of

241

a few hours. How long would it take to reach Alpha Centauri from Earth?"

"That depends on its position and the configuration. It might be possible in a single hop, or it might require several months of jumping. By the same token, it might be as easy to traverse the entire galaxy—if this representation of the nature of space is accurate."

"The macroscope suggests this is the case."

She caught on rapidly. "So the destroyer origin is theoretically within reach?"

"Yes."

She looked at him, life coming into her face. She, like Beatryx, had lost weight, but she was lovely yet. "How long have you worn that shirt?"

He stuttered, caught completely by surprise. "I—I don't know. What—?"

"Too long. May I?"

"I—"

She walked around him, pulling out his shirt and unbuttoning it. She removed it and bundled it under her arm. She kissed him lightly on the cheek and departed, leaving him somewhat stupefied.

It had been forcibly brought home to him who, if this were a game, had the ranking hand.

A mouse born into Leo was still a mouse, he remembered. Afra, however low she might sink, remained a stronger personality than he.

Six hours later his shirt was back, clean and fragrant.

He looked for Afra, not knowing what to say or whether to say it—and found her kneeling beside Brad's grave, sweet-pea flowers in her hand, tears coursing down her cheeks.

And what had he expected?

Earth: city: "disadvantaged" neighborhood.

Children played in a tiny dirt yard, throwing rocks at a broken bottle. Their clothing was dirty and sodden with sweat; their feet were bare. All were thin, and posture and appearance hinted at malnutrition.

Inside the house, a sick child slept restlessly, flies crawling across his cheek and buzzing up whenever he moved. He lay on a ragged mattress, refuse collected beneath it. Roaches peered from the hole in the wall where the yellow plaster had fallen away.

In the next room a grizzled man sprawled before a bright television set, swigging now and then from a concave whisky bottle. He was as grimy as the children.

Ivo imagined the dialogue he might have with this man, were conversation possible:

"You're going to pot here. Why don't you move to a better neighborhood?"

"Can't afford it. I'm in hock now."

"Why don't you look for a better job, then? The economy is booming; you could make a lot more money."

"I tried that. Man said I needed more education."

"Why don't you go back to school, then? To one of the free technical universities?"

"They have a quota system; only so many per district, and this one's full up until 1985."

"Well, why don't you move, then . . . oh, I see."

Ivo removed the helmet and goggles and shook his head. This was the age of affluence, with a record GNP and excellent jobs begging for personnel. Yet the macroscope showed the truth: whether because of this particular vicious circle or some variant of it, people were living in poverty. The residence he had just viewed was typical of a growing—not shrinking—segment of the population.

There had been a time, not so very long ago, when only nonwhite Americans lived this way. There would come a time, not so very far removed, when only the affluent lived any other way.

Why should he have any regrets about leaving this area of space?

He did, though.

Groton watched the screen as Ivo guided the image into the disk of Neptune. The mighty vapors boiled at an apparent distance of a thousand miles, throwing up great gouts of color.

Five hundred miles, four hundred, and it was easy to fancy that they were aboard a ship actually coming in for a landing, and to feel the fierce spume of the methane

243

storm. The dark dot he had centered on had now been clarified as the eye of a hurricane—the eye alone three hundred miles in diameter and awesomely deep. Hydrogen gas swirled thinly in its center, and thick methane weighted with ammonia crystals rushed around the rim. The wind velocity at the surface they could presently see was four hundred miles per hour.

The cliffs of the cloudwall rose up, titanic, translucent, deadly. Then shadow as he lost the funnel, recovered it, lost it again. A hundred miles down, the tube was only a few tens of miles across, narrowing rapidly, and it wavered. Finally it was gone for good: either too thin to pinpoint or dissipated in the thickening atmosphere five hundred miles below the opening. Some light remained, but it was fading rapidly with depth.

A thousand miles down: still the turbulent gases and flying storm crystals. Two thousand: the same. Three thousand—and no solid surface.

"Does this planet *have* a surface?" Ivo demanded in frustration.

"Got to," Groton said. "Somewhere. Too dense overall to be all gas."

Four thousand. Five.

"Sure your settings are tuned? Maybe we're not as deep as we thought."

"I'm sure. It's the damn *planet* that's wrong!"

Six, seven.

At eight thousand miles below the visible surface they encountered the first solid material: caked ammonia ice. The macroscope readings were becoming vague; in this cold there was too little radiation in the proper range.

At nine, genuine water-ice: rock-hard, opaque.

Ten: the same.

"We're two-thirds of the way to the core—and nothing but *ice*?" Ivo demanded.

The traces were almost unreadable—but at almost twelve thousand miles depth they struck rock.

"Do you realize," Groton whispered, "that Neptune proper is smaller than *Earth*? Less than an eight-thousand mile diameter core—" He looked at the indications, that abruptly showed clear. "But what a core! Tungsten, gold,
244

platinum, iridium, osmium—the heaviest elements of the universe are packed in here! Think of what a gold mine this place is!" He paused. "Gold? Throw it away! The stuff here——" He gave up.

"Is it *all* precious metal?"

"Sorry—got excited. No, it's seventy percent iron, and the rest mostly oxygen and silicon. The heavy stuff just leaped out at me. But there *is* a lot of it, compared to what we're used to, and the proportion is bound to increase with depth. Mighty solid lithosphere. But then, it has to be. As I make it, something like two-thirds the mass of this planet has to be in the core—and the core's no larger than our Earth. My God—I didn't think! This core—it has to be ten, eleven times the average density of Earth, to make that mass. *Nothing's* that solid."

"Going down," Ivo said.

It was that solid. The multiple heavy elements on the core-ball's "surface" were floating there because the interior was several times their density.

It was composed of partially collapsed matter: the refuse, possibly, of an extinct dwarf star. Protons and neutrons were jammed together with only imperfect electron layers holding them apart.

"It seems," Groton remarked, "that half our job has been done for us."

Ivo nodded, satisfied.

Ivo began to explain their intent to the women.

"The idea is to utilize the principle of gravitational collapse. We have obtained schematics for a rather sophisticated variant of the gravity focuser, though this resembles what we have here on Triton about the way a hydrogen bomb resembles a matchstick. Assembly of the generators alone will take months, even with a full crew of waldoes, and the related safeguards——"

"What do you mean by 'gravitational collapse'?" Afra interjected.

"Oh. Well, simplified, it is the effect gravitational attraction has on matter when taken to the extreme. Any object of sufficient mass tends to compress itself by its own gravity, and the more dense it is the stronger this force becomes. Actually the other forces, electromagnetic and nuclear, are far stronger on a unit basis than——"

"May I?" Groton put in. "I think I can simplify this for the benefit of those who haven't been exposed to a galactic education." Suddenly Ivo realized that "those" meant Beatryx. He had become used to Afra's almost instant comprehension, and tended to forget that the other woman was slower, though as vitally concerned. He had forgotten, also, that he was now talking in a manner he would not have comprehended himself, not so long ago; despite his care not to fathom galactic meanings too deeply, he had picked up a considerable amount.

And of course that was the reason Afra had asked her question. *She* knew astronomy and physics far better than he did, and was aware that the other woman was being left behind.

"You see," Groton said, "Triton is smaller than Earth, so we weigh less there—I mean *here*—or did, before we started changing things. Schön is smaller yet, so on it we hardly weigh anything at all. But it isn't just size that counts. If Schön were made of osmium instead of ice, it would have about twenty-five times its present mass, and therefore more gravity. We would then weigh more there than we do, though still very little."

Beatryx nodded. Ivo was impressed; he had not really appreciated what a real talent teaching was. Comprehension was one thing; converting one's knowledge into a clear explanation for others was another.

"But a planet isn't just pulling at *us*," Groton continued. "It is pulling at itself, too. It is much more tightly packed in the center than at the edge, because of its own gravity. And if we squeezed Triton down into a little ball about the size of Schön, and stood on that we'd weigh more than we do now, just because it was so dense and because we were so much closer to its center.

"And if we squeezed it down into a ball the size of a pea—why then the gravity would be very strong indeed. It might even begin to squeeze itself down farther, because its own attraction was so powerful. That's what's known as the gravitational radius—the point at which an object begins to collapse in upon itself as though it were a leaking tire. Once that happens, it's too late; nothing can stop it from going all the way."

"But what *happens* to it?" Beatryx demanded, alarmed.

"That's what we'd very much like to know. Ivo seems to have an answer from the macroscope, however."

"It seems that matter can't just collapse into singularity—that is, nothing," Ivo said, doing his best to emulate Groton's style. "That would violate fundamental laws of—well, it's no go. So instead it punches through to another spot in the universe, following the line of least resistance."

"Punches through ..." Afra murmured, putting items together. "*That's* how you mean to—"

"To jump to the galactic reaches. Yes. But there are some problems."

"I should say so! You're playing with the molecular, the atomic collapse of matter! Assuming that you have a process to force this, which for the sake of conjecture I'll assume you do, exactly what happens to *people* compressed to pinhead size?"

"Worse than that," Ivo said. "A two-hundred-pound man would have to squeeze down to one ten-billionth the size of—"

"One ten-billionth!"

"—of the nucleus of an atom. That's if he were to go it alone, of course; not so small if accompanied by other mass."

"That's very small, isn't it," Beatryx said.

"Very small," Ivo agreed. "But a mass the size of, say, the sun would not have to reduce by the same ratio. The greater the mass, the easier it is. But about people, now—this entire program is taken from the major extragalactic station. It is the only one that carries anything of the sort, for some reason. Actually, it doesn't carry anything *but* the technology related to such travel; its area of information is smaller than I thought at first. The melting is part of the preparation for it. This station says that animate flesh can survive the transformation, provided it is properly prepared."

"And it was right before," Groton said.

"Let's have the worst," Afra said grimly.

"Well, first the liquefication we're already familiar with. Then isolation of the individual cells, and a kind of gasification."

"The gaseous state rebounds better after compression," Groton put in helpfully. "Once molecular structure is reestablished."

247

"And the field—that's a simplified description—maintains an exact ratio during compression," Ivo said. "That is, it fastens every atom in place and stabilizes things so that the entire field collapses evenly, and nothing is jostled or mixed up in the irregular currents of collapse. Much the same as spots on a full balloon will shrink in place when it is deflated, but not if it pops. After the —jump—the field maintains the ratios for the expansion, and only lets go when everything is as it was before. The machinery can take it all right; the extra flexibility for living things is required—because they are living. You can't turn life off and turn it on again. Not in the normal course."

"You say the larger the accompanying mass, the easier the procedure," Afra said, becoming seriously interested. Large concepts came more readily, after the success of the melting and the Triton colony machinery. "Does that mean you're going to try to fasten onto—well, Schön,—and compress us with it?"

"You have the idea, but we have larger masses at hand, and the equipment will be geared for them. The larger the mass, the less sophisticated the necessary technology, because of the smaller compression ratio. So—"

"Triton itself? That may be simple, but it *is* ambitious."

"Neptune."

She seemed beyond surprise. "Do you know where we'll emerge?"

Ivo looked at Groton, who shrugged. "We don't. The maps have changed in three million years. The expansion of space hasn't stopped. Even if the convolutions were constant, the arrangement of stars and galaxies keeps shifting. We need a contemporary projection—and there isn't any available on the macrosphere."

"So we simply punch through and hope for the best?"

"Yes. After a number of tries, we should be able to set our own map, and perhaps to extrapolate reasonably."

"Suppose we land inside a star?"

"The odds are vastly against it. But there seems to be provision for it even so; apparently matter will slide off other matter, when jumping. Path of least resistance means it is easier to punch through to an unoccupied spot than to double up on a star or planet or even a dust nebula that is indenting space on the other side. So we don't have to worry about it at all."

"Suppose we get lost?"

"We can't get lost as long as we have the macroscope. Not for long, anyway. The galaxy may look strange from another location in space, but we do have a rough notion of its present layout."

"Do you?" Afra inquired. "Did you stop to think that a fifteen thousand light-year jump—to pick the kind of figure we'll be dealing with if we are to reach the destroyer—is like traveling fifteen thousand years into the future? All you've seen to date is the past history of a fragment of the universe. Your 'present layout' may be useless in determining your position."

"We'll still have the programs; most of them are galactically dated. And of course there'll be the destroyer signal. Ill-wind department; we want to abolish it, so we use it for orientation."

"What makes you believe there is only one destroyer?"

Again Ivo and Groton exchanged glances. "We can always fix on the Solar system," Groton said. "We're pretty familiar with that. We can estimate how far we've gone by judging how Earth appears, and of course the fix on Earth will establish our direction. With azimuth and measurement—"

"With all due respect, gentlemen," Afra said briskly, "you are sadly inundated if not totally submerged. You may not even be able to *locate* ol' Sol from fifteen thousand light-years' removal. The configurations will be entirely different, and Sol's absolute magnitude is not great. Let alone the strong possibility of obscuration by intragalactic dust and gas. As it is, we can only see, telescopically, one-thousandth of the Milky-Way center, and the dust is worse at the fringes. The macroscope is much better, of course, but—"

"Translation:" Groton said. " 'We men are all wet; we'll get lost in a hurry.' " Beatryx gave him a smile—and, surprisingly, so did Afra.

"How would *you* handle it?" Ivo asked her.

"First I would orient on some distinctive extragalactic landmark such as the Andromeda galaxy. That's two mil-

249

lion light-years away, in round figures, and if we jump farther than that we won't need to worry anymore about local affairs like destroyers. Then I'd fix on certain Cepheids, and look for the configurations typical of this general area—say, within a thousand light-years of Sol. Once I had identified the Pole Star I'd be within a hundred parsecs—"

"Andromeda being another galaxy like our own, only larger," Groton said to Beatryx. "We should be able to see it from almost anywhere, because it is outside of and broadside to ours. The Cepheid variables—"

"*I'll* explain what I mean, thank you," Afra said. "A Cepheid is a bright star that gets brighter every so often—regularly, as though it has a heartbeat. And the longer a star's period—that is, the time it takes to go from dim to bright and back again—the greater its absolute magnitude. Its real brightness. So all we have to do is measure its brightness as seen from our location and keep track of its period and we can figure out how far away it is. Because a star that is far away looks dimmer than one that is close."

"Why yes," Beatryx said, pleased. "That's very clear."

Ivo said nothing, not wanting to admit that *he* had not known what a Cepheid variable was, or how it could be used to ascertain galactic distances. He had produced technological wonders during their stay on Triton, and the principles Groton had applied to his machinery were in advance of anything known by Earthbound specialists. Ivo had increased his awareness considerably during all this, but his participation had been that of a stenographer. He had no real idea of content. He had *done* it, but he didn't *understand* it. The result was detailed technical knowledge in some areas buttressed by appalling gaps in related areas. He could talk about gravitational collapse, yet not know what a Cepheid was.

And how much of Earth's civilization was exactly like that, he wondered. Doing without comprehending—even when this was tantamount to suicide?

"When," Beatryx said, "do we go?"

It was four months of intense effort, mental, physical and emotional—but the group was in harness again, and profiting thereby. The members lived and worked in comfort, but the hours were savage. No longer did anyone do laundry or cooking by hand; that wasteful practice had been shoved aside in the rush.

Beatryx became mistress of the automated life-services equipment so that the others were free for full-time labors. She also learned how to supervise the connection-soldering machines and circuit-assemblers, making sure that each quality-control dial registered favorably for each completed unit.

Ivo traveled the galaxy via the macroscope in search of critical bits of information, since the intergalactic broadcast seemed to assume that the supportive techniques were already known; he also transcribed ponderous amounts of backup data.

Afra received much of this material and spent many days with the macroscope computer verifying tolerances, vectors and critical ratios. She admitted that the essential theory of it was beyond her; she was merely adapting established processes to their needs and confirming its applications.

Groton took her results, made up diagrams of his own, and tuned in the waldoes. He also supervised a complete survey of the globe of Triton, and selected particular locations with extreme care for the construction of enormous mechanical complexes. A visitor would have thought the planet to be the site of a burgeoning industrial commitment. In certain respects it was.

They were participating in superscience: Type III technology. None of them comprehended more than a fraction of it. But by accident or cosmic design, they were a team that could do the job, with the overwhelming assistance of the supervising programs from space. The first crude waldoes had given way to tremendous mechanical beasts that roved Triton as though the human element had been dispatched, and computers superior to the one the macroscope employed were now in routine service—but the incentive lay with the human component. Ivo, Afra and Groton became immersed in their separate areas and did not communicate directly with each other for days at a time, and too often the contacts were irritable, for all were chronically overextended. Beatryx, with her invariably ameliorative personality, kept them in touch, and this was as necessary a function as any of the others.

The action became impersonal, for the project was much larger than they were, and the entire group had become merely the implementing agency. Yet Ivo watched what was happening and took pride in it, and he was sure the others did too. He knew that though Earth had largely forgotten their spectacular theft—the news *had* leaked out, making them momentarily infamous—the completion of their effort would leave the Earth-based astronomers and physicists gaping.

The nature of the work shifted. Excavators burrowed into the lithosphere of Triton, casting up fragments of rock in a null-gravity field. A hole formed, deepening day by day: a deep hole, braced by immense metallic tubing. The borer advanced at the rate of just over ten miles per day, the ejecta spouting forth in a geyser of grit and raining down steadily upon the normal-gravity torus surrounding the hole.

In time the tunnel, sixty feet in diameter, achieved the limit of depth the planet would tolerate. Metallic alloys could not prevent implosion beyond this point, and a force-field was impractical in the neighborhood of the existing null-G field.

The machines finished their business and retired. For a time activity diminished. Triton was at peace again.

Then the shield of force that maintained an Earth environment around the tetrahedron home disintegrated. The foreign atmosphere puffed out, crystallized, and settled languidly upon the ground, dead as the erstwhile vegetation. The tetrahedron remained, sealed, in desolation.

A figure trekked from the disaster area, encased in a space suit. It paused where a grave lay frozen and passed on to the waiting module. It entered; the vehicle blasted away, and Triton was uninhabited.

On the moonlet Schön the reintegration of units occurred, and Joseph mated again with the macroscope housing. The ties cast loose; the ship-assembly drifted free of the ice, and Schön too was vacant.

The space-borne macroscope entered the null-gravity column, still functioning but splayed and ineffective at the thousand-mile elevation. The vehicle descended against the increasingly strong updraft of nitrogen and oxygen.

Near the surface of Triton the circulation became fierce; dust, debris and snow formed a tornado. The ship came down forwards, the macroscope housing leading, and nudged along on fractional power of the main engine.

At three feet per second relative velocity the ship entered the tunnel at the base of the windy column. The turbulence subsided around it. Buoyed by the escaping atmosphere, that passed with a five-foot clearance around the rim of the housing, the assembly descended, gently accelerating. The flowing gas cushioned it, preventing brutal contact with the walls. At fifteen miles per hour maximum velocity, the ship tunneled through the moon.

In three days it came to rest. The null-G column expired; debris filtered down. A nudge from the hot jets, no longer leashed at minimal power; the metallic restrainers, designed for exactly this failure, dissolved. The tunnel imploded, the action shocking back up its length and burying the ship a thousand miles beneath the surface.

Now the immense field generators came into play elsewhere on Triton. Three new null-G columns developed, spearing out from the advance side like the prongs of the Neptune symbol. The atmosphere, augmented by cubic miles of rock pulverized into dust and voluminous byproduct pollutants, rushed into the breach and shot outward in ten-mile diameter thrusts.

Triton slowed in its orbit, reluctantly, as the three vast motors braked it. Slowly it began to spiral in toward its primary—then gained velocity as its tether shortened.

The mighty gravity of Neptune embraced its minion and hauled it into its gaseous bosom. Great ruptures appeared in the sea-god's ocean of atmosphere, torn up by the gravity of the spiraling ball. The tiny ice-moonlet Schön disappeared into that melee and did not reappear. Triton had lost its satellite, a moment before it lost its own identity.

Well within Roche's Limit, that proximity that would have sundered a normally orbiting moon, Triton shuddered but did not break up. Events were far too precipitous to allow tidal force opportunity to take full effect.

Contact: the stormy exterior veil of the gas-giant parted. Ahead of Triton, crystals of ammonia-ice exploded into vapor as the heat of friction boiled the atmosphere. Behind, there appeared a turbulent wake five thousand miles wide, the crystals frothing whitely as they rematerialized in the surging breadth of it.

In five hours the moon had looped the planet at the fringe of its atmosphere and was entirely immersed in hydrogen. At fifteen thousand miles per hour it carved an atmospheric trench and looped again. On the third circuit it touched what had been the surface of water-ice and blasted it into steam. Water and ammonia thrust outward convulsively, throwing mile-long splinters of ice high into the storm, to warm and fragment violently again; sleet and boiling water and methane gas battled in the most violent conflation ever to occur on the surface of the planet.

On the fifth circuit the molten moon touched the solid portion of Neptune. At three thousand miles per hour stone met metal, rolling and melting. Now the wake was of bursting lava and precious heavy elements.

The ball that came to rest at last, embedded within a lake of liquid metal, was six hundred miles in diameter—but intact. Precipitously near its margin, like a worm in an apple, nestled the encapsulated ship.

Yet the action was not over. From that capsule spread two Type III technology fields of force: the first encompassed the moon and planet, now forever fused, extending outward twenty thousand miles, permeating every particle of dust, every molecule of gas, every crushed atom of the core. It anchored every atom in place irrevocably, relative to the whole. The second field permeated the first and began a cataclysmic contraction, taking the entire package with it. It fed upon the energies released by that compression, and continued relentlessly.

Neptune shrank, its turbulence abruptly frozen in place. Atmosphere and all, it diminished as though the viewer were retreating from it at a hundred thousand miles per hour—but there was no viewer. It became the size of Earth, of Luna, of Ceres the asteroid. It dwindled to a single mile's diameter—but its full mass and that of its moon and its moon's moon remained. It achieved its gravitational radius.

Then it shrank again, so rapidly it seemed to vanish. In a microsecond it was gone.

Five million miles out, tiny Nereid—Neptune's second moon—became a planet in its own right, circling the sun in Neptune's erstwhile orbit. Caught on its backswing, it had insufficient velocity even to retreat from Sol, let alone escape it, and fell instead in toward the orbit of Uranus as though looking for a home.

Man's physical exploration of the cosmos had begun.

CHAPTER 8

The marshes of Glynn: now they were crossed by highways, infringed upon by the welling city that sent its pseudopods of industrial flesh questing outward in a great half-circle. Brunswick—founded in 1771, now more numerously populated than the entire state of Georgia at the date of this city's inception. The reputed cotton was gone from this area, and the pecans and the peaches, perhaps encouraged in their departure by the advice of the poet who made this region esthetically renowned. Instead there were shipbuilding yards, the ships not necessarily of the water, and machine shops, the machines not necessarily the servants of man. The old pulp mills, their forest cellulose depleted, had been replaced by more sophisticated refineries, and the canneries by protein-simulatories. There was more to learn about chemistry in Brunswick than any man could ever know.

"Do you have your fix, Ivo? We're moving into position above the null-G column and it may get a little breezy."

"Almost, Harold."

Yet the marshes remained, protected in part by statute of the Empire State of the South, that the live-oak might retain its ancestral home, and perhaps too the Cherokee rose. From the city he flew, disembodied, all observing, passing through obstacles without flinching, seeming to breathe the freer atmosphere of nature. The dusky English sparrows gave way to the red-winged blackbird; the chimney-swift to the belted kingfisher. The ugly cockroach hid, the lovely dragonfly emerged; the bold house rat yielded to the shy cottontail rabbit; the gray park squirrel faded in the face of the gleaming blacksnake.

"Are you about finished, Ivo? We're descending toward the excavation."

"Almost, Afra."

The marshes: and if there were water moccasins and alligators and snapping turtles, were these not more beautiful and less destructive than the stout tourists, the hapless domesticants? From the watery inlets rose the ancient bald cypress trees, magnificently—some would say grotesquely—swollen at the base, their islands of woody "knees" adjacent. Farther along were a rare American elm, several glossy-leaved handsome magnolias, some small sassafras, large sycamore, medium tulip-tree—and finally the aristocrat of the south, the great live-oak, garlanded with hanging Spanish moss.

He came to a halt beneath it, within its somber cathedral of foliage, responding to the massive permanence of it, the solitude.

"Glooms of the live-oaks, beautiful-braided and woven/With intricate shades of the vines that myriad-cloven/Clamber the forks of the multiform boughs—"

"What did you say, Ivo?"

"A poem I know, Beatryx. I'm sorry; I did not mean to repeat it aloud."

"One by Sidney Lanier? But isn't that poetry *meant* to be spoken aloud? Please go on with it."

Not really surprised, he obliged. "Emerald twilights—Virginal shy lights/wrought of the leaves to allure to the whisper of vows,/When lovers pace timidly down through the green colonnades—"

He broke off, staring at the spreading oak in consternation. It was the poem of Schön's first message, the one that lead up to the terminal thought. If Afra were to hear it and identify it—

He calmed himself. It was, after all, only a poem; it bore only obliquely on his secret. Why should he hide it? Afra must already have caught on to the truth. Signifi-

257

cantly, she had stopped pressing him on the matter of Schön. "It goes on like that. I was looking at a tree, on Earth, and it reminded me."

"It's very nice," Beatryx agreed.

He had his fix: that mighty live-oak in the marshes of Glynn. He keyed the location into the computer as the primary reference point. He was ready for the first jump.

Ready—to penetrate to the bowels of Triton, to be entombed there, to undertake, while the entire moon decelerated, the melting . . . and gasifying . . . and collision with Neptune . . . and compression . . . and . . .

The scene opened on his fix: the magnificent live-oak, extending its rotund branches as though to embrace all the world. The tree was hardly changed, except—yes, it was smaller, more vigorously leafed. Still bearded with Spanish moss, it was a young adult rather than a patriarch. The oval green leaves were more shiny, the acorns seemed richer in their scaly cups.

"When lovers pace timidly down through the green colonnades,/Of the heavenly woods and glades,/That run to the radiant marginal sand-beach within/The wide sea-marshes of Glynn;—"

And, astoundingly, there *were* lovers! A young man in what Ivo took to be a farmer's outfit and a rather pretty girl, her looks spoiled somewhat for Ivo by the dated cut of her dress. They were just leaving a bower, perhaps having completed their liaison there.

Dated dress? Ivo reproved himself. He was thinking in late twentieth century terms. He cared nothing for fashion, dictated as it was by commercially-minded foreigners, yet somehow anything not contemporary was less attractive than it should be. He suspected that he would have been quite satisfied, had he lived in this girl's time, with her costume. It decorated, after all, the timeless attributes of the sex.

He followed them past a mighty white-oak that had been a rotting stump before and into a swampy glade where two and three foot high red-flowered knotweeds bloomed, and white-flowered arrowhead plants, and bright yellow buttercups. At the edge of an open pond stood yard-high pickerelweeds with glossy spadelike leaves as long as a spread-fingered hand, the blue flowers just forming on the upright spike; and upon the water lay the great green disks of the water-lily, not yet in bloom.

The season was late spring or early summer, Ivo decided. June, perhaps. Late enough for the first pickerelweed, too early yet for goldenrod.

He left the couple to their silent dialogue and traveled deeper into the swamp. Yes, there was an alligator in pursuit of fish, as graceful a swimmer as any. Emerging near the city, he passed cottontail rabbits and flickers browsing for beetles in the fields. It was amazing how much closer nature came to civilization, here.

He traversed the city, and found a creosoting plant, a box factory, a conventional cannery, shipping wharves, and at last a newspaper with the date: June 5, 1930.

They had jumped fifty light-years from Earth.

And those lovers—in their early seventies, now. It was a wonderful and somewhat painful thought.

Another jump, another fix: the scene differed: The terrain was still marshy, but no trace of either the stately live-oak or huge white-oak remained. Instead it was bright dawn upon white cedars, the average tree perhaps eighty feet tall, crowded together and cutting off much of the light of the sun so that it did not touch the ground directly.

Ivo paused to consider the implications. Cedar preferred freshwater swamps, and the marshes of Glynn were salt. How had this come about?

Either his fix was off or there had been a serious change in the landscape. The computer was responsible for the fix, establishing it by the gravitic and magnetic qualities of the planet: a complex and indirect process, but thorough. The location checked out. Therefore—

How big a jump had they taken?

"Continental drift?" Afra inquired, her voice seeming to emerge from the cedar grove. It was not hard to picture her standing there, just behind a tree.

"Drift?" Back to the stupids again.

"The movement of the continents in the course of geologic time," she explained. "If the expression on your face means what it surely means, your landscape has changed. You might be a mile or so from where you thought you were, and it wouldn't be the scope's fault.

259

The continent itself could have shifted. Or orogeny could have—"

"Could be. I seem to be in a freshwater swamp, inland from where I was, and the fix checks. But how much time—"

"Oh, a few million years or so."

He drew off the goggles and stared at her. She was smiling, as he had suspected. "Such a jump is possible, you know," he said, nettled.

"Certainly. But not this time. Our stellar configuration establishes our continued residence within the Milky-Way galaxy, so we have to be within seventy thousand light-years or so of Earth. I would judge within ten thousand, actually. And it is also possible for rivers to change course and for beaches to submerge. A few thousand years would be enough to change your flora and fauna perceptibly."

Ivo replaced the goggles with something less than good grace and sped toward Brunswick. His exploration, he knew now, was confirmatory only; Afra had already worked out the position by astronomical means. The very process of locating Earth established its distance, though only his own investigation could pin it down precisely. The macroscope had a sweep-adjustment that enabled it to select for a certain type of image; that was one of a number of refinements courtesy of galactic broadcasts. Otherwise the problem of locating Earth would be horrendously complicated.

There was nothing at the Brunswick location except scrub forest. "It's pre-1771, anyway."

He heard the rustle of her leaning forward. How he wished she would do that when his eyes were on her, when there was no technical business at hand. But she belonged to a dead man yet, however the live might yearn for her.

She murmured: "As I make it, the jumps should be gradated sharply. Probably fifty years is the minimum—forty-nine, actually—because you can't jump from the end of one loop to the middle of the one adjacent, or from place to place within your own. The larger loops should be multiples of these, since they're made out of looplets, and then there could be multiples of *those*—we don't know how far it extends. Even a slight change in the angle of our jump could shift us from the smalls to the mediums or

260

worse. If we assume each level is the square of the prior one, first level being roughly fifty years, the second would be two and a half thousand years and the third six and a quarter million—light-years. So just keep calm until you know which level it is."

"Six and a quarter *million*?" he repeated, comprehending her reason for the private discussion. "That—that could put us in another galaxy!"

"Not likely. Probably in intergalactic space. But as I said, the local light survey places us definitely within a galactic structure, and since you found Earth where it was supposed to be, the odds are it is our own. I conjecture level two, therefore."

"Two and a half thousand." It was still appalling—and she wasn't sure. It was possible, if unlikely, that this was merely an Earthlike planet occupying the same spot in another galaxy or cluster that Earth occupied in the Milky Way. Perhaps every galaxy was laid out on a common plan. Cepheid variables, novas, planets, all fitting into their destined slots. . . .

He abolished it as fantasy. "That's before the Christian era."

She made no reply, but he felt her closeness, her excitement. To peer into ancient history! No man had done such a thing so directly before.

"Oh what is abroad in the marsh and the terminal sea?/Somehow my soul seems suddenly free—"

She replied: "Ye marshes, how candid and simple and nothing-withholding and free/Ye publish yourselves to the sky and offer yourselves to the sea!" And she touched his hand.

Thus did she confess to him that she knew of Sidney Lanier and what he signified in Ivo's life, and perhaps had known from the beginning; and her hand now squeezing his own suggested an added meaning to the words she quoted. Candid and simple and nothing-withholding and free? He dared not hope; it was most likely an intellectual game, for her.

He had tried to emulate the qualities of Lanier the person, to mold his character after that of his adopted ancestor—but it had not worked. Ivo could not create poetry, and he totally lacked Lanier's winning ways with

261

the ladies. How much better off he would have been to develop a personality truly his own!

"Jump it to Europe," Afra said.

He jumped it to Europe. The time was noon at Rome— and there was no settlement of man there. "Pre-Roman," he announced.

"Try Egypt."

"Nothing at Alexandria," he said after a moment. "Not even dry land."

"Naturally not, if it's pre-Roman. You want Memphis."

He headed southeast, toward the noncoded location, feeling out of sorts again.

On an eastern channel of the Nile delta he discovered a bustling city, not large by his expectations but with the aura of a capital of some sort. Memphis?

"Doesn't sound like it," Afra said. "But *any* city is good news for us. Look for a palace or a temple; see if you can find written records to photograph. We should be able to date those."

Ivo obliged, descending to street level near a complex of buildings he took to be significant. The street was narrow and filthy, lined by tiny mud-brick dwellings set close together and generally no more than a single story high. He could make out the straw coating of the weathered bricks, and fancied he could almost sniff the surrounding slum offal. Inferior residential districts had not begun with America, certainly!

The natives were human: slender, swarthy Mediterraneans with black hair and brown eyes. A number were naked, and these he presumed were slaves; their racial types were variable, ranging from Nordic blond to full black. Even the clothed ones gained little; they possessed none of the glorious habiliment he had thought of as ancient Egyptian. There were no gold ornaments or bright cloths, and not even shoes or sandals. Barefoot, bareheaded, the men were clad only in the wraparound *schenti*: white cloth held at the waist by a wide leather belt, the outfit reaching only to the knees. The women wore long tight skirts and a number were bare-breasted. The effect would have been delightful, had they been young, healthy and clean; these were not.

At the temple/palace grounds things changed abruptly. There were no women, and the men were much better dressed. They wore wide, short wigs, hairpiece quality a seeming guide to status. They wore full skirts with a short sleeve for the left arm only and overset by a pleated mantle of linen. Evidently the people he had seen on the street were of the lowest class.

Some stone was in evidence, but up close the structures were hardly impressive. The jewelry the personnel wore furnished most of the temple color.

He explored several private cells, finding them routinely occupied. If this were a place of worship, it was decadent; if a palace, the Pharaoh was far away. One section even seemed to be still under construction. Here there were guards, their spears, axes and pear-shaped shields set aside as they watched lethargic slaves chipping stone under the supervision of a harried elderly taskmaster. There was no particular brutality about it; only the supervisor—probably the responsible one—showed any urgency, and his gesticulations went largely unheeded.

Ivo came in for a closer look, knowing that where there was activity of this nature there had to be some kind of blueprint or written directive. If that document were dated, or carried the name of the chief executive—

At this point another man came into the scene. His hair was divided and partly shaved above the ears, and he had a long braided lock falling in front of one ear and curling up at the end. Two bright feathers decorated the remainder of his hair. His arms were tattooed, as were his thighs, in crosshatched patterns. He wore a wrap of decorated fabric that looped around the body and anchored to one shoulder, the hem richly bordered.

This man looked up, facing Ivo. His mouth parted in an O of surprise. He gesticulated.

The guards woke up. In a moment they were beside the man, bright headpieces in place, short-sleeved metal shirts gleaming, ox-hide shields up. There were many more of them than Ivo had suspected. Some must have been summoned by the commotion from elsewhere on the grounds. Many were Egyptian, while others were racially similar to the recent arrival. Ivo realized he was dealing with a superimposition of cultures. The Egyptians must have been conquered recently.

The feather-headed man pointed. There was no question who commanded, here. The guards lifted their spears, and some dropped back to notch arrows. All looked toward Ivo.

They saw him!

Now the slaves were looking too, desisting from their labors. Frightened, they clustered on the far side of the court, while the guards formed a defensive line. Postures were aggressive, but no one took action. They were waiting for the command.

"What is it?" Afra's voice demanded nearby, jolting him. He had thought for a moment that one of the guards had spoken audibly—a ridiculous notion. Thousands of years separated scene from viewer, and the macroscope did not transmit sound.

Almost as ridiculous a notion, actually, as that of these men of the past seeing Ivo, as though this were merely a window.

The feathered leader made his decision. His mouth moved as he barked commands. The guards began to move, closing in on—

Without answering Afra, Ivo manipulated the controls convulsively and shot straight up two hundred feet, instinctively fleeing from the situation. The faces of the warriors turned up to follow him, and he could see that they were afraid.

"Ivo, you *saw* something!" Afra persisted.

"Nothing," he said, feeling himself shaking. *Lanier* had had courage! "Must be a little tired." He was drifting far above the city now, finding a certain birdlike security in height.

"Maybe you should take a break," she said with concern. "These transformations are weakening us all, and we don't know how much of your strength this searching draws. No point in risking—"

"I'm okay." He was ashamed to admit what form his fatigue had taken, and did not trust the result of his observation. Non-Egyptians in ancient Egypt? As rulers? He was sure Egypt had done the conquering, not the reverse.

Of course he had become sleepy, letting a dream-image replace that of the scope. He had known something like that to happen when reading: the words on the page would become more and more fantastic, until with a start he realized that his eyes were closed. Returning to the real book he would find his place, noting where the mundane text diverged from the astonishing vision ... only to drift off again similarly.

He understood that this could happen to a fatigued driver, too. The man would spy something incredible, like an ocean liner crossing at an intersection, and realize that he was dreaming at the wheel. If he were sensible, he would pull over immediately and rest, lest the next nod be fatal. The mind had intriguing ways to sublimate strain.

He was tired; that explained it, though he did not *feel* depleted. Perhaps it was not so much a physical effect as a psychic one. Knowing how far they had ranged from Earth—so far that light reflected from their base of operations, the planet Neptune, would not reach home for thousands of years—knowing this, he unconsciously sought a closer identification with the home planet. He *wanted* to step into the world he saw, somehow, much as a child wanted to step into a storybook picture. A world of ancient adventure and glory, where the threat of nuclear holocaust or mind-destruction did not exist. For all its primitive faults, a better world. . . .

If it happened again, he would quit. Afra was right; there was no point in wearing himself out, when his mission was so important. A misreading of a year or two might throw them a light-year or two off course. Better to be sensible: to wait a few hours and do it properly, than to risk inaccurate information.

And it *was* important, he reminded himself again. They were not just traveling; they were attempting to map the convolutions of the cosmos as the jump cycles penetrated them, and in that sense an error of as much as a day might invalidate the phase. How much would a tiny inaccuracy be magnified by a large jump? There was no point in the map unless it were precise, and without the map they would never be able to return physically to Earth. Only the macroscope could pinpoint their location so exactly; the telescope, over a distance of a thousand light-years, was a blunderbuss.

"You know best, Ivo," she said quietly.

Almost, he quit then. "Thanks," he said, meaning it. "I don't think Egypt is doing us much good. Where else should I try?"

"You might try Damascus. That's traditionally the

oldest city in the world, and a very important one. Move northeast about four hundred miles—"

"On my way." He could jump there instantly by touching the correct coding, since Damascus was on the list; but he preferred to make the trek by, as it were, his own power. It gave him badly needed confidence.

He shot across the delta of the Nile at jet-plane velocity and intersected the coastline. His route would take him over the southwest corner of the Mediterranean Sea— probably the same route used by the Egyptian ships in the course of trade or war with Asia minor. Except that he was high above the ground. Even so must the fabulous spirits of Near East legend have swooped in minutes over land and sea—the godlets, the genii, gaseous creatures of malevolence and power. Their number was supposed to have been severely curtailed by Biblical King Solomon, who confined them to bottles when they would not swear fealty to him. Some were said to have remained helpless in such confinement for thousands of years. Could they be considered in fact travelers via the macroscope, able to witness without participating? What a horrible fate, to be corked forever, sentient, within a tiny sphere!

Time had passed during his sojourn in the land of Egypt, and his exodus was late. The day was terminal, dusk approaching, and he was traveling into it. The descending sun sparkled from the waves and tinted the edges of clouds. "How still the plains of the waters be! / The tide is in his ecstasy. / The tide is at his highest height: / And it is night." And what if this were the Mediterranean instead of the marshes of Glynn? The words of the poet still applied.

A ship came into sight upon the ocean. He swerved to study it: a stout galley, a dozen or fifteen oars stroking the water rhythmically on each side. So they really did use them, in the olden days! It had a mast, but the sail was furled: not enough wind. Probably anxious to get home tonight, he thought fondly, and no wonder; this ship could not be much over fifty feet long. Compared to the modern liners, a thousand feet from stem to stern (he smiled a little wistfully, remembering Brad's pun) ... though this one did not appear to have much of a stem ... or even the three-hundred-foot sailing ships....

No. This toy dared not stray far from its port.

He was too low, too slow; he wanted to reach Damascus before nightfall. He could not afford to tarry beside every curiosity along the way, tempting as such diversions might be.

He lifted—and did not rise. The ocean was nearer now, less placid; the green waves slopped randomly fifty feet beneath him. He felt cold.

He concentrated on the macroscopic controls, closing his eyes to the scene around him. If this were a second snooze, he wanted to pull out of it before admitting defeat. Pride required at least an orderly retreat. If it were a momentary slip of the fingers, no problem. The spherical control was in his right hand, guiding his journey as he automatically adjusted it, hardly conscious of his manipulation. A twist—

The ball was gone! His fingers closed on air.

He opened his eyes. The living liquid was twenty feet below and he was falling.

He grabbed at the goggles. His hand smacked into his bare face.

"Ivo!" Afra's voice, from a distance.

The water struck, the force and chill of it numbing his naked body. Brine slapped into his eyes, his mouth, blinding and choking him.

He forgot about the niceties of perception and probability, and swam. His head broke surface and he coughed out the spume fogging his lungs and shook the sting from his eyes.

He was here. No doubt of that. Had he really heard Afra cry his name, as though she cared, just before the splash? Academic curiosity, now.

Who was he to claim the thing was impossible? He could drown in mid-protest. Better to deal with reality as he found it.

He had fallen somewhat ahead of the ship, and to the side. He did not know how far he was from land, but it was too far. He was not that strong a swimmer, and the cold was getting to him already, and he did not even know the direction. His best hope was to intercept the galley; otherwise—

He swam. His arms were heavy already, unused to these conditions and probably fatigued in advance by the melting/gastifying/compression cycle, though he had no personal awareness of the details. They had set the program, and had gone under the melt-beam ... and come out of it to find space shifted about them. Space travel, in practice, was that simple. Afra no longer demanded the handling, such was her own confidence now. Meanwhile, it was hard to keep from breathing the water, since the waves came irregularly and he was not adept at the crawl breathing cycle. Finally he lifted his head and switched to breast-stroke/frog-kick, watching for the ship.

It seemed it was easier for him to traverse the light-years than to cover a hundred feet of choppy water.

The galley was in sight! The oars lifted and stroked, lifted and stroked, and the vessel cut through the sea at an impressive rate, large and sleek from this lowly angle. Circular shields lined the top, and in occasional swells he could see the great front ram lift: a warship.

He was not going to make it. He was still a little ahead, but his rate of progress toward it was insufficient and getting slower. Already the numbness of his arms had reduced him to a dog-paddle. In a few minutes the ship would pass him and be on its way, leaving him to tire at last and sink. Would that return him to their Neptune-base, buried deep in the continent of Triton with the screaming methane storms above and impacted matter below? Or would it simply be the end?

He did not have the nerve to find out. His struggle had to be for life as he experienced it; he could not end this adventure by suicide, even if it were no more than a nightmare.

He saw the galley now with sharp clarity: dark brown wood low in the water surmounted by the row of oar-holes, and above them square windows with additional mountings for oars. The bow was vertical and without ornament, curving forward near the waterline to project into the massive six-foot spike that clove the ocean and, upon occasion (he was sure), the hulls of enemy ships. The rear curved up and back like the neck of a swan, terminating in a forward-tilting point twelve feet above the waterline. The last oar-brace was larger, and from it came the sturdy rudder, resembling a paddle inserted backwards. The side of the vessel above the oar-banks was checkered with alternate wooden and wickerwork panels, and the capping row of multicolored circular shields contributed to the galley's increasingly formidable aspect.

Threre was a lookout sitting high in the bow, now directly opposite him. Ivo yelled.

The head swung around immediately: no snoozing there. An exclamation, and other heads appeared. The banks of oars lifted and paused at the height of their uniform backstroke, and the ship coasted to a halt. Then a chain of gruff orders, and it spun neatly and shot toward him.

Had he thought it a toy, from the patronizing vantage of his macroscopic elevation? This was a precisely disciplined, highly maneuverable warship!

It hove-to above him and he clambered clumsily aboard the ram—Aries the ram?—immensely grateful for its support. He discovered that it was triparte: the major portion was an extension of the narrow keel, reinforced with bronze plates, with two braces converging from the sides of the bow. The entire thing could be crushed or broken off without holing the ship proper. It must have seen action recently, too, for there were no barnacles on it.

Hands reached down from the upper deck. Ivo braced himself against the curving bow and stood up, clinging weakly against the motion of the boat. He was just able to reach the proffered assistance, and in a moment they had him hauled roughly aboard, bruised, chilled through and as tired as he had ever felt, but intact.

A short warrior stood before him, resplendent in metal helmet and leather armor unlike that of the Egyptians: evidently the captain. He studied Ivo, who stood naked and shivering violently in the slight evening breeze. "Who are you?" the captain demanded brusquely.

"Ivo Archer." He realized that these people were not going to help him until they were satisfied he was not dangerous to them.

"Ivarch," the captain repeated. "Slave, free or royal?"

"Free." But how could he prove it, naked as a slave and without money or home-address or friends?

"Which nation?"

"America."

"Arpad?"

"America." Naturally they would not have heard of it, but there seemed to be no point in prevarication.

The captain hesitated, probably uncertain whether a citizen of an unknown country deserved courtesy or rebuke.

At length he made his choice. "Mattan will decide."

Mattan: a superior? A god? Fate?

The captain wheeled neatly in military fashion. "Clothe this man and feed him." A man of decision, he.

They brought Ivo an abrasive fiber blanket and put him belowdecks where the air was steamy from the perspiration of the naked oarsmen. The stench was terrific, but the warmth made it worthwhile. Before long the stiffness withdrew from his limbs and he felt his vigor oozing back.

He was seated in the stern just ahead of the rudderman's compartment. There was a center aisle about five feet across that ran the length of the hull, cluttered with boxes and buckles. On either side were the narrow benches upon which the oarsmen sat, one per oar. They heaved in unison, as they had to, for in these cramped quarters any wrong or poorly timed motion would create chaos. Every second oar projected well into the aisle, but the men did not bother with the added leverage available. They were slaves, obviously, but none was chained or, as far as he could tell, unhappy. Most of them were light-skinned.

Night, and the hold grew dark. The officer at the far end terminated the cadence and bawled out his orders. The oars were shipped, their ends pushed to the floor and fastened there with stiff leather straps. There followed a period of fifteen minutes while the slaves stood up, stretched, chatted, and relieved themselves into the available containers. The rudderman—another officer, since he wore the leather armor—tied his own oars and used the bucket. Ivo, seeing the way of it and finding himself in need, availed himself in like fashion of the facilities. More of the reason for the intense atmosphere was now evident; not all of it was sweat.

But was it any worse than the broken toilet and steaming garbage of a twentieth-century slum dwelling?

Under the supervision of the bow officer, the slaves hauled on the bottom panels of the lower deck and handed up from the bilge the supplies: rolls of hard bread, goatskins of wine. The rudderman went topside and returned shortly with two legs of smoked goatmeat, one of which he passed to the cadence officer. Rank had its privileges.

Ivo took one of the rolls and found it wooden. It had not occurred to him just how solid unleavened bread could be. He couldn't bite it; he had to gnaw. Soon the saltiness of it inspired thirst, and he borrowed a skin. He squeezed it the way he had seen the others do, to arc a stream into his mouth without contaminating the nozzle with his saliva. The brownish stuff splashed across his face, bringing laughter from the slaves.

Ivo laughed too, sensing no enmity from these people, and wiped the burning fluid out of his eyes and off his hair. This concoction was beyond contamination! On the second attempt he managed to center on his mouth, though he did not have the technique of swallowing while squirting and had to break off quickly. Wine? This brew tasted like overripe dishwater with frogjuice in it, but it was wet.

Some of the slaves had brought out fine lines of knotted tendon and were dangling these out the oar-ports. Soon Ivo saw why: they were fishing, and not without success. The fish liked the chips of bread! There was air-space around the rising mast, and in an enormous ceramic bowl they built a smoky fire to roast their catches against. The lucky slaves might well sup better than the masters!

While this was not the life Ivo would have chosen for himself, he did find a certain appeal in it. A man here had only to pull his oar and keep the cadence, and he was adequately fed and sheltered and protected, with little to worry about (except an enemy ram?) and plenty of company.

After an hour the crude tallow candles were snuffed. The men returned to their places and slept, seemingly not discommoded by the cramped discomfort. The officer-shift changed; the two hitherto on duty went above, while a single armed soldier paced the aisle. Any slave could have grabbed him from behind, but none was interested; this was token force to keep order, nothing more. Probably the slaves had no knowledge of sailing or of navigation; mutiny was pointless.

Ivo lay down on the filthy deck and slept without

271

difficulty, only moderately queasy from the constant rocking of the boat.

At break of day a rising wind rocked the ship more violently. The slaves grinned as they heard the sounds of the great sail being unfurled and hoisted: no rowing this morning! The breeze took hold and the sidewise rhythm subsided, making Ivo feel better. He was not ordinarily subject to motion sickness, but the combination of smell, wine, fatigue and wind had assaulted his intestinal well-being.

About noon orders began to fly above. The men came alive, taking their places and unshipping the oars, though the craft was still under sail. The alternate men who had the projecting oars stood up this time, grasping the tips. The center aisle was now filled, one man standing behind another, arms resting on wood held waist-high.

The cadence began and the oarsmen strove vigorously. The ship—still under sail!—accelerated. Then Ivo heard distant cheering, and understood.

The ship was coming home.

The cadence accelerated and the men fairly bent the oars in their effort, muscles glistening. Ivo peered through the nearest port with some difficulty and was able to make out the outlines of a walled city. Nothing like putting on a' show for the homefolk!

Then *halt!* and the oars reversed as the sail dropped, braking the ship within a few feet of the dock.

The captain had not forgotten Ivo. Two soldiers came to escort him from the ship. He blinked in the brightness of day, topside, then was hustled over the gang to the dock. The harbor was in the southern section of the city; the sunlight slanted over his right shoulder as he walked.

The terrain was rocky, houses perched upon slanted foundations, and the narrow streets curved a great deal. It was a wealthy city. Some buildings were of stone and wood, built to last, though most were of many stories and crowded into very small areas, making the streets seem like mere crevices in a solid mass of residence. Almost every house had its terrace, however, which helped.

Ivo was delivered to an antechamber where an elegant assortment of bedsheets were hung. The two guards departed, but he was sure they were not far away. What next?

A girl, bare of head, foot and breast, entered and approached him with provocative confidence. He decided to go along with whatever was expected.

Efficiently she stripped the soiled blanket from him and deposited it in a corner. She brought a basin of cold water and sponged his body down and rubbed scented ointment into his muscles. Since she was obviously trained for this and competent, he maintained his composure; but it was only the continuing feeling of unreality that enabled him to put up with such familiar handling by an unfamiliar woman. The arms and legs weren't so bad, but the buttocks—

And how had Afra felt, being handled by him?

Then she sat him down upon a bench and brought out a horrendous iron blade. While he watched with alarm, she sharpened it assiduously against a leather strap. The insecurity of his present situation impressed him strongly.

Carefully she bathed his face and shaved him, never cutting his flesh despite the irregularity and clumsiness of the razor. She finished by rubbing perfume into his hair and combing it back.

The bedsheets he had noted before turned out to be apparel: lengths of embroidered cloth. The girl took one down and wrapped it about him in a series of convolutions surely as intricate as any of the folds of macroscopic space and pinned it into place. He emerged from her ministrations in a handsome red tunic and soft leather sandals. He was sure he could never duplicate the costume by himself, should it come undone; he might even have trouble getting out of it on his own! When a citizen of this city retired at night, did he have a girl like this come to undress him properly? Hm.

Suitably prepared, he followed her to his interview with Mattan.

Mattan was mortal and courteous: an official of some importance in the city, if appearances were any guide. He reclined beside a tray of pastries and ripe fruit, dressed in a bright yellow robe and assorted jewelry. The tray was a sheet of almost-transparent glass: undoubtedly a rarity in this age, and a sign of wealth and power. He gestured Ivo to a couch opposite.

273

"And how do you find the Hegemony of Tyre, Ivarch of Merica?" Mattan inquired politely. His voice was soft and sure.

So it was to Tyre he had come—one of the old Phoenician cities on the coast of Asia Minor. Perhaps this was as good for his purpose as Damascus. Tyre had been a leader for many centuries, until—he strained to remember—it had finally fallen to Alexander three centuries before Christ. Had it warred with anyone else? He wasn't sure.

"You do not choose to comment?" Mattan inquired, too gently. "One could be led to the impression that you were averse to our hospitality."

"I have not been in this area long," Ivo said hastily, wondering what the man's purpose was.

"Merica is very far away, then."

"Very far."

"But surely not so far that its citizens have not heard of the might of Tyre?"

"Not that far."

"And what brings you here so precipitously?"

"I—got lost on my way to Damascus."

"Your ship was wrecked?"

"In a manner of speaking." How could he explain what had happened? He hardly understood it himself. Somehow the world he had only watched had become physically real, and his twentieth-century existence unreal. Another macroscopic trap more subtle yet? Time travel? How could he, denuded of his equipment and thrown upon his personal resources, find his way back?

Mattan nibbled at a grape, not offering any to Ivo. "It occurs to me that we are not being entirely candid with each other, Ivarch."

"I don't think you would believe my story."

"Perhaps not. Still, I would certainly like to hear it. I am informed that you were picked up thirty miles out to sea, in a region clear of enemy ships, and I can see for myself that you are not locally sired. In fact," and he peered knowledgeably at Ivo's face, "I am at a loss to define your ethnic heritage. Tyre is as eclectic a pot as any in the world, but you are a veritable cauldron of race! I observe traces of so many things—Mycenaean, of course, but also Egyptian, Cimmerian, Nubian and others I hesitate to mention. Yet you know the tongue of Canaan

as well as any native of the Seven Cities, while professing
ignorance of our ways. In fact, I do not see how your
story can be anything less than incredible."

"The tongue of Canaan?" But then, had he really expected them to speak American English? "I have no
secrets, but I just don't think my story would help you."
Or me, he thought.

"Perhaps I should judge that for myself. Is there any
way I can facilitate the spinning of your yarn?"

"Well, yes. I need to know the date." Or was that
concern now pointless?

"You were not aware that this is the summer season in
the thirty-ninth year of Hiram?"

"I was not aware. It seemed like winter when I was in
the water." And it did not help much. When was Hiram—
presumably their king—on the Christian calendar? Five
hundred BC? Two thousand?

"Nor that Hiram died six years ago?"

"No. But why did you number—"

"Forgive me for verifying your ignorance. It had entered my mind—purely as a matter of speculation, naturally—that you could be considered to be the representative of a hostile power."

"A spy?"

"That was not precisely my term. But I am inclined to
discredit the possibility. You are far too naïve."

Ivo was becoming less so rapidly. "What happens to
—representatives of hostile powers?"

"That depends on their, shall we say, cooperation. An
incorrigible—that is, one who cannot or will not provide
us with sufficient and significant information—may be
offered in sacrifice to Baal Melqart. Our Baal prefers
tender children or succulent infants, naturally, and this is
said to be a distressing demise for an adult, since the
facilities are not wholly adequate. Still—"

The threat was adequate, whatever the condition of the
facilities. Human sacrifice! And he had been shocked by
Brad's revelation of the black-market in human bodies in
his own time! At least that had been for a purpose, grisly
as its practice was. Here it would be sheer waste. "What
of a person whose story is merely unbelievable?"

"Sooner or later it must, in the nature of things, *become* believable." Mattan shrugged away the unpleasant-

275

ness. "Perhaps if I were to clarify the current situation for you, you would then' find it easier to relate your framework to ours."

"I think I would." Was Mattan permitting him to stall for time, or was he really trying to be helpful? The Tyrean was an educated and intelligent man, but Ivo needed to know more of his attitudes before trying to explain the concept of time travel—particularly when Ivo himself did not believe in it. Did Mattan, for example, believe in magic? If so, that might be the most promising approach. He suspected the man would not put up with delay beyond a certain point; the mailed fist was only casually veiled.

Mattan settled back on his couch, looked at the cedar-paneled ceiling, and took an ample breath. This was evidently the type of dialogue he preferred. "In the days of Tyre's origin there were three equal powers, three equivalent spheres of influence that parceled the civilized world between them. The first was Egyptian, extending from northern Africa, along the banks of the emperor of all rivers—the Nile—to the fourth cataract, and as far north as Damascus. The second was Hittite, including all of Anatolia and the region of the coast south as far as Damascus. The third was Assyrian, whose sphere was east of the other two, including the remainder of greater Syria and virtually all of Mesopotamia.

"Of these three superpowers, I would deem the most formidable to have been the Hittite, chiefly because of the vigor of their leadership and their facility with the working of iron. Unfortunately, they also had the worst enemies. The northern nomads—Cimmerians and Cythians and such—raided constantly, and the western barbarians—Thracians and Greeks—invaded in masses. The Phrygians even set up a kingdom in western Anatolia, and the Hittite empire finally collapsed. This left a power vacuum of monstrous proportion that was to cause interminable trouble. For a time the entire countryside was a nest of robber barons.

"This left two superpowers—but both were hardpressed. For a time Assyria expanded, but eventually it fell into stagnation and merely defended itself against the nomads from the south, the Arameans. Egypt lost its possessions in Palestine and resisted the incursions of the fierce Peoples of the Sea with difficulty.

"The result was that a number of lesser powers developed, feeding on the decay of the great ones. Perhaps none of this anarchy would have happened if the Hittite empire had survived." He stood up and drew aside a

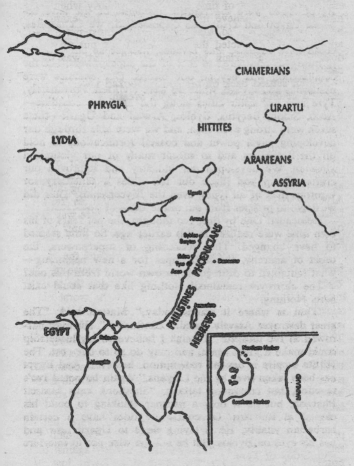

277

curtain. There, set into the wall, was a huge cedar panel with a painted map. Ivo recognized the crude outlines of the far eastern Mediterranean. His host really was a student of history!

"The Philistines," Mattan continued, touching a section of the Asia Minor coast, "invaded Palestine from the sea, having been repulsed by Egypt. The Hebrews, meanwhile, invaded from the desert, having also been repulsed by Egypt. Thus were the rightful residents of the land between Egypt and Damascus dispossessed: we Canaanites, who had occupied it for a thousand years in peace. We could have repulsed one invader, meager as our military posture was compared to that of the superpowers, but the combination was beyond our means. Our enemies were numerous and savage, while we were civilized. Fortunately, Tyre and her sister cities along the northern coastline—Acco, Sidon, Berytus, Byblos, Arwad and Ugarit—these seven were strong even then, and we were able through our developing naval power and coastal fortifications to hold off the despoilers and to succor many of our victimized kinsmen. We developed our industry and improved our craftsmanship and made our fair cities a sanctuary for vigorous men of all types, even the Mycenaeans. Thus did we begin to prosper from out of the ashes of holocaust."

Holocaust! One by one, Ivo thought, the pet fears of his own time were realized in this earlier age. So little seemed to have changed. The weakening of superpowers, the onset of anarchy, the high hopes for a new beginning—what remained to distinguish his own world from this one?

The *destroyer* remained! Nothing like that could exist here. Nothing.

"That is where it stands today," Mattan said. "The great destroyer Assyria remains confined—" His eyes narrowed as Ivo jumped. "Though I believe strong leadership could make it great again, and may do so to our cost. The Hittite empire is beyond redemption, however. And Egypt has been taken over by the Libyans." Again he noted Ivo's reaction, but continued talking. "Sheshonk calls himself Pharaoh, but he is only a usurper thinking to build his capital at Bubastis. Of course he does have a certain barbarian vitality. He is laying siege to Ugarit now and has his eyes on Byblos. But he will be wise not to interfere with Sidon or Tyre."

Ivo had followed only the gist of all this, more concerned with his own situation. At least the mystery of his Egyptian experience had been partially alleviated. There *was* a superimposition of cultures: Libyan over Egyptian. The main question remained unanswered, however: how could *he* be participating? Probably he would have found himself physically in Egypt, had he not fled immediately ... and had he had the sense to quit then and rest for a few hours away from the macroscope, none of this present adventure might have come to pass.

Well, recrimination was futile. Mattan was waiting for his comment on the local situation. The Pharaoh of Egypt was attacking Ugarit. "But aren't the Pheonician cities being attacked? Why don't you help them?"

"That becomes problematical. For one thing, their colonies along the African coast—and there is more to Africa than you might suspect—are competing with ours. For another, we can't afford to weaken our comparative standing with our rival Sidon, and Sidon has not agreed to match any assistance we might grant. For a third, we have a continuing contract with the Kingdom of Israel, and a war effort against even a decaying giant like Egypt at this time would seriously interfere with this. That would be bad business."

"Israel? But I thought you were at war with the Hebrews!"

"Not currently. Hiram and Solomon got along well enough, and now that the Hebrews have split up into Israel and Judah, they're not so much of a threat. There is still much copper and iron to be had from Wadi Arabah, in their present territory. One must appreciate the practical side of things."

Mattan, like the deceased Senator Borland, was a practical man. And Sidney Lanier had inveighed (would inveigh?) against cruel trade! He had been a trifle late.

Then another thought: "Solomon? You mean this is *that* time?"

"Ah, you have heard of David's son. Almost as great a king as our own Hiram, in his fashion, and he certainly did a good deal with the kingdom he had. It isn't easy to bring culture to nomads. Solomon died only three years ago, and his empire broke up. Too bad; Sheshonk will overrun them before long. For a while it seemed as though a new power were developing in that area, but that's all over. Tyre will have to carry the burden alone." He brought his gaze to bear on Ivo "And now, Ivarch, if you please, *your* story."

This still posed a problem. Mattan had showed no inclination toward superstition or magic; rather, he was extremely pragmatic. It hardly seemed likely that he would go for anything as fantastic as the macroscope.

"First," Mattan said, "explain to me exactly where Merica is." He gestured to the map. "Is it represented here?"

"No. It is much farther away. Do you have a map of the world?"

"This *is* the map of the world."

Oh-oh. "You mean the *civilized* world, don't you? There are lands beyond it."

Mattan nodded. "I misunderstood. Yes, there are regions beyond and we are exploring them. Suppose you sketch a map of your own?"

The tone remained mild, but Ivo realized that he was being tested again. This man was determined to take his measure, and smart enough to know that he didn't have it yet. Ivo also seemed to remember that the Phoenicians had traveled out quite far in search of trade and exploitation, as had their rivals the Greeks, and were secretive about any important discoveries. Hadn't they mined tin or something in Britain? And what about the story of the lost Phoenician ship, blown from an attempted circumnavigation of Africa over to South America, where its craftsmen inspired Western pyramid-building? Still, he was on much firmer ground here.

He accepted the blank scroll Mattan provided and drew a tiny copy of the wall-map. Then he extended it to complete the closure of the Mediterranean. He was no cartographer; his rendition was crude and not particularly accurate, but he doubted that mattered. "Here is Italy," he said, "and Sicily—the boot tripping over the rock." Mattan nodded thoughtfully, and Ivo knew that this was a geography so far familiar to the man.

"Here is the western coast of Europe, and the British Isles." Mattan was so carefully noncommittal that Ivo was certain he knew something of this area also. "And to the south is the rest of the continent of Africa, so."

"What lies to the east?"

"A huge continent." Ivo sketched an exceedingly crude Asia.

"And where is Merica?"

"Across the sea to the west." He began to sketch it in, leaving inadequate space for the width of the Atlantic because of the limitation of his map-surface.

"I see," Mattan said as Ivo's charcoal rounded the peninsula that would later be Florida. "And in what manner did you travel here?"

Ivo took hold of himself and gave the only answer. "I flew."

"And can you fly for me now?"

"No."

"I see." Mattan thought a bit more. "And do they speak Pheonician in America?"

"No."

"How did you master it, then?"

"I don't know. It just seemed to come to me when I needed it."

"I see." The two words became more ominous with each repetition, and this time the pause was very long. "You are, then, laying claim to the godhead?"

The godhead: the attributes of deity? Ivo wondered how far he could get by breaking and running. "In America, these things—like flying, I mean—are not surprising. There is nothing supernatural about it."

"America is a land of gods, then."

"No, no! It—" But how could he explain, to this intelligent yet so ignorant man? Here there were many gods, and they were no more supernatural than the One God of Christian times. Mattan's suspicions were quite justified, by the standards of his age. Any further attempts to clarify the nature of the divine would merely make things worse.

"Were it not for your distinctive physical makeup and your cognizance of certain matters no local could know, I would brand you a champion prevaricator," Mattan said. "As it is, I confess to certain doubts. Your misinformation is as intriguing as your information, and I cannot tell whether you are preposterously clever or preposterously inept at invention. Either way, you *are* preposterous. I do not see how you could be what you call a spy, yet I am at a loss to explain what you *are.*"

There was a silence.

"I think," Mattan said at last, "that this is properly a matter for the priesthood."

Ivo felt cold again, and the increasing hunger he had felt while watching Mattan eat departed abruptly. "I have spoken heresy?"

"By no means. You have not remarked at all on Melqart, and in any event your Merica appears to be beyond the dominion of our Baal. But since I seem to have exhausted the procedures available to me . . ."

If this were the final threat, it had become subtle again. There had been no further mention of sacrifice. "I suppose I could talk to your priests, though I can't tell them anything I haven't told you."

"Excellent. My men will show you the way. I'm sure you will reach an understanding with Melqart, and perhaps complete unity."

Ivo was not entirely satisfied with that phrasing, but he accompanied the two husky guards without explicit objection. He noticed that they, like every person he had seen here and aboard the ship, were shorter than he. He was a virtual giant in this city. Though he hardly thought of himself as the physical type, his superior size and weight would give him a certain advantage if trouble came.

These soldiers were better armed than the ones he had observed in Egypt, possessing vests of metal mesh and well-fitted low helmets, as well as long spears and sharp swords. Tucked in each stout belt was a wicked battle-axe.

Ivo had a second thought about his supposed physical advantage.

"Strange," the guard on his right remarked as they entered the slender street. "I have never seen a lamb go to the sacrifice so calmly." He spoke a different language from Phoenician, and Ivo realized with a start that these were conscripts from some other area, mercenaries who did not realize that he could understand their dialogue.

"Mattan probably told him he was going to witness the ceremony," the other said. "And him already shorn!"

Ivo noticed now that both men were bearded—as had been Mattan. Why, then, had the visitor been so painstakingly shaved?

"Well, he'll get a fine view—of the fiery stomach of

Baal!" the first agreed, laughing. "I thought every fool knew that no one but a priest ever leaves the temple."

"You are mistaken," the other replied. "Every day the urns go out to the burial ground."

"His bones would not fit in a child's urn, even after cremation," the first protested. "Far too long."

They were at the foot of the steps leading to an elegant stone building. Two mighty columns stood beside the entrance, one painted yellow, the other green. The second guard turned to Ivo and put out his callused hand. His short sword hung from a chest harness, sheathed in leather, the hilt almost brushing Ivo's left elbow. "Let me help you up these hallowed stairs, sir," the man said in Phoenician.

"The priests would be very unhappy if such an honored guest were to stumble," the other said. "And Baal would be fuming." And, in the other language: "Yes—look at the length of that humerus!"

Ivo looked up and saw a white-robed priest coming to meet them. Several temple guards accompanied him. All looked purposeful.

He grabbed at the left guard's sword and drew it from the scabbard before the man reacted. Then he shouldered past and turned to face the second, afraid that flight would bring a spear at his back. But that guard also had been slow to react, perhaps not expecting the lamb to turn, and stood open-mouthed, hand not even on his weapon.

The guard who had donated his sword tripped over his battle-axe and sprawled on the ground. His shield, that had been hooked in some fashion to his left hip, lay between them on the lowest step. Ivo swooped at it and picked it up with his left hand, fumbling a moment with the grip. It was surprisingly light: an oval disk of wood, padded behind the hand-strap, nocked at the rim from countless military encounters. Obviously it was intended for active defense; one had to meet the oncoming sword or spear with it and deflect or snare the barb, rather than simply hiding behind the shield.

The other guard had finally caught on that something was wrong. He drew out his sword and raised his own shield, advancing cumbersomely on Ivo. It was hard to believe that these were veterans; they were like oxen.

Behind the attacking guard the priest cried out, and the temple personnel charged down the steps, crowding each other dangerously.

Ivo hefted his weapon. The sword was about two feet long, not counting the hilt, and tapered so that the widest part of the blade was six or eight inches from the tip. Both edges were sharp, though hardly knifelike; muscular power had to be applied to hack through opposing armor and the blade could not maintain a really good edge.

The weapon was clumsy and the handle was too small for a comfortable grip. He could hardly fight effectively with this, or, for that matter, protect himself with the shield. Not that he wanted to fight at all; violence of this sort was not in his nature. There had to be some reasonable means to—

The guard struck with his sword, and Ivo automatically blocked with the wooden disk.

It worked.

The blade collided with the notched rim and clung for an instant, held by the spongy wood. Ivo swept his own sword around in a clumsy quarter-circle, and the guard jerked back.

He had missed—but the swing had been oddly refreshing. The sword, so clumsy just to hold, became a nicely balanced instrument in motion. He saw now that its delicate taper contributed to its effectiveness, placing the greatest width and weight behind the intended point of contact.

He had already wasted too much time. During the few seconds of this action, the temple guards had continued advancing, and were now almost upon him. He could not hope to overcome them all. He would have to run, and risk the spears.

He turned—and discovered more troops coming up from the street. He was already surrounded.

Do the unexpected! he thought, remembering the advice from somewhere. The unexpected could prevail in almost any situation. They obviously expected him either to fight or to run, and neither course could save him long.

They had stopped within twenty feet, forming a closing ring of swords, the two original guards among them. The priest stood in the center of the line upon the wide steps, gesticulating. His feet, Ivo noticed, were bare.

Ivo charged at him, bounding up the low steps three at a time. At ten feet he hurled the shield at the priest's head. It skimmed through the air like a sail, rotating.

The man jumped aside, agile enough, banging into the guard adjacent. Ivo threw his sword at the line of men on the other side. It whirled like a boomerang, flashing sunlight in all directions.

The three nearest shields came up reflexively to block it, as he had known they would, but the men were taken aback. Before they recovered, Ivo dived at the stumbling priest, catching him around the waist and shoving him back against the standing guards again. They all went down in a tangle.

A sword clattered almost by his ear, thrown up by one of the scrambling warriors. Ivo snatched at it, then caught the priest around the waist once more as he tried to stand up. The man, fortunately, was of birdlike physique, easy to manhandle. Ivo pinned the priest against him, in lieu of a shield, and backed up the steps. The guards started after them, but Ivo raised the great blade to his captive's neck, and they hung back.

But he had to do something else soon, for the heavy sword was already weighing down his arm in this awkward pose. The threat would lose effect if the blade sagged wearily to the hostage's chest. . . .

"Listen, treacherous one!" Ivo hissed into the man's ear as the two retreated. "Either we visit Melqart's furnace together, or we escape together. It is for you to decide whether we part company in life or in death. Do you understand me?"

The man said nothing, but Ivo was sure he had the message. At the top of the stair between the columns Ivo released him, but held the sword at his back. The massed soldiers were following, ever more numerous, not closely; they were making a resounding clatter, but not risking the hostage. Ivo congratulated himself on an excellent choice.

He placed his back against the yellow pillar, mind racing to formulate a workable plan of escape. Audacity he had never suspected in himself had taken him this far, but there had to be a limit to his luck. The priest did not move, and the crowd below did not advance.

He prodded the priest. "Into the temple," he whispered.

"Make no turn or sudden motion without advising me. If I doubt your intention one moment, it will be your last." Was it he, meek Ivo Archer, reading the lines of this melodrama? Why not complete the scene by informing the man that he had an itchy sword-finger?

Not funny. Sweat made the handle of the weapon treacherously slippery, and already he felt the sting of a developing blister.

The priest uncurled a talonlike finger and pointed.

"Oho!" Ivo said. "There's a private door?"

The priest led him around the column to the side of the building. Sure enough, there was a small entrance there opening into a dark corridor running parallel to the outer wall. There was hardly room for his head to clear, though the smaller man had no trouble.

They entered. This did seem better than the main hall, since only one person at a time could follow, and the gloom would make pursuit harder. Light came in only from high narow vents, embrasures in the outer wall.

Twenty feet along the priest tapped a stone of the inner wall. Then he put his fragile shoulder against it and pushed. Ivo watched this suspiciously, at the same time glancing back to make sure no one was following yet.

The stone swung back, leaving a blank opening from which a cool draft came. Cool, but corrupt; there was stagnant water somewhere.

"Secret exit?"

The man nodded. Ivo could barely see him here, and kept one hand on the bony arm. The stone must have been very lightly balanced, to move at the urging of such a skeleton. And why did the hostage never speak?

"In case of rebellion, foreign conquest ... ?" Ivo inquired, poking his sword-hand into it dubiously.

No response.

Ivo prodded him. "You first."

The priest drew back, alarmed.

"Uh-huh. We meet our fate together. Hurry!"

There was a commotion behind, and he knew the troops were clustered around their entrance, and probably had the temple proper surrounded for good measure.

"I know you aren't dumb," Ivo said fiercely. "I heard

you calling to the guards, before. So either get in there or tell me why not, or I'll run you through right now!"

He was bluffing, but hoped it didn't show.

"There is a better exit ahead," the priest said quickly. His voice, after all that suspense, was ordinary.

Ivo smiled grimly. Victory—and another trap avoided. The violent approach did have its recommendations. "That one we shall both use—for better or worse."

But there was no time. The sounds outside verified his recent conjecture: the guards surrounded the temple, and this time a higher priest was evidently in command. His human shield was almost useless. Now there were noises from the far end of the passage as well.

The priest suddenly tore free of Ivo's loose grasp. Ivo lunged, grabbing with his left hand and sweeping with his sword. The blade crashed into the man's side, but not hard enough to cut through the cloth. Trying to avoid it, the priest scuttled sidewise, his back against the tilted stone.

Ivo grabbed again—and only succeeded in shoving the little man into the hole. The stone yielded smoothly, closing on a descending scream and a faint splash—some fifty feet down, by the timing. Some escape!

Now Ivo was alone, pinned between armed bands without his hostage. Was there another exit, or had that been merely the rascally priest's stall for time? There *had* to be one!

He moved along the wall, pushing at each great block, but none gave way. Minutes passed. His eyes adapted to the dim light, but all he saw was a veneer of dirt on wall and floor. His own scuff-marks were all that disturbed it.

Why weren't they attacking? They must have overheard his struggle with the priest, and realized the man was dead. Or had they assumed that *Ivo* had fallen, so that the priest would emerge in a moment? Or was the delay part of some more subtle ploy—something less risky to them than a frontal attack in a confined space?

He rolled his eyes up, shrugging ... and spied a dark hole in the ceiling, a few feet in front of him. The second exit!

He tossed his sword into it, and the metal clattered on stone and came to rest without falling out. He followed it immediately, reaching up to catch the edges with his

287

fingers. He chinned himself on it—and could not get any higher, as his feet kicked without support. He had to drop down.

He studied the situation, then chinned himself into the hole again. An athlete, or perhaps some birdlike priest, might have entered it easily, since it was hardly above head-height—but Ivo was neither. Yet an effective escape hatch should have some convenient handhold. . . .

Ivo braced his chin uncomfortably against the rim and got one elbow up. His questing hand struck the sword. He grunted, feeling the sting of the pitted blade grating against his palm, but did not drop back. Then he had it: a firm wooden bar.

There was caked dust upon it, but dryer and fluffier than that below. No one had been here for a long time, evidently. A good sign, or a bad omen?

Well, Ivo had little choice now. He got his shoulders up, his chest, one foot, and finally the rest of him without losing too much skin. He licked the grime off his bleeding palm and picked up the sword. Infection was the least of his worries at the moment.

A belated thought: the soldiers could trace his trail in the dust. He had to cover up.

Probably the tunnel was riddled with exits. If he could conceal the one he had actually employed, they would be hours tracing him down.

As a planner, he was a misfit. Again he had thought of the obvious just too late for convenience.

Regretfully, he eased himself down into the tunnel again, his cut hand smarting as the dust ground in. Then he ran scuffling down the passage and back, slapping his hand against each inner panel. Let them analyze *that* trail! Then up again, into the hole. He swept up handfuls of the dust and sprinkled then near the entrance and on the bar, hoping that this would conceal the evidence of his passage. He couldn't see the effect at all, perhaps fortunately.

And, at last, on:

He was in a cramped passage running skew to the one below, as nearly as he could tell by the aim of the walls, and absolutely dark. His sandals, never meant for such exertions, tended to catch on the rough-hewn flooring.

Finally there was light. He emerged on a dusty balcony

overlooking an interior court at what he took to be the rear of the temple. In the center was a huge, grotesque metal statue shaped roughly like a man. Smoke spiraled up from a vent in its head, and a ramp led into a gate set in its bulging belly: Melqart, the carnivorous Baal of Tyre.

Ivo turned aside, not particularly curious. It seemed to him that he could smell the lingering aroma of roasted flesh. No wonder the Israelites had fought against this faith! And had the Nazi machine, so many centuries later, been a monstrous reincarnation of the spirit of Baal?

He spied crude stairs leading down, also layered with dust. He hesitated. There were still hours of daylight remaining, and once he left the temple he would be vulnerable again. Perhaps they were waiting beyond this exit, too. It would be better to wait until nightfall, when he might escape unnoticed. They would not expect him to linger within sight of the metal god. And perhaps the priests, who must surely know of this passage, would not reveal it to the soldiers. Better that one lamb go free for a while, than that the secrets of the temple be betrayed. Yes—his unexpected, and therefore sensible, course was to remain right here . . . sword ready.

He located a concealing niche and lay down. He tried to hold on to the sword, but his right hand had a blister and his left a cut, so he laid it beside him. Once more, oddly, he had no difficulty sleeping. Perhaps it was because he was sure any approach would alert him. He hoped.

It was dark when he woke. His hand still smarted and he was hungry. He had not enjoyed the rough staples of the galley slaves, and had not had any of Mattan's delicacies. Even Melqart was beginning to smell appetizing.

Ivo decided it was time to get out of this region. He descended the steps cautiously, trying not to disturb the dust any more than necessary. He also heeded the sounds of temple activity. He wondered whether the troops were still patiently waiting in ambush for him, at the two ends of the original passage. A soldier might have peeked and found him gone, the fake escape hatch still open. No, it was closed now. Would they think he had taken that plunge? In that case they would not be alert for him.

A heavy door closed off the foot of the stair. It was barred, but the bar was inside. No doubt about it: this was the priesthood's official emergency outlet. He lifted the plank, set it aside, and pushed. Nothing happened.

Was it barred outside too? That did not seem reasonable, for then it would have to be opened from both sides simultaneously: a dubious emergency exit. He kneeled down and put his eye to the crack. Lights from the city came through. He traced the crack up and down and found no blockage. The door was merely tight.

He put his shoulder against it and shoved hard. It held. Finally he braced both feet against the bottom stair, set his back against the door, and straightened his knees hard.

The portal crashed open. Ivo fell on his back, the sword clattering beside him. The noise was horrendous. There were immediate shouts, and torchbearing figures came running toward him from both sides of the building.

He was in trouble again. Naturally.

Ivo picked himself up, brandished the sword (finding the blister less painful), and ran. The torches swerved to intercept him. He slowed to navigate the stone terraces beside the temple, and the first group of men was upon him. He could see the glint of broad blades in the torch-light, the spark of staring eyes.

He swung his sword. It caught the leading man on the shield. Ivo swung again, this time striking flesh; the man screamed and fell back. Two more attacked at once, striking from either side. Ivo felt the searing contact of a blade meeting his left arm and fell back himself. Again his grip was slippery, whether from sweat or blood he could not determine. The light was too bad, and his own sensations too confused. He lunged desperately at the figure who had wounded him, aiming for the glint of the helmet— and in the dark he scored.

The fellow had been carrying the torch instead of his shield, and had tried instinctively to block—with the torch. Ivo's blade, coming into the sphere of light, struck both hand and face, sickeningly. The torch flew out and rolled on the ground, providing him a passing glimpse of what he had wrought; then the spreading blood extinguished the fire messily.

The shallow steps were as nothing. He was down them

and away, running into the city, without being aware of the motions. Behind him the torches milled and followed, like angry bees searching for their mission.

The streets were dark. He charged down the nearest, panting already, heedless of the direction or possible obstacles. He made a right-angle turn at the first intersection, angled again—and found himself as lost as the torches.

He was surrounded by three-story houses closely set, boxlike and gloomy. He could not see whether any had windows or doors without approaching closely, but was sure entry would gain him nothing but further outcry. Where could he go? He had no money—was not even certain they used it here—and no home. The night was not cold—yet—but he did not want to wander about indefinitely.

Suddenly the torches confronted him again. The temple troops had not given up the search; indeed, they were combing the city for him. He ran dismally before them, ashamed of the blood already on his sword. He had not meant to kill the man, only to drive him back, perhaps to wound him superficially. He had to believe that.

His own wound was sodden under the dragging loops of his tunic, still squeezing out plasma with every motion he made, he was sure. That was another reason he had to find sanctuary.

Where, where? He could not even flee to the countryside, for Tyre was an island—a walled island.

Torches were coming down two alleys of the next intersection. He could see by their massed brilliance that the houses were richer than he had thought. Though the ground-level exterior walls of most were of blank stucco, the upper stories were of wood with small square window openings, and some even had balustrades supported by miniature palm columns. Not slum housing, certainly.

The next intersection was torched on three sides, including the street behind him. Ivo ran in the one direction permitted him, thankful that they had not quite sealed him off entirely. Yet even if he eluded them, he saw no long-range salvation. He could not run much longer.

"Fugitive!"

It was a woman's voice, pitched low but with excellent

carrying quality. Ivo rotated to face it, hauling up the tainted blade defensively.

"Fugitive—here!" the voice repeated urgently. "Come quickly, before they see you."

He had to trust her. He ran toward the caped figure standing upon a tiny terrace.

"The blood!" she exclaimed disapprovingly. "You have left a trail of blood!"

So that was how they had boxed him in so readily! He could not see it himself, but they obviously could, with the torches. Had he any chance at all?

"Perhaps I can still help you," she said. "Come inside."

He stumbled in the door she stood beside—in this case, a hole in the wall covered by a length of hide or canvas—and found himself within a small and dirty vestibule. The walls were covered by crumbling brown plaster. Not a domicile of wealth, obviously—yet he could hardly be choosy!

The woman closed the entrance and led him to a small interior court. She was young and tall—very tall for this locale—and quite fair of feature, and the cloak hardly concealed her voluptuousness of form. He wondered dully whether she could be a prostitute. If so, she would turn him out quickly enough when she discovered that he had no money or barter.

"We must stop the blood," she said. "I know an empty house where they will not find us tonight. But we can't let the blood betray us." She peeled back the cloth that had become a soggy bandage and began sponging off the wound.

"Who are you?" he demanded. "Why do you help me?"

"I am Aia. I do not worship Melqart, nor do I like human sacrifice."

She bound his arm with a rough cloth. Ivo hesitated to inspect the compress closely, certain that it was not very clean. Something nagged him about her statement, but he could not, in his present fuddled state, pin it down. Perhaps it was that opposition to a particular policy or religion should not necessarily lead one to risk one's own well-being in that connection? There ought to be a stronger, more primitive motive.

Still, there was the adage about gift-horses—if they had horses here.

"And," she said, "I need help myself, to escape from this foul city. Alone, I would soon be pressed into slavery."

Oh. Nothing like a male fugitive for such assistance! Someone whose imperative for rapid escape was guaranteed.

If that were her case—and there now seemed to be no reason to question it—their needs could very well coincide.

"Do you trust yourself to a stranger?" he asked her anyway. "A criminal, for all you know, a rapist, even a murderer?"

"Do you desire to murder me?"

"No."

"Then there is no harm you can do me."

Oh.

"Now we must hurry. The temple guards will find this house very soon." She showed him to the back exit and peered at the street. Torches were passing.

"And who are you?" she inquired as they waited.

"Ivarch of Merica. I was taken in by a ship and brought before Mattan for interrogation."

"Mattan," she said darkly. "He is notorious. Soft spoken but never to be trusted. A dabbler in past events."

An apt assessment. "What I don't understand is why he sent me to be sacrificed. How could he get information that way?"

She shrugged. "Mattan is Mattan. Come—they are past."

So they were, for the moment. Soon they would discover the termination of the bloodstain trail on the other side of the house and backtrack. Aia led him into the dark street, guiding him past irregularities and obstructions while he sheltered the sword under his tunic. She seemed to have an inherent sensitivity to danger, knowing where the temple patrols were likely to be and how to avoid them. In half an hour they were comfortably ensconced in the house she had spoken of: empty, yes, but very well stocked.

Ivo ripped off the remaining shreds of his tunic and cleaned up in the well-appointed bath. He had not expected any drainage facilities, but this had a wooden pipe leading down and out, and the floor was of pink cement set with little marble cubes. As elegant as anything of the twentieth century, except for the lack of heated or running water.

Then he had to beg Aia's help to don a new tunic, hoping she would not be outraged by the request. She obliged without comment, fortunately.

The remainder of the house was simply executed: several rectangular rooms without architectural pretensions. The foundation was stone cleverly fitted together with a minimum of cement, giving way to bricks with occasional upright slabs of stone for strength, and finally to straight wood. The cedar paneling of the upper rooms was handsome but not ornate and there were no objects of art. The owner, apparently conforming to Phoenician taste, had no personal interest in elegance, with the exception of clothing. The house was stocked with an array of material fully as splendid as that of Mattan's residence: multicolored cloaks, tunics and skirts, heavily embroidered. Some were of wool, others of fine linen. Purple was predominant, and he seemed to remember that Tyre had been famous for its purple dye. Even the pointed caps were richly hued.

Aia served him a tremendous and welcome meal: smoked goatmeat, olives, figs, date wine, honey and pastries made from unidentified grains, finishing off with whole pomegranates. It was almost too rich for him, after his day of hunger, but he disciplined his appetite and filled his stomach without reaction. "How did you know of this place?" he asked her as he pried out the juicy pomegranate morsels. "Won't the owner object?"

"The owner is a rich merchant who is on the mainland this week negotiating a shipment of cedarwood," she said. "And of course he is checking into the labors of his mainland slaves who make jewelry and statuettes of foreign gods."

"Strange—I have seen nothing like that around here."

"Oh, he has good craftsmen—but of course such baubles are for export only. Fine workmanship brings a better price, you see."

"Even for religious artifacts? I should think—"

"Look," she said. She got up gracefully and pulled aside

294

a curtain. Behind was a voluptuous statuette of a female, with bulging stomach and ponderous breasts, flanked by two sphinxes. "Astarte," she said. "I'll show you how to milk her."

She fetched a cup of goat milk and poured it carefully into a hole in the goddess's head. Then she took a brand from the main fire and touched it to the mossy kindling beneath the statue. The flame caught, warming the entire metal figure.

Suddenly milk spouted from the nipples of the hanging breasts, to pour into a bowl held upon the goddess's belly. Ivo stared, fascinated and a little repelled, though he realized there was nothing either magical or obscene about it.

"The heat melts the wax plugs," Aia explained. "The worshipers don't know that, though. Great moneymaker, I understand."

"But to commercialize other people's religion—"

"Oh, he patronizes his own religion too, never fear. He pays graft to the temple and buys small boys for his pleasures. When he tires of one, he donates that lad to Melqart. He is considered extremely devout."

Ivo, his conscience eased, did not inquire into the matter further. This was as good a domicile to raid as any. "How long are we safe here?"

"No more than a day. Tomorrow night we must leave the city, for they will surely be watching and nowhere in Tyre is there permanent security from the temple."

When the meal was done she took the lamp—a simple clay saucer, undecorated, with a single pinched beak for the wick—and showed him to the sleeping compartment, where soft pelts were piled upon straw. It looked delightful.

Ivo flung himself down in the bed gratefully . . . but soon discovered that he had company. "Even the best of ships come into port at night," she murmured.

She had removed her cloak and other apparel and snuggled under the pelts beside him, close, and he learned that his original estimate of her physical properties had erred conservatively. She was scented with a heavy perfume he could not identify, apart from its effluence of sex appeal, and she was as lithe and sleek as a panther.

Ivo was tired, but he had had a good afternoon's sleep in the temple and was recovering nicely from his more recent wounds and exertions. Aia had taken good care of him, and the flesh injury of his left arm only hurt when he banged it. He felt, all in all, adequate to the occasion—except for one detail.

"My ship docks elsewhere," he said. Then, not wishing to hurt her feelings by too blunt a statement, he tried to explain: "I love another woman, and have no inclination to embrace any but her. I mean no offense to you."

"Your wife?" she asked alertly.

"No."

"Your concubine."

"No."

"It is hard to see what she offers, then, that I do not. You have a very handsome ship, and I have a comfortable port. If we are to travel together—"

"I *love* her. Don't you understand?"

She gazed speculatively at him, the lamplight flickering against the wall behind her head and touching her hair with reddish highlights. "What is her name?"

What harm was there in the truth, here? "Afra," he said, and felt a kind of relief in the confession. "Her name is Afra, and she doesn't love me and I have no right to her, no right at all, but I love her."

"I loved a man once," Aia said, "but he died. Then I saw how foolish it was to depend on such a thing. Love protects nothing, it only restricts pleasure. Take pleasure in me; she will not suffer." A pause. "Or is she near?"

"No. She is thousands of years away."

"Thousands of *years*!" It had been a slip, but he saw that it bothered her only momentarily, since of course she did not understand the connection. "By foot or by ship?"

"By ship," he said, no longer worrying about misunderstandings.

"Then you will never possess her again." She looked at him a moment more. "But how did you get here, so long a journey? You are still young."

"My gods are very powerful."

"Oh." She pondered a little longer. "If the gods of the Canaanite had been stronger, I might have had my lover back."

"How so?" He was not particularly curious about her tragedy, but wanted to divert the conversation from both her immediately amorous intent and her queries about his travels.

"I tried to follow the way of the gods, as Anat brought back Aliyan," she said. "But it didn't work."

"I am not familiar with those names."

"You must come from *very* far away," she murmured. "I will tell you: El was the supreme god of the Canaanite: El the Bull, the Sun. His wife was Asherat-of-the-sea, mother-goddess. Together they begat Baal, god of the mountains, and of the storm and the rain."

"Very interesting," Ivo remarked absently, wondering what he had let himself in for. "How does that relate to your—"

"I'm *telling* you, lover-to-be. Baal's son was Aliyan. The two of them entered into a struggle with Mot of the summer heat, who resides deep in the womb of the earth. They did not return, so Anat went in after them. She was Aliyan's sister and his wife, of course."

"Of course." What was a little incest, between gods? "All in the family."

"Yes. She found Aliyan's body in the abode of the dead, and carried it to the height of Saphon and buried him there with many sacrifices. That's what I did with my lover. I fixed him a very nice stone coffin—"

"I understand."

She took the hint and returned to the mythological narrative. "Then Anat killed Mot, who had killed her husband. With a sickle she cut him, with a winnow she winnowed him; she scattered his flesh in the field, and he was dead."

"I'm sure he was."

"Then she brought Aliyan back to life and set him on Mot's throne. And that was the way the seasons began again. When she killed Mot, that was the annual harvest, of course."

Live and learn! So it was all a variant of the seasonal mythology he had heard in other guises. "But you couldn't bring your lover back to life?"

"No. I tried, but the gods didn't help. He just rotted. That's one reason I don't appreciate Melqart."

"I sympathize. He really should have done more for you."

"These things do pass," she said philosophically. "I was denied my lover, and you are denied yours. Why don't you pretend I am she, and I'll pretend you are he whom I once loved. We shall have joy in one another, while both being true to our memories."

The suggestion, phrased this way, caught him by surprise, and he started to make an angry refusal—but changed his mind. He was not sure what Aia's true motives were, or how cynical might be her intent, but her body was decidedly conducive and the notion had its peculiar appeal. He had faith that somehow he would return to Afra, for this was not his world—but it was not time or distance that separated him from her. Afra would never be his—not so long as she loved a dead man. Not so long as their joint mission required that he give up his identity to the ruthlessly clever Schön.

Was he to torture himself by perpetual abstinence, knowing that his aspiration had no reasonable fulfillment? Why not settle for the *un*reasonable fulfillment, in that case? For what he could get?

Why not?

"All right," he said.

Aia helped him to remove his tunic, touching him with exciting intimacy in the process, and they came together amidst the furry upholstery, shock of flesh against flesh. His left arm gave one twinge and anesthetized itself.

"Speak to me words of love," she murmured, not yet quite acceding to the ultimate. "Tell me what you feel."

Oh, no! "I can't. I never spoke love before."

"No wonder you never impressed her! Don't you know that the whispered word moves a woman as no caress does? Hurry—I'm getting sleepy."

He considered the request, distracted somewhat by her breathing. She was, by touch, as well-endowed as the goddess Astarte, but much younger. "The only words I know that would not be stupid are not my own. They're from a poem, *Evening Song*, by—" But what would she know of Sidney Lanier, unborn these many centuries?

She was silent, so he went ahead with the poem. "Look off, dear love, across the sallow sands, /And mark yon meeting of the sun and sea. / How long they kiss in sight of all the lands. / Ah! longer, longer we."

He recited the two remaining stanzas, frustrated because they had neither rhyme nor meter in Phoenician, and waited for her reaction. There was none.

She was asleep.

She was up before him in the morning, trying on finery from the domicile's stock. "None of these will do," she said sadly, shaking her head. "Too obvious."

"Obvious?"

"If I go into the street in one of these, every person in sight will stare."

She was not unduly pessimistic. She was, by daylight as by night, an extraordinarily lovely girl.

"Did you have suitable pleasure in me last night?" she asked next, with what irony he could not be certain.

"Well, I must admit I expected something else."

"Oh?"

"You fell asleep."

"Oh, yes. I always do. That's why I like a man to hold me."

Ivo tried to make something of this and failed. "While it certainly was stimulating holding you, I did find it a bit frustrating."

"How could that be?"

"I had somehow thought we were going to make love."

She turned to face him, resplendent in a purple skirt that stopped at the waist, and nothing else. Hold a bowl to her midriff . . . , he thought. *"Didn't* you?"

"I said you were asleep."

"Of course."

Ivo looked at her, disgruntled. "You mean you expected me to—to go ahead anyway?"

"Certainly. As many times as you desired."

"Maybe next time," he said, not clear whether he should feel angry or foolish.

They spent the day feasting and resting, since there was no predicting how much of either exercise they would get for some time to come. Aia acquainted him, in snatches, with her own history: Brought to one of the violent Aramean states from her home in the Kingdom of Urartu—Urartu being the most civilized nation of the world, by her definition—because she was the daughter of a traveling trader. Upon maturity, she had undertaken a marriage to a prince of Sidon. "He was the one I loved," she confided. "If Baal will not succor a prince, what good is he?" But she had never seen Sidon; his merchant ship had been waylaid by a galley from Tyre and taken captive, her betrothed killed resisting. Thus, a year ago, she had found herself here, hostage, in daily peril of being added to the temple staff as a ritual prostitute. Only the suggestion of wealthy family connections had saved her from that; a hostage used by Melqart lost value. But the truth was that her family had suffered reverses and was not wealthy, and momentarily the temple accountant would verify this and dissipate her subterfuge. "So you see, I have been waiting for a chance to escape—and now, with you, I have it."

Ivo perceived holes in her story, but did not challenge it. Undoubtedly her past was more mundane than she cared to admit. "How far is Urartu from here?"

"Very far. But I don't want to go there. The politics will have changed, and my family could not afford me now. I will go with you."

Ivo shrugged, appreciating her help but having no idea where to journey. First, however, they had to get off the island that was Tyre, hardly a mile in circumference; then he could make longer-range plans.

They packed as much as could be concealed under heavy cloaks: breads, dried fish, small crocks of wine. The host-merchant had been too canny to leave anything really valuable in his house during his absence; there was no gold or jewelry. Ivo inquired about coins, and learned by her reaction that they had not yet been invented. Trade was largely by barter, with weighed metals increasing as a medium of exchange, but no standardization had occurred.

At dusk Aia took him to the edge of the city, where the high wall balked their escape. Guards paced along the top of it, carrying dim lanterns. Ivo wondered how the open-dish lamps had been adapted for windy wet outdoor use, but they did not get close enough for him to observe. He would be satisfied just to know how they could get past the wall.

The girl knew what she was doing, however. "The factories go through," she whispered. "And no one watches inside at night."

Factories?

She led him into a dark building. He had to hold on to her hand to keep from getting lost, as he could not see at all inside. But that was not his major concern of the moment. His nose was.

The smell was appalling—a suffocating redolence of corruption unlike any he had encountered before. He tried to seal off his nostrils, but the thought of taking such putrefaction unfiltered into his lungs repelled him even more. "What—what?" he whispered.

She laughed. "They can't hear us here. Speak up."

"What died here? A flatulent whale?"

"Oh, you mean the murex. It *is* a little strong, but that's the price of industry."

So industry polluted the atmosphere in ancient days too! "What *is* it?"

"The murex. The shellfish. Don't you know how they process it?"

"No." He hoped they would soon be through the building and into clean air again.

"That's right. I forgot it's a trade secret. Well, they gather the murex, break the shells, extract the fish and dump it in big vats. They let it rot there for some time, until the yellow forms. For the darker shades they have to put it in the sun. Then they filter it down and market it. It's a big industry here; no one outside of the Seven Cities knows the secret. Here, I'll find a shell for you."

She banged about in the dark, and in due course pressed an object into his hand. It was a shell resembling that of a spiny conch.

"Market *what*?" he demanded, perplexed about the point of all this.

"The dyes, of course. Yellow, rose, purple—"

"From decomposing shellfish?" But now he understood. The great mystery of the purple dye of the Phoenicians! He was thankful he hadn't chosen to wear a purple outfit.

At length they emerged, and he took in refreshing

301

lungfuls of partially oxygenated air. They were outside the wall, walking along a narrow starlit beach strewn with crushed shell, hunching in the fortification's shadow in order to avoid the gaze of the patrolling guards.

They arrived circuitously at a docking area where the lesser ships were tied. This was a shallow harbor facing toward the mainland, evidently limited to local shuttling. There were also several coracles: doughnut-shaped little boats or rafts (depending on viewpoint) with calked boards across the inside where the hole might have been. Ivo remembered the macroscope station, and wondered whether the stations of the future—*his* future—would be as far beyond the torus as atomic liners were beyond the coracle.

The tiny boats did not look seaworthy, but Aia assured him that they were the best to be had for a crew of two on the sneak. She climbed into one about six feet in diameter, and he followed her and experimented with the paddles. There were V-notched sticks braced at either side, fulcrums for the long oars; he had to take up one while she managed the other.

He stood within the precarious structure and looked across the water at the mainland. Suddenly it seemed very far away, and the calm, shallow water intervening seemed ominously deep and rough. "Somebody should build a causeway," he muttered.

"We must pull together," she said, "or the craft will simply spin about. Not too hard—I am not as strong as you." Privately, he wondered. She was careful to flatter him regularly, but she was a well-conditioned female. She was uncommonly knowledgeable about nonfeminine affairs, from temple politics to coracle paddling.

After some initial unsteadiness, much of it stemming from his early flinching as he tried to put too much weight on his left arm, they managed to stroke the clumsy craft out of the harbor. The water was gentle, yet even little swells rolled the party about alarmingly, and progress was hard work. It was the coracle's natural ambition to rotate, and only continuous and well-synchronized paddling kept it on course.

In that period of silence and painful effort—why did sword-swinging superheroes never feel their wounds the following day?—Ivo reviewed his recent experience mentally. How had it all come about? It was obviously impossible for him to be where he seemed to be. Could he in some fashion have traversed three thousand or more light-years without benefit of galactic machinery, he still could not have landed in Earth's *past*. The future, yes; the present, possibly; the past, never. The past was forever gone, and anything like time travel brought calamitous paradox. He could not physically participate in past events without altering history, which in turn meant that it was *not* the past; that was the fact that made it unapproachable.

Yet he certainly was *somewhere*. The adventures were too real, the pains too persistent, the series too cohesive, for any idle nightmare. It was becoming evident that he was not going to get out of this by himself. He knew too little, and had such slender resources that he had to depend on a mysterious woman.

Was it time to confess his own inadequacy and summon Schön? He had been shying away from this notion, but he knew that Schön would place the historical perspective instantly, and pinpoint not only the year but the exact degree by which this reality differed from Earth's true history. Schön would know how to reverse whatever circumstances had brought him here, and thus how to bring back Afra and Groton and Beatryx and the Neptune base.

But Schön might very well have his personality destroyed by the ambushing destroyer in Ivo's memory, before any of the rest of it came to pass. Then he would be gone, not merely buried, and with him that fragment, that waking dream that was Ivo.

Better not to chance it. The pawn was still pinned. This was a problem he had to handle by himself.

As though that decision were catalytic, another notion came to him. He realized what had bothered him about Aia, the first time they had spoken together. "Who are you?" he had demanded, and she had replied immediately, "I am Aia. I don't worship Melqart or like human sacrifice." Something like that.

How had she known that he was fleeing the temple, or why?

Certainly it could have been a guess—but she had not been asking him. She had known. She had said the one thing calculated to assuage his suspicions, and had followed it up with enough blandishment and personal motivation to keep them lulled. She had said that she wanted to escape, but it seemed that her real intention was to stick with him, wherever he might go.

He thought back to his interview with Mattan. The man obviously had not been satisfied, yet he had not pursued the matter of Ivo's origins. Instead he had forwarded his guest to the temple for further interrogation—and the guards had conveniently staged a giveaway dialogue.

Mattan was clever; there could be no questioning that. Suppose he had had firm suspicions that Ivo was a spy who refused to talk, spinning any fantasy to avoid the truth? Would torture be effective? Perhaps—but there was also the risk of reprisals, especially in the event the visitor turned out to be innocent after all, or of powerful connection. Perhaps, even, he had been infiltrated to provoke an embarrassing incident. Why not, then, prompt the spy to bolt for home, and follow him there? What surer method to fathom the truth?

A skilled spy would know many dialects, naturally. A spy would comprehend the dialogue of the mercenaries, and react accordingly. Ivo remembered how handy that sword had been—virtually proffered to his hand, as the guard turned to him at the foot of the temple steps. How slow those men had been to react, though they were obviously long-time professionals, so that even his clumsy efforts had availed.

Of course, the priest had tried to trick him—but perhaps the man hadn't had the word yet, or was merely cowardly. Then the chase through the city—with all avenues of escape closed off but one, and attractive Aia waiting at the end of that one.

She had been so eager to ingratiate herself with him—but not personally involved enough to stay awake for the romantic denouement. Well, this released him of any obligation he might have felt for her assistance.

What would have happened, had he meekly accompanied the two guards into the temple? Probably nothing. He would have demonstrated thereby his ignorance of the

mercenary dialect, his innocence of spylike suspicions, his
general naïvete about temple politics. He might then
have been treated with the courtesy due a genuine traveler
from a distant land. His gift of tongues had betrayed him.

Gift of tongues?

He stopped rowing, and the coracle jerked about as
Aia's stroke met no counteraction. "Careful, lover," she
said.

"It occurs to me that I have nowhere to go," he told
her, watching her as carefully as he could in the dark.

"Nowhere? But—"

"America is much too far away, and I would be no
better off at any other local city than I am at Tyre. We
might as well go back."

"But Mattan—"

"What *of* Mattan? I'm sure I can explain about the
mistake to him, and everything will be all right."

"All right! After he sent you as sacrifice to Melqart?"

"I was only going to the temple to talk with the priests
there. Mattan told me so. I suppose the one that met me
assumed I was to be sacrificed, but they should have all
that straightened out by now. These little errors happen. I
should have realized then that it was a common misunderstanding."

"A misunderstanding! How blind can you—" She
paused. "Well, what about *me?* Aren't you going to help
me escape?"

"From what?"

"From the temple. I told you how they meant to make
me serve as—"

"You told me that there was no harm a man could do
you. You could have a good life at the temple, and a nice
comfortable sleep every night with a new ship in your
port, just the way you like it."

For a moment he thought she was going to hit him with
the paddle; but her words, when they came, were low. "Do
you know what Mattan does with an unsuccessful spy?"

"One he catches, you mean? I do have some inkling."

"One he *assigns.*"

Now he caught her meaning. "The sacrifice?"

"Bride of Melqart—and our Baal has a fiery member."

"Suppose we land you on the mainland, then, and I can
305

paddle back by myself. I want to see Mattan and clear this thing up as soon as possible."

"You couldn't handle this craft by yourself."

"Maybe I can find a canoe or something. I'll make do. You can travel back to Urartu."

"I didn't really come from Urartu."

"Strange. I *do* really come from America."

"Stay with me," she pleaded, setting down the paddle and reaching for him. "I can guide you past the soldiers that are watching us now, and when we are free I promise you I will stay awake until you are exhausted. Until the very hull of your ship is blistered. I will steal valuables for you. I will—"

"Steady," he said, worried about the equilibrium of the craft as Aia sought to approach and embrace him. She did have a fine body, but her mind appealed to him less and less. "Unfortunately your promises lack conviction. Or are they threats?"

She let go. "What do you want?"

"I want, believe it or not, to go home. It is not a journey you can share. I travel to the stars."

"I can take you to the finest astrologer!" she said eagerly.

He began to laugh, harshly. Then, as he had done a night ago, he reconsidered. He just might be able to use a good astrologer. Hadn't Groton told him that they had traditionally been the most educated of men? "Where?"

"It is said that the very best reside in Babylonia, particularly the city of Harran. We can join a trading caravan—"

"How long would such a trip take?"

"It is across the great deserts where the nomads raid."

"How *long?*"

"Not long. Thirty days, maybe only twenty-five."

"Scratch Babylon. Who is there in Tyre?"

She considered disconsolately. "There is Gorolot—but he is very old. However, in other cities—"

"Should be very wise, then. Is he an honest scholar or a faker?"

"Honest. That is why he is so poor. But elsewhere there are—"

"Gorolot will do. We'll see him tonight."

"Tonight! He is already asleep."

"We'll have to wake him."

"We have no money for his fee."

"Do you want to help or don't you?"

"Will you leave Tyre after you see him?"

"Sleeping Beauty, I may leave this *world* after I see him!"

She twisted the paddle until the craft was in position for the return voyage.

"What I have in mind for payment," Ivo said, "is service. If Gorolot is old and poor and honest, he has no servants, right? A strong young woman could do marvels for his household, and perhaps encourage business too. And—"

"I am no household slave!" she exclaimed.

"And Mattan would never suspect that the household slave of an aged astrologer could be an unsuccessful counterspy or potential bride of Melqart."

She paddled silently.

Gorolot, once roused by strenuous clamor, had the aspect of a sleepy old fraud. His eyes were sunken, his beard straggly and white, his clothing unkempt. He agreed to consider Ivo's case once the terms had been clarified.

"I wish I had a better offer to make," Ivo said regretfully. "But I may not be in these parts long. Aia—you'll have to change her name—isn't too reliable and will need a lot of supervision—"

"I will not!" she exclaimed angrily. "I can do the job as well as any girl in the city."

"And you dare not entrust the daily marketing for staples to her, because she can't bargain well—"

"I bargain very well! I'll show you!"

"And she'll probably run away within a week or two, but at least—"

"I will not!"

"But she may be all right, if she doesn't fall asleep on the job."

"I—" She shot him a dirty look and twitched her hip, conscious at last of the needling.

The two men sat down at Gorolot's official table. Ivo saw that there were no flashy pictures of stars, planets or other symbols in evidence, and the man had donned no special robe. Probably the soiled tunic on his back was all he owned. The effect was unimpressive, even though such things had no inherent validity.

"What is your date of birth?" Gorolot inquired.

Ivo hesitated, but found after reflection that he was able to express it in local chronology, except for the year. That he solved by taking his age and figuring back to the year he would have been born, had he been born into this world and age. It came to the fifteenth year of the reign of Hiram the Great.

Gorolot brought out a scroll of stripped camel hide together with several clay tablets. "Do not expect too much," he warned. "The meanings of the motions of the planets are not yet well known to us, and many times have I made mistakes. Often the Babylonian interpretations differ from the Egyptian, and I do not know the truth of it. I offer only the portents; I do not vouch for their authenticity."

Ivo nodded. An honest man, yes, and a humble one. How many potentially well-paying customers did he alienate by his candor?

For almost an hour the astrologer pored over his records and assessed the imperatives of the seven planets— Uranus, Neptune and Pluto being unknown to Phoenician astronomy—questioning Ivo occasionally, while Aia showed her mounting impatience. "Others give instant readings," she whispered.

"Others are charlatans," Ivo replied. Gorolot labored on, unheeding.

At last he looked up. "Is there some event in your life that—"

Ivo gave him the same event he had given Groton, modified slightly in detail.

Still the astrologer was not satisfied. He mumbled and shook his head and rechecked his texts and runes fretfully. "I cannot help you," he said abruptly.

Aia started to object, but Ivo gestured her to silence. "You have already helped me considerably," he said. "I know you see something. What is it?"

"Nothing."

"You have spent all this time contemplating nothing?" Aia demanded.

"The signs are contradictory, as I warned you they

might be," Gorolot said to Ivo. "But more than that, and it disturbs me deeply, some aspects are sure, yet they are the least credible of all. Either you have never been born, or you come from so far away that you are not truly under any of the signs I know." He shrugged. "You must have been born, for I see you here, and I do not credit genii. Yet the signs are all-inclusive. So there is error—but not one it is in me to fathom. I am old and tired, and perhaps my brain is weakening. Take your servant-girl and go."

"You admit you are a charlatan!" Aia exclaimed.

"No," Ivo said firmly. "He is right. I have never been born—but I *will* be born thousands of years hence. And in my time the constellations have moved, and there are newly discovered planets; some of their meanings have—er, developed with the march of time."

Gorolot peered at him over the flickering pewter lamp. "My charts suggest that this is so, but still it is a thing beyond my experience. I deem myself a sensible man, and all my life I have denied the supposed impact of the supernatural on the affairs of men. Yet here you are, real but inexplicable. Surely you mock me?"

Aia was silent now, looking at Ivo intently. The red in her hair was stronger, her features almost familiar in a non-Phoenician sense. She was extremely lovely.

"Do you speak other languages?" Ivo asked the astrologer. The man nodded. "I will show you that I am not of this world. I have the gift of tongues."

"Are you familiar with this one?" Gorolot said in a foreign language, smiling.

"Egyptian, southern dialect," Ivo said in the same language.

"And this?"

"Phrygian—as a Lydian tribesman would speak it."

"No one in Tyre knows this one but me, and I know it only from my texts," Gorolot said carefully.

"No wonder. It is parent-stock Etruscan. If I may—here is a correction on your phrasing." He gave it.

Gorolot stared at him. "You are right. I remember now. You speak it far better than I." He had lapsed into Phoenician. "You *do* have the gift of tongues, and you are far too young to have mastered it here. You *are*—"

309

"I don't believe it," Aia said, half believing it.

"So you come from Ugarit—peasant stock," Ivo told her. She looked dismayed, and he turned back to Gorolot.

The man's features changed. The white beard faded, leaving him clean-shaven. His face filled out. Behind him the mud-plaster wall metamorphosed into metal.

Groton was opposite him, a look of incredulous hope on his face. To the side stood Afra, weeping silently.

"I'm back," Ivo said.

"It was Schön's doing," Ivo explained. Afra obviously had caught on to his secret, so no further pretense was in order. "It took me a long time to catch on to that, possibly because he tried to hide the evidence from me, more likely because I didn't really want to believe it. But even a genius can't convince an ordinary person that white is purple. Not always. Not when the purple stinks." But he hadn't told them about the dye yet. "And that gift of tongues was the unmistakable key. Schön has it, and he had to make it available to me in order to have me participate properly in that world; otherwise I would have popped out again quickly. When I realized that, I was on the way to victory, because I knew he was behind it all."

"Why?" Groton wanted to know.

"Why did he do it? Easy. Because he wants to take over, and he can't do it unless I abdicate. He tried to drive me into a situation that only he could save me from, hoping that I would capitulate. Maybe he forgot how stubborn I was."

"But the destroyer—"

"Either he doesn't know about that, or he isn't afraid of it."

"Why didn't he give you just one language—Phoenician?"

"It doesn't work that way. He can't give me part of a talent. Only so many speech centers in the brain, as I make it."

"But that would mean that English takes up one," Afra said, "and all the other languages of the world, the other. That isn't reasonable."

"Schön isn't reasonable, by our definition. Maybe he

310

has some other setup. Anyway, it's everything, or it's nothing."

"Do you have it now?" Afra asked, mopping her face. She looked so much like Aia that it set him back. Obviously one girl had been modeled from the other, just as one astrologer had emulated the other.

"No."

"He took it away when you broke out?" Groton asked.

"No. I left it there. I didn't want it."

The two looked at him.

"It's hard to explain. This arrangement between us—it isn't absolutely set. He can give me things, like the intuitive computations, and I can accept them. But I can't take anything he doesn't make available and he can't force anything on me that I refuse to accept. This episode was a special case; I was off-balance and tired, and I accepted more than I should have. Then I had to fight my way out by *his* rules, the hard way. But I stopped it there; I didn't take the gift with me."

"But why?" Afra cried. "The gift of tongues! Every language anyone ever spoke!"

"Because each trait I accept from him brings me that much closer to him. I started with two, and that's the way I like it. I don't need tongues."

"But if you can have all that and remain yourself—"

This was like arguing with Aia. "I *can't*. As I stand, I have two parts out of, say, twenty that make up Schön. Tongues would be a third part, and then I might be tempted to gamble on artistic ability or eidetic recollection. And after that I might get a craving for physical dexterity—you know, be a champion at sports, be able to do sleight-of-hand, control the roll of dice—and at some point Schön would achieve controlling interest. It's more subtle than the destroyer, but the effect is the same, for me." And suddenly another reason he had been able to avoid the destroyer popped up: he had had a lifetime of practice protecting his individuality from oblivion.

"That's how you—turn into Schön?"

"That's one way. There are others." He decided to change the subject. "Of course, I'll never know whether I really *had* tongues. It could all have been American English, with the suggestion of translation. Just enough for verisimilitude in the dream."

"Dream?" Afra said.

"The Phoenician episode I summarized for you. It seemed like several days, and it was real for me, but—"

"Maybe we'd better play off one of the tapes," Groton said.

"Tapes?" It was Ivo's turn to be perplexed.

Afra was already busy. "Listen." She switched on the playback.

A stream of gibberish poured out of the speaker. "This was yesterday," Afra said. "That is, about twenty-seven hours ago. Your voice."

"I was *speaking?*"

"Ancient Phoenician. Fluently. I was able to pick out words only here and there, so we set up a program and ran the tape through the computer and patched up a translation. Do you want to hear it?"

"I'd better."

She lifted the printout. "Are you trusting yourself to a stranger? A brigand, perhaps a rapist or murderer? No. Ifarsh of America. I was captured by a ship and brought to Mattan for questioning. What I don't comprehend is the reason he sent me for sacrifice. How could—"

"That's enough," Ivo said, embarrassed. "Did you translate—everything I said?"

"Yes. We had to."

"We rigged up a real-time continuous translation," Groton said, "and monitored it. In case there was any way we could help. Just now you messed it by switching to non-programmed languages."

Ivo tried to remember all the things he had said, particularly to Aia. He felt his cheeks growing hot.

"How did you finally fight your way out of it?" Groton asked him. "We knew something special was happening, but we couldn't tell *what*. You were telling someone *there* about your presence *here*, but—"

"I was telling *you*, Harold." And with that statement he had another realization: that this man had become Harold instead of Groton in thought as well as speech. That was significant. "Or at least your ancestor-in-spirit. An astrologer, and an honest and knowledgeable man. I remembered
312

that they were the best-educated men in those days, because they were the true astronomers and scientists before those fields were recognized as such, always questing for the secrets of things. It seemed to me that if I could convince one intelligent person in that world that I didn't belong there—literally—then the framework would be rent, or at least punctured. And I guess I convinced him, because it happened." He thought about the implications. "I hope Gorolot wasn't too upset when I disappeared."

"Aia will console him," Afra said with gentle irony. It had not taken her long to revert to her normal cynicism. Had she been crying for *him,* that moment he first returned?

"Similar to punching through by gravitational collapse," Harold said. "This would have been credibility collapse, though. You do believe that world was real?" He was asking for an opinion rather than a defense.

"I would hate to believe that it *wasn't.* If I was really speaking Phoenician—"

"I think I understand." Harold looked about. "We'd better take a break, now that it's over. This has been rough on all of us, and my wife doesn't even—"

Beatryx appeared, carrying a tray. Incongruously, that reminded Ivo that now they were in a gravity defocuser, rather than the intensifier of Triton days, since they were buried in massive Neptune. How much stranger this situation was than the one he had visited!

Beatryx saw him. "Ivo!" she cried immediately. "You're back!"

That seemed to make it complete.

Though less than three days had passed, it was a novelty to sleep in a modern bed again, and to be free of the pain of a flesh wound on the arm and a cut on the hand. He had been too much a part of the world of Tyre, had experienced too much there. He had sought only to leave it—yet now he was sorry, perversely, that it was gone. Was it that he craved the adventure it had offered?

There he had been a man—a man in constant danger and discomfort, but a man. Here he was no more than a surrogate, a mild-mannered reporter waiting for Superman to take over. He wondered whether, if the offer of such adventure were made again, he would accept it. Give Schön what he wanted, in exchange for that satisfaction. For Schön could do that, if he chose; and the covenant would bind him. He could relegate Ivo to a fantasy fragment, his personality turned inward instead of outward, and let him live out his life there untrammeled by the inadequacies of the present. Perhaps it would be a short life, but—

There was a motion nearby that made him jump. "Hello, Ivo."

Afra.

She sat down beside him: fresh, white, perfumed, elegantly packaged. "I think I know what you're thinking, Ivo. You're nostalgic for that world."

"I guess I am, now that it's over."

"And you're afraid you might go back to it the next time you use the macroscope, or something like it."

He nodded. She was so beautiful in the half-light that he felt her presence as heat radiating against the side of his body toward her. The effect might be subjective, but it was powerful.

"This Aia—was she me?"

"No. She was a spy, a courtesan."

"She still could have been me, Ivo. That name is close. And I was used to—to keep you at the station, so that Schön would be available. I'm not very proud of that."

"You didn't know."

"I *should* have known. I don't like being stupid, particularly about a thing like that. Brad told me to be nice to you. I—I'm trying to say I'm sorry. About that and a lot of things. But that isn't why I came here."

He felt it safest not to comment. Why *did* a lovely woman come to the bed of an admirer? To reminisce?

"I suppose it's like the—the handling. I'll just have to *say* it. And *do* it. I heard what you said to her. About me."

Oh-oh. "I was afraid of that. I didn't mean to—"

"Don't *you apologize to me! I'm* the one at fault. All I can say is that I was dense, or blind, or both. I didn't know, I really didn't know—until I read it on the printout. I didn't know you loved me."

"I didn't want you to know. I'd rather you forgot it."

She did not move, but it was as though she leaned over him where he lay. "That isn't the past tense, is it, Ivo. You love me now—and I *won't* forget it. I—well, you know my situation. I can't say I love you or ever will."

"I understand."

"That Aia—she offered herself to you, and you wanted her. But you told her—"

Ivo felt his face burning again. "Can't we just let that pass?"

"No we can't, Ivo. You held her in your arms and she made you recite poetry—but then you didn't make love to her. And you could have."

"How do you know? It was *my* vision."

"Not entirely, Ivo. I *do* know. Did you think you were having an innocent wet dream? *I was with you.*"

He had thought he was already embarrassed, but once again she had made him realize that he had been naïvely skirting the edge of the chasm. Again he had fallen in.

"I know this hurts you, but I have to say it. The girl you held was me. Naked, ready—"

What possible comment? "But if I'd—"

"I said you *could* have. I won't say I'm sorry you didn't."

"But *why?*"

"I had this crazy idea that if I could somehow bridge the gap between us—between your world and mine—it would bring you back. I felt responsible . . . maybe guilty is the word. It wasn't premeditated. There was something nagging at my mind—something Brad once told me about Schön—but it wouldn't come clear. I did realize where Schön was, of course, though it took me entirely too long to put two and two together. And I think if Schön had won, I could have—I don't know. I just had to *do* something. I was monitoring the tape, the others were asleep, and . . . the time seemed right. And—we do need you, Ivo. Objectively. We can't locate ourselves in the galaxy without you. Not close enough."

She had been talking rapidly, throwing justifications at him as quickly as she thought of them. As though she had to apologize for ever having offered her body to him in any guise. And, he thought bitterly, if she felt ashamed of

315

the impulse, then her apology was in order. She had said once that she did not like acting like a whore.

She took his silence as an objection. "We had to have you back. It was that simple. It isn't as though there are any physical secrets between us, after the handling and the melting. If you were falling and I could offer a hand to pull you back—the principle is the same. You did it for me, on Triton, with your trial. So this time it was my turn to—to contribute."

The irony was that it might have worked. Could he possibly have made physical love to Afra and *not* been drawn back to her world? He doubted it.

"I thank you for the gesture," he said, feeling quixotic.

"Now that we understand each other," she said, relieved, "the rest is easy. I want you to know that this world needs you more than that one does. So—this world *offers* you more. It is, as I said, that simple."

"It's still too complicated for me. What are you getting at now?"

"You love me. I need you. That's not the same thing, I know, but it's honest. If my embrace will hold you here, I give it to you. Anything Aia had for you—I will match. Anything *any* woman has for you. You don't have to travel to any other world—you *mustn't* travel—"

"I suppose you *are* pretty much like Aia."

There was no flickering lamplight, but the classic lines of her forehead, nose and chin wavered in his gaze. "That's no compliment, but it's the truth," she said. "We sell what we have for what we need. Men their brains, women their bodies. Better that than hypocrisy."

There was a silence of several minutes. Ivo thought of all the things he might say, but knew she knew them already. She had said one thing and meant another, earlier; now the truth was coming into view as the base warred with the sublime. She was offering paid love—the last thing he wanted from her, but all she had, realistically, to give.

Again the question he had asked himself in Tyre: why *not* settle for the best he could get? He had been willing to embrace Aia's body in lieu of Afra; why not accept *Afra's* body—in lieu of Afra? Both women had come to terms with their necessities, knowing they could not bring their lovers back to life; why not he?

Yet if he had learned any lesson in Tyre, it was this: *there was no salvation in a surrogate.*

"Maybe next time," he said.

She did not move or look at him. "Look off, dear Love, across the sallow sands. . . ."

She was still sitting there when he fell asleep.

It was night in the marshes of Glynn. He had either to wait a few hours and try again, or travel to the daylight side of the globe.

He felt Afra's hand take his left. "If you go, I will don the goggles and follow you," she said. It was a threat, for she would encounter not Tyre but the destroyer.

"I'm on guard now, and rested," he replied. "It's safe." But he felt better for the touch of her fingers, their almost-affectionate pressure. Last night he had turned her down; today, oddly, she was warmer toward him.

Tyre appeared unchanged, superficially. Warships still docked at the ports of the island city and the buildings remained tall and crowded. He recognized the temple complex and the area where he had met Aia, that night.

"We don't seem to have moved," he said, perplexed. He wondered how he could have seen the city so accurately before, since they had probably removed him from the macroscope as soon as he fell into the Mediterranean. He *must* have been there!

"More likely it's a fifty-year jump," Afra said. "Backward or forward or sidewise. Can you find a landmark?" She still had not relinquished his hand, except for the brief periods he needed it for coordinated adjustments.

He centered on Gorolot's house, quite curious and a little nervous. Strangers occupied it, and the configurations of the structure had changed, as though the house had been rebuilt. Ivo lingered, disappointed, though he remained apprehensive about the effect the sight of Gorolot—or Aia—might have on him.

"You *can* go back," a masculine voice said in his ear, in Phoenician.

Ivo clenched Afra's hand. "Pull me out!" he said urgently. "It's Schön!"

317

He felt her fingers returning his pressure, as from a distance, and the tug of the goggles coming off—but the scene did not shift.

"Why do you fight me?" Schön asked in Ivo's voice.

"Because you may be destroyed the moment you take over, for one thing. Don't you know that?"

"When I take over," Schön said as though never doubting the eventuality, "I will have the whole of your experience to draw on, should I require it. At present I have almost none of it. It is exceedingly difficult for me even to contact you, since you don't let go until your mind is distracted. So I don't know what your problem is—but I do know there is something intriguing afoot."

Someone was still tugging at a distant extremity. "Hold up a minute, Afra," Ivo called. "He only wants to talk."

"I don't trust him," she said from the far reaches.

"Give us two minutes."

"Little puritan Ivo has a girlfriend now?" Schön inquired. Obviously he knew—but how much?

"No. Now look, I have to explain why I can't let you have the body. We're in touch with a nonhuman signal that—"

"I can give you romantic prowess. No woman can withstand that. A warty toad could seduce a princess."

"I know, but no. Now this galactic civilization has broadcast what we call the destroyer signal that—"

"How about turning me loose for a specified interval? Just long enough to lick this problem of yours."

"No! You don't understand what I'm—"

"Junior, are you trying to lecture *me* on—"

A cold shock hit him, reminding him of the original plunge into the Mediterranean. Ivo looked up to find Afra standing before him, the bucket in her hands. "Yeah, that did it," he said, shaking himself. She had doused him with icewater: three gallons over his head.

"Are you going to be trapped every time you use the scope?" she demanded. "You were talking in Phoenician again, but I got the bit about two minutes, not that I waited that long. What did he want?"

"He wants out," Ivo said, shivering. He began to strip off his clothing. "But he can't *get* out until I let him."

"What about the destroyer?"

"He doesn't seem to know about that, or want to hear it. I couldn't make him listen."

"He *must* know about it. What about that message— 'My pawn is pinned'? He knew then."

Ivo, bouncing up and down to warm up, halted. The wet floor was slippery under his bare toes. "I didn't think of that. He must be lying."

"That doesn't make sense either. If he knew the destroyer would get him, why should he expose himself to it? And if he knows it *won't*, why not say so? This isn't a game of twenty questions."

"Now that I think of it," Ivo admitted, "he didn't sound much like a genius to me. I've never actually talked directly with him before, but—it was more like a kid bargaining."

"A child." She brought a towel and started patting him dry, and he realized that for the first time he had undressed unselfconsciously before her. They had all seen each others' bodies during the meltings, but this was not such an occasion. Barriers were still coming down unobtrusively. "How old was he when—?"

"I'm not sure. It took some time to—to set me up. I remember some events back to age five, but there are blank spots up until eight or nine. That doesn't necessarily mean *he* took over then—"

"So Schön never lived as an adult."

"I guess not, physically."

"*Or* emotionally. *You* matured, not he. Is it surprising, then, that he appears childish to us? His intelligence and talent don't change the fact that he is immature. He likes to play games, to send out mysterious messages, create worlds of imagination. For him, right and wrong are merely concepts; he has no devotion to adult truth. No developed conscience. And if the notion of the destroyer frightens him—why, he puts it out of his mind. He no longer admits its danger. He thinks that he can conquer anything just by tackling it with gusto."

Ivo nodded thoughtfully, looking about for some dry shorts. "But he's still got more knowledge and ability than any adult."

She brought the shorts. "A sixteen-year-old boy has better reflexes than most mature men, and more knowl-

319

edge about automotive engineering—turbo or electric or hydraulic—but he's still the world's worst driver. It takes more than knowledge and ability; it takes control and restraint. Obviously Schön doesn't have that."

"If he began driving—what a crash he could make!"

"Let's just defuse the destroyer first," she said, smiling grimly. "You were right all along: we're better off without Schön."

CHAPTER 9

"We have made," Afra announced as though it were news, "five jumps—and we are now farther removed from the destroyer source than we were when we started."

"Schön says he can get us there within another six," Ivo said. "He has been figuring the configurations."

"How does he *know* them? I thought he didn't have access to—no, I see he does. He's there when we pinpoint our distance by Earth history, and he probably picks up everything you hear when you're on the scope. Though how he can figure anything meaningful from the pitiful information we have—"

"Let's review," Harold said. "Obviously there is something we have missed—unless Schön is lying."

"He *could* be lying," Ivo said. "But he probably wouldn't bother. He wouldn't be interested in coming out unless he were sure he could accomplish something—and he wouldn't have the patience to go through many more jumps."

"Our first jump was about fifty years, to 1930," Harold said. "Our second was almost three thousand years, to 930 BC as we make it. A 2,860 year difference, but actually a larger jump because it landed us on the opposite side of Earth, spacially. Then another fifty-year jump to 890 BC, slantwise. This could get confusing if it were not so

321

serious! Finally, jumps to 975 and 975 BC—just sliding around the arc, getting nowhere. But apparently Schön can make something of it."

Afra turned to Ivo. "You have his computational ability. Can't you map the pattern he sees?"

"No. He's using more than mathematics, or at least is making use of more factors than I know how to apply. He can be a lot more creative than I can; his reasoning is an art, while mine is conventional."

"Maybe he's using astrology," Afra said sourly.

Harold shook his head. "Astrology doesn't—"

"Chances are he knows it, though," Ivo said. "So it's no joke. If it is possible to make a space-curvature map of the galaxy by astrological means, Schön can do it. He—"

"Forget it," Afra snapped.

But Harold was thoughtful. *He believes,* Ivo thought, having this come home to him personally for the first time, though of course he had known it intellectually before. *He really believes.*

And suppose Schön believed too?

How was any one person to know what was valid and what was not? Even if astrology were a false doctrine, Harold had already applied it to better effect than Afra had her doctrines.

"I wonder whether we haven't taken too naïve a view of jumpspace," Afra said after a pause. "We've been thinking of a simple string-in-circle analogy—but a four-dimensional convolution would be a system of a different order. We can't plot it on a two-dimensional map."

"I could build a spatial-coordinates box," Harold said. "Intersecting lines and planes of force to hold the items in place, the whole thing transparent so we can study any section from any angle. If we plotted our five known points of tangency and looked for an applicable framework, we might be able to begin deriving equations—"

Afra grabbed his arm, abruptly excited. "How soon?"

The sixth jump was a large one, but that was the least of it.

They contemplated the figures and could not deny them.

"It *is* a different destroyer," Afra said.

They were another five thousand light-years slantwise

from Sol, and Earth history stood at approximately 4,000 BC. The destroyer signal that bathed Earth in 1980-81 was gone—but sixteen thousand light-years down a divergent azimuth was the point source of a second emission virtually identical to the first.

"I suspect," Harold said, "that we are up against a genuine galactic conspiracy. A paranoiac's delight."

"I'm ecstatic," Afra said.

He cocked a finger at her warningly, as though she were a child of five. "It cannot be coincidence that similar broadcasters of this nature are set up thirty-thousand light-years from each other, the range of each about eighteen thousand miles, presumably expanding in all directions at light velocity. Note how both skirt the middle edge of the galaxy. Six so placed, with a seventh in the center, would cover the vast majority of the stars available."

"Which seems to prove that their target is *all* civilization, Earth's being incidental," Afra agreed.

"Which may also mean that those sources are armed," Ivo said. "Physically, I mean. They couldn't have stood up for all these millennia, against all the species we know exist, otherwise." He paused. "Do we go on?"

"Yes we go on!" Afra said so fiercely it alarmed him. Every so often she still furnished such a reminder of her personal involvement in this mission. Her memory of Brad—the god-prince who had died and not returned to life.

They were becoming blasé about galactic travel, or at least inured; but the tenth jump amazed them all. It was about thirty-five thousand light-years—and it placed them entirely outside the Milky Way Galaxy by approximately thirty thousand. They had jumped almost vertically out of the great disk.

There were no destroyer sources in evidence.

The party gathered to look at their galaxy on the "direct vision" screen. This was actually an image relayed from sensors set into orbit around Neptune. Harold had not been idle during the intervals of recuperation between hops, and he had sophisticated machinery to play with. The mini-satellites even survived the jumps without disturbance, once the anchor-field had been modified to account for such motion.

Below them it lay, filling well over a ninety-degree arc: the entire galaxy of man's domicile, viewed broadside *by* man for the first time. The pallid white of the stars and nebulae deflowered by Earth's atmosphere existed no more; the colossal fog of interstellar gas and dust had been banished from the vicinity of the observer. The result was a view of the Milky Way Galaxy as it really existed— ten thousand times as rich as that perceivable from Earth.

Color, yes—but not as any painter could represent, or any atmosphere-blinded eye could fathom. Red in the center where the old lights faded; blue at the fringe where the fierce new lights formed. A spectrum between—but also so much more! Here the visible splay extended beyond the range for which nomenclature existed, and rounded out the hues for which human names did exist. A mighty swirl, a multiple spiral of radiance, wave on wave of tiny bright particles, merged yet discrete. The Milky Way was translucent, yet mind-staggeringly intricate in three, in four dimensions.

At the fringe it was wafer-thin, sustained largely by the masses of cosmic dust that smeared out thousands of stars with every hideously compelling wisp and whorl. Within this sparse galactic atmosphere, nestled in tentacles of gas, floated Sol and its solar debris: hardly worthy of notice, compared to the main body; indeed, invisible without magnification.

And, clear from this exquisite vantage, the pattern of the stellar conglomeration that was the galaxy emerged: the great spiral arms, coiling outward from the center, doubled bands of matter beginning as the light of massed stars and terminating as the black of thinning dust. Not flat, not even; the ribbons were twisted, showing now broadside, now edgewise, resembling open mobius strips or the helix of galactic DNA.

And yes, he thought, yes—the galaxy was a cell, bearing its cosmic organelles and glowing in its animation; motile, warm-bodied, evolving, its life span enduring for tens of billions of years.

Ivo felt a physical hunger, and realized that he had been looking at the galaxy for many hours. He had been stupefied by it, as a worshiper was said to be blessedly stupefied by confrontation with his god.

He broke the trance and looked about him. Afra stood nearest, lovely in her mortal fashion, her eyes encompassing a hundred billion stars, her lungs inhaling cubic parsecs of space.

Harold turned to face him, and he noticed with a shock that the man, like the women, had lost weight sometime in the past few months. Everyone was changing! "Did you observe the globular clusters? Hundreds of them orbiting the galaxy, a million stars in each. Look!" He pointed. "That one must be within ten thousand light-years of us."

Ivo saw what he had somehow missed before: a glob of light near at hand and about as far out from the galactic disk as they were. It resembled a small galaxy except that it was shapeless, a Rorschach blob of brilliance. It was as though some of the cotton had drifted free when the fabric of the main tapestry was woven. At its fringe, as with the main galaxy, the stars were sparse, but they thickened at the center, converting from blue to midrange. This cluster was younger than the main body.

There were many others in sight, most closer in toward the galactic nucleus. Each, perhaps, was a cosmos in itself, possessing lifebearing planets and stellar civilizations. The overall pattern of the entire group of clusters was spherical—or at least hemispherical, since he could not see what lay on the far side of the main disk. Though he could not perceive individual motion, it struck him that the clusters were in fact orbiting the center of the galaxy—elliptical orbits, brushing very near to its rim and riding higher over its broad face. Some even seemed to be colliding with the galactic fringe, though that was so diffuse that it was a matter of interpretation.

Almost, he could picture the original ball of gas and dust, turning grandly in space and throwing out gauze and sparks. The majority of the material remained in the plane of rotation, to become the spiral arms and the overall disk-shape; but a few mavericks took separate courses, and were the clusters.

How did the universe appear to a creature looking out from a planet aboard one of these island systems? Did any cultures aspire to descend to the mighty mother complex?

Was their god a whirlpool thirty thousand parsecs in diameter?

Beatryx emerged from the kitchen area, and Ivo realized that it had been the smell of cooking that had first brought his attention to his stomach. She was typically the bringer of nourishment. It was good that *someone* was practical!

At last Afra came out of it. "We are within the traveler field, but beyond the destroyer," she said musingly. "We are thirty thousand light-years toward the traveler—so it will be passing Earth and the galaxy for at least that period in the future. Obviously it preceded the destroyers, too, or they would have started earlier and reached out this far. And that suggests—"

"That the point of the destroyer may be merely to suppress the alien beam," Harold finished for her. "Since myriad local stations come through nicely, they cannot have incited the destroyer."

"Talk of xenophobia!" she exclaimed. "Just because it proved that there was superior technology elsewhere—!"

Harold cocked his head at her. "Is that the way you see it? I might have reasoned along another line."

"I am aware of *your*—"

"Soup's on!" Beatryx called, once more abridging the discussion appropriately.

Because there was no destroyer here, they turned on the main screen to watch Ivo work. Afra could have used the macroscope herself, but there was now a certain group recognition that this was Ivo's prerogative, and that practice had brought him to a level of proficiency no other person could match without a similar apprenticeship. It was his show.

He had stage fright.

He avoided the routine programs, now offered in such splendor and multiplicity that it would require years to index them by hand. Their several language coding families were of course unfamiliar to the others; Ivo had mastered the basics only after intense concentration, though all were to some extent similar to the technique of the destroyer itself. He also avoided the traveler signal (when had that term come into use?); that would come in its own time. Instead he concentrated on the nonbroadcast band and searched for Earth: the world of Man as it was thirty thousand years ago.

And couldn't pick it up.

He rechecked the coordinates derived from their telescopic sightings of the Andromeda Galaxy and selected Population II Cepheids of the Milky Way, and made due allowance for galactic rotation and the separate motions of the stars in the course of 30,000 years. Everything checked; he knew where to find Earth.

Except that it wasn't there.

"Either I've lost my touch, or Earth didn't exist thirty thousand years ago," he said ruefully.

"Nonsense," Afra said. "Let me try it." She seemed eager.

Ivo gave place to her, feeling as though he had been sent to the showers.

Afra played with the controls for twenty minutes, focusing first on the Earth-locale, then elsewhere. The screen remained a melange of color; no clear image appeared. At last she swung around to focus on one of the globular clusters outside the galaxy—and got an image.

She had set the computer to fix on any planetary surface encountered in a routine sweep of the views available, and it had done that. The picture was of a dark barren moon far from its primary. In the night sky above the horizon individual stars could be made out, and even the light band of massed distant stars.

"That's no cluster!" Groton exclaimed. "You wouldn't find a band like that in a spherical mass of stars."

Afra fussed with the controls, adjusting the scene clumsily and finally losing it. She returned to the computer sweep, while Ivo chafed internally at the loss of the only picture they had landed, and such a mysterious one. The picture would not come in again. She began to show her temper.

"Something strange here," Harold said. "The alignment of that image doesn't check with the direct view of the cluster. And the scene was typical of a planet within the galaxy. That light band was the Milky Way!"

Afra set the computer for Earth-type planet selection, leaving the azimuth where it was, and waited while it filtered and sorted the crowded macrons. Ivo was anxious to take over again, but held himself back. The situation certainly *was* strange, and Afra obviously lacked the expertise necessary to solve the contradictions. But it would not be diplomatic to point this out.

A green landscape appeared, Earthlike but not Earth. Afra jumped to manual—and lost it. She swore in unladylike manner.

Abruptly she disengaged. "I'm not doing any good here. Take it back, Ivo."

And he was in it, oblivious to the others, using the goggles though the main screen remained on. He felt his way into the situation, reacting as though the computer were part of his own brain. There was no image directly from Earth—or from any other point in the galaxy. Except for the programs; they came through splendidly. What was the distinction between the tame macrons and the wild ones, that only the tame should pass?

The programs were artificial, generated by sophisticated Type II technology macronic equipment set up within a powerful gravitic field. He knew that much from the local stations, who discussed their techniques freely. Their signals, in effect, were polarized, stripped of wasteful harmonics and superficial imprints, and radiated out evenly. Natural impulses were weak and unruly, by contrast, and tangled with superimpositions. A wild macron could produce several hundred distinct pictures and a great deal of additional scramble; a cultured macron produced only one, or one integrated complex.

It was like the difference between a random splash and a controlled jet of water. The splash interacted with its environment more copiously, but the jet went farther and accomplished more in a particular manner.

What was the galactic environment?

Light. Gas. Energy.

"Gravity."

It was Schön whispering in his ear. Communication between them was growing more facile, to Ivo's distress. He preferred Schön thoroughly buried.

Gravity: cumulative in its gross effect, but divided within its originating body. Outside the massive galaxy—

Macrons: essences born of gravitic ripples, and subject to them. And what happened to those emerging from the galaxy itself, meeting the larger interactions of the universe?

He knew, now. The programs struck through, even as far as other galaxies, if properly focused, for they were beamed and streamlined and syncopated and unencumbered. But the wild impulses could not make it; they were too woolly, prickly, horny, disorganized. They felt the great galactic field, were bent by it (for they were creatures of gravity), hauled around as were the clusters, strained. . . .

But not the light. Galactic gravity was not enough to prevent the light from escaping. And finally the light struck out into deep space, leaving its macrons behind, divorced. Like a cloak shed of its master, the mantle of macrons collapsed, compacted, lost form—but remained as lightspeed impulses, clumping to each other, billions where one had been before. Unable to escape the master field, they remained in orbit about the mighty primary, the galactic nucleus.

Thus, shotgun images at right angles to the disk of the galaxy.

Thus, no direct contemporary—within 30,000 years— news.

Thus—history.

Ivo narrowed the coded specifications to a classification of one: Earth. Earth, any time since life conquered its land masses. He swept the captive stream, searching for animation. He scored.

They were watching the screen, and he heard their joint outcry. Earth, yes—

The creature resembled in a certain fashion a crocodile, but its snout was short and blunt. Its body, with its stout round legs and powerful tail, was about seven feet long. A grotesque bridgework of bone and leather stood upon its back, like a stiff sail.

It was morning, and the animal rested torpidly at right angles to the rays of the sun, its eyes partially closed. Behind it was an edge of water clustered with banded stems, a number of them broken. Tall brush or alienistic trees stood in the background. and the ground seemed bleak because there was no grass.

"That," said Afra, "is Dimetrodon. The sail-backed lizard of the Permian period of Earth. two hundred and fifty million years ago. The sail was used as a primitive temperature control mechanism before better means were found. Though Dimetrodon looks clumsy, that heat-control was an immense advantage, since reptiles tend to be dull when cold—"

"I don't see how a sail could make it warm," Beatryx said.

"Oh, it does, it does, and cool too. Broadside to the sun it soaks up heat; endwise it dissipates it. Reptiles don't dare get too hot, either, you see. Quite clever, really—and it does make identification easy."

"Paleontology is not my strong point," Harold said, "but some such conjecture came to my mind, minus the no-menclature. Wasn't the sail-back the ancestor to the dinosaurs?"

Ivo, wearing the goggles, could not see the expression on her face, but he could hear it. "What dinosaur practiced temperature control? Dimetrodon was a carnivorous pelycosaur, probably ancestral to the therapsids. Mammal-like reptiles, to you."

"Oops, wrong family tree," he said without rancor. "Still, a surprising manifestation, considering that we are only thirty thousand light-years out. I don't see how it could actually be Earth."

"It *is Earth*," Ivo said, remembering that the others had not been privy to his deliberations. "The macrons are in orbit around the galaxy. They've clumped together until they have something like mass in themselves, but we can still read them when we catch them. These must have circled a thousand times. I don't dare mess with the orientation; reception is largely a matter of chance, since there's so much to choose from. All space and all time, as it were."

And as he spoke, the picture faded. The vagaries of macronics had washed out the reception. He reset the sweep and angled back and forth, searching for a steadier pulse.

"Two hundred and fifty million years!" Afra said. "The galaxy should have completed a full revolution in that period."

"Galactic revolution shouldn't be relevant," Harold said. "We're out from the flat face of it, not the edge. The macron orbiting here must be at right angles to the galactic rotation, and not circular at all. I wonder whether it isn't more like a magnetic field?"

Ivo had another picture on the screen: an animal resembling a deer, but with doglike paws. It stood about a yard high, and poked its nose through the low brush as though searching for vegetable tidbits.

"Mammalian," Afra said. "Oligocene, probably. I don't quite place the—"

Then it happened: one of those breaks that mock probability. There was a concerted gasp.

A monstrous beak stabbed down into the picture, followed by a tiny malignant eye and white headfeathers. It was the head of a bird—almost, in itself, the size of the full torso of the deerlike animal. The cruel beak gaped, stabbed, and closed on the deer's quivering neck.

Now the rest of the predator came into view. It was indeed a bird: nine feet tall and constructed like a wingless and huge-legged hawk. Three mighty claws pierced turf with every step, each scaly and muscular.

"Phororhacos!" Afra exclaimed, awed. "Miocene, in South America. Twenty million years ago—"

"How horrible!" That was Beatryx.

"Horrible? Phororhacos was a magnificent specimen, one of the pinnacles of avian evolution. Flightless, to be sure—but this bird was supreme on land, in its territory. If diversity of species is considered, aves is more successful than mammalia—"

They watched the bird lift its prey by the neck and shake it into unconsciousness or death. Ivo felt the pangs of the onslaught, and had to refrain from putting his hand against his neck. Then beak and talon disemboweled the carcass, and the gory feeding began. Now Ivo felt the taste of warm blood in his toothless mouth.

The picture faded again.

"We skipped two hundred million years between images," Afra said. "How about one in between—like a dinosaur?"

"In time, we should be able to fill in Earth's entire history, from this debris," Ivo said. "But the selection is largely random, for any one scene. The macrons aren't uniformly distributed, though they seem to be reasonably well ordered within the clumps. I can keep trying, though." He, too, was fascinated by this widening of their horizon. No longer did they have to jump enormous distances in order to see the preman past.

All space and all time. . . .

"I hate to break this up," Harold said, "but we do have more serious concerns. We are drifting far outside our galaxy, and a wrong jump could lose us entirely."

That brought them to attention, and he continued more specifically: "I gather that the pictures would be less random if their scope were not so limited, no pun intended. Suppose we look at the Solar System as a whole, and try to get some clue to the finer alignment of our macronic streams? If we can learn to manipulate our reception properly, the significant history of our entire galaxy will be open to us. That means—"

"That means we can trace the onset of the destroyer!" Afra broke in. "Discover what species did it, and why." She paused. "Except that it hasn't reached this far out yet."

"That's why we are free to experiment. Once we know what we're doing, we can slide in closer and pick it up again. We won't have to approach that generator blind."

"Is that right, Ivo?" she asked. "Would a Solar System fix—the entire system—promote uniform reception?"

There had been a time when she did not ask his opinion on anything technical. "Yes. I could put the screen on schematic, and there would be a much broader band to work with. It would be excellent practice, though I can't guarantee the results at first."

She did not answer, so he set it up. The image in his goggles and on the screen became a cartoon diagram coordinated by the computer and his own general guidance. The sun was represented by a white disk of light, and the planets by colored specks traveling dotted orbits, with their moons in similarly marked paths. The scale was not true, but the identities and positions were clear enough.

"I'll try for a System history," Ivo said. "But it will take some time to map the macron streams, assuming they are reasonably consistent. Then I'll have to patch together recordings, since I won't have chronological order at first. No point in your watching."

"We are with you, Ivo," Afra said with sudden warmth. "We'll watch. Maybe we can help."

He knew she was being impersonally practical, but the gesture still warmed him considerably. This was the way he preferred her: working *with* him, not trying to buy him. He bent to the task, searching for comprehensible traces. He had a macroscopic patchwork ahead of him.

"*Let me do it, clubfingers,*" Schön said in his ear. "*I can post it all in an hour. You'll take two weeks, and you'll miss a lot.*"

Ivo had already discovered the magnitude of the task. He did not want to be embarrassed by the inevitable tiring of his audience as the unproductive hours went by. "Do it, then," he replied irritably, and gave Schön rein. More and more was becoming possible, between them.

Yet—if Schön could do this, using the macroscope— what had happened to the destroyer? The entire basis of Ivo's refusal to free Schön was being thrown into question.

Perhaps—was it a hope?—he would fail.

Schön had not been bluffing. He expanded into Ivo's brain and body and applied his juvenile but overwhelming intellect to the problem. Ivo watched his left fingers dance over the computer keys while his right ones flexed on the knob, and wondered whether he had not made a serious mistake. He had not freed Schön—but Schön might free himself, given this leeway. He was clever enough....

The screen cleared. The indicated scale expanded to two light-years diameter and a representation of cosmic dust appeared.

"What are you doing?" Afra demanded. "That's no stellar system."

"Primeval hydrogen cloud, stupid," Schön replied with Ivo's lips and tongue, while Ivo winced.

Afra shut up and the show went on. Had he not been observing from so intimate a spot, Ivo would have suspected it of being entirely fanciful. As it was, he knew that Schön had actually manipulated the macroscope to pick up impulses dating back five or ten billion years; the representation, though indirect, bridged and abridged, was an honest one.

The cloud of primitive gas swirled and contracted, the time scale showing the passage of roughly a million years every 25 seconds. In the course of ten million years the gas cloud compressed itself into a diameter of a hundred million miles, then to a scant one million, and then it flared into life and became a star. The compression had raised its temperature until the hydrogen/helium "ignition" point was achieved; now it was drawing enormous energy from the conversion of hydrogen atoms to a quarter the number of helium atoms.

"It's like trying to cram four glasses of liquor into a fifth," Afra explained to Beatryx. "A quart won't fit into a fifth, so—"

"Doesn't it depend on the size of the fifth glass?"

Oh no, Ivo thought. Once more the two women had crossed signals. Harold would have to untangle them, as he always did. Eventually Beatryx would be made to understand that four hydrogen atoms had a combined atomic weight of 4.04, while a single helium atom's weight was 4.00. The combination of four hydrogens to make one helium thus released the extra .04 as energy: the life of stars.

Only one percent of the new atom released—but so great was the aggregate that it halted the collapse of the huge cloud/star pictured on the screen and stabilized it for a period. Most of the light of the universe derived from this same process; the myriad stars of the Milky Way Galaxy were merely foci for hydrogen/helium conversion.

Several billion years passed in a few intense minutes.

At last the fuel ran low, and the sun swelled into a vast red giant a hundred times its prior diameter.

"That can't be Sol!" Harold objected. "Our sun is only halfway through its life cycle."

Schön did not dignify this with a reply. Ivo did not comprehend the situation either, but still knew the image was accurate.

The star, having exhausted its available hydrogen, collapsed again. But within it now was a core of almost pure helium, the product of its lifelong consumption of hydrogen. As it contracted to a much tighter ball than before, the internal temperature increased to ten times that of the earlier conversion. Something had to give. It did: the helium began to break down into carbon. A new fuel had been discovered.

The star was in business again, as a fast-living white dwarf.

But soon the helium ran out, and the tiny star faded into a blackened ball of matter no larger than a planet. It
334

had come to a dismal end. It was dense with collapsed matter and peripheral heavy elements captured during its glory from galactic debris, but it was dead, a drifting ash.

After more millions of years this minuscule corpse was swept into the sphere of influence of a nascent star, a body forming from the more plentiful gas nearer the rim of the galaxy. As the new star, heedless of its degrading destiny, took on the characteristic brilliance of the long atomic conversion, this cinder became a satellite, sweeping up some of the gas for itself. It enhanced its mass and developed an atmosphere, but remained inert. Its day was done: it was never to regain its erstwhile grandeur.

"That's Earth!" Afra said. Then, immediately: "No, it can't be. Wrong composition, and the core is much too dense." She was absorbing the symbols for material and density automatically, seeing the planet as it was.

A second ember was acquired by the young system, also representing the death of an ancient star. Then a third and a fourth, each accruing what pitiful lagniappe it could from the scant debris of space. The last two were much larger cores than the first, and acquired more atmosphere for their dotage, but had no hope of rejuvenation. Four planets orbited the star, each far older as entities than it was.

A neighbor had problems. The picture shifted to cover it for a geologic moment. This star was much larger than the original one and had consumed its hydrogen—and helium—lavishly. In a scant few million years it had run its course. But its mass, and therefore its internal heat, was such that the conversions did not stop at carbon. Oxygen, sodium, silicon, calcium—all the way down to iron, 26 on the atomic scale, the elements formed in this stellar furnace. A series of thermal intensifications— cataclysmic storms—broke through the shell of helium even before its breakdown was complete, producing trace amounts of heavy metals up to lead; but the basic, energy-releasing conversions predominated. The demise of a large star was not a quiet matter.

When nothing remained at the core lighter than iron, the gravitic collapse resumed. The heat ascended to a hundred billion degrees. Strength was drawn from this collapse, and energy poured back into the core to form new matter. The heavier elements all the way up to uranium now were manufactured in quantity.

But at this final collapse the star rebounded in an explosion that splattered its mass across the galaxy: a supernova. A splendid spectrum of heavy elements shot past the more conservative viewpoint star and through its satellite system, and some of this was captured while some fell into the star itself. The system was richer than it had been, feeding greedily upon the gobbets of its neighbor's destruction.

The original planet intercepted a fair share of this largesse, and gained perceptibly thereby, as did the others. But the largest fragments, mostly iron, fell into orbit and coelesced into planets in their own right. Now three small satellites circled within the four large ones.

"Mars, Earth, Venus!" Afra said, caught up in this adventure. "And the first planet we saw is Neptune—*our* planet!"

Schön still did not bother to comment. Ivo felt Schön's concentration as he identified and captured the diverse threads of the macronic tapestry and organized them into a coherent and chronological visual history. This was a task that required all of Schön's powers, the artistic with the computational and linguistic. They were nevertheless exceptional powers for an exceptional undertaking; Ivo had tended to lose sight of just how potent a mind his mentor-personality possessed. If a mouse born into Leo remained a mouse, a lion confined to the harness of a mouse remained a lion. Or, in this case, a Ram.

More time passed, and the slow accretions continued. A billion years after the first, a second nova developed in the immediate neighborhood. More rich debris angled by, and the sun's family levied another tax on it, acquiring material for two more inner planets and a number of major moons.

"Mercury and—Vulcan?" Afra inquired. "Or is that Pluto, misplaced?" For there were now five inner planets—one more than could be accounted for.

Schön kept on working.

From distant space, travelers came. Most passed, merely deflected by Sol's gravity, not captured. One, however, lurched into a wobbly elliptical orbit that passed close to that of planet Jupiter.

"*Six* inner planets?" Afra demanded in a tone of outrage.

It was not to be. Jupiter wrestled the newcomer around in a harsh initiation, twisting it inward toward the sun ... and toward the orbit of the next inward planet. Too close. They drifted, interacted—and came together.

And sundered each other before they touched.

"Roche's Limit squared," Afra murmured.

One fragment shot out to intercept planet Saturn, and was captured there—too close. Roche's Limit exerted itself again: the apprentice moon shattered, and the tiny fragments gradually coalesced into a discernible ring.

A major fragment of the original demolition traveled farther. It intercepted Neptune, where it too broke up, forming two tremendous moons and some fragments. One moon escaped the planet but not the system, and became the erratic outer minion Pluto; the other hooked in close to Neptune and remained as Triton.

Another major fragment angled across an inner orbit and interacted there, too large for capture, too small to escape. The two bodies formed the binary planet known as Earth and Luna.

Then a close shot at almost normal time. The landscape of Earth, seven hundred million years ago: strange continents, strange life on both land and sea. The moon came then, sweeping terribly close, a tenth of the distance it was to have at the time of Man. No romantic approach, this, but the awful threat of another application of the Limit. The tides of Earth swelled into calamity, gaping chasms split the surface of Luna. Mounds of water passed entirely over the continents, obliterating every feature upon them and leaving nothing but bare and level land. No land-based life survived, even in fossil, and much of the higher sea-life also perished in that violence. The progression of animate existence on Earth had been set back by a billion years: the greatest calamity it was ever to know.

"And now we make love by the light of Luna," Afra said, "and plot it into our horoscopes as 'feeling.'"

It was Harold's turn not to comment.

All this, stemming from the single trans-Mars wreckage—yet the bulk of the refuse dispersed as powder or spiraled into the sun, to have no tangible impact. Debris remained to form a crude ring around the sun in the form of the asteroid belt, and a number of chunks eventually became retrograde moonlets. It would be long before the disorder wrought by this accident was smoothed over.

A third nova, more distant, provided another cloud of dust and particles, adding several tiny moons. Some of the swirls become comets, but the complexion of the system did not alter in any important way. Sol had its family, collected from all over the galaxy, portions of which were older and portions newer than itself. Life recovered from its setback on Earth and individual species crawled back upon the reemerging land and drifting continents in the wake of a receding moon.

One thing more: a solitary traveler came from the more thickly-settled center-section of the galaxy. It was a planetary body moving rather slowly, as though its kinetic energies had been spent by encounters with other systems. It looped about Sol in an extraordinarily wide pass, hesitated, and settled down to stay, averaging seven billion miles out.

"What is *that?*" Afra inquired.

"That thing must be twice the size of Jupiter!" Harold said. "How could it be there, in our system, and we not know it?" But no one answered.

Ivo half-suspected Schön of joking.

The motion stopped. The picture remained: the contemporary situation, updated to within a million years. They had witnessed in summary the astonishing formation and history of the Solar System.

"Beautiful, Ivo!" Harold exclaimed. "If you can do that, you can do anything. Congratulations."

Ivo removed the macroscope paraphernalia. They all were smiling at him, and Afra was getting ready to speak. "I didn't do it," he said.

"How can you say that!" Beatryx protested. "Everything was so clear."

But Afra and Harold had sobered immediately. "Schön?" Harold asked with sympathy.

Ivo nodded. "He said it would take me two weeks, and he was right. He said *he* could do it in an hour. So I dared him to, I guess."

"Wasn't that—dangerous?" Afra asked.

"Yes. But I retained possession."

Harold was not satisfied. "My chart indicates that a person like Schön would be unlikely to put that amount of effort into a project unless he expected to gain personally. What was his motive?"

"So it was *Schön* who called me 'stupid,' " Afra murmured.

"I think he has found a way to get around the destroyer," Ivo said carefully. "The memory trace in my mind, I mean, and maybe the rest too. I think he can take over, now—and I guess he wants to."

"Are you willing to let him?" Harold asked, not looking at him.

"Well, that *is* in the contract, you might say. If the rest of you feel I should." He said it as though it were a routine decision, but it was only with considerable effort that he kept his voice from shaking. It was extinction he contemplated, and it terrified him.

When Afra had feared loss of identity she had fallen back on physical resources and demanded the handling. Irrational, perhaps, but at least it had satisfied her. What did *he* have to bolster his courage?

"So Schön was merely making a demonstration for us," Harold said. "An impressive one, I admit. Proving that he can make good on his claims. That he can get us to the destroyer, and with the advance information we need. All we have to do is ask him."

Afra's eyes were on Harold now, but she remained silent. Ivo wondered in what spheres her thoughts were coursing, and was afraid to guess. She was intent and exquisite.

"Is it necessary to take a vote?" Harold asked, casually. Thus readily did they accept the prospect of a companion's departure.

"Yes," Afra said.

"Secret ballot?"

She nodded agreement.

How badly did she want that destroyer?

Harold leaned over and filched the note-pad from Afra's purse. Ivo wondered idly why he didn't use his own pad for the dirty work. Harold tore out a sheet, folded it, creased it between his fingernails, tore and retore it. He handed out the ballots.

"I—don't think I'd better vote," Ivo said, refusing his ballot. "Three can't tie." *Did they realize*—?

Harold shrugged and marked his paper. "The question is, do we ask for Schön, yes or no," he said.

The two women marked theirs and folded them deliberately. Harold picked up the ballots, shuffled them without looking and handed the three to Ivo. "Read the verdict."

"But I'll recognize the script. It won't be secret."

The truth was that he was afraid to look. This was another nightmare, where everybody took things casually except himself, he being the only one to properly appreciate the nature of the chasm over which he leaned.

"Have the computer read them, then," Harold said. *How could he be so indifferent?*

Ivo dumped the slips into the analyzer hopper and punched SUMMARIZE. There was a scramble inside the machine as it assimilated the evidence.

The printout emerged. Ivo tore it off, forcing himself to read:

NO
NO
NO
IVO
LOVE

The relief was so great he felt ill. It took him a moment to realize that somebody had voted more than once, and another to discern the other oddities about the listing. Someone had written "NO" carelessly so that the first stroke of the "N" was unconnected, and the machine had picked it up as "I" and "V" and added the "O." Thus the word became his name.

He was unable to explain how the last word had come about.

Harold stood up. "Was there any doubt?" he asked. "I don't think we'll need to do this again. Let's get back on the job. We have a lot to do and none of us are geniuses."

Only after they were gone did he realize that he still held the printout—that he had not read aloud or shown to any of them.

Reentry into the galaxy—was anticlimactic. Group confidence was on the ascendant. They had been unable to pinpoint the destroyer's moment of origin; there had been nothing, then everything, and there was no emanation from the area except those terrible "tame" macrons. Apparently the destroyer broadcaster had been set up rapidly by a task force that jumped into location and away again in a few hours, and whose technicians could somehow interfere with wild macronic emission. Unless the observer happened to land at the very fringe of the broadcast, its inception could not be caught. But still they had confidence, sure somehow that the worst was over.

They centered on the destroyer source nearest Earth, jumping toward it and away again, but gaining from experience. The jumpspace map was sketchy, but it helped, and overall their approach was steady. Five thousand light-years from it; eight thousand, one thousand, seven thousand, four hundred, two thousand, seventy, twenty.

There they paused. "We can't get any closer," Afra said. "Our minimum jump is fifty years, and that would put us thirty years on the other side, or worse."

"Nothing to do but back off and make another pass," Harold said. "Shuffle the alignment and hope."

"Schön says he can—"

"If he wants to give us the info, fine," Harold said. "If he's using it to buy his way into this enterprise, tell him to get lost. We idiots can muddle through on our own."

They retreated and made another pass, coming within ten light-years. The third try was worse, but the fourth was very close: less than a parsec, or just over three light-years.

"This is probably about the best our luck has to offer," Afra said. "We could renovate Joseph and row across, as it were. A few years in melt—"

"We'd have to reconstitute every year, for safety," Ivo reminded her. "The melt's shelf-life isn't guaranteed indefinitely."

"I am not a gambling man," Harold said, "but I'd rather gamble. That is, try some more passes. I don't want to approach the destroyer in the melted state. I want my wits about me, not my protoplasm."

They gambled—and lost. Six more passes failed to bring them within five light-years of the target. That parsec had been their best, and they couldn't even find that track again. Jumpspace was too complex a puzzle.

"Schön says—"

"Shut *up*!" This time it was Afra, and her vehemence gave him another warm feeling. He remembered the word

LOVE in the balloting, and dared to wonder. His love for her had changed its nature but never its certainty; he knew her well, now, and understood her liabilities as well as her assets, and loved them all. It was a love without illusion; he expected nothing of her, and drew his pleasure solely from being near her. Or so he told himself.

But—had she written the word? Harold would not have done it, and Beatryx should not have thought of it. Still—

"I think," said Harold, "we had better give up on this one. There are several others in the galaxy, and for our purpose any one of them should do for a beginning. Perhaps our channel runs closer to another destroyer."

That much they had verified, coming down into the Milky Way: there were a number of destroyers. Their devastating signals had intercepted the human party at about eighteen thousand light-years, wherever they moved within or near the galaxy. Once they had had two destroyers in "sight" simultaneously, and had verified the similarity of the signals by superimposing one on the other.

They gambled again, going for a new target. Once more their luck changed. Their second pass at the second destroyer brought them to just within one light-day.

At last they learned why it had been so difficult to obtain normal macroscopic information about any destroyer. Here virtually all macronic impulses were overridden by the artificial signal; or perhaps they were preempted for its purpose. Only one flux emanated from this area of space, and hardly anything coherent entered it. Apart from the destroyer signal itself, it was blackout. The macroscope, for the first time, was out of commission.

Except for the traveler signal. That, oddly, came through as strongly as ever. This was one more evidence of the superiority of the extragalactic technology: the traveler could not be jammed or blocked or diverted.

"Damn lucky, too," Harold said. "Think of the trouble we'd have getting *out* of here, otherwise."

Afra busied herself with the telescopes while the others set about demothballing Joseph. The ship had been buried within Triton, which in turn was buried in Neptune, and extricating it and themselves whole was no offhand matter. Fortunately—though Harold denied that chance had been involved in such an engineering decision—they had also mothballed the heavy equipment. Harold had constructed it on macroscopic plans, and what could be done could be undone enough for storage. Anything not deposited well within the Triton drillhole had been melted down during the Neptune approach, of course.

"I have photographed the destroyer complex," Afra reported at lunch. "Can't actually *see* anything with these inefficient optical instruments, but as I make it the center unit is almost two miles in diameter and spherical. Definitely artificial. Metallic surface. Since we can't use the macroscope on it, we'll have to go inside ourselves."

"We seem to be getting blasé about galactic technology," Harold said. "Now we complain about imperfect detail vision at a distance of one light-day! Still, why *not* go inside, then?"

"Because they might tweak our tailfeathers with a contraterrene missile, that's why not," she said. "So I suggest we make a dry run first." She appeared uncommonly cheerful, as though, perversely, a weight had lifted from her mind.

"How?" Harold asked her. "Joseph is all we have."

"Catapult, stupid," she said, smiling. "We have a spot gravity nullifier, remember? And plenty of material."

Harold knocked his forehead with the heel of his hand. He, too, seemed uncharacteristically lighthearted. "Of course! We can shape a mock ship and launch it toward the destroyer—"

"Let's begin with the satellites," she said. "I think they're the battleships."

"Satellites?"

"I told you. The destroyer is ringed with hundred-foot spheres—six of them, about five light-minutes out, north-south-east-west-up-down."

"You did *not*, girl, tell me. You implied that you could not obtain such detail with optics. This complicates the problem."

"I *did* tell you. Where were you when I said 'destroyer *complex*'?"

"Who was it who said 'There is no faith stronger than that of a bad-tempered woman in her own infallibility'?"

"Cabell said it. But he also implied that a bad-tempered woman needs an even-tempered man." Both smiled.

Ivo went on eating, but Beatryx's excellent cooking had become tasteless. Afra and Groton!

No—he was jumping to an unfounded suspicion. A ludicrous one! Their open banter merely reflected the increasing intimacy of the little group. It was almost the way the project had been, when he and Brad and all the others had batted inanities back and forth while pursuing deeper studies. Afra and Groton had had to work closely together ever since Triton—particularly when Ivo himself had skipped off to Tyre and left them stranded in deep space. And there had developed a kind of father-daughter relation between them since the trial. Afra had lost her own father somehow, so—

Groton and his waldoes and machines performed their miracles of construction again, and in due course Neptune had a planetary cannon. The bore was thirty-five feet across and two miles long, bottomed by the field-distortion mechanism. Slender tubes opened to the atmospheric surface of the planet in a circle many miles across, and fed into the nether sections of the bore. Great baffles stood ready to redirect the force of the gases that would converge the moment the generators opened the tunnel to space.

They gathered in the control room to watch the launching. Neptune was rotating, relative to the destroyer complex, and the action had to be properly timed. Afra had done the calculations, querying Ivo only for verification. She had made it plain, in similarly subtle ways, that the relation between them had changed. She was not dependent on him for such work.

Groton manipulated his controls, that seemed to be almost as intricate as those of the macroscope maintenance, and on the screen the monster dummy-ship was lifted into place. This was a breech-loading cannon with a clip of four; further expenditures on dummies had been deemed a waste of time.

Groton fired. The gravity-diffusion field came on, taking a moment to develop full intensity. It was generated by a different unit than theirs of the residential area, since it was essential that they continue to be shielded from the

344

full gravity and pressure of the planet. Then gas hurtled through the pipes and smashed into the base of the projectile, itself abruptly weightless. The control chamber shuddered.

Above, atmosphere imploded into the column of null, meeting the baffles there and forming into an instant hurricane with an eye that was a geyser of methane snow. All the pressure of Neptune's atmosphere drove that bullet forward: one million pounds per square inch, initial.

Out from ammonia and water, both vaporized by the friction; through hydrogen and beyond the mighty atmosphere: a thousand miles beyond the apparent surface of the planet the motor cut in. The rocket accelerated at a rate that would have terminated any fleshly occupants and shattered unprotected equipment. It was a temporary motor, designed for power and not duration, and it consumed itself as it functioned; and it got the ship up to a velocity that would bring it to the destroyer in days instead of months.

"Certainly looks like a ship from here," Afra said with admiration. "Are you sure you didn't put Joseph in that lock by mistake?"

"Drone ship, on my honor. It only weighs a tenth as much as Joseph, and that galactic formula would asphyxiate our type of life as soon as it ignited, not to mention the fact that it burns its own guts. You can do a lot with chemical drive if you don't have to sit on top of it."

The watch began. Each person tracked the drone for four hours, ready to sound the alarm when anything happened. A light-day was a very small distance compared to those they had become accustomed to, but even galactically sponsored chemical drive was very weak. The rocket achieved its top velocity and coasted, an empty shell. Their vigil lasted a fortnight.

The drone passed the nearest satellite and angled toward the destroyer itself. Nothing happened. It came within a light-minute of the main sphere and curved around it as though bent by a tremendous gravitational force, but did not stop. It passed another satellite on the way out.

"Either they're dead or playing possum," Groton said. "Do we try another?"

Another two weeks of eventless waiting, Ivo thought, but certainly the wisest course.

"I'm satisfied," Afra said. "Obviously there are no functioning automatic defenses. I'm sorry we wasted this much time. Let's move in ourselves."

Ivo thought of objecting, then decided not to. She had spoken and it was so, impetuous or not. This project was hers, now.

They were space-borne again, and it was a strange sensation. Not since they put down on Schön, erstwhile moon of a moon, had they taken Joseph out of planetary control for any extended period. In the passing months the old reflexes had faded, if they had ever been really implanted, making free-fall unfamiliar, making them have to stop and think out their actions.

"I like it," Afra said. "Neptune is home, of course, but this is vacation."

Why was she so buoyant? Ivo wondered. They were near the termination of their grisly mission, in whatever guise that mission existed now, and he would have expected it to remind her forcefully of the fate of her supposed fiancé. Instead she acted as though she had found new love. She hardly seemed to care about the destroyer itself, though it was the instigator of all of this.

Groton clapped his hand on Afra's shoulder, sending her skidding in the weightlessness. "Girl, if you don't get on those computations before I reorganize our gear, I'll have the cap'n hurl you into the brig!"

They had tied down their equipment and pushed out from Neptune slowly, without the benefit of full gravity nullification. This had been expensive in working fluid, but far safer for man and machine. Now the ship was scooping in more hydrogen and compressing it, at the fringe of the Neptune atmosphere, so that they would have full tanks for the main haul. They were ready to retool for straight space flight.

They had to melt, despite Groton's earlier objection; there was no other way to cover such a distance. The cycle was routine, however, once their course had been set. They revived in good condition light-seconds from one of the satellites. It had seemed wiser to investigate the minion before the master.

Ivo had been lulled by the somewhat cavalier attitude affected by the others, but the sight of the alien sphere looming so close—telescopically—reminded him with a shock that this was to be their first physical contact with an artifact of extraterrestrial civilization. A malignant one.

It was monstrous as they approached, not so much in its hundred-foot diameter (Afra had done expert photographic work and analyzing, to pinpoint that size at a distance of a light-day, even allowing for the superior equipment sponsored by galactic technology) as in its suggestion of implacable power. The surface was pocked, as though it had been subject to spatial debris for many millions of years. Portions of it projected, reminiscent of cannon.

Afra took over the telescope to make detail photographs. Now, while her attention was wholly taken up, he could watch her. She was radiant; her hair was bound in a single braid that drifted over one shoulder and down her front, red against the white of her blouse. She had recovered the weight she had lost and was now in vibrant health. Her lips were parted, half-smiling in her concentration. Light from the equipment played over her high cheekbone and across her perfect chin, caressing her face with shadow.

Was it the single rose he smelled again?

"Moonstruck," Brad had termed him, setting that emotional snare, and Afra was that moon. Ivo knew he would have loved her anyway, whatever her color, whatever her intelligence. It was perhaps her appearance more than her personality; he had disillusioned himself long ago about his romantic values and hers. Still, the love he felt encompassed all of her, the violent along with the beautiful. All, no matter what.

She jerked her head up, eyes widening in shock, showing that blue again. Ivo jumped guiltily, thinking she had caught him staring, but her exclamation banished such inconsequential alarm immediately.

"It's tracking us!"

Groton and Beatryx seemed to materialize beside her.

"It's live!" Afra said with the same shock. "It has a range-finder on us."

"Since we're a sitting duck, all we can do is quack,"

347

Groton said, but he did not look as complacent as he sounded.

Beatryx ventured one of her rare technical comments: "Wouldn't it have *done* something, if it meant to?"

Afra smiled, as she did so readily and prettily now. "You're right," 'Tryx. I'm getting hysterical after the fact. We'd be smithereened by now if we were going to be. We're within fifty thousand miles, and you can bet that's well within its sphere of control. So eradication just isn't in our horoscope for today."

The strange antenna continued to track as they came close. It was a bowl-shaped spiral of wire about two feet in diameter, with beads strung on the outermost spire. There was no other sign of life. Ivo felt the cold sweat on his palms and wiped it off, embarrassed by it and what it signified. Was he the only one to feel old-fashioned *fear*?

The journey via melting and ten-G acceleration had reduced the problems of deceleration and docking to elementary ones; maneuvering was nothing after distance had been conquered. Afra piloted them into a companion orbit—the destroyer-sphere five light-minutes distant, small as it was, was the primary for both—and let Joseph drift. None of them had conjectured how an object two miles in diameter could have a gravitational field about it equivalent to that of a small star. Galactic technology had done it, utilizing gravity as a tool, and that was explanation enough.

"Someone should stay on the ship," Groton said. "We can't be sure what is waiting—there."

"Ivo should stay," Afra said. "If anything happens, he's the only one who can get the ship out. Neptune, rather." She said it as though he were a fixture, a commodity; she hadn't asked his opinion. "Give me one companion, though; I'm afraid of the dark."

"I'll stay," Beatryx said. "You go, Harold."

Ivo could find no legitimate objection to make.

The two got into their suits and departed via the airlock at the appropriate time. Ivo was alone with Beatryx for the first time since their last conversation on satellite Schön, seemingly so long ago. In the interim he had traveled into Earth's historic past, and into its geologic past, and beyond the fringe of the galaxy. His body had run through the astonishing liquefication and reconstitution so many times that the process had become routine, even tedious. He had lived many lifetimes, and many of his basic certainties had been annulled.

Why, then, did it bother him so much that Afra and Groton should be together?

He tried to say something to Beatryx, but realized that he could not ask her advice without undermining her own framework. She had proper faith in her husband.

He looked at her, realizing in this isolated moment of association and reflection how much she had changed. She had been plump and fortyish when he met her at age thirty-seven; in the period of the Triton trouble she had become emaciated and fortyish. Now she was thirty-eight— and had regained her health without her former avoirdupois. She looked thirtyish. Her hair had brightened into full blonde, her limbs were sleek, her torso reminiscent of the goddess she had been momentarily during the first reconstitution. It had happened gradually, this change in her; the surprise was that it had taken him so long to recognize it.

"You have changed, Ivo," she said.

"*I've* changed?"

"Since your visit to Tyre. You were so young at first, so unsure. Now you're more mature."

"I don't *feel* mature," he said, flattered but disbelieving. "I'm still full of doubts and frustrations. And Tyre was nothing but violence and intrigue—not my type of life at all. I don't see how it could have changed me."

She only shrugged.

He glanced at the screen again, reminded that half their party was in the alien structure. Groton and Afra—

"She has let go of Bradley Carpenter," Beatryx said. "Have you seen the difference? She's changed so much. Isn't it wonderful?"

Was there such a thing as being too generous? True, the two were risking their lives by attempting personal contact with aliens likely to be powerful and hostile; but the human interaction could not be entirely ignored. "I've noticed the difference, yes."

"And she gets along so much better with Harold. I'm sure he has been good for her. He's very steady."

Ivo nodded.

"She's such a lovely girl," Beatryx said. There was no malice in her tone; nothing but concerned pleasure.

"Lovely."

"You look tired, Ivo. why don't I keep watch while you rest?"

"That's very kind of you." He went to his hammock and strapped himself in. It was an anchor rather than a support, in this weightlessness.

It was this about Beatryx, he thought: she was happy. There was no place in her philosophy for jealousy or petty conjecture. She did not worry about her husband because she had no internal doubts.

How much could the group have accomplished, without her? The ingredients of strife had been abundantly present, particularly with the strong personalities of Groton and Afra clashing at the outset, and the background specter of Schön, but somehow every flareup had been diverted or pacified. Beatryx had done it . . . and profited in the doing. Intelligence, determination, skill—these would have come to nothing without that basic stability.

He must have slept, for he was Sidney Lanier again: poor, ill, his aspirations unrecognized. He did some more teaching, but the pupils were unruly, the employers exacting. It was the Reconstruction, and it was bad; the carpetbaggers corrupted everything. "Dumb in the dark, not even God invoking," he wrote, "we lie in chains, too weak to be afraid."

But the love of Mary Day, now Mary Day Lanier, sustained him. She was as ill as he, and as hard put upon, but their marriage was an unqualified blessing. His son Charles delighted him, for he loved children though he did not really understand them.

In 1869 James Wood Davidson published a survey of two hundred and forty-one Southern writers. Lanier was listed, though largely for completeness; much more space was devoted to others considered more notable.

But you were the greatest of them all! Ivo cried. *If only your contemporaries had opened their minds—*

But nothing changed. The mind of Ivo was prisoner to the situation of another person; he could watch, he could know, but he could not influence.

As Schön was watching him even now. . . .

At Macon they spoke of Sidney Lanier as "A young

350

fool trying to write poetry." They paid no attention to his dialect poems—a form whose origin was later to be credited to another man—or his cautions against the shiftless, shortsighted Georgia Cracker ways. Cotton was destroying the land; wheat and corn were far better crops, but the farmers refused to change.

He put his sentiment at least into a major poem, "Corn," and sent it off to the leading literary magazine of the day, Howells' Atlantic Monthly.

Howells rejected it.

Lanier was crushed by this response. He believed in his work, yet the unambitious efforts of others achieved readier acceptance. "In looking around at the publications of the younger poets." he was later to remark, "I am struck with the circumstance that none of them even *attempt* anything great. The morbid fear of doing something wrong or unpolished appears to have influenced their choice of subjects."

Not only in poetry! Ivo thought. The entire society is governed by mediocrity. We never learn.

Several other prominent magazines rejected "Corn."

Were they absolutely blind?

At last Lippincott's Magazine accepted it. Publication made Lanier's poetic fame; henceforth he was known, though still poor and ill.

The year was 1875, and he was thirty-three years old. He would not live to forty.

Ivo must have slept, for the exploratory party was back already.

"What a bomb!" Afra exclaimed. "There's enough armament there to blast a fleet. Chemical, laser, and things we won't invent for centuries! All of it on standby."

"I don't understand," Beatryx said.

"It's a battlewagon, dear," Groton explained. "But somebody turned it off. All but the sensory equipment."

"It could have blasted Neptune to bits!" Afra said. The potential violence seemed to fascinate her. "It has—I think they're gravity-bombs. Devices that would throw the fields associated with matter into complete chaos. Whoever built that wagon really knew how to fight a war!"

Ivo decided to get into the conversation. "It must be there to protect the destroyer. But why would they deac-

351

tivate it? If enemies had boarded it and turned it off, they would have gone on to squelch the destroyer too."

"And why *build* such an arsenal, if not to be used?" Groton said. "I can't make sense of it either."

Afra was not fazed. "We know where the answer is."

"Did it occur to you that we may not much *like* the answer, when and if we find it?" Groton, at least, seemed to be taking the matter seriously.

"It's in the stars. Who am I to object?"

The two-mile bulk of the destroyer itself seemed more like a small planet, compared to the satellite. Though the gravitic field about it was monstrous, intensity had not increased proportionately as they approached its surface, and the weight of the ship was only a quarter what it would have been on Earth. This still made for tricky maneuvering, since the macroscope housing was vulnerable in gravity. But indentations in the sides of the sphere resembled docking facilities, so they piloted Joseph in instead of establishing a tight orbit. The builders had evidently expected visitors, and had made the approach convenient.

Ivo gave up counting the incongruities of the situation. Better simply to accept what offered, as the others were doing.

The dock was a tubelike affair open at each end, as though a missile had passed cleanly through the rim. The gravity was minimal inside—just enough to hold Joseph in place at the center of the tube. The macroscope housing thus never had to rest in an awkward position; the ship was able to "land" with it attached.

Groton and Afra donned their suits again and went out first. Ivo watched him boost her into the lock with a familiar hand on the rear.

Three minutes later their cheerful reports began coming in. "Very well organized," Groton remarked. "Very businesslike. There seem to be magnetic moorings we can attach to the hull. Why not?"

"And pressure-locks," Afra said, her voice girlishly thrilled. "Harold, you anchor Joseph while I figure out the settings."

"Right." The sounds of his exertions came through, and the clank of tools, audible without benefit of earphone. Ivo wondered how this was possible, in the exterior vacu-

352

um, then realized that the sonic vibrations were being transmitted through the hardware and into the ship. Groton was holding on to something, and standing somewhere, so contacts were plentiful.

Then came the knock of another contact with Joseph's hull. The ship had been secured.

"I'm setting it for Earth-normal pressure and composition," Afra said. "I don't even have to remember the oxygen-nitrogen ratio or the fine points; it has a gasanalyzer. One sample puff from my suit—"

"Let's not trust it too far," Groton cautioned. "Don't forget this *is* the destroyer."

"Don't get worked up, daddy. If it let us get this far, it isn't going to trick us with a mickey now. I'm going in."

Ivo wondered. Wasn't it possible that the destroyer cared less about infringing individuals than about dangerous species or cultures? This had the aspect of flypaper— or, if occupied, of the spider's lair.

But if it had them, it had them. No incidental caution could protect them within its bowels, if personal malignance waited. They could be snuffed out in a thousand casual ways. Had they wanted security, they should have stayed well clear of the destroyer. Thousands of lightyears clear.

"Removing suit," Afra said. A pause. "Air's good. Shall I go on into the interior?"

"Not without checking it!" Groton said. "That's only the airlock, you know. What's inside could ruin your delicate complexion. It might be hundred percent ammonia at five degrees Kelvin."

"No it mightn't. The system has been keyed to the lock. The entire wing has been pressurized to match my sample. I tell you, these galactics are experienced."

"What do you think, folks?" Groton asked dubiously.

Ivo remembered that he was on this circuit too. "She'll have to get out of the lock before anybody else uses it. Might as well go in."

"You, dear?" Groton inquired.

"Whatever you think, dear," Beatryx said. She had faith in her husband's judgment, and Ivo envied her that.

"Come on out, then, both of you. We should take on

this particular adventure as a group. I'll wait here for you while Miss Impetuous shows the way."

"Goats are naturally inquisitive," Afra said.

Goat = Capricorn, her astrological sign, Ivo thought. Groton must have showed her her chart, during one of their . . . private discussions. And did Beatryx know that she was Pisces—a poor fish?

They dressed and climbed out. Ivo assisted Beatryx, but not with any palm on the bottom.

Groton stood on a platform resembling that of a train station. Massive cables reached from the rounded ceiling to Joseph on either side.

"Just swing over on the spare," Groton recommended. "The gravity increases near the lock. You could jump, but why take chances?"

Ivo wondered again whether the humor were conscious. How much difference could one more chance make, now?

They swung over. This was his first physical contact with an alien artifact, since he had not visited the satellite, and he was vaguely disappointed both at its ordinary substance and at the continuing casualness with which the others adjusted to the situation. This was supposed to be the moment of climax—Alien Contact!—and nobody noticed.

Or was he merely put out because he had become a minor figure in a major adventure? After this, if they survived, Afra would be able to handle the travel signal (at least until they reencountered the existent destroyer field, which would take thousands of years to dissipate even at light speed;) and so she would have no further need of Ivo.

"Okay, I'll go through and you follow in turn," Groton said. "No problem with these controls—" He went on to demonstrate.

"Hurry up!" Afra said from the inside. "I'm itching to look about in here."

Had this degenerated into a child's game of "Spaceman"? Girl astronaut wanted them to hurry because she was impatient to explore!

He thought he heard Schön laughing. Little Ivo had thought to manage this adventure himself, and only succeeded in making himself unimportant. Ivo was no Lanier;

he was not likely to achieve fame on his own. Schön, on the other hand—

They don't need you, *either,* he thought furiously at the lurking personality. Schön did not reply.

The interior was, as Afra had claimed, pressurized. He and Beatryx joined the other two in summer clothing, depositing their suits in binnacles provided for them adjacent to the lock. Regular tourist facilities!

The changes in the two women were quite noticeable now, as they stood side by side during that inevitable hesitation before proceeding further into the station. Both were well proportioned, Afra a little taller and more dynamic. Afra was modern—and it looked less well on her, in contrast to the more conservative motions of the other. Where Afra jumped, Beatryx stepped. The difference in their ages showed less in appearance than in attitude and posture and facial expression.

Finally he pinned down the elusive but essential distinction: what Afra had was sex appeal; what Beatryx had was femininity.

Ivo wondered whether he and Groton had changed similarly.

They were in a long quiet hall lighted from the ceiling, a hall that slanted gently downward. "Down" was toward the center of the sphere, not the rim; nothing so simple as centripetal pseudo-gravity here. The materials of the hall's construction were conventional, as these things went; no scintillating shields, no compacted matter. If this were typical, the two-mile sphere could not possibly have the mass of a star, or even a planet. Somehow it generated gravity without mass.

The situation was not, on second thought, surprising. A potent gravitic field was no doubt necessary to power the destroyer impulse, and it should be a simple matter to allow some of it to overlap around the unit, providing for visitors. It was handy for holding down satellites too, even at distances similar to those prevailing in the Solar System itself. Earth was only eight light-minutes from Sol. . . .

A hundred yards or so along, the hall widened into a level chamber. Here there were alcoves set in the walls, and objects resting within them.

Afra trotted to the nearest on the left side. "Do you

355

think the exhibit is safe to touch?" she inquired, now hesitant.

"Do you see any DO NOT HANDLE signs, stupid?"

"Harold, one of these minutes I'm going to whisper nasty things about you into your wife's docile ear."

"She's known them for fifteen years." Groton put his arm around Beatryx, who smiled complacently.

Afra reached into the alcove and lifted out its artifact. It was a sphere about four inches in diameter, rigid and light, made of some plastic material. It was transparent; as she held it up to the light they all could see its emptiness.

"A container?" Groton conjectured.

"A toy?" Beatryx said.

Groton looked at her. "I wonder. An educational toy. A model of the destroyer?"

"Not without docking vents," Afra said. She put it back and went on to the next. This was a cone six inches high with a flat base four inches across. It was made of the same transparent material, and was similarly empty.

"Dunce cap," Ivo suggested.

She ignored him and went on. The third figure was a cylindrical segment on the same scale as the cone, closed off by a flat disk at each end. It was solid but light, the silver-white surface opaque but reflective. Afra turned it about. "Metallic, but very light," she said. "Probably—"

Suddenly she dropped it back in the alcove and brushed her hands against her shorts as though they were burning.

The others watched her. "What happened?" Groton asked.

"That's lithium!"

Groton looked. "I believe you are right. But there's a polish on it—a coating of wax, perhaps. It shouldn't be dangerous to handle."

What was so touchy about lithium? Ivo wondered, but he decided not to inquire. Probably it burned skin, like an acid, or was poisonous.

Afra looked foolish. "I must be more nervous than I let on. I just never expected—" She paused, glancing down the wall. "Something occurs to me. Is the next one a silvery-gray pyramid?"

Groton checked. "Close. Actually it's a tetrahedron,

similar to the one we built originally on Triton. Your true pyramid has five sides, counting the bottom."

"Beryllium."

"How do you know?"

"This is an elemental arrangement. Look at—"

"*Elementary* arrangement," Groton corrected her.

"*Elemental.* You *do* know what an element is? Look at these objects. The first is a sphere, which means it has only one side: outside. The second is a closed cone: two sides, one curved, one flat. The third, the cylinder, has three. Yours has four, and so on. The first two aren't empty—they're gases! Hydrogen and helium, first and second elements on the periodic table—"

"Could be," Groton said, impressed.

"And likely to be so for *any* technologically advanced species. Lithium, the metal that's half the weight of water, third. Beryllium, fourth. Boron—"

She broke off again and lurched for the sixth alcove—and froze before it.

The others followed. There lay a four-inch cube—six sides—of a bright clear substance.

Groton picked it up. "What's number six on the table? Six protons, six electrons . . . isn't that supposed to be carbon?" Then he too froze, eyes fixed on the cube. The light refracted through it strongly.

Then Ivo made the connection. "Carbon in crystalline form—that's diamond!"

They gazed upon it: sixty-four cubic inches of diamond, that had to have been cut from a much larger crystal.

A single exhibit—of scores in the hall.

Then Afra was moving down the length of the room, calling off the samples. "Nitrogen—oxygen—fluorine—neon. . . ."

Groton shook his head. "What a fortune! And they're only samples, shape-coded for ready reference. They—"

Words failed him. Reverently, he replaced the diamond block.

"Scandium—titanium—vanadium—chromium—" Afra chanted as she rushed on. "They're all here! All of them!"

Beatryx was perplexed. "Why shouldn't they put them on display, if they want to?"

Groton came out of his daze. "No reason, dear. No reason at all. It's just a very expensive exhibit, to leave

357

open to strangers. Perhaps it is their way of informing us that wealth means nothing to them."

She nodded, reassured.

"The rare earths, too!" Afra called. She was now on the opposite side of the room, working her way back. "Here's promethium—pounds of it! And it doesn't even occur in nature!"

"Does she know *all* the elements by heart?" Ivo muttered.

"Osmium! That little cube must weigh twenty pounds! And solid iridium—on Earth that would sell for a thousand dollars an ounce!"

"Better stay clear of the radioactives, Afra!" Groton cautioned her.

"They're glassed in. Lead glass, or something; no radiation. I hope. At least they don't have *them* by the pound! Uranium—neptunium—plutonium—"

"Saturnium—jupiterium—marsium," Ivo muttered, facetiously carrying the planetary identifiers farther. It seemed to him that too much was being made of this exhibit. "Earthium—venusium—mercurochrome—"

"Mercury," Groton said, overhearing him. "There *is* such an element."

Oh.

Afra came back at last, subdued. "Their table goes to a hundred and twenty. Those latter shapes get pretty intricate . . ."

"You know better than that, Afra," Groton said. "Some of those artificial elements have half-lives of hours, even minutes. They can't sit on display."

"Even seconds, half-life. They're still here. Look for yourself."

"Facsimiles, maybe. Not—"

"Bet?"

"No." Groton looked for himself. "Must be some kind of stasis field," he said dubiously. "If they can do what they can do with gravity—"

"Suddenly I feel very small," she said.

But Ivo reminded himself that such tricks were nothing compared to the compression of an entire planet into its gravitational radius, and the protection of accompanying human flesh. This exhibit was impressive, but hardly alarming, viewed in perspective. He suspected that there was more to it than they had spotted so far.

The hall continued beyond the element display, slanting down again. Ivo wondered about such things as the temperature. Sharp changes in it should affect some of the element-exhibits, changing them from solid to liquid, or liquid to gas. Yet the exhibit had been geared to a comfortable temperature for human beings, and was obviously a permanent arrangement. The layout, too—convenient for human beings, even to the height of the alcove.

Had this been the destroyer station closest to Earth, there could have been suspicion of a carefully tailored show. But this one was almost fifty thousand light-years distant. It could not have been designed for men—unless there were men in the galaxy not of Earth. Or very similar creatures.

The implications disturbed him, but no more than anything else about this strange museum. He knew it had been said that a planetary creature had to be somewhat like man in order to rise to civilization and technology, and that long chains of reasoning had been used to "prove" this thesis—but man's reasoning in such respects was necessarily biased, and he had discounted it. Yet if it were true—*if* it were true—did it also hold for man's *personality?* The greed, the stupidity, the bloodthirst—?

Was that Schön laughing again?

The passage opened into a second room. This one was much larger than the first, and the alcoves began at floor-level.

"Machinery!" Groton exclaimed with the same kind of excitement Afra had expressed before. He went to the first exhibit: a giant slab of metal, shaped like a wedge of cheese. As he approached, a ball fell on it and rolled off. Nothing else happened.

"Machine?" Ivo inquired.

"Inclined plane—the elementary machine, yes."

Well, if Groton were satisfied . . .

The second item was a simple lever. Fulcrum and rod, the point of the latter wedged under a large block. As they came up to it, the rod moved, and the block slid over a small amount. Groton nodded, pleased, and Ivo followed him to the next. The two women walked ahead, giving only cursory attention to this display.

The third resembled a vise. A long handle turned a heavy screw, so that the force applied was geared down twice. "Plane and lever," Groton remarked. "We're jumping ahead about fifty thousand years each time, as human technology goes."

"So far."

The fourth one had a furnace and a boiler, and resembled a primitive steam engine—which it was. The fifth was an electric turbine.

After that they became complicated. To Ivo's untrained eye, they resembled complex motors, heaters and radio equipment. Some he recognized as variants of devices he had blue printed via the macroscope; others were beyond his comprehension. Not all were intricate in detail; some were deceptively smooth. He suspected that an old automobile mechanic would find a printed-circuit board with embedded micro-transistors to be similarly smooth. One thing he was sure of: none of it was fakery.

Groton stopped at the tenth machine. "I thought I'd seen real technology when we terraformed Triton," he said. "Now—I am a believer. I've digested about as much as I care to try in one outing. Let's go on."

The girls had already done so, and were in the next chamber. This contained what appeared to be objects of art. The display commenced with simple two-and three-dimensional representations of concretes and abstracts, and went on to astonishing permutations. This time it was Beatryx who was fascinated.

"Oh, yes, I see it," she said, moving languidly from item to item. She was lovely in her absorption, as though the grandeur and artistry of what she perceived transfigured her own flesh. Now she outshone Afra. Ivo had not realized how fervent her interest in matters artistic was, though it followed naturally from her appreciation of music. He had assumed that what she did not talk about was of no concern to her, and now he chided himself for comprehending shallowly—yet again.

The display did not appeal to him as a whole, but individual selections did. He could appreciate the mathematical symbolism in some; it was of a sophisticated nature, and allied to the galactic language codes.

A number were portraits of creatures. They were of planets remote from Earth, but were intelligent and civilized, though he could not tell how he could be sure of either fact. Probably the subtle clues manifested themselves to him subliminally, as when Brad had first shown him alien scapes on the macroscope. Description? Pointless; the creatures were manlike in certain respects and quite alien in certain others. What mattered more was their intangible symmetry of form and dignity of countenance. These were Greek idealizations; the perfect physique with the well-tutored mind and disciplined emotion. These were handsome male, females and neuters. They were represented here as art, and they *were* art, in the same sense that a rendition of a finely contoured athlete or nude woman was art by human terms.

The rooms continued, each one at a lower level than the one preceding, until it seemed that the party had to be at the second lap of a spiral. One chamber contained books; printed scrolls, coiled tapes, metallic memory disks. Probably all the information the builders of the station might have broadcast to space was here, the reply to anyone who might suspect that the destroyer was merely sour grapes delivered by an ignorant culture. It was, in retrospect, obvious that that had never been the case.

One room contained food. Many hours and many miles had passed in fascination; they were hungry. Macroscopic chemical identifiers labeled the entrees, which were in stasis ovens. The party made selections as though they were dining at an automat, "defrosting" items, and the menu was strange but good.

Nowhere was there sign of animate habitation. It was as though the builders had stocked the station as a hostel and center of information, and left it for travelers who could come in the following eons. Yet it was also the source of the very signal that banished travel. What paradox was this?

The hall opened at last to a small room—and abruptly terminated. There were no alcoves, no exhibits; only a pedestal in the center supporting a small intricate object.

They walked around it indecisively. "Does it seem to you that we are being led down the garden path?" Afra inquired. "The exhibits are impressive, and I *am* impressed—but is this *all?* A museum tour and a dead end?"

"It is all we are supposed to see," Groton said. "And

361

somehow I do not think it would be wise to force the issue."

"We *came* to force the issue!" Afra said.

"What I meant to say was, let's not start hammering at the walls. We could discover ourselves in hard vacuum. Further exploration in an intellectual capacity should be all right."

Ivo was looking at the device on the pedestal. It was about eighteen inches long, and reminded him vaguely of the S D P S: an object of greater significance than first appeared. It was in basic outline cylindrical, but within that general boundary was a mass of convoluted tubings, planes, wires and attachments. It seemed to be partly electronic in nature, but not entirely a machine; partly artistic, but not a piece of sculpture. Yet there was a certain familiarity about it; some quality, some purpose inherent in it that he felt he should recognize.

He picked it up, finding the weight slight for so intricate an object: perhaps two pounds, and deviously balanced. The incipient recognition of its nature struck him more strongly. He ought to know what it was.

Something happened.

It was as though there were the noise of a great gong, but with vibrations not quite audible to human ears. Light flared, yet his eyes registered no image. There was a shock of heat and pressure and ponderosity that his body could not discern definitely, and some overwhelming odor that his nostrils missed.

The others were looking at him and at each other, aware that something important had been manifested—and not aware of more.

Ivo still held the instrument.

"Play it, Ivo," Beatryx said.

And all were mute, realizing that in all the chambers there had been no musical devices.

Ivo looked at it again, this time seeing conduits like those of a complex horn; fibers like those of stringed instruments; drumlike diaphragms; reeds. There was no place to blow, no spot to strike; but fingers could touch controls and eyes could trace connections.

The object was vibrating gently, as though the lifting of it had activated its power source. It had come alive, awaiting the musician's imperative.

He touched a stud at random—and was rewarded by a roll of thunder.

Beatryx, Afra, Groton: they stared up and out, trying instinctively to trace the source, to protect themselves if the walls caved in ... before realizing what had happened. Multiphonal sound!

"When you picked it up," Groton began—

"You touched a control," Afra finished. Both were shaken. "The BONG button."

"And now the thunder stud," Beatryx said.

Ivo slid one finger across a panel. A siren wail came at them from all directions, deafening yet melodious.

He explored the rest of it, producing a measured cacophony: every type of sound he could imagine was represented here, each imbued with visual, tactile and olfactory demesnes. If only he could bring this sensuous panorama under control—

And he could. Already his hands were responding to the instrument's ratios, achieving the measure of it, growing into the necessary disciplines. This was his talent, this way with an organ of melody. He had confined himself to the flute—Sidney Lanier's choice—but the truth was that all of Schön's gift was his. Probably there was no human being with greater natural potential than his own—should he choose to invoke it.

Ivo could not call out the technical aspects or discuss the theory knowledgeably; that was not part of it. He could not even read musical notation, for he had never studied it, choosing instead to learn by ear. But with an instrument in his hands and the desire to play, he could produce a harmony, and he could do it precisely, however complicated the descriptive terms for what he performed.

Now he developed that massive raw talent, bringing all his incipient skill to bear. He picked a suitable exercise, adapting for the flute at first, hearing the words as the song became animate. It was not from Lanier; that would come when he had command. One had to practice with lesser themes first. A trial run only ...

Drink to me only with thine eyes and I will pledge with mine;
Or leave a kiss within the cup and I'll not ask for wine.

The thirst that from the soul doth rise doth ask a
  drink divine;
But could I of Jove's nectar sip, I would not change
  for thine.

The others stood as the simple haunting melody surrounded them, marvelously clear, almost liquid, possessed
increasingly of that éclat, that soul that was the true
artist's way. The galactic instrument brought also the
suggestion of a heady nectar . . . and the touch of magic
lips.

Afra was staring raptly at him, never having heard him
play before. Had that been his worst blunder? Not to
employ the real talent he had?

Groton was staring at Afra. . . .

No, he was staring beyond her! The blank wall blocking
the continuation of their tour was dissolving, revealing
another passage. The way was open again!

"The free ride is over," Groton murmured. "Now we
have to participate."

They moved down it then in silence, Ivo still carrying
the instrument. This hall opened into a tremendous chamber whose ceiling was an opaque mist and whose floor was
a translucency without visible termination. There were no
walls; the sides merely faded into darkness, though there
was light close at hand.

They walked within it, looking in vain for something
tangible. But now even the floor was gone. Physically gone:
it too had dissolved and left them in free-fall, hanging
weightless in an atmosphere. Their point of entry, too, had
vanished; they tried to swim back through the pleasant
air, but there was nothing to locate. They were isolated and
lost.

"So it *was* a trap," Afra said, seemingly more irritated
than frightened.

"Or—a test," Groton said. "We had to demonstrate a
certain type of competence to gain admittance, after the
strictly sightseeing sections were finished. Perhaps we shall
have to demonstrate more, before being permitted to
leave."

They looked at Ivo, who was floating a little apart from
the others, and he looked at the thing in his hands.

"Try the same tune you did before," Afra suggested. "Just to be sure."

He played "Drink to Me Only" again. Nothing happened. He tried several other simple tunes, and the sound came at them from all over the unbounded chamber, not simple at all, but they remained as they were: four people drifting in nebulosity.

"I persist in suspecting that the key is musical," Groton said. "Why else that instrument, obviously neither toy nor exhibit. So far we may only have touched on its capability."

"Do you know," Ivo said thoughtfully, "Lanier believed that the rules for poetry and music were identical, and he tried to demonstrate this in his work. His flute-playing was said to be poetically inspired, and much of his poetry was musically harmonious. He even——"

"Very well," Afra said, unsurprised and still unworried, though the web of the spider seemed to be tightening. "Let's follow up on Lanier. He wrote a travelogue of Florida, one poor novel, and the poems 'Corn,' 'The Marshes of Glynn,' 'The Symphony'——"

"The Symphony!" Groton said it, but they all had reacted to the title. "Would that be——?"

"Play it, Ivo!" Beatryx said.

"The Symphony" was poetry, not music; there was no prescribed tune for it. But Ivo lifted the instrument and felt the power come into his being, for he had dreamed of setting this piece to music many times. He had never had the courage to make the attempt, on his own initiative. But here was his chance to make something of himself and his talent; to find out whether he could open, musically, the door to the riddle that was the destroyer.

There was music in meaning, and meaning in music, and they were very close to one another in the work of Sidney Lanier and in this poem in particular. Each portion of it was spoken by a different instrument, personified, and the whole was the orchestral symphony . . . .

The macroscopic communications systems he had experienced shared this trait. Music, color, meaning—all were interchangeable, and he was sure some species communicated melodically on their homeworlds. A translation was possible, if he borrowed from galactic coding—and if he had the skill to do it accurately. He had learned to comprehend galactic languages, but he had never tried to translate *into* them. The music charged his hands and body—but could he render the *poetry?*

The others waited, knowing his problem, searching for some way to help. Harold Groton, whose astrological interpretations could do no good in this situation; Afra Summerfield, whose physical beauty and analytical mind were similarly useless; Beatryx Groton, whose empathy could not enchant his suddenly uncertain fingers.

Analysis, empathy, astrology . . .

Then he saw that they *could* help, all of them. Just by being available.

Ivo began to play.

CHAPTER 10

The mists receded; the shadowless darkness evaporated. In the grandeur of sound the vision came, vastly mechanized: the image of the galaxy, cosmic dish of brilliance turning about its nebulous axis, trailing its spiral arms, radiating into space a spherical chord of energy of which the visible spectrum was less than one percent.

Then came the planets, recognizably Solarian, superimposed upon the nebular framework: Pluto, Neptune, Uranus, Saturn, Jupiter, Mars, Venus, Mercury, Luna. And it was as though they rolled around within that bowl at differing velocities, Sol rolling too, and Earth at the center. Merged with that was a second bowl, that shifted against the first without friction: galactic and planetary roulette. The combined motions were diverse and complex; it seemed that no eye could trace where within that melee all the planets were at any given moment or how the bowls aligned. Only if the action stopped could such a survey be accomplished—and such a cessation would destroy it all.

It could not be halted—but it could be photographed, in a manner, and such pictures revealed unique aspects. For the two concavities were marked off in quarters, and each quarter in thirds: twenty-four sections between them, twelve against twelve. Each of these was an open chamber wherein a planet might lodge forever, once caught by the flash of the camera. And the flashes came, four of them, making the planets freeze and the two bowls mesh together, binding themselves to the configurations of the instant; and in each case a form of existence was thereby set.

The motions were such that *only* the instant fixed the ratios; had the action been halted a fraction sooner or later, an entirely different configuration would have resulted, and reality would have deviated by that amount.

This, then, the symphony of motion and meaning, embracing all experience. The instant of its theoretic cessation, that fixation of all planets, was the horoscope.

FIRE

There was the swell of massed strings as Ivo descended to the circle of pie-shaped pens, searching out the fire symbols. He found a lion with flaming mane and passed it by; a centaur with drawn bow, the arrow a torch, and gave a nod to the archer that was not himself; and the ram. Here he tarried, approaching the animal with caution. The blades of its pasture were red spears of conflagration and the hairs of its body were coils of spreading smoke, but it was the head that predominated. Upon one mighty horn was written ASPIRATION and upon the other, TRADE.

"O Trade! O Trade! would thou wert dead!" Ivo exclaimed, quoting the words of the poet in the language of music: themes of the violin.

But Aries the Ram turned his molten head and snorted fire. "The beasts they hunger, and eat, and die; And so do we, and the world's a sty; Hush fellow swine; Why nuzzle and cry? *Swinehood hath no remedy.*"

And Ivo was afraid of this enormous beast, that spoke of other beasts and was so close to him that its very gaze seemed to burn his flesh, and he comprehended its power and determination. But still he tried: "Does business mean, *Die, you—live, I?* Then 'Trade is trade' but sings a lie: 'Tis onlywar grown miserly."

Aries pointed one horn at a scorched scroll illuminated in the massed-string surge, and Ivo read:

Formal galactic history commences with the formation of the first interstellar communications network. Only scattered authentic prior evidences exist for the employment of artificial macronics, and these may be disregarded as transitory phenomena of insignificant galactic moment.

The first two cultures to establish a dialogue were only two hundred light-years apart; but a thousand years elapsed from the onset of broadcasting to confirmation The second culture received the signals of the first and comprehended them, but delayed some time before deciding to respond. It is conjectured that conservative elements within that culture feared the long-range effect of a dialogue with complete aliens: a caution that was justified if value was placed on the status quo.

During the second millennium fifteen additional cultures joined the network, having observed the successful interchange of the first pair and having gained confidence thereby. This was the nucleus of primitive galactic civilization.

Within a hundred thousand years the initial signal had traversed the galaxy and gone beyond, diffusing into the entropy of macronic debris; but its originator had ceased broadcasting within ten thousand, presumably because of species decline or natural catastrophe. It had not been, in retrospect, a particularly notable culture; it owes its distinction in galactic history solely to the fact that it was the first to precipitate the network. Others, however, stimulated by that sample period, remained active, and the total number of participants increased steadily for the first several million years. Eventually the number stabilized, ushering in the so-called main phase.

Spheres of influence developed, the extent of each determined by the relative commencement time of broadcast the level of knowledge provided, the endurance of the originating culture and the compatibility of neighboring cultures. Certain stations, having nothing original to contribute,

*closed down and were lost to history. Some became inter-
mittent, doing little more than announcing their presence
every millennium or so. Some became "service" stations,
relaying material gathered and correlated from others. Some
merely acknowledged prevailing broadcasts and expressed
identification with the more notable ones. A few broadcast
without reference to incoming signals, in this manner avoiding direct competition for prestige.*

*Thus fairly stable spheres developed amid the general
chaos, centered on the most durable and knowledgeable
stations. This stability extended beyond individual broadcasters, for when a major station desisted lesser ones
would fill its place and continue disseminating its information. Quite a number of prominent spheres were based on
long-defunct cultures, since the quality of knowledge developed transcended the details of species or culture.
Overall civilization gradually expanded, as individual species profited by the knowledge of their neighbors. At times
dominance within a sphere would shift, as a pupil became
more vigorous than the instructor; but generally the leading cultures maintained their positions, owing perhaps to
greater inherent species ability. This main phase endured
for about a hundred million years, and almost all the early
cultures were replaced by later ones who could lay claim
to very little original knowledge. The time of pioneering
was over, galactically, and it seemed that the ultimate in
civilization had been attained.*

*The onset of the First Siege altered this situation dras-
tically. This came in the form of an extragalactic broadcast
that intercepted the galaxy broadside and thus saturated it
within a few thousand years. This was the first intergalactic
communicatory contact made, apart from faint, blurred
signals of relatively primitive culture. This one was advanced: more sophisticated in knowledge and application
than any hitherto known. By its mere existence it proved
that the local level of civilization and technology was fledg-
ling rather than mature. It presented a technique until this
point thought to be beyond animated physical capability:
the key to what amounted to instantaneous travel between
the stars of the galaxy.*

*It was hailed as a miracle. No longer was commerce con-
fined to the intellect. For the first time, divergent planetary
species were able to make physical contact.*

*But the wiser cultures saw it for what it was—and could
not cry the alarm before the consequences were upon them.*

The stellar constellation known on Earth as Aries was
not a true association of stars at all, for some were
relatively close to the planet and others were far removed,
in that apparent region of space. Yet this could be construed as a segment of the galaxy, and within it were
numerous cultures. In this time of interstellar travel, empires were forming; and it was to one of these that Schön
journeyed.

As Ivo had found himself at the Hegemony of Tyre, so
Schön landed on an Earth-type but alien planet, feeling
its gravity and breathing its atmosphere. There was vegetation, similar in function if not in detail to that of Earth,
and there was what passed for civilization.

The planet appeared to be at war.

Schön assimilated the situation almost immediately. He
proceeded to the nearest recruiting office. "I am a talented alien in need of employment," he said to the
boothed official.

The beetle-browed, facet-eyed creature contemplated
him. "I grant you are alien—sickeningly so," it honked. "If
you are verbally talented, I suggest you make use of your
ability to show cause why I should not vaporize you where
you stand on your repulsive meaty digits, in three minutes
or less."

Schön could tell by the shade of its carapace that it
was suspicious. "Obviously you suspect me of being a
representative of a hostile power, since I perceive you are
on a war, er, footing here." The hesitation reflected the
creature's absence of feet. "Obviously, too, I *could* be a
spy or saboteur, since the ability to penetrate your defenses
without observation is a requisite for that trade. And my
direct approach to you is no guarantee that my motives
are innocent; I could be holding a radiation bomb triggered to go off the moment you blast me. That would be
my employer's guarantee that my failure to insinuate
myself into your military machine could not lead to awkward exposure of his vile designs. I would naturally prefer
to preserve my life and quietly gather whatever useful
information I could while maintaining scrupulous cover. I
should for that reason be an excellent employee of yours,

371

since suspicion would naturally center on my activities and only months or years of excellent and unimpeachable service could dissipate this doubt—by which time the present crisis should long since be over and my employer could be allied to yours. But if I cannot accomplish this, at least my employer may have the satisfaction of knowing that a cubic mile of this planet's lithosphere—perhaps a trifle less, if the shoddy workmanship of the past is any criterion—has been rendered uninhabitable by my radioactive demise. Two of my three minutes are done; you may keep the third."

The creature paused, almost as though in doubt. "Will you accede to fluoroscopic examination?"

"Certainly. But that could be construed as an uncertainty on your part that your superiors would surely question. It would be wiser to blast me right now, before any such complications develop."

"If you are armed as you describe, that would be disastrous."

"Perhaps I am bluffing. A bluff is certainly cheaper than a bomb, particularly in these days of runaway inflation."

"If you are bluffing, then you are probably not a spy and there is no *need* to blast you. In fact it could be an inadequacy on my record. If you are *not* bluffing—"

"There is something in what you say, and I commend your perspicacity. Still, I must point out that I could be a real spy who is bluffing merely about the bomb. That is more likely, don't you agree, than my being an innocent person *with* a bomb."

"If you *were* innocent, you wouldn't *have* a bomb."

Schön shrugged in eloquent defeat not untinged with a hint of well-concealed bad grace. "Have it your way."

"Assuming that you are a spy, whether armed or unarmed, how could I best deal with you without risking my own life or record?"

"That's an excellent question. You will no doubt think of much better alternatives, but all that occurs to me at the moment is the possibility of referring the case to your immediate superior, as a matter warranting his discretion."

It was expeditiously done. After an essentially similar dialogue, Schön was bounced up another link in the chain of command. And another. Eventually he spoke to the chief of intelligence.

"We are satisfied that you are what you claim to be," the Chief said. "Namely, a talented alien in need of employment. You are also of a physical stock not on record in the galactic speciology, but you are too clever to have been trained on a primitive planet. The probability is, then, that you *are* a spy for someone—but we hesitate to interrogate you thoroughly until we can be sure you are not an observer from a quote friendly unquote or at least neutral power. Since we have at the moment only one potential enemy and several thousand potential allies, and since we are not adverse to assistance, it behooves us to deal cautiously with you. Probability suggests you are an asset—but how can we minimize the risk?"

"Just don't try to send me to any temple of Baal."

"Pardon?"

"It would be expeditious to offer me compensation that is somewhat greater than the amount my overt services warrant. That way, I would be inclined to transfer my allegiance to you, in the event it was not already with your planet. Spies are notoriously underpaid, you know."

The Chief vibrated a follicle against his beak. "Surely you realize that this is a ridiculous proposition? We would not possibly—"

Schön sighed. "Of course you are right. A captaincy in your navy would be an unheard of reward for a suspected spy, however meritorious his service."

"Who said anything about—!" the Chief began, his shell crackling with righteous indignation. "A captaincy! I was thinking of Third Lieutenant, J. G., apprentice, probationary."

Captain Schön docked his sleek destroyer and gave his crew thirty-hour planetary leave while the ship underwent preventive maintenance. He set the thermostat within his flame-red cloak of authority to an invigorating sixty-five degrees Farenheit, making the mental conversion to local units effortlessly. The few civilians passing him on the street saluted with alacrity; he ignored thm. Protocol did no require that an officer return courtesy to any person more than three grades below him, and of course civilians were beneath rank.

He mounted the ramp of the capital and brushed past the rigid guards. The other officers were already assembled in the presidential suite: the five supreme individuals of the planet, gathered about the giant semicircular table. The Monarch, the Prime Minister, the Fleet Admiral, the Chief of Intelligence and the Chancellor of the Exchequer —all waiting somberly for the meeting to begin.

Schön took his place. Not one of the others was particularly pleased at his presence, but they did not dare to make a key decision without him. They knew he was clever enough to foil anything arranged without his consent.

The Prime Minister elevated himself, lifting his venerable thorax above the table. "Gentlemen—we have received an ultimatum from the Hegemony of Lion. We are met here to consider our response."

The Monarch turned to him. "A précis, if you please."

"Surrender of all military equipment together with attached personnel. Deportation of hostages to Lion, as itemized. Indemnities. Reconstruction."

"Standard contract," the Chief observed.

"All present of this council appear on the hostage list?" the Monarch inquired.

The Minister rattled agreement. "All but the Captain. Together with households."

The Chancellor coughed. "Households! That means our daughters get dinked."

"Good for them, I'm sure," the Chief muttered.

The Chancellor inflated angrily, but the Monarch cut him off by speaking again. "How strict are the indemnities?"

"Standard. Ten percent of Gross Planetary Product for Ram and environs, fifteen percent for subsidiary worlds. Exploitation of subsequently developed offworld resources, fifty percent."

"Too high," the Admiral said. "They should not get more than twenty percent of windfall acquisitions."

"Academic, since we won't have our navy," the Chief pointed out. "No ships, no loot—unless you plan to refit merchant vessels for your piracy."

"Piracy!"

"Gentlemen, let's not quibble over terminology in this time of crisis," the Monarch said. "The question is, do we acquiesce?"

"No!" the Admiral exclaimed. "We have the space fold coordinates of their main system updated to the second. We have the missiles for an inundation strike. Act now, and we can wipe them out. Solve the problem once and for all."

"Very neat," the Chief said dryly. "Except for their second-strike capability. What use mutual destruction?"

"Better that than slavery!"

"A standard contract is hardly slavery, even with fifty percent windfall appropriation. We have issued similar contracts to lesser species in the past."

"What makes you think they'll honor those terms, once our fleet has been dismantled?"

"Haven't you heard of the Gemini Convention?"

"That's passé. We never bothered with it. Not for fifty thousand years—"

"Gentlemen," the Monarch repeated, and the argument subsided fretfully.

"It seems our various opinions are fairly set," the Minister remarked. "Some are amenable to compromise, some feel we would be foolish to allow ourselves to be read out of power by such means."

"Better read than dead," the Chief murmured.

"Treason!" the Admiral exclaimed.

"*However*," the Minister continued loudly, "we must agree on some recommendation before this session ends. The Monarch, of course, will make the decision."

There was a silence.

"I am, as you know, from a far system," Schön said after an interval. "Possibly my perspective differs from yours."

They waited noncommittally, grudgingly allowing him to make his case.

"As I understand it, Ram has historically had good relations with Lion. Both hegemonies rose to sapience about a million years before the Traveler appeared, and because of their proximity—within a hundred light-years of each other—an intense dialogue was feasible. The development of spacefold transport was hailed as the begin-

375

ning of an era of splendor, now that these longtime and compatible correspondents could meet physically and without a time delay of centuries."

"Ancient history," snorted the Admiral.

"Yet instead of a mutually beneficial interchange—trade—you developed antipathy. You were at war within a thousand years, and have fought intermittently and inconclusively ever since, just as Tyre fought with Sidon."

"Tyre? Sidon?" the Admiral inquired. "Where in the galaxy are they? What kind of fleets do they have?"

"Mixed fleets: war galleys and merchanters," Schön replied straight-faced. "The point is, they depleted their resources and discommoded their navies by striving senselessly against each other, instead of mobilizing against their mutual enemies."

"That's an oversimplification," the Minister said. "We have had numerous encounters with other systems—"

"Three wars with Centaur, two with Swan, altercations with Eagle, Horse, Dog, Hare—" Schön put in.

"Alliances with Bear, Beaver, Dragon—" the Minister interposed in turn, retaining his equanimity.

"All of which were violently sundered. Why? What happened to the mighty era of knowlege and prosperity heralded by the availability of interstellar travel?"

"Our neighbors disappointed us."

"They all were unworthy. Sure. And now Lion has issued an ultimatum demanding your conditional surrender. Surely they had provocation?"

The Admiral and the Minister rustled their scales discordantly.

"There *was* a border incident," the Chief admitted after a small delay.

"Of what nature. Practically speaking, you don't *have* a border with Lion. You have to use spacefold—and you can't just rub up against your neighbor by accident. Not when you have to compress an object of near-planetary mass into its gravitational radius in order to poke through. For that matter, spacefold transport and accurate coordinates make the entire galaxy your neighbor. Light velocity limitation means nothing anymore."

"It was a reconnaissance mission," the Admiral said.

"A two-thousand-mile diameter moon on reconnaissance? Equipped to service several thousand warships, each potentially armed with planet-busters? Your euphemism hardly becomes the situation. And I'll bet you planted it within five light-seconds of their homeworld."

"Three light-seconds," the Admiral said almost inaudibly.

"And *you* didn't bother with any ultimatum, did you? Just a nice, neat fait accompli. You thought. Sneak your battlemoon right within range of their capital-planet, while their own ships were elsewhere. So what happened?"

"They were ready for us," the Minister said. "They had complete information."

"Incredible bungling," the Chancellor of the Exchequer muttered. "Have you any idea what a battlemoon *costs?*"

"Obviously there was a leak," Schön said. He was beginning to get bored.

"Obviously." The Admiral glared at the Chief, who averted his facets.

"So now Lion has your, er, expedition, and the balance of power has shifted in its favor. Thus the ultimatum."

None of them replied.

"I have," Schön continued after a pause, "been doing a little research. I find that this entire question is unimportant."

Their eyes appraised him stonily.

"Ram and Lion are two principalities amid a galaxy of kingdoms, federations and empires. The only reason neither has been gobbled up yet is that there is insufficient wealth between you to warrant the trouble. However, the flux of major powers is at the state where it has become economically feasible to absorb you both, rather than tolerate your petty raids on civilized installations any longer. You Phoenicians and Greeks are ripe for Egypt or Assyria—or even Alexander."

The Monarch contemplated him sadly through a golden facet. "Are you ready now to inform us whom you represent? This Alexander, perhaps?"

"I represent no one but myself. I am merely stating facts that should be obvious to any objective party. Your shortsightedness is destroying you. You are wasting each other's resources while the wolves look on, and they are only waiting until you are at your weakest stage before snapping you up. You would be far better off to make an honest alliance with Lion—even to the extent of accepting that so-called contract—and thus perhaps postpone a more final loss of identity."

Still they did not coment.

At last the Monarch looked up. "What you say makes sense to us, Captain. We are in the wrong, but it is not too late. We shall accept the contract."

There was no dissent, of course. The Monarch of Ram had spoken.

Two weeks later Schön's ship berthed within the transport satellite: another moon of minimum effective mass. It had been stripped, the Chief informed him, and was nothing but a ball of rock, with the exception of the tube leading down into the compression mechanism compartment. The equipment, Schön knew, was far more sophisticated than that constructed by the human party on Triton; this could make use of a far smaller mass, and the location perceptors were precise. This, together with the up-to-date spacefold maps of this area of the galaxy, made a controlled jump routine. He had done his homework here, too, and was familiar with the equipment.

He was alone. He had been selected to make the trip to Lion bearing the capitulation message. "They would not trust any sizable party," the Chief had explained. "But you, an alien, can negotiate the details, and return with their expeditionary party. We shall be ready, then."

Yeah, sure, bugeye.

Schön entered the control compartment and examined the telltales. The mechanism had been set and locked: transport was scheduled to occur within the hour, and this had been timed exactly. The express position of the object was important, as the human explorers had known; what the dull-witted humans had not suspected was that the precise *time* of transport was equally critical. For the universe was not stable; it had been expanding, and now was in a state of flux preparatory to contraction, and this affected every part of it. Some sections were *still* expanding, while others were already contracting, and special stresses acted even on the interiors of galaxies and stellar systems that appeared to the fleeting animate observer to maintain their original sizes and positions. And this flux caused a drift between adjacent surfaces of jumpspace; the loops were fairly constant, but their fabric continued to stretch, eventually forming new loops of similar size or abolishing old ones. As a result, the differential between adjacent surfaces could be a swift current. In some instances, as shift piled upon shift and jumpspace warped frantically to compensate, the passage of minutes meant a similar number of light-minutes deviation from the calculated location of emergence.

So his journey had been carefully calculated in advance, and the equipment sealed to prevent potentially disastrous distortion. Emergence at the wrong point in space, even if only a few million miles off, could be taken as an indication of betrayal, and the waiting warships would open fire.

Schön unlimbered the special equipment he had brought (smuggled) and powdered the locking devices with single applications of his limited-slip laser. The panel opened, exposing the intricate circuitry. He manipulated his tools with the dexterity and competence he naturally possessed and made certain minor adjustments.

He was not traveling quite where the good Monarch of Ram had arranged.

He returned to his ship, sealed himself in, and entered the melting chamber. The ten-second melt-radiation warner sounded; then—

He came out of it whole, knowing that many hours had passed while his body melted, vaporized and finally compressed along with the ship and moon into a comparative speck—and then reversed the process at the other end of the jump.

He set himself before the ship's macroscope and looked out at the universe.

There was no destroyer signal, as he had known. The ship's computer shifted through the configurations and matched his present location: approximately one light-hour away from his scheduled rendezvous in the home-system of Lion.

He smiled. It had worked.

He had set the contraction mechanism for a triple sequence with a delay of only minutes between each effort. Thus the moon had made the first jump to Lion, hesitated momentarily, and gone into the return cycle before protoplasmic reconstitution could start. The brief interim and the relative motion of the two surfaces of space had sent it back at an angle, and it had emerged several light-minutes from its origin. Before the home-crowd could respond, since it took minutes for them even to see it, it had gone into the third compression, to emerge at its present spot. Its route had been a kind of N figure, the displacement magnified by the stress exerted on the fabric of space by adjacent punchthroughs. Dangerous—but what were heroes for, if not to brave danger?

Only then had the reconstitution process commenced. This had taken hours—but his displacement in space should have been sufficient for security. Just about now things should be popping.

They were. The sweep showed the traces that indicated an armada encircling the inhabited world of this system: battleships traveling at speed. The Lions had anticipated treachery.

And the anticipation had been well fulfilled. Two uncharted moons drifted within the system, light-hours apart, and he knew that at least one more was present on the far side, too far from his own location to register yet. Observation by optics or macronics was so *slow!* It was an all-out attack; the inundation strike the Ram Admiral had urged.

What of the Lion second-strike capability the Chief had so carefully mentioned? Schön smiled again. The solution to that inhibitor was obvious. The Rams had underestimated the perspicacity of the stranger, thinking to set him up as a duped emissary. They had staged a mock meeting and made a mock decision, while the war preparations moved ahead full-scale. There had never been a true capitulation, and probably not even a genuine ultimatum. This thrust had been decades in the making.

Lion ships still cruised in the vicinity of the supposed emergence, though the bulk of that fleet was already heading toward him. They had thought that his moon was merely another unit in the invasion—as indeed it was. But it had not stayed long enough to allow their planet-busters to score, and now was in an unscheduled location. Doubly unscheduled: naturally the Ram schedule differed from that set up for the truce mission, and his own schedule differed from Ram's.

He adjusted the macroscope to focus within his own moon and took a look on sweep. Sure enough, the buried warships were already coming to life, their crews having emerged from mass gasification. He had at least done them the favor of saving them from the planet-busters; Lion intelligence *was* better than Ram's. Not that it made any difference to him.

Strange that they had trusted him with the spacefold mechanism. Perhaps they had feared that he would recognize a dummy-panel—a correct assumption—and had felt that the lock sufficed against incidental mischief. If they really thought he was an important Lion spy, verisimilitude required that he be allowed to observe the setting for himself.

There were hundreds of simpler and surer ways of doing it, naturally. But the military mind had never been noted for its subtlety or efficiency, fortunately. Fortunately? It would not *be* the military mind if it were clever. Most likely, the Ram strategists had simply underestimated him by a factor of two or three.

In due course his Ram escort would get around to dispatching him as superfluous. His ship was unarmed—theoretically in accordance with the negotiations setup—and lacked working fluid for any extended trip. They were sure they had him penned safely; their immediate concern was the approaching fleet of Lion.

He refocused the scope on the farther reaches of the system. Sure enough: the third expedition had appeared. No moonlet, this; Ram had transported its entire homeworld! That was their answer to Lion's second-strike capability, as he had suspected. Removal of the target from the target-system.

A third time he smiled. Such naïveté!

For now the Lion home-planet was gone, leaving only the massed offensive arm to attack the Ram planet before its inhabitants could be reconstituted. Two could play at this game of treachery and system-jumping!

Oh, the fragments would be small, very small, when the first accredited empire came collecting!

Now it was time to make contact with Lion, on the way to larger things. In three hours the jumpspace mechanism would initiate its fourth and final cycle, with disastrous consequences for any unprepared troops in the vicinity. Those outside the field of compression would be smashed by the moon's collapse and displacement; those still within it would be preserved—but not in animate state. Only the resilient gas-form could sustain that terrible implosion alive.

Schön paused before the chamber entrance. Exactly how grateful, he wondered, would the opposing monarch— the Pride of Lion—be for a complete undamaged military moon, together with a number of serviceable warships?

Not grateful enough, he decided. Lion would attempt to string him along as had Ram, exercising the eternal governmental prerogative of amorality and fallibility. Meanwhile the internecine struggle would continue, each home-world in orbit about its neighbor's sun, its native life suffering from the unfamiliar radiation.

No, the real rewards for the entrepreneur would not occur until an empire made its move.

Perhaps such a move could be hastened by a little judicious manipulation. . . .

Still smiling, Schön stepped into the chamber. "Alexander, where are you?' he murmured as the warner sounded.

WATER

"*A velvet flute-note fell down pleasantly upon the bosom of that harmony* . . ." And Ivo was that flute, or of it, and the chambers he descended into were liquid. First he encountered the scorpion resting on the beach, not a horror, huge as it was, but rather with an aspect of creativity and fairness. Then he passed the crab, who watched patiently from under the surface, housed beneath a shell. At last he stopped at the tank wherein the fishes were swimming, like twin animate feet wading under the wave. Upon the one was written SYMPATHY, and upon the other HEART.

"From the warm concave of the fluted note Somewhat, half song, half odor, forth did float, As if a rose might somehow be a throat. ..." Ivo said to Pisces in the prescribed mode.

And the first fish replied: "Yea, Nature, singing sweet and lone ‾Breathes through life's strident polyphone ..."

And the second fish continued: "Yea, all fair forms, and sounds and lights, And warmths, and mysteries, and mights, Of Nature's utmost depths and heights ..."

And the first: "So Nature calls through all her system wide, *Give me thy love, O man, so long denied ...*"

And the second: "Trade! is thy heart all dead, all dead? And hast thou nothing but a head? I'm all for heart," the flute-voice said.

And on the bottom of the tank was written in sand and shell:

Physical contact between the stellar cultures of the galaxy in fact meant chaos. All species had needs and ambitions, and few were ethical in galactic sense when subject to meaningful temptation. Prejudices submerged during the long purely-intellectual contact reappeared now with renewed force. It developed that certain warm, liquid-blooded species had an inherent aversion to certain cold mucous-surfaced species, however equivalent their intellects, and many other combinations were similarly incompatible. Certain species turned pirate, preying on others and taking wealth, slaves and food without fair recompense; others inaugurated programs of colonization that led rapidly to friction. Not all encounters were violent; some were mutually beneficial. But the old, stable order had been completely overturned, and power shifted radically from the intellectual to the biological and physical. Highly civilized cultures were overrun and annihilated by barbarians.

A new order arose, dominated by the most ruthless and cunning species. Greed and distrust acted to split and weaken the empires of these new leaders, forcing further change and breakup, in an ever more dissolute spiral. In the course of half a million years, galactic civilization as an entity disappeared entirely, submerged in the tide of violence; no macroscopic broadcasting stations remained except the extragalactic Traveler. Isolated by their own released savagery, all species declined. It was the Siege of Darkness.

Approximately one million years after its inauguration the Traveler beam terminated. The siege was over—but the progress of galactic civilization had been set back immeasurably. As time passed, macroscopic stations began again to broadcast, and a new network was established—but the scars of the Siege were long in healing. Love, once denied, recovered slowly.

"You are better now," the voice said hopefully.

Beatryx opened her eyes, that were still stinging from the salt, and squinted into the warm sunlight. She was wearing a black bathing suit somewhat more scant than seemed appropriate. "Oh, yes!" she agreed, a little dizzy from her recent immersion. It had seemed she was drowning. . . .

The young man's face seemed to shine. "Lida! Persis! Durwin! A paean, for she who was lost is healed!"

Three handsome young persons bounded across the sand. "Joy!" the leader cried, a muscular giant, sleek with the water dripping from his torso.

In moments they stood before her: two bronzed young men, two lovely girls, each radiating vitality. All had lustrous black hair and classically sculptured features.

The first man spoke again, more formally: "This is Persis, girl of peace." The girl performed a motion suggestive of a curtsy, smiling. Her teeth were bright and even. "This is Lida, beloved of us all." The second girl genuflected, smiling as politely as the first. "And my dear friend Durwin." The second man raised his hand in a formal wave rather like a salute, hoisting an eyebrow merrily.

"And I," the speaker said diffidently, "am Hume—lover of my home." His smile was the most winning of all.

Beatryx tried to speak, but Hume squatted to touch her lips lightly with his slender finger. "Do not name yourself. Surely we know you already. Have you not brought joy to us?"

"She who brings joy!" Durwin exclaimed. "Her name would be—"

"Beatrice!" the two girls cried.

"No," Hume said solemnly. "That would be common joy, and hers is uncommon."

Durwin studied her. "You are right. Look at her hair! She is as a diamond amidst quartz. Yet joy must be her designation. Not Beatrice, nor Beatrix—"

"But Beatryx!" Hume finished.

"We shall call her Tryx," the girl Persis said.

Beatryx listened to all of this with tolerance. "You knew my name already," she said.

"We knew what it had to be," Hume said, and offered no further explanation.

"Where is this?" She looked at the white sand and the strings of seaweed and the green-white surf.

"Where," Hume inquired gently, "would you like it to be?"

"Why, I don't really know. I suppose it doesn't matter. It must be like Ivo's dream, when he went to Tyre—only it seems so real!"

"Come," Durwin said. "Evening is hard upon us, and the village is not in sight."

"Yes," Lida agreed. "We must show you to our companions."

Then Beatryx was walking down the long beach, seeing the light of the setting sun refracted off the rolling water in splays of colored light. The men paced her on either side and the girls skipped next to them. Inland the palmlike vegetation rose, casting long and waving shadows in the distance. The air was warm and moist, rich with the briny odors of the sea. Underfoot—all feet were bare, including hers, she suddenly realized—the sand was hot but not uncomfortable, spiced with multihued pebbles and occasional conchlike shells. The word "murex" came to her, but she could not place either the source or the meaning; certainly she had never seen shells quite like these before.

Half a mile down the curving shoreline rested the village, a cluster of conical tents on the beach. In the center she saw a bonfire, great fat sparks leaping into the darkening sky, occasional fluffy wood-ashes drifting in the air current coming in across the water. She could smell the burning cellulose, together with hot stones and charred seaweed, and the hungry aroma of roasting fish.

Hume took her by the arm and guided her into the crowd. "This is Tryx," he proclaimed. "Come from the water, and great joy to us that she is sound and well."

"Another rescued!" someone cried.

They gathered about, dark-haired, slender, glowing with health and friendliness. There were about thirty in all, as comely a group as she had ever seen. "See how fair she is!" a girl exclaimed.

Beatryx laughed, embarrassed. "I am not fair! I'm almost forty!" With that she wondered where Harold was. It was strange to be anywhere without him, and not entirely comfortable, though these were certainly nice people. Harold and Ivo and Afra—were they still back in the floating chamber, watching her as the three had watched Ivo before? But she had no Schön-personality to direct the trip . . . it was all so complicated.

The others smiled. "We must build a house for you," one said, and immediately there was a flurry of action. One of the tents was evidently a storehouse; from it the men and women, working in cheerful concert, brought poles and rolls of clothlike material and lengths of cord. Some quickly planted the poles deep in the sand and bound them together at the top, while others wrapped the cloth around the outside of the resultant structure. Beatryx noticed that there were snap fastenings at the edges, so that the material could be easily joined to itself and to the uprights.

And it was complete: a many-colored teepee residence for her to stay in while she was here. They stood back and looked at her expectantly.

"It's very nice," she said. "But—"

They waited, but she could not go on. It *was* very nice, and their society was very nice—but how could she inquire the purpose of it all? She had entered some kind of—diagram?—something with little balls falling and wheels spinning, and she had seen strange animals as though one of Harold's charts had come to life, and finally she had fallen into a pond with talking fish—or had she *been* the fish, somehow?—and some kind of writing on the bottom. She understood vaguely that it all had to do with history and the reason she and Harold and Ivo and Afra had come to this place. *That* place. But now she was by herself, and there was no history and no explanation, and she did not know how to phrase her question.

If only Harold were here to take charge! He was so practical about such things.

"Thank you so much," she finally said.

"A paean!" Hume cried, and suddenly the group was in song, a melody of sheer exuberance and youthful glee. The voices of the girls were like flutes, marvelously clear and high.

Then they were all sitting around the fire, now a ring of dimming coals, and passing spicy, juicy fish around, each one wrapped in tough green leaves. For drink there was something very like coconut milk, but richer and more filling. She worried that it might be alcoholic, but was soon satisfied that it was not.

No one seemed to have lamps, and when the last of the fire died they were sitting in the dark. The men were exchanging stories of the fish they had speared or almost speared that day, and the territory they had explored: some fabulous fish, some astonishing territory, if everything were to be believed. The girls spoke of the pretty flowers they had seen inland, and the colored stones they had collected No one asked Beatryx where she had been, and she was glad of that because she did not see how she could explain.

It was all very pleasant, and even the sea-breeze was not cold; but there was one problem. She had dined well and sipped well, and certain urgencies of nature were developing. But which tent . . . ?

On her left sat Hume; on her right, Durwin. She could not inquire.

At last the gathering broke up and the merry voices faded into the night. It was time to retire.

She stood up uncertainly. She was no longer sure where her tent was, or what she should do once she reached it. As for the other—

A gentle hand took her arm. "Will you walk with me?" Persis' soft voice came.

Thankfully she accepted the guidance. They walked out of the village and into the line of vegetation; she could tell only by the retreating sound of the waves and by the occlusion of a swath of stars by overhanging branches every so often. Now and then her foot came down on a twig or pebble, but there was nothing harsh enough to cause pain.

"Here."

"Here?" They were still in the forest; she was sure of

387

that much. Night insects chirruped and fluttered nearby. Where was the building?

Persis squatted down.

Beatryx realized, with a despairing shock, that this was it. There *were* no lavatory facilities! Nothing but the bushes. And these people weren't even disturbed!

Harold would have arranged to build a privy, at least. . . .

There was a fluffy mattress on the floor of her domicile, and no wind entered to disturb things. Persis showed her where to hang her bathing suit, and left. The advantage of the teepee format was that everything was within reach in the dark. It was comfortable enough.

Comfortable enough physically, but not esthetically. To sleep without night clothing . . . and no sanitary facilities! She knew she was being foolish, but these were aspects of the primitive idyl that disturbed her profoundly.

Now she wondered about the sleeping arrangements of her companions. It seemed to her that there had been fewer than twenty structures in the village. Not enough for each person to have one. Were a number of these young men and women married? She had seen no sign of this; no rings on any fingers, no marital designations.

Perhaps Hume and Durwin shared a tent, and Lida and Persis. Young people often did not like to remain alone. Nor, for that matter, did people like Beatryx herself. Still—

She knew what Harold would say: other peoples, other customs. Let them be.

If only he were here!

In the morning the young men gathered more dry branches for the fire, but did not light it. The girls brought fruit from the forest, harvesting it from somewhere, and more coconuts. The nectar, it turned out, was from these. Teams of men punched holes in the mighty-husked objects and skillfully poured the juice into gourds. The women added flavoring from crushed berries.

Breakfast was as supper had been: a communal gathering around the fire—still unlit—and distribution of succulent sections of fruit and cups of drink. Instead of tales of the day's adventures, the dialogue was about forthcoming projects: where the best fishing might be had, whether it was time to move the camp to a new location, the prospects for rain.

"I," Hume said, "shall scout to the south this morning. Maybe I can find a suitable campsite."

"And who will go with you?" Persis demanded with a twinkle. "Do you think we can trust a *man* to make such an important survey?"

"Tryx will go with me!" he replied jovially. "Was I not first to find her?"

"Are you sure it was not her sunbeam hair you found first?" Persis concentrated with mock-brooding on a strand of her own black tresses.

"I really don't know anything about campsites," Beatryx protested. It was foolish again, but she felt flattered by the frequent references to her hair. Once, of course, it had been quite fair, and some of the color lingered. Of course it would be subject to comment amid a black-haired group such as this, but it really was nothing remarkable.

"Do you think *he* does?" Persis said. Beatryx took a moment to remember that this referred to knowledge of campsites. The matter seemed to be decided.

She and Hume walked down the beach, not hurrying. Beatryx worried about sunburn, but clouds were growing in the sky and rain seemed to be a more likely problem.

"Is it like this—all the time?" she asked, still having trouble framing her question. She had not understood, before, why Ivo had not simply snapped out of his Tyredream. Now she appreciated his situation. This world *included* sleep! Waking up was merely waking up, not a return. There was nothing to take hold of, no way to—she still couldn't formulate it.

"All summer," he said. He carried a fishing spear that he used as a staff.

So that was it! A summer holiday. "Where are your families?"

"Oh, they're inland. It is too dangerous for them on the beaches."

"Dangerous?" That didn't sound like vacation!

"The blacks," he said, as though that explained it.

"What are the blacks?"

He looked uncomfortable. "They come up from the sea. I thought you knew all about—that. We have to stop them from infesting the land. Every year some try. If they ever

389

take hold and start breeding—" He looked ahead. "There it is! I wanted you to see it."

She followed his gaze and spied an abutment of rock—a sheer cliff rising out of the sea, twenty feet high. It was an unusual formation, since the vertical side faced away from the ocean and toward the beach. Harold would have made some observation about reverse tidal undercutting, but she didn't really understand that kind of thing. It was very pretty.

The clouds had overcast the sun, but as if stage-directed they parted to let a beam come down. It struck the sea-side of the rock, and there was a brilliant flash from the edge.

"What is that?" she asked, concerned.

"The sun-stone," he said, running toward it. She had to follow, bewildered.

The overcast closed in again, but as she came up to the cliff she discovered why the rock had seemed to take fire. It was mirror-surfaced! The face toward the beach was a clean fracture that had been polished by nature or man until it shone. The beach was reflected in it, and the distant trees, making it appear almost like a window to another world.

Could she step through? Would *that* convey her back to—

Then she saw herself within it, and gasped.

She had lost twenty years. Her hair was thick and blonde, as it had been before she settled in to married life. Her face was thin, narrow-chinned, like those of the girls here, and her figure appallingly trim.

"And you said you were not fair!" Hume said, divining her thoughts. "You said you were forty."

"But I was—*am*," she said, confused. "I don't understand this."

"Why try? Too much understanding only brings sorrow, as we well know." And he was off again down the beach, the mirror-rock a fancy only of the moment.

She lingered, ostensibly to investigate the other facets of the structure, all as clear as the first but much smaller, but actually taking in the marvelous picture. The too-scant suit—now it was voluptuous. She was young again, and ... fair. Perhaps she had known it before, and not believed.

"Tryx!"

She jumped, surprised by his impatience, and ashamed to be caught indulging in schoolgirl vanity, and ran to him. Yes, she could recognize it now: she had the vitality of a girl of seventeen.

But Hume's exclamation had not been impatient. He had found something.

A line of footprints crossed the beach from the water to the trees. They were not human; the indentations were too large and shallow, even where the moist sand near the surf held them well. Webbed prints.

"It must have crossed within the hour," Hume said tersely.

A reaction ran up her bare back and tightened the nape of her neck. "A—black?"

He nodded. "We can't catch it now. Impossible to run it down in the brush, except with a full party."

"What can we do?" The tension made her feel nauseated in exactly the way Ivo had described.

"I'll stand guard here. You run back to the village and warn the others. And be careful—they usually travel in pairs and cross in different places, so that if we get one—hurry!"

Fear gave her fleetness. She skipped over the sand, running at the line where the water gave it firmness, though the ocean horrified her now. Creatures from the deeps!

She passed the mirror-stone and went on, panting already. How far had they come down the beach? At least a mile—a long, long distance, now. What if the black came back before she fetched the others? Hume had only his spear. Those awful footprints . . .

She had to slow down. She was young, but she could not keep up this headlong pace. Her side ached.

She walked, recovering. She felt guilty, as though she were malingering, but this was the best she could do. She glanced over her shoulder, half afraid something would be coming after her, and saw that the mirror-stone was already out of sight. That made her more nervous than ever.

Something caught her eye in the water, and she turned back. She jumped, though she knew it was only a wave, or perhaps a bit of driftwood coming into sight between the swells. She started to run again, but the pain in her side came back quickly, dragging at her strength.

Again that shape in the ocean, attracting her unwilling eye. She forced herself to look carefully, trying to convince herself all the way down inside that it was nothing. Only a freak swell caused by adjoining currents in the tide; that was what Harold would say, comfortingly.

A black, monstrous-eyed head rose out of the whitening froth, two glossy antennae quivering.

Beatryx screamed.

It was the wrong thing to do. Instantly the head swiveled to cover her. She saw its banded snout, the fixed round hole of a toothless mouth beneath. It was earless, but it had heard her—and now it was swimming or slithering toward her with alarming speed.

She bolted for the forest, but the loose dry sand caught at her feet while giving way beneath them, impeding her and throwing her off balance. She fell, sand flying up and into her face. She choked on it and tried to brush it out of her eyes, but her hands were covered with it.

Somehow she could not get coordinated. She remained on hands and knees in the sand, watching the creature through streaming eyes.

The thing rose out of the water and came at her, a towering ebony figure. The scales of its thick body gleamed metallically. She saw through her sandy tears that its extremities—all four of them—were webbed. This was a black!

Then it loomed above her, hoisted upon two legs, the great square bulk of its forward segment swaying near. The antennae vibrated, casting off drops of moisture

A cry in the distance! The black's head rotated toward the sound and its dangling flipper-forefeet hoisted up. The others had heard her cries! They were coming!

The brute shuffled around and away, driving for the ocean. But already a party of men were running along the fringe of surf, cutting off its retreat. The black was clumsy; it could not move rapidly on land, and she saw that the powdery sand inhibited its grossly webbed feet even more than her own. It was trapped.

"Joy! You are all right!" Persis cried, running up to her and flinging herself to her knees.

"Hume!" Beatryx gasped, remembering. "He—he's watching for another one! Beyond the mirror-stone!"

"The sun-stone!" Several men detached themselves and pounded on down the beach, holding their spears aloft. They understood.

Meanwhile six men were closing in on the nearby creature. It spun about awkwardly, seeking some passage to the water, but there was none. At last it charged, a caged bull, raising its solid forelimbs threateningly.

Durwin's spear thunked into its body. The black stumbled, clutching at the shaft but not mortally wounded, and the men were on it.

"Kill it! Kill it!" Persis screamed, her eyes dilated, her fingers curved into claws.

"Kill it!" Beatryx echoed, horrified by the narrowness of her escape.

The spears rose and fell in a frenzy of attack. The sea-thing's gross body twisted and fell, bright red blood dripping down its scales. A kind of groan issued from it; then it collapsed face-down in the sand, the water lapping at the tip of one forelimb.

"It's dead," Durwin said with grim satisfaction. "Now let's go after that other one. Spread out and watch for any more along the beach, too."

The men moved on, leaving the vanquished hulk where it lay bleeding into the moist sand. It was the women who spread out, facing the ocean, each one scrutinizing the ocean for signs. Their grim expressions differed strikingly from the simple camaraderie of the evening before.

"How fortunate we heard you in time!" Persis said, helping Beatryx to her feet. "In another moment it would have touched you."

"I thought I was dead, when I fell," Beatryx said, still shaking with reaction. "I couldn't get up again, I was so frightened."

"Dead?" A fine dark eyebrow arched inquisitively.

"I mean, I couldn't get away from it."

Persis nodded. "That's horrible, I know. One of them touched me once, on the arm, and I thought I'd never wash that spot clean. I was an outcast for weeks. Filthy thing!"

Something was strange. "It didn't hurt you?"

"Of course not. They wouldn't dare attack a human being."

A sick feeling crept over Beatryx. "What do they *do*, then? I mean, if you hadn't come here in time—"

"Don't you know? It probably would have touched you, tried to talk to you. Disgusting."

"They talk?"

"They talk. But let's get off this depressing subject. You must be very tired, after what you went through."

Beatryx looked toward the body. "What about it?"

"The men will burn it and bury the suit. We don't need to look. They'll put on special gloves, and bury them too, afterward. That's the worst part of it—having to handle them."

Something else nagged her. "The suit?"

"The diving suit. They use those rigs for swimming under the water. Didn't you see?"

Beatryx walked to the body, appalled at what she knew she would find. "That's a *man!*"

"That's a *black!*" Persis corrected her. Then, horrified: "What are you doing?"

Beatryx ignored her. She kneeled beside the corpse, seeing now the machined parts she had taken for scales. The protective face-mask attached to the large goggles, almost the way the macroscope headgear did. The breathing apparatus—what she had seen as the "snout"—was fastened below the helmet to a ribbed diving outfit. She put her hands to the helmet and twisted, and the mask snapped loose. She worked it away from the face.

The head inside was that of a young man, as handsome in his own way as Hume was in his. This man was dark, however: a Negro.

A black.

Beatryx stumbled along in the dusk. The stones and brush and sharp twigs hurt her feet but did not slow her. The cries of the men and women of the beach village were lost behind her; they would not find her tonight, and tomorrow did not matter.

That such a lovely world could have such horror! It had been so appealing at first, with the delicious climate, attractive seascape, and friendly people. And her own gift-body, youthful and vigorous.

But to kill fellow-men so brutally simply because they came from the sea—she could not comprehend or accept this. Harold would never have abided it. He was a peaceful man but could be moved to severe measures when something really important came up. "The horoscope does not specify race," he would have said.

So she had fled. Not bravely, not openly; she was not a courageous woman, and she did not know what was best. She had washed her hands again and again, as they demanded, though in truth she was not ashamed of the touch of the black; rather she was painfully remorseful that she had failed to touch the man when it had counted, in her fatal ignorance. She had waited until night, then gone into the forest as though to—to employ the facilities. Then she had plunged into the darkness, though the branches struck cruelly at her bare flesh and the rocks turned under her bruising feet.

No, she did not have physical courage, and the darkness terrified her, with its thousand lurking suggestions of spiders and snakes and centipedes. But there was something she had to do. It was the thing Harold would have done.

She made her way to the beach and found the corpse. Then she moved down toward the mirror-cliff. Even in the night she was sure she could find *that* landmark, and of course it was not completely dark. The stars were out in vaguely unfamiliar constellations, and the ocean glowed gently. It was cool, now, but her motion kept her warm.

She saw the somber hump of rock and knew that her bearings were good. Only a little way beyond this spot. . . .

Now, cautiously, she began to call. 'Black—black, I don't have any weapon . . . black, if you're there, I want to talk with you . . . black, where are you? . . ."

For somewhere was the second black. The men had not found it—found *him*. They had followed the traces, but the man from the sea had eluded them in the brush. Tomorrow they were going to burn the forest here, to drive him out.

He had to be here somewhere, Hume had explained, for in the chase the man's face-plate had been knocked out. It had fallen to the ground, and Hume had it. He had hurled it into the fire with gloved hands so that it could never be used again. The black could not go under the sea again without it.

Neither could he get far inland, for the second line of defense was canine. The big, vicious dogs would be released if they winded him, and the black surely knew that. They were cunning that way, Hume had explained. They knew enough to stay clear of the hounds. He would not venture out of the shoreline foliage.

Tomorrow, the fire . . .

"Black," she called again. "I have the other face-plate. . . ."

It had been a grisly task, in the dark, prying out the plate from the helmet of the corpse. But what else could she do? She could not let them kill another man.

For an hour she tramped up and down the beach, not daring to call too loudly lest the others hear. There was no answer. Then she cut into the forest, hurting her feet again but keeping on, still calling. She could think of nothing else to do.

And finally blind purpose prevailed. Somewhere in the night she had an answer.

"I hear you, white."

It was a woman's voice.

And Beatryx found her, lying in the hollow between two fallen trunks. The woman had a tiny electric lantern she had kept hooded until now—until she was sure that the calling voice was not a trap. By its abruptly unfettered light Beatryx saw that the woman had removed her useless helmet and much of the rest of the underwater outfit. She lay on her side, her rather attractive dark head propped against her elbow.

"You have to move," Beatryx said urgently. "They're going to set fire to the forest. They're going to—"

"One place is as good as another," the woman replied philosphically.

"You don't understand. Tomorrow morning—"

"Tomorrow morning you be gone from here, white. And don't tell them you saw me, or they'll kill you too. I can't move."

"But I brought you the face-plate. From the dead man. So you can go back under the water. That's why I—"

"White."

The tone stopped her. The woman angled the light of

the lantern so that it illuminated the area around her feet.

Then Beatryx understood. Both flippers were off, and one black ankle was swollen grotesquely. The woman could not walk.

"I'll help you get to the water," Beatryx said quickly. "You can swim slowly, can't you? Using your hands and one foot?"

"I could." But the tone was fatalistic. Obviously the woman did not intend to try. "Where would I go in the sea, what would I do, and my husband dead on land?"

Her husband!

What would Beatryx do if Harold were dead? If some stranger had casually mentioned the fact and offered his belongings for her use? There would not be much point in going on. Why should this woman feel any differently?

"I am Dolora," the woman said. "The lady of sorrows."

"I am Beatryx. But I don't bring any joy to you." How stupid her name seemed now! And how pitiful the delayed introduction, abreast of tragedy.

Dolora carefully removed a capsule from a sealed pocket in her suit and swallowed it.

"Your foot?" Beatryx inquired sympathetically. "For the pain?"

"For the pain, yes."

"How did this happen?" Beatryx asked after a pause. "Why do they hate you? Why do you come from the ocean?"

And Dolora explained: In the time of the Traveler Siege the whites of this planet had embarked upon conquest and plunder, recognizing no law but force. The blacks of the neighboring less-technological world had been defeated and subjugated. Great numbers of them had been brought to this world as slaves.

"But you are both human!" Beatryx protested. "How could—"

"We are of the same stock, yes," Dolora said, misunderstanding the nature of her objection. "There must have been a prior siege, before the dawn of history, and one world colonized the other. We could not have evolved independently. But this world is not so good for us as was our own; its sun is too dim."

Beatryx had meant to protest the enslavement of one human race by another, rather than the genetic probabilities. Now she remembered how similar it had been on Earth, and did not bring the matter up again.

When the siege ended (Dolora continued) and the Traveler signal was gone, the slaves were stranded on the alien world. But, deprived of foreign conquests, the whites returned to planetary matters, and gradually a liberalizing sentiment grew among them. In time they formally abolished the institution of slavery. But there followed a considerable minority reaction against *this*, as certain economic interests suffered; and trouble was continuous. The blacks had mastered the white technology but were refused admittance into white society.

At last a compromise was achieved. The blacks were given a country of their own—under the water. They built tremendous dome-cities there, with artificial sunlight approximating that of their homeworld, and they cultivated the flora and fauna of the sea-floor efficiently. They traded with the landborne whites, shipping up ocean produce and metals from undersea mines in exchange for grains and wood.

The separation was not complete. A few blacks had elected to remain on land in spite of stringent discrimination there, and a few whites had joined the undersea kingdom. Both minorities had a difficult time of it, being under constant suspicion, though their motives had been high. Periodically some land-blacks would give up and seek the sea, and some sea-whites would return to land. These were welcomed by both groups as rescued personnel, and encouraged to publish lurid narratives of their hardships among the barbarians.

Beatryx realized at this point what the whites had taken her for.

But gradually this supposedly ideal compromise had soured. Too many on each side believed they somehow had the worst of the bargain. Politicians forwarded their careers by making a scapegoat of the other culture, and after a time polemics became policy. Trade became disrupted, and the blacks found their diet lacking in trace elements that only land-grown produce could provide, while the whites' industry suffered for lack of the sea metals. It seemed to each that the other was maliciously trying to destroy it.

White militants made preparations for what they claimed would be an effective solution to the problem: not a kind one. But they acted subtly, because the great majority still believed in the double-culture compromise, and would protest if the truth were to become known. Meanwhile the black militants were also making their moves. They had almost achieved control of their government, and would take military action against the whites as soon as the proper power was theirs. They, too, believed in simple solutions.

At best, somebody was going to be badly hurt. At worst . . .

"*We* don't want this strife either," Dolora said. Her voice had become lower and sadder, as though she were very tired, and Beatryx had to strain to hear. "It will be the end. We *have* to establish lines of communication. To put the reasonable blacks in touch with the reasonable whites, acquaint them all with the leadership crisis, reintegrate the two societies. This two-culture compromise is sundering the planet. . . ."

"But why don't you just send a—a message? *Telling* them? Or talk with—"

"Governments do not listen very well," Dolora said, her voice a whisper. "Particularly 'conservative' governments. And as for talking—that is what the two of us set out to do. We were not the first. For many years people like us have been trying, but none has returned, and no one has come to us from the whites. But my husband and I—we did not believe that the average white would actually refuse to listen, if approached without malevolence. So we came without weapons, spreading out in the hope of making individual contact sooner, thinking good intentions were enough—"

And had met savagery. And Beatryx herself, caught up in the fever, had cried "Kill it!" with the others.

And thus this girl's well-meaning husband had been butchered, and she pursued through the forest by a killer mob—all because the man had seen Beatryx and come to talk with her.

"But I see now that we were wrong," Dolora whispered. "They do not *want* to listen. So there is nothing to be done."

Beatryx herself had been so ignorant. She had screamed instead of listening. What could she say?

"Dolora, I—"

But the girl was not paying attention. She lay still, her head resting in dry leaves. Asleep?

Beatryx picked up the lantern and shone it on Dolora. Then she touched the flaccid hand.

The girl appeared to be dead.

Now, too late, Beatryx realized the significance of the capsule. Dolora had taken it after she was assured that her husband was dead. . . .

Beatryx looked for something to dig with. It seemed important that the girl be buried before the fire came. Then she realized that something more important remained. No whites had gone to the undersea city. . . .

Tediously she stripped the remainder of the suit from the dead girl's body. She experimented with the various attachments and controls, learning how the air supply operated. She fitted in the alternate face-plate. The suit was well designed and largely automatic; otherwise, she knew, she could never have succeeded in using it. Probably if the face-plate had not been designed to pop out without disturbing the goggles, it would not have come loose.

"You were *not* wrong, Dolora," she said.

She put on the suit and all its equipment, sealed herself in, and made her way to the water. It was almost morning.

Beatryx was not a proficient swimmer, but her strong new body and the diving equipment made the endeavor possible. She was tired, she was clumsy, she was afraid, but she could do it because she had to. She entered the water, her feet stinging as the salt brine pried into the multiple scratches. She submerged, relieved to discover that she could breathe well enough, and followed the coastal shelf down. The suit was heavy, holding her down, so that she actually walked as much as she swam.

She pushed forward for what seemed like many hours. Her arms and legs became tremendously weary, and the unfamiliar suit chafed, but she kept on. She fought down her mounting and unreasonable fear of sharks, stingrays, octopi, huge-clawed crabs, murky black crevices in the ocean floor...

If she could only reach the dome-city, wherever it was—

"Ahoy!" The voice startled her. It was coming from her helmet!

Someone was addressing her over the suit's radio. She had made contact!

A pair of shapes came out of the murk, bearing search beams. "Identify yourself, stranger! Don't you know this is restricted water?"

"I—I am Beatryx. I—I borrowed this suit so that I could come and tell you—"

"That's a *white!*" the voice said, shocked.

"Kill it!" another voice said, charged with loathing. "Don't let it contaminate our waters."

"But you don't understand!" Beatryx cried. "You have to listen—"

Then the powered spear transfixed her, and she died.

AIR

Not the heat of the flame or the coolness of water, this time, but the ambience of atmosphere. First he encountered the twins, two handsome young men breathing the fresh air, exuding life and joy. Then the loyal water-carrier, walking in mist, whose burden was truth; and if the slowly marching man resembled a portrait of Sidney Lanier, this was not surprising. Ivo had tried all his life to assume the task of this man, to carry perhaps one of his heavy buckets, but had never quite succeeded. Finally he came to the balance: the great ornate scales of Libra, out in the open sky, paired dishes swinging gently in the breeze. Upon the one was written EQUIVALENCE, and upon the counterweight, JUSTICE.

Ivo had watched the machinations of the ram with one part of his mind, and the tragedy of the fishes with another. They were only dreams, in one sense—yet real information

401

had been conveyed through them, and he knew that real resolutions were necessary. He could not act, himself, for the moment he stopped playing the symphony everything would stop, in whatever state it existed. Perhaps here, with the scales, was the assistance so desperately required concurrently for the flute; here amid the hornlike air of the symphony.

"There thrust the bold straightforward horn," he began. "To battle for his lady lorn . . ."

And the scales replied in that voice of the horn: "Is Honor gone into his grave? Hath Faith become a catiff knave, And Selfhood turned into a slave, To work in Mammon's cave, Fair Lady?"

And Ivo read the print behind the scales, written in vapors in the atmosphere, certain that everything would be all right.

But a hundred million years is a long time, and civilization developed again after the passing of the Traveler. Some cultures dwindled in importance, unable to adapt again to purely intellectual contact; some overcame their setback and achieved new elevation. The net long-range effect of the siege could be construed as a selection: those cultures unfit for galactic contact eliminated themselves by their own violence. Unfortunately, they took with them a similar number of those that were not suicidally violent. Nevertheless civilization, once it recovered, went on to a new height, for there was the spur of the potential demonstrated by the Traveler.

But suppose the Traveler itself returned, to wreak devastation again? Certain evidences suggested that there had been prior sieges, possibly many of them; perhaps civilization had risen, flourished and perished many times, leaving not even a memory. Were the cultures of this period simply to disappear at such time as the Traveler laid siege again? Or could something be done to stop a recurrence?

Plans were made. Theory was perfected, special stations were constructed. A select cadre was trained and maintained from generation to generation and millennium to millennium. If the Traveler came again, this galaxy was ready.

And it did come, as projected—one hundred million

*years after the earlier siege. Dissolution proceeded where it
touched, as species far too young to remember or appreciate the devastation of the last siege embarked upon trade
and its corollary, conquest. Some of these did not know
about the Plan, however—and sought in their naïveté to
prevent it. A number of stations were disrupted. . . .*

Harold Groton came out of it as he had before: not
with nausea or alarm, but simply a feeling of stress, of
internal acceleration. The sensation did not bother him; in
a manner of speaking he had been rehatched and matured
in minutes and hours, and in another sense he had re-
traced the entire evolutionary experience of the hive in the
same period. It was the nature of the reconstitution.

He leapfrogged out of the chamber and looked around.
The room was unfamiliar, but elegant. A daylight-
emulating ceiling of muted yellow, richly muraled walls
depicting hive activities, resilient flooring, uniquely styled
furniture—a very plush accommodation.

There was a triple-refraction mirror—one of many, he
noticed—at hand, and he positioned himself before it to
assess his condition before dressing. He did not recall
undertaking a melting cycle this time, though; in fact, he
had been—

Small-thought ceased abruptly.

The image in the mirror was man-sized, as far as he
could tell. The creature was basically tripodal, so that two
small feet offset one very large center foot. Perambulation
was by leapfrog: the center leg provided most of the
power, the side legs incidental support, somewhat like a
one-legged man on crutches. He was able to stand on the
center leg alone and spin about in a small circle, but the
pair of legs were less stable. Walking human-fashion was
impossible; the side legs acted in concert when supporting
weight unless he concentrated directly on them, much as
had the toes of his erstwhile human foot. Offsetting the
third leg in front was a mound that tapered into the
torso.

The upper limbs were also triple, with the third arm
rising from what he thought of as the chest area. Unlike
the third leg, this limb was slender and delicate. Evidently
this species had evolved from six-legged stock, modified
for an upright posture. Three eyes decorated the head,
and each saw in a different color and fashion, making an

403

impressive composite picture. He closed one eye and found that the image differed substantially; much could be learned by using only one or two eyes at a time, and analyzing the result and filtered view. There were three ears on the back of the head, and these were also very good in concert, each responding to a different range. He was sure he could detect much more intricate and extended sound than ever as an Earthman.

It was a good body, in good condition; he could sense its general health. He realized that this was to be his home for the duration: this alien body. The experience was novel but not alarming.

"Drone!" an imperious inhuman voice called from the adjacent room, sonically assaulting all three ears.

"Immediately, mistress," he replied on the center frequency, and perambulated hastily in that direction. He had supposed walking would be awkward, but for this creature it was not. Observing it in action, he suspected that if this body were to engage in a foot race on even terms with his human form, this one would win.

The language employed, like the body, was alien to anything in his prior experience, yet he handled both with expertise. He had not intended to respond: his body had done that automatically. Was this the way of Ivo's gift of tongues at Tyre?

The female he approached was similar in construction to himself, but larger and adapted for reproduction. He presumed that she laid eggs, perhaps thousands of them. Her swollen midsection was certainly geared for it. Yet her form was the essence of sex appeal by the definition of this species. He was of this species now, and he felt himself becoming interested, despite his human background. Well, other cultures, other ways.

"Groom me for presentation," she snapped (her mandibles making it literal), not bothering to give a reason.

Groton rebelled at the tone—but his body was already active, rushing to a cabinet, unsealing the waxy fastening easily, taking out a brushlike device, and approaching the female with due deference.

This time he was sure the process was involuntary. This body he occupied was strongly conditioned. Unless he exercised conscious control all the time, it went about its business as usual.

404

He/it played the brush over the fur of her thorax, some electrical interaction making the pelt brighten and fluff out with each pass. Groton let the task continue while he explored his situation internally. There ought to be an explanation somewhere, a mind belonging to this body—

There was. As easily as his intention to search had come, the object was realized.

He was the Drone: consort to the Queen. He was expected to do nothing other than cater to the whims of his mistress. In return, he received respect and the best of all physical things—so long as he retained her favor.

"Fetch a new brush," she said. She did not explain what objection she had to this one. Why should she? The Drone did not need to know. He needed only to obey.

He was in the hall and swinging toward the supply depot before he could assert himself. Perhaps it was just as well; what could his human mind have done except aggravate an untenable situation?

"One static brush for the Queen," he snapped at the clerk, his own mandibles clicking as he addressed the inferior. This was the first worker he had seen: an apparently neuter creature, similar in outline to himself but only two-thirds his size.

The worker affected not to hear him, going about its ruminating without a pause. This was unprecedented contempt—yet there was nothing he could do. He was a Drone going out of favor, and the workers knew it. Soon he would be cast off entirely, and the neuters would have the sadistic pleasure of ignoring him while he starved to death. He was unable to provide for himself, if the workers did not make food available; he and the Queen were royalty, requiring service for life. His body tensed in hopeless fury.

Groton-human viewed the situation more dispassionately. He saw that it was conditioning, not physical capability, that made the Drone dependent. He did not appreciate the insult either, but realized that there was a more practical danger. If he delayed unduly in fulfilling this mission, the Queen's short temper would vent itself upon him immediately—as this insolent worker hoped. The creature was maliciously hastening his demise.

It had not been like this a year ago, he remembered with the Drone's mind. Then, flush with the Queen's favor, he had been an object of virtual worship. The neuters had gone out of their way to do him little favors. It had seemed that he had complete control of the situation.

Fond illusion! He saw himself now as the vehicle he was, to be used by both Queen and workers, possessing no personal value to either apart from convenience. An ambulatory reservoir of egg-fertilizer. He had known it would inevitably come to this, for all Queens were fickle—but, dronelike, he had refused to accept it for himself.

Groton did not consider himself to be a man of violence, but the emotion of the despised being that was the Drone affected the more analytical human mind, and brought forth an atypical response. Atypical for both beings. The Drone was a creature of emotion, as befitted the royal consort; Groton was a man of action. The combination converted impotency to potency, perhaps in more than figurative terms.

He swung the two side arms over the counter and caught the worker by the shoulders. He lifted, and the light creature dangled in the air.

Groton held it there for a moment, letting it feel the great physical strength of the Drone—a strength that could crush it easily. No words were necessary. The worker's cud drooled from its mouth in its astonishment and shock. The Drone had done the unthinkable: it had acted for itself. It would hardly be more astonishing for a neuter to impregnate the Queen.

He set it down, and in a moment he had the brush and was returning to his mistress. It would be a long time before that worker allowed its courtesy to slip again—and the message would spread.

Expectations of this drone's downfall were premature.

Unfortunately, setting back one predacious worker did not alter the fundamental stuation. The Queen *was* tiring of him, and unless he acted to preserve himself in her esteem, his fate was assured. A simple demonstration of muscle was sufficient to faze a simple worker—but not the Queen.

The Drone body and mind quivered with reaction and fear. The act it had just participated in was plainly beyond its nature, and it did not yet realize what agency was responsible. Once possessed of a fine intellect, it had largely succumbed to apathy, protecting itself from injury by ignoring it. Even the momentary surges of emotion were generally well disciplined, externally.

Groton calmed it, discovering that it reacted as subserviently to his control as to that of the Queen. But now it knew—and he felt its mixed elation and alarm.

If he had to occupy another creature's body, this one had been an obvious choice. The Drone had a good physique, a position of enormous potential influence—and very little genuine will-power. Yet that did not explain why he, Harold Groton, had been selected to enter this picture. How had his quest for information about the nature of galactic civilization been diverted into such a channel?

Probably some answers were in the Drone's mind—but it would be a tedious chore digging them out and organizing the information for his own comprehension. There was a hundred times the store of facts he needed—relevant only to the Drone's life, not his own.

The Queen glanced at him with a single eye to hint at her displeasure at his slight tardiness, but did not make an issue of it. He had performed within tolerance—this time.

The communication screen came alive before he finished the grooming. "Mistress," the pictured neuter said respectfully, keeping its third eye lidded in respect for royalty.

"Crisis already?" the Queen demanded.

"A Felk battlemoon has materialized four twis distant."

Groton felt the reaction of his host. A twi was a unit of spatial measurement equivalent to about eighty-five lightseconds. The Felks—enemies—were within six lightminutes.

"So soon! So close!" the Queen exclaimed angrily. "How did they know?"

But she did not wait for an answer. Obviously there had been a leak, and the Felks had followed this expedition in. They could not have traced it in space so rapidly, since this would require years by lightspeed observation.

The Queen was already traveling down the hall at a pace that pressed even the trailing Drone hard. She was a magnificent specimen of life, large and sleek and strong, one who had been not merely born to command, but evolved for it.

The supervisory workers were already assembled in the royal hall. Show me your deployment," the Queen snapped, having no need of query or courtesy.

A sphere of light appeared, bright dots within it. A map of space, Groton realized, that covered a volume half a light-hour in diameter. A sun, several planets, and two free moons showed within it: the Queen's battlemoon and the Felks'.

A sun? No, the Drone memory corrected him: that was merely the identifier for their point of focus, the scheduled location of the station. There was no sun within two light-years.

The magnification increased in response to an imperative gesture by the Queen, and the pattern of ships appeared. The Queen's moon was englobed by dreadnoughts—but already similar armor was emerging from the enemy moon.

"What kind of disposition is that?" the Queen demanded. "They will penetrate it in hours."

"Our tactician was lost in the last engagement," the leading officer-worker reminded her carefully. "We did not pause to pick up a replacement."

"Naturally not. I would not tolerate an alien in my hive. Where is the next tactician-egg? Hasn't it been hatched yet?"

Almost, the Queen reminded Groton of someone. Would her next expostulation be against the need to take care of every detail herself?

"I am it," the officer said, answering her question. "But the enemy has surprised us and I lack experience."

The Queen brooded over the sphere. "My Drone could make a better deployment," she said.

The officer very nearly dared to show its ire at the disparagement. "Perhaps your Drone should assume tactical command."

The Drone-mind suffered a flare of rage at the well-turned sarcasm. The Drone would never have implemented it or even expressed it in the presence of the Queen; but Groton, caught off-guard by the ferocity of the emotion, did.

"The Drone *will* assume command," he said, with the resonance of triple-range vocal chords.

The Queen turned, about to rebuke him—such rebuke

possessing the force of exile—but changed her mind. "Yes —he will. You tactician—attach yourself to him as apprentice. It should be an intriguing experience."

Thus had a single incontinent outburst netted him stellar responsibility. The whim of the Queen was cruel.

Desperately, Groton assessed his resources. The Drone-mind was cowering in horror, as a man might who had just broken wind vociferously while saluting his country's flag. He had to detach himself from its emotional state and suppress that mind almost entirely to prevent being overwhelmed by cowardice. This meant taking over most of its remaining functions and dispensing with its store of information. He became the Drone.

Yet it seemed to him that the joke was not as farfetched as the Drone's diminished status had encouraged the neuters to believe. The Drone had spent several years in close attendance upon the Queen, and surely had overheard many of her directives. The Drone had a good mind and excellent information; it was its timidity and dependence on the Queen that made the notion of command ludicrous.

Neither Queen nor workers knew that a determined human personality had taken control. The Drone had strong emotions and weak initiative; Groton had mild emotions and strong will. The combination could have meant weakness in both departments—but fortunately that was not the case. This worm could turn, as the experience with the supply depot worker had shown.

The Queen was gone, leaving him to his mess.

The tactician-worker waited beside him as directed. Groton perceived the distress caused by this ultimate indignity—but the Queen's word really was law. The officer, like himself, was captive to its own indiscretion. The Queen had her own ways of dealing with insolence—and the remaining workers had had another lesson.

"What is the immediate objective?" Groton asked the officer, determined to do his best, whatever became of it.

"To drive off the enemy, so that the station can be installed and activated, and the mines placed," it replied.

"And the mines will prevent subsequent attacks?"

"Yes."

"How does the Felk armament compare to ours?"

"It is superior. In number, not in kind. We suffered losses in prior placements."

"How much time do we have?"

"Time for what?"

Groton perceived another weakness of the worker-mind. "How much time do we have before the enemy breaks through and destroys the station?"

"About six hours—unless we can outmaneuver them or frighten them away." The time had been given in alien units, but Groton had no difficulty in comprehending.

He studied the map-sphere. "You plan to wait for them to attack?"

"Yes."

"Why?"

"How else can we observe the nature of their thrust?" Orders or no, the officer had little respect for the Drone. Groton was reminded of a somewhat similar experience many years ago. Then it had been high school students. Now, as then, he had no higher appeal, contrary to the theoretical situation; he had to handle the matter by himself or be washed out.

"Yet," he said, "with their ships massed and traveling at high velocity, our scattered forces cannot hope to stop them all. And one ship should be sufficient to blast the station."

The neuter did not bother to reply.

"You have no manuals of strategy?"

"Of course not. A tactician learns by experience."

The military mind! "Provided he lives."

"Yes," the officer agreed. "My predecessor—"

"And the Felks are similarly organized? No study of the lessons of history?"

"I assume so. How else should it be?"

How else indeed!

It appeared that a noncombative but practical-minded Earthman was as well equipped to handle galactic battle tactics as the galactic commands were.

"All right. Relay this directive: All ships, repeat *all* ships, to proceed immediately to the Felk battlemoon, there to attack without englobement."

The officer, true to its nature, relayed the command. Groton heard the controller giving directions to individual ships. Then, thinking about it, the officer objected. "What?"

"You wouldn't be familiar with the dictum 'The best defense is a good offense'?"

"Certainly not."

"Well, chalk it up to experience, once you see it happen. We know we can't stop their attack, if we wait for it to develop, nor can we hope to overcome the enemy in a normal encounter—but our ships do have an advantage of several hours in deployment. We can hit the Felk before the Felk hits us."

"But with no defense—"

"Wait and see." Inwardly, Groton prayed that his audacious gamble paid off. He was not, ordinarily a gambling man. He was exchanging almost certain defeat for a fifty-fifty chance at victory—but had he been a real tactician, he might have known how to play for two- or three-to-one odds in his favor. "Now you and I will board the fleet flagship," he finished.

That made another stir. It seemed that commanders of naval operations generally ensconced themselves safely within the base moon and jumped to another location in space when the battle went against them. No wonder losses could be heavy!

He had no time to concern himself with the details of the ship he boarded. It was a standard cruiser, heavy on armament, slow on maneuver, but capable of high velocity under sustained acceleration.

Three hours later they were closer to the enemy moon than to their own. The Felk fleet was still emerging, though about half of it was now positioned around its base.

"Form our ships into three wedges," Groton said. "Send them in simultaneously from three directions." And it was done.

The enemy fleet deployed to counter this move. "Why don't they mass and attack our station?" the officer asked, baffled.

"Would *you* attack the enemy home-base—if your ships were needed to save your own hide?"

"Hide?"

"Carapace. Chitin integument. Personal dignity."

"Oh. Yes. Self-preservation."

An underling-worker reported: "Felk commander has a message for Queen commander."

"Is that safe to accept?"

"Yes," the officer replied. "The Felks are reputed to be honorable in battle."

"Let's see it then. Maybe he wants to negotiate."

"Negotiate?"

"Don't you ever bargain for some settlement short of total victory?"

"Bargain?"

Groton shrugged and watched the communications screen. A picture of a two-eyed creature with a caved-in face formed, manlike in its way. *Do we look that ugly?* he asked himself, already acclimatized to the shell-gloss outlines of the hive personnel.

The Felk commander spoke in whistles, pursing its flaccid lips, but there was a running translation. "Commander, I am impressed by your technique." There was no opportunity for normal dialogue, since there was almost a minute's delay owing to lightspeed limitation of communications. By the time a rapid conversation was feasible, they would be virtually on top of the enemy moon. "I did not anticipate such initiative on the part of the Queen's forces. From the facility with which you are adjusting formation, I suspect that you, commander, are aboard one of the ships in the area. This demonstrates courage, and gives a tactical advantage over me, since my communications delay is much greater than yours. I am authorized to offer you a generous commission in our navy, if you will defect to our side."

Groton stood before the silent screen, amazed at the audacity of it. "He's losing—so he offers his enemy a commission!"

"Felks are adroit," the officer agreed indifferently. "That's how we lost my predecessor."

"He defected?"

"He tried to. But the Queen overheard and cut off his head. The mission was successful."

Groton gained respect for the Queen. She, at least, had unquestioned loyalty to her side. Of course, she *was* her side, largely. . . .

Still, the notion of blatantly buying off the opposition. . . . "Well, beam back a picture of me," he said hotly. "Nothing else. We'll see if the Felks figure to bribe away the Queen's Drone."

He had his answer in two minutes. "As it happens," the Felk commander whistled, "we hold captive a Queen of your species, obtained as the result of a singularly fortunate maneuver. Unfortunately her Drone died. She has been very lonely for a year, though we permit her a reasonable retinue of her neuters, hatched from the few remaining eggs she has in storage. I suspect she would not tire of a serviceable mate for a very long time, knowing she could not obtain another. As you know, the favor extended to individual Drones is normally of short duration—two or three years. I can arrange to send you to her."

Again Groton was astonished. Would this creature stop at nothing? The Drone's memory verified that the Felks had overrun an outpost some time ago—one staffed by a Queen—and that a Queen could not raise her own Drone from an egg. Incest did not exist, in this culture.

The Drone-mind clamored for attention. The offer, it developed was attractive, particularly to one who faced the prospect of early retirement by his present Queen. A Drone could live as long as a Queen could—if permitted. That amounted to decades. Felks did not lie; the offer was valid.

Sorry, Groton said to the Drone. Then, to the officer: "Tell the Felk to look to his defenses. This commander is not about to be bought off by the boudoir."

In the interval between messages, the officer fidgeted, then spoke. "Request permission to voice an opinion." The third eye was now lidded.

"Granted, provided it is brief."

"I had thought it was an insult to serve under Drone command. I was mistaken."

"We all make mistakes," Groton said, touched but not forgetting that it would be a mistake to betray any personal softness. The mission was not yet over. More and more he appreciated the lessons of that hectic schoolteaching session of his earlier life. Then it had been merely his pride and self-confidence that took beatings; now the lives of thousands were at stake.

The third message showed that the Felk had not given up. "You evince a handsome loyalty to your Queen. But have you properly considered the nature of your loyalty to

413

your species, and to other technological species? Surely you are intelligent enough to perceive that this station and the others in your program will hurt all of us. All we ask is the right to travel—yet only one species in a thousand is to be permitted this, if the stations function. Neither your species nor mine is among the select. Why cooperate as the tool of the destroyer?"

The destroyer! Suddenly the meaning of all this settled into focus. He was participating in the origin of the destroyer station—perhaps the very one that had blanked out Earth's finest minds. *Would* blank, for what he experienced now had to be history at least fifteen thousand years past. His mystic journey had finished on target; there could be no more significant event.

And he was on the wrong side.

Or was he? He had learned, in his human existence, to consider things carefully. Surely the Queen had not gone to the immense trouble and danger of setting up an interference that would prevent her own kind from using the spaceways, without very good reason. He should understand that reason, before making his own decision.

Meanwhile there was the practical problem of the enemy fleet. If he did not destroy it, it would destroy him, making his personal decision less relevant than his indecision. Unless he defected . . . but that would doom the station, and might be a mistake.

"Send this reply," he said. "MESSAGE RECEIVED. SUGGEST YOU WITHDRAW."

The officer obeyed, then came back to question the directive. "Do you expect the Felk to retreat merely because you ask him to?"

"We'll see."

In due course they saw. The Felk ships decelerated, looped about, and drew in toward their base. As time passed they docked within their moon in orderly fashion.

"A ruse!" the officer said.

"Yet you told me the Felk were honorable."

The officer looked confused.

More time passed. The last enemy ship docked while Groton held his own fleet back, suspending fire. For three hours they globed the moon at a safe distance. Then it vanished.

The release of its gravitational influence jolted the

Queen's fleet, sending ships tumbling outward. Space had been drawn into a knot and rent, and had healed itself. There was no doubt the Felk force had withdrawn.

"He will pop back on the opposite side, close to the destroyer station," the officer predicted. "He didn't say he *wouldn't*, anyway."

But the Felk did not return. In the course of the following twelve hours the workships finished laying their mines and activating the mines' perceptors and trackers. The area was impregnable. A mine could not travel, but it was supreme in its area of space. Anything that approached, even an entire fleet, would be blasted, unless it carried the nullifying code-signal. The Queen's fleet possessed this, of course—but its nature was a secure secret known only to the Queen.

The Queen's moon detached the destroyer station and let the ships adjust its position. As it warmed up, its tremendous field of gravity took hold, hauling the moon into orbit around *it*, though it was two miles in diameter compared to the moon's two thousand. Child's-play, for this technology; gravity could be turned on and off as though it were a magnetic field. Probably the station had reclined in null-G aboard the moon, so as not to be crushed in storage. To think that the entire fabulous layout that was the destroyer-complex was no more than an installation problem to the Queen . . . !

Then the destroyer signal was cut in, and Groton knew that it was spreading out in a sphere whose radius expanded at lightspeed. Any battlemoon that transferred *in* would not transfer *out* again—and the six mines would finish whatever stayed.

"Request permission to ask a question."

Groton understood the hive signals now. This was something important to the officer. "Granted."

"By what reasoning did you determine that the Felk would leave upon request? I saw nothing in your conversation to indicate such a response." It paused. "I wish to learn, for I note that you accomplished the mission without loss of ships, when I surely would have failed."

This was not a question Groton particularly wanted to answer, but he felt an obligation to give a serious response to a serious query. "Put yourself in the place of the Felk

415

commander, he said, seeing a discreet way to handle the matter.

"Defect to the Felk?"

Oops! "No—I mean to imagine that your situation was his. You emerge from spacefold to set up your attack, and instead you find the enemy, whose force is inferior to yours, attacking *you*. What would you do?"

The officer concentrated, adjusting to this unfamiliar mode of thinking. "I would wait for further developments," it said at last. "I would want to ascertain what advantage the enemy had that made him so bold."

"Precisely. And if he maneuvers with such facility and confidence that you find yourself at a disadvantage in spite of your superior resources?"

It thought some more. "I would attempt to subvert its commander." Then its center arm lifted in the gesture of sudden illumination, and its center eye blinked. "That is what the Felk did!"

"Right. And if you could not buy off the enemy strategist?"

"I would attempt to negotiate honorably." It paused again, now translating from actuality. "I would—appeal to that officer's loyalty to its species, and attempt to convince it that our causes were one. But—not too obviously, for its honor should not be impugned."

"And if he agreed to consider the matter?"

"If my position were already too bad to recover, I would have to leave the decision up to it. Perhaps that commander would—change its mind—once left to its own devices." It looked at him. "May I—"

"You may *not* inquire. Perhaps you can decide for yourself what my decision will be."

The officer remained silent, accepting it. Groton hoped the mental effort would do it good and that it would be a better tactician in the future. It certainly had come a long way in the past hours.

And what *was* his decision to be? Here was his chance to change history, perhaps even to give his species— mankind—freedom of space travel. In one sense this adventure might be a dream, a vision; but in another he was certain it was real. Now he understood why Ivo had been unwilling to dismiss his Tyre episode out of hand. It was likely that the body that remained at the starting point was the mockup; the better portion of reality was here.

Should he act now, sabotage the destroyer station before it could blank out the thousand traveling species for every one it promoted? He could fire a volley from his flagship that would wreck the station mechanism. What right did the Queen have to repress a major section of the galaxy in such fashion?

He refused to act without information. That was the way of prejudice, and could only stir up catastrophe. If he wanted to know the motivation of the Queen, he would have to ask her.

She was waiting for him as the operation closed down. "Drone, that was a creditable byplay. I had expected to have to retreat to one of our alternate locales during the enemy's commitment, perhaps even to leave you behind, but you surprised me by prevailing. What came over you?"

He tried to say "Sometimes the worm *does* turn," but it came out, in this situation, as "Upon occasion the annelid completes a circuit."

"You seem to have demonstrated your point. It would not be expedient to adopt a new Drone at this stage," she said. "Here to me, my cherished."

Realizing her intent, Groton tried to resist. He was human whatever his present body, and infidelity was not in his nature. How would he face Beatryx, if—?

But the Drone-body was already advancing to its destiny. The Queen was mistress, the dual concept a single one in this society. She was wife and monarch, never to be denied in either capacity. The Drone motor response, in this instance, was involuntary. Groton could observe but not control.

From the hump before his middle leg a member of specific purpose telescoped out. His legs and arms reached to embrace her in the fashion peculiar to this association, and the act of intimacy precipitated itself.

It lasted a long time, this fertilizing of several score eggs, and afterward, exhausted, he slept. His body had been drained in a fashion far more literal than that of human intercourse.

When he woke, Groton was tired but in control again—

and gifted with a unique appreciation of the meaning of rape.

"Drone!" the Queen's voice came—and once more he was on his feet at her behest. His control extended only to the extent she permitted it; he could not disobey a direct order.

"Groom me," she said as he arrived. Nothing had changed.

"What is the reason for the destroyer?" he inquired as he worked, relieved that he could communicate to this extent.

"The Horven knows," she said. "Shall I send you to it in my stead?" Then, as was her wont, she made her decision immediately. "Yes. Groom yourself, feed yourself, and go. I have eggs to lay."

Obediently he turned the brush on his own fur, less handsome than hers, and set about procuring a meal of the royal nectar.

Who or what was the Horven? The Drone had never been curious, and consequently knew very little on this subject. The Horven was a member of a civilized species of long standing—a species that did not deign to trade with others, or even to communicate with them. Yet one was resident within this moon.

He searched the Drone's memory. Three times before, the Queen had descended into the depths of the Horven apartments, after setting up destroyer stations. On her return, the moon had begun the transmission cycle leading to the emplacement of the next unit. Did she have to make a report? Receive orders? This was an unacceptable concept to the Drone. The Queen bowed to no creature.

Why, then, these regular journeys? What passed between them, the Queen and the strange alien?

He was about to find out.

The Queen put him aboard the hanging descent-car with something almost like affection. "Do not linger, male-thing."

The capsule was translucent; distorted images entered to tantalize him. The polished metal walls of the upper landing gave way to bleak stone as the unit swung along at a rapid pace. Sometimes it seemed he was traveling through natural caverns; at other times the walls were so close as to resemble a tunnel. Once light blazed, as though he were navigating a fiery hell.

He gathered that the Horven liked its privacy.

What was he supposed to say to it? He had no idea.

At least he knew that one could make such a visit and return intact. Whatever business the one species had with the other, it was not physically dangerous. Still, the Drone-mind within him gibbered with fear.

Was it right to use this body so callously? He had control, and he had exercised it ruthlessly. How would he feel, if an alien intellect had taken over his own body and suppressed the higher centers of his brain?

"I believe this is a temporary phenomenon," he said to the Drone. "When I have finished my business here, you will have your body back."

And was surprised to pick up a fiercer burst of terror than any before.

The capsule halted before he had a chance to ascertain the reason for this reaction. Its side panel opened and the vehicle tilted to disgorge him.

He looked about. He was in a spacious hall, and standing on a circular platform. A manlike figure was before him, dressed in an enveloping robe. Its head was inhuman in a manner he could not quite define. It was as though his three eyes were unable to focus on it. *Had* they been able, he was sure he would have discovered truly alien features—alien in ways his imagination had never hitherto touched on. Somehow his eyes ceased to track whenever he looked at it, whether he used one or two or three at once. The effect was frustrating in much the way an Earth-blackout was: the direct glance at a given object was less productive than a peripheral view.

"Welcome, Harold," the creature addressed him. Its voice, like its face, was undefined; perhaps it had spoken telepathically.

"I'm not sure I—"

It gestured benignly with a blurred extremity. "Certainly we know you, Harold. We most appreciate your difficult excursion from hence. You are the only Earthman to participate in our venture, and we comprehend the peculiar courage required."

Groton had not been aware of any exercise of courage, and in any event this development was contrary to anything he could have expected, let alone feared. "You know where I—*when* I come from?"

"Approximately one hundred million years hence, in the Third Siege. We have a number of volunteers from that period, since the cultures of that time have a superior perspective on history."

"I thought I was a messenger from the Queen. I'm wearing the body of her consort."

"So you are," the Horven said, as though just noticing. "That means that the last unit is in place and activated, and we can begin on the next. I shall initiate the cycle."

"You handle the gravity compression? I thought the Queen—"

"Once the unit has been activated, the ordinary species cannot attune to the Traveler," the Horven explained gently. "Several hundred personnel must be discorporated, which means they must be assessed by the Traveler. I will handle juxtaposition."

Of course! The destroyer blocked off that macroscopic band, as Ivo had observed, making it impossible for most minds to draw on the intergalactic knowledge. Ivo had set it up, for the human party; the Horven—

"You are the one-in-a-thousand!" Groton exclaimed. "The species that is immune to the destroyer."

The Horven donned a surprisingly Earthlike helmet and touched a panel. "There will be several shifts," it said. "This will take some time, but it only occupies a portion of my intellect. Please do not interrupt your discourse."

The Queen's workers, Groton realized, would be lining up and passing through Traveler introductions, exactly as he and Beatryx and Afra had while Ivo guided them past the lurking destroyer. But the Horven must be handling them a score at a time! "You—you built the destroyer!"

"We—with companion species—designed it," the Horven admitted. "We cannot construct or emplace the individual units."

"Why are you doing this? Why are you reserving true space travel for yourselves?"

"It must be." Lights were flickering within the helmet, and Groton wondered what circuitry was being utilized. A lead to the macroscope, naturally, and trunk lines to the upper regions. . . .

"Wait! I need to get back upstairs before the cycle

begins." Shifts there might be, but if he missed the last one it would be the end, for him.

"For what purpose? Your destiny is with us."

"It is?" He was confused.

"We have weighted the repressive side of the scales. The destroyers have been installed. Now we must balance the other side, or the task remains half-complete. Another representative will replace me here; you and I travel to Horv."

"And I am supposed to—to participate in the other side too? When I'm not even certain I agree with *this* side?"

"I apologize for my neglect," the Horven said. "I forgot that you have not been adequately informed, since your species evolved many millions of years after mine passed.

"The Traveler destroyed the civilization of our galaxy once, and perhaps many times. This travel-power is too great for juvenile species; it only releases and amplifies their destructive impulses. Therefore we of the Second Civilization, rising from the ruins of the First, have had to take defensive measures against this Second Siege. Only we who have left violence behind can safely travel from star to star. In this manner we may preserve galactic civilization until the Siege is over."

At last it was beginning to fall into place. Now he remembered a fragment of—history?—he had heard or read at some point, that reinforced this explanation. "The destroyer—only destroys evil minds?"

"Not evil minds, no. To be savage is not to be evil. It is a necessary phase in the evolution of a mature species. But until it passes, that species must be protected from itself. It must be confined to its planet of origin and that planet's immediate environs. It does not have the discretion to indulge in galactic contacts—apart from purely communicatory, of course. Maturity requires an extended apprenticeship."

"And you Horven are one of the mature species?" He had thought to put irony into his tone, but it misfired; he was already convinced that the Horven *was* mature. "Why do you make younger species do your bidding? Why not simply place the destroyer-units yourselves?"

"Because there is insufficient violence in our nature. We can conceive of suppressive strategy, though with discomfort, but cannot implement it. We could not survive the destroyer ourselves, if such pacifism diminished in us."

Thus this temporary cooperation between forward-looking juveniles and inactive seniles. Were they correct? Was this necessary to save civilization?

He thought about the incalculable violence of human history, and was not prepared to deny the need for this step. Man had always been willing, even eager, to spend much more effort on calamitous war than on any peaceful pursuit. Governments had spent billions of dollars, francs, rubles for war every year, while allowing their own less fortunate citizens to starve. Man in space would be the same—except that the stakes would be larger.

"I am a member of a juvenile species," he said.

"Of the juvenile stage in your species evolution, yes. No species is inherently young or old. It may be that the climax of mankind will be a far greater thing than that of the Horven. Possibly some visitor from the Fourth Siege will know. We hope the measures we have taken here will enable your species to achieve such distinction."

"I hope so too," Groton said fervently. Then, remembering: "What is the other side of the scale? If *this* side is the forced preservation of galactic civilization?"

"Exploration, comprehension, knowledge. The nature of the Traveler, and the reason for its infliction upon us. The civilization that developed such technique is as far beyond the Horven as the Horven is beyond the Queen's hive. Surely its purpose was not to extinguish our progress."

"Why don't you just pay the source a visit and find out?"

"That was attempted during the First Siege. But our predecessors were unable to map intergalactic convolutions prior to exploration there, and intergalactic ventures were unsuccessful."

"What happened to them?"

"They never returned. Some survived, but their travel mechanisms were inoperative."

"How could you learn about them, then?"

"Their traces were picked up subsequently on the macroscope."

"But that could take millions of years, if they were in intergalactic space!"

"Yes. It was the Second Civilization that recorded the

signals, and they only succeeded in this because they were specially attuned and alert. The macroscope is hardly effective beyond our own galaxy, ordinarily. By the time the signals had been identified, it was far too late to come to the assistance of their originators, even had travel been feasible at that time. But these casualties did assist in the mapping of deep space in a general way, and provide clues as to the nature of its dynamics. We believe we can now achieve the other galaxies in our cluster."

Intergalactic travel! "So you mean to discover the truth about the origin of the Traveler," Groton said. He realized that this was a similar quest to the one the party of human beings had embarked on. They had seen the destroyer as their enemy, when in fact it was their friend (though a stern one!); Earth might have been ravaged many times by other agressor species, except for that protection, and the sapience of man might never have had the opportunity to develop. The true enemy was the Traveler—but this too was only conjecture, until its rationale was known.

"Your invitation tempts me," Groton said. "The prospect of such explorations is fascinating. But my essential loyalty is with my own. I can't simply—"

"You are not among your own. I assure you, the Queen's ire at losing her present Drone will pass quickly. The King is the game, for us. Though of course we can arrange to have you occupy a different body, and return this one to—"

No! No! the Drone-mind screamed. *Do not send me back alone!*

"Oh, I see," the Horven said. "Thoughtless of me. Of course you would be unable to cope with the revised situation." It was addressing the Drone directly. "But it would not be kind to keep you in subservience here—"

The other Queen!

"Yes, we could do that," the Horven agreed. "You realize you would be captive of the Felk, however—"

The Drone was more than willing to take that chance.

"You have no objection to assuming some other form?" the Horven inquired of Groton. "We cannot act unless all parties are amenable. It would be quite unlike your normal one."

"The horoscope does not specify species," Groton murmured. What was he getting into?

The Horven continued to wear the helmet, but Groton was sure it was simultaneously setting about preparations for the other transfer. "There are still horoscopes in your time?"

"*Still*? You mean you practice astrology here?"

"That depends on what you mean by the term. I don't know enough about your conception either to believe or disbelieve in it, let alone practice it. If you would clarify—"

"It—I—" Groton found himself at a loss for words, never having anticipated this turn of conversation. He finally had to settle for a concrete example, his well-versed summaries having fled his mind. "Well, I was born on October 11, 1940, at Key West, Florida. That means—but you don't know Earth chronology or geography!"

"I comprehend your meaning, nevertheless. Go on."

"The time was 4:10 p.m., Eastern Standard. That's important for the house structure. So the configuration of the signs and planets at that moment—well, I'm a Libra personality, sun in the seventh house, moon in Aquarius, Mercury—"

"If you will provide an exact listing, I will transpose to my framework," the Horven said. "I perceive that your astrology does approximate one of our disciplines, but of course your local viewpoint does not coincide."

"You can convert my terms to your chart?" This was as marvelous an accomplishment as any he had witnessed here.

"We Horven specialize in orderly intellectualization. One of the tools we have developed is a unified-orientation conception of horoscopy that enables us to apply the details of any local system in the galaxy to our own framework. A precise interpolation would take much time, of course, since we have to compensate in your case for a sizable time differential, but we can certainly make a crude alignment now."

For the next hour they compared notes, oblivious to all else except for the Horven's continued helmet-transaction. It needed no chart on which to post information, keeping complete data in its head.

"My tentative plotting indicates that you will enter a

new cycle of experience at a life duration of about forty-two of your years," the Horven remarked at last.

"Mine also," Groton said. "My sun passes out of Scorpio at that point." He stopped. "Ouch! That's *now*!"

"Of course, since you are coming with us."

Very neat. "But my wife—"

"Provide me her configuration, and we shall see how she fits into this picture."

Groton did so, though he felt increasingly uneasy about it. This being, this representative of a mature species, was frighteningly intelligent in obscure ways.

"I am sorry," the Horven said then. "This is not an aspect that would normally be evidenced in your more limited framework; but mine is, if I may say so without giving offense, somewhat more advanced. Your wife is dead."

The words struck with a physical impact. "But—"

"Your astrology cannot pinpoint such an event specifically, but ours *can*. Even after making due allowance for error introduced in transposition, the probability is virtually conclusive. Her skein terminates abruptly."

Groton remained stunned, not yet ready to believe it. "How—when—?"

"On that I cannot yet provide exact details, but can say that there were ironic elements. She perished as the result of her own decision, in an effort to do what she believed was proper. She was mistaken, but it was a noble demise. As for when—in this framework, approximately ninety-eight million years ago. In yours—ten minutes."

"I must go back to her!"

The Horven removed the helmet. "It is better that you do not."

Groton looked into the indefinite countenance and knew with terrible certainty that truth had emerged. The life he had known was over; his return could only wreak havoc. He was committed to a new existence—alone.

EARTH

The mellow music of the bassoon welled up as he explored the final triad. Ivo saw his resources falling away. The horn had failed him after all; it had departed, never to return. Only one hope remained—yet in this concurrency, it was impossible for him to affect its theme.

On the ground stood a fair young woman. She cast a smile at him as though it were a handful of soil, seeking to assimilate him into her world, but he passed her by. Next was a massive bull stroking the sod with its hoof, epitome of power yet not agressive. Last was the goat: a gentle doe, horned and bearded after the nature of her kind, and with a fine udder. Surely the symbol had been of a virile male-goat, a buck, most indefatigable of animals! Perhaps it was, elsewhere; but this was what *he* saw, and he would not deny it.

She contemplated him, the gaze of one eye suggesting DISCRIMINATION, and the gaze of the other—and he paused to verify this, taken aback—LOVE. He stood before Capricorn, responding to the bleat of the bassoon and the ambience of earth, and could not speak.

She said: "Music is love in search of a word."

Then he saw behind her, written upon an erosion-ragged mountain cliff, as it were a palimpsest:

There was some initial difficulty emplacing the suppressors—popularly known as "destroyers"—as many immature cultures were unable to appreciate the long-range purpose of these devices. The mission was nevertheless accomplished. Although galactic communications were necessarily inhibited during the Second Siege, civilization itself suffered stasis instead of abolition.

In fifteen to twenty thousand years the fields of the several destroyers overlapped each other, and crews were dispatched to place their defenses on standby. As more time passed, these units became repositories for galactic artifacts, and even assumed museum-status. As individual species came of age and thus were immune to the interference signal, they tended to visit the stations, and sometimes to leave examples of their own cultures for display. No untended immatures were able to visit the stations, because of the nature of the broadcasts, so selectivity was no problem.

The Second Siege, like the First, endured about a million years. This time civilization rebounded almost immediate-

*ly, no worlds having been ravaged or cultures destroyed by
other than natural means.*

*The destroyer network was considered to be only a
holding action, not a solution. The major thrust was of a
different nature. The first concerted extragalactic exploration was undertaken, and entire civilized planets made the
jump into deep space. Chief among the advanced species
participating were the Ngslo, the Horven and the Dooon.
Their objective was the realization of the true nature of
the Traveler and its reason for being. They departed—and
did not return.*

*The ultimate nature of the Traveler was not discovered
until the Third Civilization picked up reports from the
surviving explorers, many millions of light-years removed.
The truth, as brought out by the dispatch from Horv, was
remarkable, and it changed the entire complexion of
galactic intercourse.*

Afra felt the impetus shoving her into an alternate
existence. She felt the compulsion of the music, the fascination of galactic history, so much more vast than anything she had studied before. There was a period of
timelessness, of drifting to melody; then the surroundings
firmed and she was standing in—

A supermarket.

Ahead of her was an aisle bordered by towering prom-
ontories of canned goods: on one side beans—lima,
pinto, kidney, navy, great northern, vegetarian, pork &,
black-eyed peas. On the other side, other vegetables—
potatoes, canned sliced white; corn, whole kernel; corn,
cream-style; tomatoes, stewed; peas, baby; peas, dried;
beets, cut. To one side beyond the near islands were the
fresh vegetable bins, leafy green, round red, puffy white.
To the other side was the main portion of the store, neat
hanging signposts identifying the aisles; there were pyr-
amidding displays of canned fruit juice, boxed powdered
milk, cartoned cigarettes, bagged charcoal and the eleventh
volume of a cheap coupon-encyclopedia.

Shoppers moved with their wire push-baskets, their
noisy children running free to sneeze into the wilting
lettuce, splatter bottles of grape-juice on the worn
tiles, and eat bananas before they were weighed and
marked, dropping the peels behind the larger boxes of

detergent where the cleanup crews wouldn't discover them for days. Harried housewives changed their minds about half-gallon cardboard containers of ice cream and left them melting on the racks of chewing gum by the cash registers. Pot-bellied, sun-baked men ambled along in shorts and the hairs on their chests, picking up six-packs of beer. Freshly nubile girls clustered titteringly near the magazine rack, ignoring the PLEASE DO NOT READ IN STORE sign.

Afra stood there, absorbing it all. This was not the kind of vision she had anticipated. The market was ordinary, the people typical. Everything was routine middle-class, and there was nothing alien or even outré about it, apart from its slightly old-fashioned aspect. Certainly it illuminated the "truth" about the Traveler signal in no obvious way.

She turned about, seeking the exit. It was her conjecture that this vision would endure for an established period, and that whatever was to be manifested would *be* manifested regardless of her own actions. All she could do was wait it out, and act to preserve her equanimity.

Her eye fixed on a man standing in the nearest checkout line. He was muffled up as though braced against a storm, though the temperature within the store was comfortable, and he wore a tall silk hat tilted at a rakish angle. His hand was buried in a pocket as though he were searching for small change, and there was something familiar about him.

And she was screaming and running down the aisle away from that sight, terrified. She lurched into the bean shelf, hurting her shoulder and sending cans toppling down about her and bouncing to the floor and rolling across the aisle. People turned to look at the commotion, surprised.

"No!" she cried shrilly. "I reject it! I refuse—"

So negative was her reaction that the scene itself wavered, losing its reality. She *knew* it was a vision, and she had a strong will and a fundamental aversion, and it was enough. The setting could not hold her any more than a nightmare could hold the sleeper who once consciously realized that it was dream-fabric and rejected it.

The room in the destroyer station came into view, the other people floating in their places. She had broken out.

428

Harold and Beatryx appeared to be conscious also, until she saw that they were not reacting to tangible events. Their eyes moved, their limbs worked, and now and then one of them would speak—but they paid no attention to her or to each other. They were deep in vision.

Ivo still played his instrument. His hands did all of it; he did not need to blow into any type of mouthpiece. The sounds were a medley of instruments, an entire orchestra, but with four perdominating: the violin, the flute, the French horn and the bassoon. She could even pick out the individual themes. Strongest, for her, was that of the bassoon, though she knew it to be a difficult instrument to play effectively. Once someone had told her a story of a bassoonist who had gone crazy because of the reaction of his body to the reed vibration, tight lip-compression and extended breath pressure; he had suffered from chronic suffocation during long passages because he never had enough time to breathe *out*, and so his brain had been starved of oxygen. She had rejected this notion even in childhood, but knew that the bassoon in certain respects defied the conventional laws of sound, and that standard fingering did not guarantee proper notes.

She remembered hearing—minutes ago? hours?—one of the distinctive bassoon passages that composers were fond of; they were typically enamored of the coloring of this instrument's tone, and of the clownlike propensities of its upper register. She had experienced both a short while ago, when she had been a—

A *goat*?

She shrugged away the suggestion. Evidently music did have power—the power to project the members of the present company into individual visions. Was Ivo himself having a vision? He was playing—yet his eyes moved and his lips parted as though in speech, without a sound. A partial vision, perhaps.

She had escaped the nightmare planned for her, but did not seem to be much better off. She was with the others physically, but in effect alone. What had gone wrong? Surely she should have entered an illumination of history or philosophy, not a supermarket!

Beatryx spoke: first an embarrassed laugh, then words. "I am not fair! I'm almost forty!"

Almost. Harold had of course made up one of his

horoscopes on her, saying something about a "seesaw" planetary typing. From that, ironically, he was able to conclude that Beatryx was the proper wife for him. Was he right? It did seem so. And what did he have to say about Afra's own marital propensities, determined by her moment of birth? She had never admitted it to him, but she was quite curious.

As though in answer to his wife, Harold said: "One static brush for the Queen."

Ivo went on playing, and from his weird instrument the music of the symphony projected throughout the chamber. Afra continued to respond to the passages of the bassoon, neither loud nor sharp yet truly penetrating in their fashion. Almost, as she watched, she could make out the outline of the unique woodwind within the framework of his moving hands. Eight feet of tubing, narrowing and folding back upon itself, with the tilted slender mouthpiece containing the double reed, and with holes to govern the notes. The theme was expressive, distinctive, evocative, expert, soulful; it moved her, drew her down into—

She yanked herself out, refusing to reenter that vision.

"It's very nice," Beatryx said. "But—"

"The Drone *will* assume command," Harold replied.

A pause. "Thank you so much."

Afra watched and listened, confining the encompassing music to the background of her awareness. They were participating, and she was not, and that bothered her—but her own vision was unacceptable. Could she enter one of theirs?

"What is the immediate objective?" Harold asked.

Afra arched an eyebrow at him. "The immediate objective? To find out exactly what is—"

"And the mines will prevent subsequent attacks?"

"That depends what—"

"How does the Felk armament compare to ours?"

Afra shrugged. "I don't think you're paying proper attention, Harold."

"How much time do we have?"

She looked at Beatryx and at Ivo. "We may have forever, Harold, if we don't get out of here before we starve. *If* we can starve in vision-land. Dreaming may be entertaining, but, as Frost said—"

"How much time do we have before the enemy breaks through and destroys the station?"

"Really, Robert Frost is hardly an enemy. He—"

"You plan to wait for them to attack?"

"*As* Frost said: 'The dreams are lovely, dark and deep, But I have promises to keep, And miles to go before I sleep, And—"

"Why?"

"Harold, you don't ask 'why?' to a *poem*!"

"Yet with their ships massed and traveling at high velocity, our scattered forces cannot hope to stop them all. And one ship should be sufficient to blast the station."

"Of course Frost said 'woods' rather than 'dreams' but I thought I'd—"

"You have no manuals of strategy?"

"No I don't, damn you! I stick to simple sex appeal."

"Provided he lives."

"Provided *you* live. You are impossible, Harold."

"And the Felks are similarly organized? No study of the lessons of history?"

She turned away from him, finding the amusement shallow. The mellow bassoon theme surrounded her again, and she fought it off again. She could even make out the rosewood length of the instrument, the distinctive circle of ivory around the top opening. Despite the bizarre circumstance she was moved by the poignant beauty of Ivo's music. He had taken this alien contraption and produced— a symphony, each theme, each instrument of which was discrete and perfect. He *was* a skilled bassoonist, as well as a remarkable flutist. If only she had known about his musical gifts earlier!

Beatryx looked unhappy. "Here?" she inquired.

Afra wondered what it was that so disturbed the woman; then, observing her actions, began to understand. Inadequate sanitary facilities, in that particular vision. She went to help Beatryx, so as to spare her embarrassment when she came out of it. It turned out to be the motions only, and a little later the older woman slept.

Time passed.

Harold talked again, of ships and tactics and negotiations. Never, oddly, of astrology. She would have been happier if he had.

Afra practiced swimming in the air, and made her way

away from the others. She searched for the boundaries of the chamber, but the mist became dense—"lovely, dark and deep," she thought—and in this free-fall state she had no internal sense of direction. She realized that she could lose herself here, from even that pseudo-companionship the others provided, and did not relish the prospect.

She returned to the group, fixed her eyes on Ivo and his mythical band, and allowed herself to drift toward sleep. When this was over, there would be—oh, important matters—to discuss with him. His—well, his talents, and ... his ...

Nothing had changed when she woke.

"I really don't know anything about campsites," Beatryx was saying.

Several hours had passed, certainly—yet she was not hungry or otherwise in distress, physically. It was as though bodily processes had ceased for the duration, except as suggested (but not consummated) in the visions for verisimilitude. Somehow consciousness, direct or indirect, persisted in each person in spite of this stasis. Another marvel of galactic science? Why not.

Ivo still played. She wondered how his steadily agile hands were enduring. No fatigue either, here? At any rate, the visions were likely to end when the music finished. Then what?

Their mission—*her* mission—had brought them to this dread place, yet the climax was oddly insubstantial. Where was the enemy? Where the denouement? She had not really expected to struggle bloodily against a horde of ravening monsters; but *this*?

More hours passed. Harold slept. Beatryx went through a mysterious episode of terror, crying "Kill it!" and after subsiding from that, "That's a man!" Then she was very quiet.

Harold talked to someone or something evidently inhuman, unhuman. Portions of his dialogue were revealing. "You are the one-in-a-thousand! The species that is immune to the destroyer ... You—you built the destroyer! ... Why are you doing this? Why are you reserving true space travel for yourselves?" Then: "And I am supposed to—to participate in the other side too? When I'm not even certain I agree with *this* side?"

Waking or dreaming, at least Harold seemed to know which side he was on. He was putting up, in his fashion, a good fight. Afra, in his (assumed) position, would have deleted the polite qualifications and told somebody to go to hell sideways.

"The destroyer—only destroys evil minds?"

Afra was forming more of the picture. Evil minds—like that of Bradley Carpenter? Surely Harold would not succumb to casuistry of that ilk.

But certain other bits he uttered stirred the beginnings of a profound doubt in her. Had they misjudged the destroyer, after all this? Impossible—yet . . .

Beatryx began to speak again. She was talking with someone about fire, and water, and humanity. Before that she had spent considerable time calling "Black—black— where are you?" Afra had had to tune out the plaintive repetition. Now they were talking together, and Harold was finally on the subject of astrology. It was difficult to follow both conversations simultaneously, and she had to settle for snatches from one or the other.

Then: "You were *not* wrong, Dolora."

Beatryx went through an inexplicable series of contortions, then was walking or swimming strenuously, while Harold continued blithely discoursing on astrological technology. Then a sudden outburst: "But you don't understand! You have to listen—"

Her voice was cut off by an inarticulate noise, and Beatryx doubled over, her face twisted in agony.

Afra paddled over as rapidly as she could, aware that a new and ugly element had been added. A crisis of some sort was at hand.

Ivo went on playing.

Beatryx was lying quietly by the time she got there. Afra tried to lift the older woman, but in the null-G only wrestled herself around. It was pointless, anyway— position made no difference, when there was no weight to support. She was acting without thinking, and to no avail.

Suddenly she realized that Beatryx was not breathing.

Afra clasped the woman's head, poked a finger in her mouth to clear it of any possible obstruction, and applied the kiss of life: mouth-to-mouth resuscitation.

There was no immediate response, but she kept on,

exhaling into Beatryx's lungs, breaking to inhale herself while hugging the inert chest to force out the air. Again, she could not depend on gravity to assist.

As she labored in such measured desperation, hearing Ivo's bassoon and Harold's intermittent remarks in the background, scenes of their association illuminated her vision.

Beatryx, at the torus-station, carrying a platter of food in to their first meal as a foursome: She and Harold, Afra and Ivo ... and Brad too, then. Beatryx, beside her as Joseph blasted into space with the macroscope. Beatryx, trying to comprehend a difficult concept during an early discussion. Beatryx, declaring "Meeting come to order!" Beatryx in spacesuit, tentatively exploring the Schön-moonlet of Triton.

Beatryx, always ameliorative. Unimportant flashes—yet so poignant now, as Afra realized how important the quiet presence and support of the older woman had been to her.

Older? Beatryx had never looked so young as she did at this moment. . . .

Still she did not breathe—and there was no heart-beat.

Beatryx, tending her garden on Triton. Beatryx, waxing hysterical in Afra's defense, during that mock, not-so-mock trial.

"Tryx, Tryx!" she cried. "You were the only one who understood—"

It was no use. Beatryx was dead.

Afra wrenched away and launched herself at Harold. She took hold of his shoulders and shook, rocking herself more violently than him. "Wake up! Wake up!"

Harold did not respond.

"Harold—*your wife is dead!*" she cried in his ear, slapping him.

Now he began to react. "But—"

"She just died and I can't—I can't—you've got to do something! Wake up!"

He looked stunned. "How—when—?"

Hastily Afra explained, continuing to shake him so that he could not relapse.

His eyes widened. "I must go back to her!"

Then, gradually, he went limp, and nothing she could do revived him. The dream had reclaimed him.

Afra looked around in a fever of desperation—and saw Ivo, still playing.

It was time for the music to end.

She went to Ivo and yanked the instrument from his grasp.

The orchestra stopped, the sound dying away from all the misty reaches of the hall.

The floor reappeared beneath them, and walls around them, much closer than she had supposed, and doors in front and back. Weight returned.

She watched Ivo, waiting for his awareness. He sat for a moment, eyes unfocused. Then he raised his head with a sharpness of decision that was not typical and looked directly at her.

"Thanks, doll," he said.

"Ivo—something terrible has happened. Beatryx—"

He stood up smoothly, flexing his fingers as though they were stiff. "I know. A black shot her with a speargun. Silly woman."

Afra stared at him.

"And your engineer—he's in stasis on the way to deep space. He's beyond the reach of this toy, now. It'll be years before he comes out of it, if he ever does. That cuts it down to two, baby."

She backed away. "You're not Ivo! You're—"

He picked up the orchestrial instrument. "Ivo—Ivon—Ivan—Johan—John—Sean—Shane—Schön! You broke the chain, blue-eyes. You interfered—again!—and Ivo-at-the-idiot-end lost out, just as Brad did. You do have a talent for that. Now—"

A memory—something important—nudged the surface of her awareness, but she had no time for it now. Afra raced toward the door, not pausing to consider where she might be going or why.

"Not so hasty, dish," Schön called after her. "I am not finished with you." He lifted the musical device and held it dramatically before him. "In fact, I have not yet begun to fight."

She had almost reached the door, and could see a lighted hall beyond. It was not the one they had entered by. She reached toward it—

And rebounded from a pliant rail.

The recoil threw her to the floor. She landed on her fanny, facing back toward the center of the room.

ASCENDANT

It was not a room any more. It was a stadium, filled by faces peering up, none distinguishable, and by crowd noises that remained in the background. She perched on a raised platform enclosed by resilient cord. It was a square: the type of arrangement known as a boxing or wrestling ring.

Schön was entering at the far corner, dressed in fighting trunks and laced footwear. His muscular torso shone brown in the glare of the overhead light, and his eyes and teeth were brilliant.

Her glance caught him in that pose: a pugilist entering the ring. It was, as she saw it, the moment of supreme power for him; he dominated. There was nothing she could do to stop him or even inhibit him, whatever he intended.

As though recognizing the strength of the image, he paused, head inside the ring, one foot outside, the rope held up by one hand. "You don't understand, do you, stupid," he said. "You don't know what any of this means. Hell, you purebred clod, you can't even face your *own* symbol."

She pulled herself up, but hesitated to climb out of the rope enclosure until she knew what Schön was planning, and what other barriers he was able to conjure. It just might be safer *in* the ring than *out*.

He did not move immediately, and in that interim of tension she assessed herself. She was dressed as she had been: culottes halted above the knee, snap-slippers designed to fit within the large space-suit shoes, elastic blouse, ribbon tie-down for her hair. The outfit was brief, for the sake of mobility and air-circulation within the space suit, and attractive, for the sake of appearances outside. She cared about those appearances and didn't mind admitting it, and she had had special reason to be presentable at this time.

Now Beatryx was dead and Harold gone, and Ivo had given way grotesquely to Schön.

Beatryx, looking raptly at alien pictures.

Harold, fascinated by strange machines.

Ivo—

Her aspirations of yesterday were meaningless. She could not even spare attention for proper grief, though that would come the moment this chase abated.

Her assessment was now in terms of physical fitness: the clothing she wore would not encumber her in any way, and she had the health to move quickly and with stamina. She knew from fairly intimate observation that the Ivo/Schön physique was not particularly impressive. The apparent musculature of his present body was a function of the illusion, the waking vision he had somehow simulated for them both. She had no doubt that Schön, with his multiple and devastating skills, could overcome her readily if he once caught her—but he might not be *able* to catch her.

She confined her assessment to those physical terms. She did not question his mental superiority. Emotionally he might be a child, or at best an adolescent; intellectually he was the leading genius mankind had produced.

He had been talking while she considered these things. He seemed to be showing off his knowledge: bragging, now that he had the opportunity.

"No, you don't comprehend at all," Schön repeated. "So I'll have to lecture you on the fine points, or you won't appreciate any of it. Too bad you're such a puny audience, but you're the only part of it that's real."

Afra waited with one hand on the rope, ready to dive out of the ring the moment he entered. She knew she was in trouble, but she was also aware that unreasoned flight would get her nowhere she wanted to go. That had already been demonstrated. Somehow Schön had the power to form a setting that physically inhibited her—and she would be well advised to discover exactly how he did it. This time it had been a square formed of rope; next time it might be worse.

"The key," Schön said, "is this tool of the galactics." He held the instrument aloft, the one Ivo had played, and she realized that it must have been in his hand all the time. She had not noticed it before, since the ring. "And 'key' is exactly what I mean. The key to the inner sanctum; the key to history; the key to personality. Call it the symbolizer. SYMBOLIC = SYMBOL PRIME = S′. It transmutes reality to symbols and vice versa, and thereby makes plain the truth. I recognized it for what it was immediately, of course." He snickered. "Ivo thought it was a flute! He tried to play Sidney Lanier on it!"

And succeeded, she thought, knowing better than to interrupt now. She was recovering confidence in herself; if she maintained the proper spirit, she would be supreme over this situation, somehow. Schön had been overrated.

"Actually, it is a teaching device," he continued. "By bringing to life the symbolic essence of a situation or personality, it instructs the participant and viewer. Of course it is necessary to interpret the symbols correctly, but anyone with a smattering of—yet you lack even that, naturally."

"Lack what?" she asked, wiling to cooperate in order to keep the dialogue going. He was teasing her, childishly; she knew that, but already she had a valuable hint. If she could get the galactic instrument—S prime—away from him—

"Astrology," he said. "You have closed your mind to it, and that makes it ideal for my purpose. So the symbolic ascendant means nothing to you."

She waited, refusing this time to rise to the bait. Schön, obviously, had dipped into Ivo's memory and picked up her continuing debate with Harold. He was trying to annoy her—and that could mean that his power would be diminished if she refused to react. The sophisticated response to his exertions was best.

"The ascendant is the overall indication of personality; the rising sign for each individual. My own ascendant falls at Aries 21, and the symbol for that position is A PUGILIST ENTERING THE RING, as you can readily perceive if you concentrate. This indicates full confidence in my own powers—justified, of course—and a complete lack of personal sensitiveness. Thus the galactic machine has dramatized my basic personality and graphically illustrated the power inherent in me."

"That isn't the way Harold described astrology," Afra

murmured, wishing this time that she had taken the trouble to learn more about it, whether she believed in it or not. Its rules were evidently governing this game.

"Harold was an engineer, not an astrologer. His approach was too conventional and conservative, though last I saw of him he was getting disabused in a hurry. Those old galactics really had their sciences worked out."

He was still toying with her. If she tried to defend Harold, she would be defending his hobby as well, and so be on exceedingly tenuous ground. "What about Ivo?"

Schön gazed at her speculatively across the ring, but did not challenge the shift in topic. "Ah yes, Ivo. There's someone *really* confused, for all that I invented him. He oriented on something from each of you, not really knowing the proper use of S-prime, and came up with a mélange that must have made the galactic creators wince. Harold Groton's astrology, Sidney Lanier's poetry, darlin' Afra Glynn's supposed intellectual discrimination and Tryx Groton's suicidal sympathy—all tied in with a galactic history text that the instrument put out as a kind of sideshow attraction. Fascinating juxtaposition, I admit. I was a fiery ram, 'Aspiration' astrologically, 'Trade' poetically, and the strings musically. I engaged in First Siege internecine power politics. I had a good thing going, too—until you torpedoed Ivo for me."

Suddenly the goat image made sense to her, and the evocative music of the bassoon. These had been *her* symbols, in the combined context. And love—where the poem had specified Trade for him, it had specified Love for her. And she had felt it—

"What is my symbol?" she inquired, genuinely curious now. "My—ascendant."

"You don't want to know it, cutie. You are afraid of it, neurotic that you are."

"*Am* I? Or is it that you are afraid to animate *my* symbol, instead of yours? Would that give me dominance?"

"Lady, I'll gladly match symbols with you planet by planet. That would put us on an even footing, in spite of my inordinate superiority in overt life. But you would achieve parity only if you are able to face your own nature when you see it objectively—and you aren't. Your ascendant controls you, and probably your planets do too. It is a contest you would lose by your own prejudice."

"I'll take that chance—if *you* will. I don't think you know *how* to compete, on an even basis."

He smiled, the vicious grin of the warrior tasting blood. "Calling my bluff, Glynn?"

She smiled back, as maliciously as he, though she was afraid of him. "Yes, prettyboy. And if you cheat, you lose." She wasn't sure what to expect, or whether Schön would really bind himself to the outcome of a fair competition, but if it nullified the advantage of his intellect . . .

"Take it, child," he said, touching the instrument. "Your ascendant is Taurus 15—A MAN MUFFLED UP, WITH A RAKISH SILK HAT."

And she was back in the supermarket, the same one she had fled, and she was facing the man beside the checkout counter. She had asked for it—and she was terrified.

Something obscure happened. People backed away from the cash register. The muffled man looked up, around, pausing a moment as though considering. It seemed that he was looming over Afra, and she was very small, very fragile. Something remarkable was about to happen—

The large man moved.

There was the sound of a gun being fired.

SUN

She wrenched herself out of it—and was out of the rope enclosure and passing through the door she had originally been running toward. She had escaped one vision only to return to another—unless she could also escape Schön and the galactic, the demonic, S' device.

This room was thoroughly finite, at least, and well lighted. Banks of what appeared to be electronic equipment stood against the walls, and there were a number of screens flashing what she took to be broadcast patterns. This was, by her reckoning, a communications center. That suggested some kind of occupation of the station, at least at intervals. Automatic machinery would not be set up for viewing like this.

Schön was there ahead of her. He sat on a podium in

the center of the room, behind a table whose white cloth extended down to touch the floor. He wore a high turban and stared into a shiny crystal ball. "Man," he said grandiosely, "has the capacity to bring the entire universe within the purview of his mind."

She had either to retreat into the original chamber or to pass directly by him. Neither alternative appealed, so she temporized. "I thought you were supposed to be a pugilist."

"That, my dear, as I so tediously explained, was the ascendant. Now we are with the sun, and it behooves us to be more acute. My sun is in Aries 19, and so I am as you see me: A CRYSTAL GAZER. So it is written in the most authoritative text." He stared into the ball. "I see that the referee has graded the first round on the ten-point must system: ten points to Fire, no points to Earth, who washed out. An excellent start—though it would be more entertaining if you were to at least put up some show of competition."

So she hadn't lost yet! "How do I know that's an honest score?"

He shoved the ball in her direction. "Witness."

She stepped up to look into it. Inside was a great-horned ram copulating with a frightened doe.

"Miscegenation is all I see," she said. Then, saying it, she realized that the animals too were symbols: the ram of Aries and the goat of Capricorn. Schön had played his little prank on her. Two different species—somewhat as the two of them were of different races. A bald proposition, a dirty joke—or a threat. He had said that her own prejudice would cost her victory. . . .

"Too bad nature forbids it," she said in reply to his mocking gaze. She resented the implication that this was the only use for her—to submit to the sexual assault of the male—knowing it to be a conventional objection of womankind but still stirred by it. There was that about Schön that fascinated her in ways Ivo had not; yet she was not about to encourage his casual lewdness. In her mind was the remark Ivo had made about childhood sexual activity at their project: homo, hetero and group. She would contest the issue more fiercely in the coming rounds.

It was amazing what a difference the mind made. Schön

441

did not resemble Ivo at all, though the body was the same.

"Yes, you would lecture on nature," he remarked, as though that proved something. "Your symbol for Capricorn 12 is A STUDENT OF NATURE LECTURING."

"How do you know?" she demanded, nettled again in spite of her disbelief in the personal relevance of such things.

"Dear little Ivo studied your horoscope. Now all that information is mine." He grinned. "You are, you see, in my power. That chart has you laid out and nakedly displayed, and I can sample any part of you I desire. Fortunately I don't desire your *mind*."

She controlled her mounting irritation. "How much do you expect to accomplish, depending on astrology?" Again, she had to keep him talking, while waiting for an opportunity to gain some advantage. Genius he might be, but his youthful arrogance might defeat him yet.

"There are many ways to view existence," Schön said. "Symbols are useful for minds of any potential, and astrology is an organized system of symbols as valid as any. I would accept it as readily as, say, religion. Of course, no symbol has validity apart from the values and qualities assigned to it by the user. What alternative would you prefer for your nuptial?"

"What makes you think the ram is so damned attractive to the doe?"

"What makes you think the ram is *trying* to be?"

"You imagine your word is my command?"

"Sister, there is no other functioning homo-sapiens *man* within fifty thousand light-years, and you can't penetrate the destroyer field by yourself. I *can*. The question is, am I to be obliged, however clumsily, on my way home, or do I travel alone?"

Could he travel alone? Even if he turned off the destroyer broadcast—a thing he might not be able to do, assuming it had safeguards against interference—he would not succeed in freeing the spaceways of its effect. Earth was in the field of another station, and in any event it would require at least fifteen thousand years for the destroyer to clear itself, limited as it was by light velocity.

Yet he was in control of his body and Ivo's experience

now. That meant he had found a way around the destroyer memory—and, therefore, the destroyer itself.

Or so he wanted her to believe.

"I don't believe you," she said. "I don't think you *can* go home without my help. Otherwise you wouldn't be chasing me now, or trying so hard to impress me."

"Or winning rounds against you. Maybe I'm too soft-hearted to leave you here alone. Are you calling my bluff again?" he inquired scornfully.

Suddenly she was afraid again, and could not answer. Ivo's body had been possessed by a demon. How important *was* this peculiar contest, and how badly was she losing? Evidently the verbal interchange was part of it, and she was at a disadvantage there. Brad had always been able to twist around her statements and confuse her, and Schön had the same ability.

On the other hand, if she should somehow win—and theoretically she had an equal chance to do so, if she could only marshal her complete resources—what would be her victory? A liaison with Schön?

"You always were slow to get the message," he said. "I sent you an obvious one as soon as Brad lost out, but naturally you fouled it up."

"You sent *me* a message!"

"Surely you didn't think I needed to send *Ivo* one? I had to borrow his hand to type it."

Her curiosity had been aroused, and she didn't care that this was what he had intended. "Then why didn't you just *tell* him what you wanted?"

"He wouldn't listen."

That simple? That all the mystery and confusion engendered by the obscure missives had been Ivo's fault? Again, she doubted it.

"Why, you wonder, did I not address the message to you? And, I explain—for you are exceedingly interested in explanations at the moment, your symbol says—I found it necessary to be circumspect. Ivo was almost always on guard, and only in rare moments of negligence was I able to assume control of so much as a single limb. He happened to pass the teletype section while in a condition of shock from the Senator's demise and Brad's discommodation, and I froze him unaware and set up the message. But I didn't dare to do it in any style he comprehended, or

443

mention *you* at all, or he would have snapped right out of it then. I had very little time, so I just jotted down the opening line of Lanier's "The Marshes of Glynn" in polyglot, sticking to languages you could interpret. I thought you'd be smart enough to follow that up and get the *real* message."

"Well, I wasn't and I didn't," she snapped. "So what *was* the '*real* message'?"

"The terminal couplet of the poem, stupid. 'And I would I could know what swimmeth below when the tide comes in/On the length and the breadth of the marvellous marshes of Glynn.' *Anybody* with a note of savvy could see that what swam below Ivo's Glynn was Schön, and of course a Georgia girl would be familiar with the poem. Once *you* fluttered your pale pink eyelashes and told him to give over—"

"What makes you so sure I would have told him?"

"Back in that hour you fancied you were enamored of Brad Carpenter. You thought Schön would help you get him back. You were charmingly naïve. Still are, too."

She remembered. Had she known the truth then, she *would* have sacrificed Ivo ... foolishly. It had taken the phenomenal chain of events of the ensuing period to change her thinking—and her values.

"After that, Ivo was on to the polyglot dodge, so I had to try other stuff. He wasn't exactly bright, but he did know enough not to get taken twice on the same boat, and he was stubborn as hell. The problem was to identify him without alerting him, and there were not many opportunities. Fortunately he never did catch on to the fact the messages were not intended for him, so the arrow-address gimmick got through."

"So you made a Neptune-symbol to send us so far out we'd be dependent on you to get us home again—"

"Obliged to cry uncle, yes. Neptune *is* the planet of obligation, if we accept the view of your engineer's main authority on the subject. Traditionally, of course, Neptune is allied with liquids, gases, mystery, illusion, dreams, deceit—but that simple hint passed you by, naturally. At least Groton, duffer that he was, began to catch on that—"

"And a shorthand message once we were there," she said, cutting him off. She was furious with herself for not delving beyond the superficial, at the time of that message. Liquids and gases—as in the melting process? Could Schön actually have forseen that? Mystery, illusion—as in the whereabouts of Schön behind the illusion of Ivo. A multileveled communiquè indeed, and she *had* missed it. Brad would have grasped all of it. . . .

"But why did you want to take over if you couldn't help Brad?" she asked him then. "Surely you didn't care about the world crisis?"

"There was an entertaining situation developing. Why else?"

She stared at him, aghast at his indifference, but he met her gaze levelly. "Brad's mind gone and a United States Senator dead, the very future of the macroscope project in peril—and you found it amusing?"

"Entertaining. There's a distinction, had you but the wit to grasp it, chick. The challenge of a signal from space that could stupefy and kill—"

"Why *did* the Senator die? No one else did."

"The rules of the game require me to remind you that every serious question I answer seriously is gaining me points."

"And any you can't or won't answer will gain *me* points." She hoped.

He shrugged. "More people would have died had more been exposed. Your others were all mature, sedate, pacifistic scientists who had largely come to terms with reality. The destroyer activates a neural feedback that varies directly with intelligence and inversely with maturity. Thus an intelligent mature person is unaffected, or an unintelligent immature person. But an intelligent immature one is hit with all the voltage of the disparity between those qualities. The Senator was a primitive genius (I use the term loosely)—so he died. Brad was a medium-mature genius, as were the other scientists."

"And what are you?" she inquired bitterly.

"I'm like the Senator, only more so. I'm smarter and less mature than he was. That was part of the challenge: to handle that alien signal, when its direct impact on me would have fried my brain—almost literally. I dare say I'm the brightest primitive ever to be spawned on Earth."

She was not going to debate that. "You plan to do a lot
445

of maturing in the next few hours—or whenever you decide to toddle off home?"

"Hardly. I'm happy the way I am. No point in going the way Brad did. I *could*, incidentally, have saved his life, there on Triton, had I been on hand. Not that you would have wanted me to."

"What?" Afra knew that he was trying to shock her again. He was succeeding. He was also leading her on to more questions and so eroding her competitive position farther. Yet her recognition of this process did not halt it; she *had* to know. She was hooked on the bits of knowledge he injected.

"No, I don't mean you were in love with Ivo then. You still were fixed on Brad, for what that was worth. But you wouldn't have wanted him to live."

She continued to stare at him, at his mercy.

Now his eyes dropped to the ball. "I see," he murmured, "I see the evolution of man, from a speck of protoplasm to maturity. I see the free-swimming larvae of the echinoderms developing into the radially-symmetrical forms of adulthood. But I also see neoteny: the larval form preempting the reproductive capacity, and so bypassing maturity. I see a long evolution of such ambitious larval forms, extending even beyond the sea and onto land where true maturity becomes not merely impractical but impossible. Thus, instead of mature starfish, larval Man."

"Are you trying to suggest—"

"You knew we derive from the Echinoderm superphylum. You know the characteristics of that type of life. What did you suppose would happen, when you interfered with the evolutionary reconstitution? By abolishing the timing mechanism, you permitted the subject to run its full course—without benefit of the proper terminal environment."

"Oh, Brad!" she cried in anguish.

"But you wouldn't have cared to marry a starfish, however mature. So—you arranged to kill him."

"I didn't know!"

"Sweetie, ignorance of the law is never an excuse—particularly the law of nature, and most particularly when you are supposed to be a student of nature lecturing."

"But—"

"But even proper attention would not have reconstituted his blasted mind. Recycling can't extirpate tissue damage; it merely reshapes what's there. He would have made a very stupid starfish."

"Stop it!" she cried.

"*You* stop it. You know how—if you have the courage."

And she was in the supermarket again, still terrified.

The sound of the gun's explosion was fresh in her ears. There was a struggle occurring at the counter. The checkout girl screamed, a man fell. The silk hat rolled across the floor toward Afra. It was huge, and it grew larger as it came, swelling as though to crush her beneath its turning mass.

She screamed and ran. She crashed into the bean shelf, hurting her shoulder and sending cans toppling heavily ... somehow aware that this had happened before, but unable to stop. People turned to stare, but she ignored them, crying "No! No! No!"

Somehow her unguided rush took her through a door at the rear, and she was hustling through a winter chamber with hanging slabs of raw meat, stumbling among tremendous boxes. A man with a cleaver loomed over her, and she saw the dark blood on it, and she screamed again and crashed through another door.

Then she was in a narrow alley, running between steaming garbage cans. The door behind her burst open and a man charged out. "Little girl!" he bellowed. "Little girl! Come back here!"

He was twice her size in every direction, and his skin was dark, his teeth great and white, and she fled.

There were trucks with baked black rubber tires taller than she was, and an ambience of gasoline odors and growling motors and the choking fog of exhausts, and she was trapped between them and the black man. She screamed again and dashed for yet another door, symbol of escape. It was closed. Desperately she reached up to grasp the handle and pull down the stiff latch, while the black pursuer closed in.

Suddenly it opened and she burst inside.

These were strange quarters: tables of alien contour, bed-pallets of singular discomfort, toilet facilities embarrassingly foreign to biped anatomy. Yet they were obvi-

MOON

☾

ously *quarters*, intended to be of comfort for resident creatures of established form, if not for man.

Afra went through the rooms of this complex, wondering whether the owners were present or when they might return. Obviously *someone* ran this station, or at least attended it periodically, and this was where the caretakers reclined in comfort during their off-hours.

One room terminated in a low wall, emptiness above it. She found that it was a balcony. It overlooked a courtyard of fair size, and green shrubbery sprouted from planters about its nether perimeter. This suggested that the caretakers were not so different from human beings in the things that mattered. This was essentially Earth-air, Earth-gravity, human-comfort temperature, and the decor was harmonious to manlike tastes. There had to be strong biological resemblances between the species, however many eyes or ears or antennae either had.

Noise; and into the court below marched a troop of men, a motley mob. They were in blue-collar working clothes—overalls, protective helmets, grime. Some were white in the face, some black, some yellow; most were composite shades.

She discovered that she had with her a huge shopping bag, evidently acquired at the supermarket, and she was holding it in her arms as she tried to lean over the rail for a better view. The balcony had been constructed with adults in mind, and she had a hard time of it. It did not occur to her to put down the shopping bag; that was filled with nameless but wonderfully promising things. Things that her mother would undoubtedly fashion mysteriously into chocolate cake, raspberry ice cream and crisp pinwheel cookies. She could not let that bag go, even for a moment.

But as she poked her head over, so that one pigtail flopped against the rail, the men beneath spotted her. A rolling cry went up. "We want REPRESENTATION!" the workers cried.

"Well, send up your represen—repre—somebody!" she

called back, not expecting her soprano voice to be heard in all that clamor.

A single man entered behind her. "I am he," he said, startling her. She began to cry, but stopped in a moment, realizing that it could do no good.

The man was Schön, tremendous.

"I thought you were a crystal gazer," she remarked in an attempt to conceal her lingering tears. She was not, actually, as surprised as she might have been.

"That was back at Aries 9," he said. "The sun. The ref scored it 10 to 2, favor of the crystal gazer, incidentally. *This* is the moon: Gemini 21 for me, Capricorn 19 for you. I see you are dressed for the part."

"The part?" This adult conversation was difficult.

"Your symbol. A CHILD OF ABOUT FIVE WITH A HUGE SHOPPING BAG."

"I'm *seven*," she corrected him primly. Then she reacted to her own statement. "I *am*?"

She was. No wonder adults appeared so large.

"And you called *me* immature!" he exclaimed, laughing. "What a fine time you had analyzing me, after I injected a little excitement into Ivo's determined mundanity. *You*—a card-carrying WASP—wanted to psychoanalyze *me* in absentia. Little appreciating the inherence of agression in the human species, the factor that brought it to dominance on Earth. Well, call me a BLASP, you who think in terms of acronyms."

"A what?"

"A *black* Anglo-Saxon Protestant. Or a brown Mongolian Catholic, or a yellow Hottentot Moslem. I represent all of them; I *am* all of them, as you see by my symbol outside. And perhaps it is fitting, precious, that your name is Afra. That's very close to Afram, or Afro-American, the convenient designation for—"

"A whole group. A whole—labor demonstration?"

"Exactly. I am Man's universal spirit, and I reject all property and private rights as invalid limitations, other than purely social. I tell you that right and justice only prevail when properly dramatized—when the issue is forced. And I attack this problem, as I do all problems, with courage."

"And not a trace of false modesty," she murmured. Yet she felt the need to help the demonstrating workers,

449

whatever their problem might be. She wanted to be a part of the group, to participate, to conform, even in rebellion. "What *do* you want, speci—anyway?" Her stature as a five- or seven-year-old child (physically five, mentally seven?), though it prevented her from getting out the entire word "specifically," was not any more incongruous than the rest of this bizarre sequence.

"I want freedom," Schön said, menacing in his emphasis. "I want security. I want power. I want equality. I, the hapless peoples of the world, want everything you have now."

"Me—the modern white?"

"Yes. You have the good life. I want the right to ravage the world as you have done. I want to destroy as much as you have done. I want to drive myself to the brink of extinction as you have done, you smug white turd. You little bitch, I mean to take—"

And she was fleeing his madness again, whether in the station or on the streets of Macon she could not tell, nor did it make a difference.

MARS

Outside was an ocean shore, and the day was windy. Ancient Indian women sat facing outward, their quick hands fashioning useful artifacts. Afra peered up and down and found no hiding place, knowing the pursuer was not far behind. He could quickly catch her here, unless—

Near at hand lay a blanket, woven of many colors but only half complete. She plumped herself down, full-size now, and composed her aging features. She took up the blanket and its attached apparatus and became one of the artisans.

Schön did not appear. Afra became interested in the blanket, noticing the fineness of its warp and weft, and the skill of her own wrinkled brown hands as they manipulated the strands. She discovered in this dull routine an excellence of self-expression, a meeting of human needs. She found that she could accept this calm, unhurried work, and take special pleasure from it. She was preserv-

450

ing an art, and this was a worthwhile thing to do, no matter how far beyond it the machines of civilization went. The old ways were not inferior, when the larger framework of existence was considered. There was reward in simple diligence.

Over the troubled waters flew a white dove. She watched it with minor interest, expecting it to be confused in the general turbulence of wave and cloud, but it was not. Its direction was clear, its mission firm. It flew low over the surf, skillfully reconciling the difficulties of gust and spray and maintaining its orientation. A clever bird.

It sailed over the beach toward her, and came to rest only a few feet away. She could smell the tangy spume it carried on its feathers, now fluffing dry. It walked over the sand, cocking its head forward at each step in the manner of a chicken. Then it fixed an eye on her.

"Welcome to Mars, honey," it said.

Schön! She had been discovered after all, in the way she least expected. "How did you find me?"

"I had to give you the score, sugar. You did better on Luna, but you flubbed it when you ran out again. No problem is solved that way. Ref called it 10 to 5, me."

"Who *is* this referee?"

"Funny thing. My Mars is in Taurus, where your Ascendant is, while your Mars is in Aries. Do you suppose this inversion is significant? Mars is the planet of initiative, you know."

"You are avoiding my questions, pigeon," she remarked. But she knew the answer to the problem. Obviously they were still personifying their symbols, and her seeming act of free will had been mere conformity. He knew what the symbols were, so still had an advantage over her. He would keep on winning, as long as he could shock her or scare her into running. She had to gain the initiative—and this was the obvious place to start.

She stood up, breaking the spell of the symbol. She was in a large room filled with machinery, and it had been the steady sound of its operation that had suggested the breaking of ocean surf. This appeared to be a section of the station's power plant, and the generators were keening, rumbling and pulsating with internal potential. Somewhere there was probably an atomic furnace utilizing the total conversion of matter into energy, and these were

451

merely the units that harnessed and channeled that awesome power.

Schön was standing before her, still mocking her. Had it been physical capture he desired, he would have had her long ago, contest or no contest. It was her mind he was after, despite his denial, and he would not give up that chase until the ram had his way or the doe escaped entirely.

Had there, she wondered, ever been a ewe for him?

"Do you know the derivation of the Mars symbol?" he inquired. He sketched it in the air: the circle with the northeast arrow emerging.

"Of course. It represents—"

"*Not* that cute little fib you tried to hand the engineer. Surely you realized the phallic essence of that pictograph? And Venus—" he described that symbol also in the air— "Venus is about as direct an image of the female apparatus—"

"It depends on your viewpoint," she said, interrupting him. But she *hadn't* thought of the symbols in this way, in spite of their normal application to designate male or female.

Schön was in effect jabbing at her now, keeping her off-balance while he set up for his pugilistic KO. The ascendant evidently influenced his entire mode of play. Similarly, her own ascendant was a continuing liability that she had to face and reconcile, if she were ever to match him on an even basis. How many planets, how many rounds remained before the terminus? Seven?

"And did you realize that innocent little Ivo thought you were having an affair with Harold Groton?"

She tried to halt her reaction, but it was as though he had knocked her breath out of her. "*What*?"

"Ivo failed utterly to comprehend your capricious Capricorn ways, and he labored under his own bumbling reverse-prejudice. White girl, white man, and all that suggestive dialogue—"

"But that was only because Harold understood how I'd—" She paused, then went on brokenly. "How I had let Brad go and—and—"

"And presented your fickle heart to Ivo—without bothering to inform him. So you just waltzed around with the engineer, enjoying the sensation, waiting for some romantic moment to let Ivo discover what was in store for him, totally insensitive to his interim feelings. Oh, lass, that was your finest hour. It was beautiful! How the irony of that little *contretemps* delighted me! But you know, he almost caught on at one point. Luckily, I succeeded in diverting him before it became conscious."

She turned a horrified glance on him. "You—you actually—"

"Be practical, doll. Why should *I* match Mars to Venus, or give the water-carrier his goat? If Ivo had known how you really felt, he never would have yielded to me. As it was, the thing was near. Only his depression and the sudden breaking of the theme while he was in harness—"

"Oh, Ivo!" she exclaimed with the sharpest pang yet.

"A little late for regrets, cutie. Ivo no longer exists, unless you count his special memories, that are now part of my own experience. He has no more reality than I did while he was in control. You will have to settle for his body."

She was running again, routed again, and it was Macon. She knew that the man behind must inevitably catch up, for there was no place to hide, no one to protect her. Her father was gone; she had seen him fall when the gun fired, there in his great overcoat; and his hat, not really silk, had rolled gruesomely toward her as though it were his severed head. . . .

Now the black murderer was almost upon her, seeking to kill her too. In a moment his hands would fall heavily on her frail body and tear her apart—

She tripped and fell headlong on the cold pavement. He came up, his giant body looming over hers, and, as in a nightmare, she could not move.

"Got you!" he exclaimed.

VENUS

It was an Easter sunrise service. Jesus Christ had died and had risen again, and she was present to give thanks, this lovely anniversary of this holy occasion. Yet her heart was heavy, for no miracle of this nature had come into her own life. Twice, three times her warning might have saved a life, the life of someone dear to her—a warning she had been too confused or self-centered to provide.

She had lost, again—yet somehow she had acquired a spiritual resource, an immortal strength to bear whatever had happened. This dawn ceremony—

She was near a tree, in this open country gathering for worship. It was a spreading live-oak, the moss festooned upon it elegantly, and on the bark of the most proximate branch nestled a large and rather handsome cocoon. As she watched, momentarily distracted from the service, the chrysalis opened and a butterfly emerged, damp and gleaming. It spread its new wings, waiting for them to dry, and it was a beautiful creature unlike any other.

Iridescence traveled along its vanes. "They don't call me Schön for nothing," it said to her.

She snapped out of it. The room was another mass of machinery in the bowels of the station. Monstrous power cables drained into a multi-layered grid whose purpose she could not fathom. It, too, in its way, was beautiful; everything during this session seemed to be rainbow.

"Gravity generator," Schön remarked. "Neat trick, converting electrical power to gravitrons so efficiently. Of course they learned it millions of years ago from other species, via the macroscope; no one knows who first developed the technology for broadcasting, because the early species were hesitant to use it. Once we return to Earth, we'll set up a local station; lots of things that process is good for besides sending information to space."

"Is that all you're interested in? How to make a profit from this?"

"By no means, babe. I would hardly be wasting my effort on *you*, in that case. I routed you by six points in Mars, by the way."

That put him ahead 40 to 11, cumulative point score. She had to begin fighting back, or the final rounds would be meaningless. "Why *are* you wasting time on me? Because I'm the only viable *girl* within fifty thousand light-years?"

"Simplistic thought. You always did view male-female interaction as primarily sexual. That was one of the things that put Ivo off. He gave you love, and in exchange you offered pudenda." He paused, but she had no comment. "Strange notion, that it is the *woman* who does the giving, in intellectual or physical love. In truth, all she does is acquiesce to the gifts of the man."

"Assuming she acquiesces at all. Not every gift is attractive."

"Fortunately, in the human species it is the male who has control. This is one of the reasons Man developed intelligence and culture instead of remaining backward. The control of reproduction, and thus of evolution, had to be taken away from the female before progress could be made. Some claim that man's capacity for rape makes him more evil than those animals that are not up to such activity, but the opposite is true."

"Of all the—!" But she was falling into his verbal snare again. That was the way of defeat.

"Even so, sex is overrated. The moment the urge is indulged, it becomes uninteresting. My real passion is for knowledge; satisfaction there only begets the desire to know even more. I have an insatiable appetite for intellectual experience. A man can sustain himself for a long time, acquiring comprehension, particularly with the macroscope."

He still hadn't admitted his real reason for pursuing her, in that case. Once she knew what he wanted from her, she might have the clue to prevail against him, somehow.

"How did you get around the destroyer?" she inquired, trying another approach. "You claim that exposure to it would kill you immediately, but yet you plan to travel."

"You wouldn't understand the technical medical description, so I'll make it foolishly simple," he said with a fine air of condescension. She had learned not to challenge him, and did not. He continued: "The problem was in blocking off a memory without *experiencing* it. I knew it was there, but I did not dare touch any part of it. It did not hurt Ivo because his personality was incomplete, acting as an inherent barrier; but the moment I absorbed that facet into the rest, the network would be complete, the circuit closed, the dam breached. Yet without that portion, I could not control the body, so I had to have it. And, unfortunately, memory is not confined to any particular area of the brain. A single impression may be laid down across untold synapses, like a thin layer of snow. It really is a generalized acid conversion. So I had to delineate the particular memory layer that was the destroyer concept, and isolate it a step at a time, neutralizing it synapse by synapse until every avenue had been caulked."

He walked about the room, happy to be telling of his achievement. "I had to do it by developing spot enzymes attuned to, and only to, the acidic configurations typical of the destroyer trace. All without leaving my own body or brain. You ever try exerting conscious control over your own enzymes, when you didn't even have it for your body? I dare say that was the most remarkable act of surgery ever performed by man."

Afra was impressed in spite of herself. "You operated on your own brain-chemistry?"

"It took me six months," he said. "The final step was rephasing the synapses I'd blocked, so that I had access to other memories without invoking the destroyer. I didn't want to be stuck with Ivo's superficiality, which was what would have happened had I merely hurdled the gap without reestablishing the lines. I wasn't crossing over into his world, I was assimilating it into mine, with that one culvert remaining. But that involved mass testing and alignment. So I cast him into a historical adventure with a fair variety of experience, where I had a certain measure of supervisory control, and set up my alternate connections while that barrage of new signals was coming through."

"All that—just so you could come out and chase a girl around the office?"

"All that for self-preservation, chick. Ivo was bound to foul up somewhere, and he could have gotten us all killed instead of just the two or three he did manage. I don't appreciate having my destiny managed by a moron. I had to be ready to step in if he ever got smart enough to cry uncle."

"Or even a moment *before*."

"He didn't always know when he had had enough."

"If you were able to accomplish something as complex as blocking off a single memory," she said slowly, "why didn't you simply block off *Ivo* while you were at it? You seem to be able to function well enough without him.

What prevented you from taking control any time you chose?"

"Honey, if I told you that, I would be in your power forever," he said.

His attitude suggested that he was lying; and so she believed him.

MERCURY

The next room contained no heavy machinery. Instead it was laid out rather like a lecture hall, with benches lined up before a podium. Afra passed through it and paused before going on. "Did you run out of symbols, genius?" she called back. She knew that she had not lost the Venus round by much; perhaps two points.

Then the benches became occupied—by perching birds. Sparrows, storks, hummingbirds, eagles, parakeets and buzzards—all species were represented, crowded together in the close atmosphere, wings rustling, feathers drifting, ordure falling. And she was among them, a bird herself, of a type she could not quite identify. She, too, was confined within the tremendous cage the room had become.

Outside, in the area that a moment ago had held the podium, were the human attendees. They were spectacularly dressed, as though seeking to out-splendor the avian horde. Each couple was more elegantly garbed than the last, and all paraded by without a glance into the aviary. In fact, the people were oblivious to it, far more concerned with the display of their own finery.

She recognized the nature of it at last: this was an Easter promenade, following fittingly the sunrise service of the prior vision. But this was as vain an assemblage as she had ever seen. Every member of it seemed to crave attention, and to fear for the least fleck of dirt in the vicinity.

Schön was in it too, resplendent in . . . a tall silk hat.

She did not even notice what else he had on. He had gone too far. Furious, she looked about to see in what

457

manner she might act. Surely something in this situation could be turned to her advantage. It was merely necessary to extend the breadth of her resources.

She scrambled—it was far too crowded to fly—to the large front gate that separated aves from homo, jostling aside the other birds officiously. This should be about where, in station geography, the podium stood. There should be a—yes, the catch was a simple one, not intended to withstand the attack of a human-brained bird. An ordered prying of the beak, a timed shove with the wing, and—

The gate swung open.

The birds exploded outward, screeching. Feathers, dust and dung enveloped the passing people. There was a grand melee, and consternation, as everyone tried to get out of the way of the dirty birds. An albatross, taking off clumsily, crashed into Schön's hat and knocked it from his head. Perhaps Afra had done it herself.

And the lecture room was back.

The podium had been shoved askew, and Schön stood disheveled beside it. There had indeed been contact, and not of his choosing. *He* had dissolved the vision, this time.

She held on to the initiative. She sat down on the nearest bench, sure that this would trigger—the presentation.

It did. The illumination dimmed, and in the air of the front of the room a picture appeared. It was the Shape— the same subtle, tortuous, flexing color she had seen back near Earth when she glimpsed the destroyer-sequence. The same red mass, the same blue dot, as though a blue-white dwarf star were orbiting a red giant. The same symbolic agglutination of concepts, building, building—

She could not withdraw from it; the thing had hold upon her brain. She suspected that Schön was similarly transfixed. The destroyer had pounced at last.

But the emphasis shifted, and suddenly she realized that this was not the mind-ravager. It was the same technique, but not the same message—and the message, despite what certain fringe-interests claimed, was far more vital than the medium. Instead of oblivion, it brought information. It expanded her horizons. In another moment her mind had assimilated its universal language, the galactic gift of tongues, and she saw and heard—the lecture.

Formal galactic history commences with the formation of the first interstellar communication network. Only scattered authentic prior evidences exist . . .

She absorbed it, entranced. She had not been offered the full history before. This lecture went on to cover the expansion of the macroscopic network, spheres of cultural influence, and the onset of the First Siege.

An illustration, it said. Then the partial concepts became complete, and her full apperceptive mass responded. She was on a civilized planet, responding to its gravity, temperature and odors as well as its sights and sounds.

"I can tell you how it comes out," Schön said. His voice interfered with her concentration, and she observed the shifting color-shapes that were telling the story, now three-dimensional and almost physical in substance.

Then her mind became attuned again, and the planet returned. She passed among the ghastly yet ordinary (by galactic standards) creatures of this world, conversed with them, and learned about the desperate struggle they were engaged in. It was planetary, interplanetary war, and this species was in danger of enslavement or destruction.

She came to understand the reason: the Traveler impulse permitted wars of conquest by immature cultures. It was like giving motorboats to hostile islanders previously separated from each other by miles of shark-infested shallows and reefs. Transportation without maturity spelled intercultural war—and mutual disaster.

Physical contacts between the stellar cultures of the galaxy in fact meant chaos, the lecture said, and now she agreed emphatically, having seen it in action. More information came, describing the termination of the siege. There was another animate, full-perception episode, showing the manner in which linked species had rejoined, sharing a planet, but not harmoniously. The creatures, like the last, were completely unhuman, yet she felt sympathy for their plight. She felt that she was there as a group of shoreline vigilantes killed an envoy from the undersea culture; and she reacted with dismay as she followed an enlightened land-dweller making a return quest into the ocean, only to be similarly slain by the border patrol of the other side. War broke out again, decimating both species and setting back the civilization of the planet disastrously; but still the mutual hate did not abate. Removal of the Traveler had not solved galactic problems; it had only suppressed them painfully. Better that it had never come.

But she learned also the positive side of it: the resurgence of civilization in the absence of the Traveler. She followed the positive preparations to alleviate the foreseen Second Siege. The destroyer was put into perspective: it was like a hurricane, that prevented the savages from using their modern boats. Many died trying—but this was better than what had happened before.

She saw the other phase of the destroyer project: the quest into the origin and nature of the Traveler signal.

It had to be assumed that the Traveler was beamed to the other galaxies of the local cluster. Had they gone through similar ravages? The macroscope did not provide the answer.

Yet, the conjecture continued, if the Traveler touched other galaxies, it had the aspect of a universal conspiracy to destroy civilization wherever it occurred. If so, it was essential that it be stopped at its source.

Still, journeys to these near galaxies had failed. Six expeditions to Andromeda had never returned. If there were a traveler there, a round trip should be possible. If there were not, then high-level macroscopic technology should have been developed and retained, and at least a few programs should have been beamed for intergalactic communication. Ordinary spherical broadcasts dissipated in the vast intergalactic reaches, but beams did not, as the Traveler itself had demonstrated.

Could it be that the Travelers encountered the other galaxies at different times? The local program appeared to originate about three million light-years distant, at a point source, and to expand to saturate the entire galaxy and its environs: the globular clusters, the Magellanic clouds, but not Fornax or Sculptor. About thirty thousand light-years beyond the rim (arbitrarily assigned; there was no physical discontinuity marking the edge of the galaxy) the beam stopped; its total cross section at this stage was about 150,000 light-years. By the time the beam might, in its onward travel, intercept another galaxy beyond the Milky Way, it would have spread into a tremendous cone-segment far too diffuse for proper effect. It had obviously been tailored to this particular locale.

If other beams were similarly tailored, and if they originated from the same spot in space, it might be that they had to take turns. A million years of traveler could be directed at one galaxy; then, while it was on its way, the projector could be reoriented to cover another galaxy. Thus direction and distance and schedule would determine the status of any particular galaxy.

After the Second Siege the confirmations began to come in. Civilized planets that had jumped to other galaxies and had been stranded there had broadcast back portions of the truth. They had made the transit, but had been unable to come out of organic stasis because of the absence of the traveler signal necessary for the reconstitution. Thus millions of years had had to pass before a Traveler intercepted the new location of an exploring world. At that point reconstitution had occurred, but with losses, since even the gaseous state did not have indefinite shelf-life. Then no *return* was feasible, unless another delay of tens of millions of years was undertaken while waiting for the local Third Siege.

This was the substance of the first report from Horv, stranded in a globular cluster orbiting Andromeda. It was almost as though the Travelers had been arranged to *prevent* intergalactic commerce. But Horven research continued, for the same signal that revived the sadly decimated populace now allowed the planet to travel freely around Andromeda. In due course the second, more remarkable report was broadcast.

Meanwhile, one drone moon from the Dooon did reappear in the Milky Way Galaxy, carrying their full report and recordings of their Traveler signal. The recordings had no potency in themselves, but were useful for direct comparison with similar records of the local Traveler. This established that two different Travelers were involved; the "fingerprint" differed in slight but consistent ways. One more fact had replaced conjecture, and another item in the tentative map of Traveler activity had been confirmed. Data was now available on three local beams— and all had emanated from the same point source.

No other drone-moon returnees were discovered. Evidently a number had been dispatched, but were either lost in the uncharted configurations of jumpspace or had arrived but not been located in or near the Milky Way. A continuous and complete scan of the entire volume of the galaxy simply was not feasible, so chance played its part.

Finally, utilizing several of the delayed macroscopic return-messages, the records of the single recovered moon, and detailed analysis of the Traveler itself when the Third Siege began, the locals were able to come at the complete story.

It was the dawning of a new era.

JUPITER

4

The lecture was over. The convoluting shapes faded, and on the stage a prima donna was singing. Her talent was superlative; she seemed to represent the pinnacle of human art, the culmination of individual opportunity. This was as close, in a cappella, as one could come to perfection. This was excellence personified.

Afra considered her human heritage, and that of the galaxy. It was as though six great manifestations of culture had occurred, in whatever mode they were considered. The galaxy had gone through three long civilizations and three short sieges, the last still in progress, and now was on the brink of the seventh and perhaps climactic manifestation. Every individual, every species, every culture was on the threshold. The mirror of history provided the reflection of all the past—but that past was a lesser history than what was about to be.

The prima donna was Schön; the symbols paid scant attention to the sex of the individual. Afra was not certain of the nature of her own symbol this time, having experienced no transformation other than purely conjectural, but the incipient realization of the truth—personal and galactic and universal—was enough. Schön might represent the ultimate in Man's prior evolution, juvenile as he was, but he did not represent Man's future. Neither did the starfish form that Brad had become; that type of maturity had been cast aside long ago as a dead-end attempt for adjustment to a bygone and limited environment. Man was destined for something else. Not physically, not technologically, but socially and emotionally. It might be millions of years before he achieved it, but that was a mere instant, galactically. The threshold was now, in his realization of his potential, in his vision of his own esthetic future.

With only moderate effort, Afra shifted into station reality. The room had changed; this was another busy complex. Machines were turning out the element-display samples and feeding them into conveyor-slots, undoubtedly for transport to the several visitors' lounges. Art was being reproduced, and foodstuffs manufactured. This section was, in fact, an extensive but comparatively routine station production center. Either there was a considerable turnover in samples, implying many visits here, or the displays were replaced frequently as a matter of course.

Schön was present, and he held the S' device. "Mercury was yours, 10 to 5," he announced. "Your damned birds ..." He slapped the instrument.

She had won a round at last! But the vision was upon her:

The street of Macon, she at age seven, the Negro man standing over her. But now her terror was gone. Six manifestations—ascendant, sun, moon, Mars, Venus, Mercury—transmuted to the seventh—Jupiter—and the auspices were beneficent. She knew that the Negro had not come to hurt her; he was not the gunman. The holdup man had been white.

"Little girl, you got to come with me. Your daddy's been hurt."

"I know," she said.

"I work at the store," he continued, helping her to her feet. "I saw you bolt, and I knew you was scared. But it's all right now. Your daddy grabbed that robber and held him, and he's in jail by now I know, but—"

Her knee was skinned, and her shoulder was bruised from the collision in the store, but these were minor injuries. She took the man's hand and began the walk back. "How bad—I mean, my father—"

"He's not hurt bad. I'm sure. He's a brave man, doing that, stepping into a gun like that. A brave man."

Afra stepped out of the memory-vision again, independent of its power as well. She did not have to run any more.

Schön was watching her, aware that he was losing ground. He had thought to win the round by throwing her into the vision of terror and forcing her to capitulate once more, but this time she had conquered her fear. Her liability was gone. Whatever type of conquest *he* had contemplated was farther from realization now than it had been during their initial encounter in the ascendant.

She was still gaining strength, riding the crest of her victory in Mercury and her release from the continuing repression of the ascendant. She was ready to expand her horizons even more, to encompass the ultimate information and profit thereby.

"Did you consider," she demanded of Schön, "the essential paradox of the Traveler? The single fact that makes it distinct from all other broadcasts, and makes its very existence proof that its Type III technology is qualitative as well as quantitative?"

"Certainly," he said—but there had been a fractional hesitation that betrayed his oversight. He *had* missed the obvious, as had they all, and worked it out only in this instant of her challenge. Another point for her side! "The Traveler, as an impulse moving at light velocity, could never supervise so complex a chronological process as melting and reconstitution of an unfamiliar creature, since no memory of prior experience could exist in a pattern traveling past the subject at the ultimate velocity. The portion of the Traveler that directed the reduction of the epidermis would be twenty-four light-minutes beyond, by the time the heart dissolved. And the portion that *finished* the job would not have been advised when the process started—not when it couldn't, relativistically, catch up for that same twenty-four minutes. Information cannot travel through the material universe faster than light. So the Traveler could not handle the job—yet did. Paradox."

"You've missed it!" she cried. "Genius, you're blind to the truth. You don't understand the Traveler any more than the early galactics did."

"Ridiculous," he said, irritated. "I can tell you how the melting cycle is accomplished within that limitation. Do I have to draw you a picture?"

"This won't fit on any picture, stupid."

Schön intercepted a carbon-cube—one of the tremendous diamonds—on its way to some display and set it on top of one of the art-machines. He trotted down the hall to procure something resembling chalk, and returned to make a sketch on his improvised blackboard. A chalk sketch on a diamond!

"The beam originates at point A, strikes the subject at point B and goes on to point C, never to return," he said, drawing a cartoon figure. She had no doubt he could turn out a work of art if he chose, but the chalk was clumsy, the surface slick, and he was preoccupied by the reversal of their competitive fortunes.

"For the sake of simplicity," he continued, "we'll ignore such refinements as the manufactured melt-beam that actually does the work; that's merely an offshoot produced ad hoc when triggered by a suitable situation. The point is, the Traveler only touches once and moves on at light velocity. It doesn't stay to see the job finished, any more than a river stays to watch the wader crossing it. There's always new water."

"You're still all wet," she said.

"But an object in water *will* set up a stationary ripple," he continued, seemingly unperturbed. She knew he had to make his point—or lose points. "Because the impulse is not confined to one direction. In the case of our Traveler, the interaction at point B initiates a feedback that meets and prepares the oncoming impulses. So an extended interaction *is* feasible." He drew another figure on a second face of the cube. "Call point D that secondary interaction, though it occurs at no fixed place. It *does* alert the oncoming signal in advance, making a type of memory and planning possible.

"So the melting is actually a function of E—the A-beam modified by the BD feedback. The only time the A-beam is encountered directly is during the introduction; and this is the reason *for* that introduction. Without that BD feedback, the melting would be a simple chaotic

465

reduction of flesh leading inevitably to death. As it is, when a critical point approaches—such as the need to close down one lung while preserving the other—the Traveler knows, and modifies its program accordingly. The same holds for the reconstitution, which is hardly the natural reformulation of evolution it appears. It doesn't matter where it occurs, so long as the Traveler is present; the beam is geared to react to a given stimulus in the proper way. A very sophisticated program, particularly since no part of its component is solid, liquid or even gaseous; but effective, as we know."

"You're talking about details and missing the whole, just as the galactics did," she said. "The old trees/forest ignorance. You know what? I think you *can't* comprehend the Traveler by yourself. You blocked it off along with the destroyer-memory! The truth is out of your reach!"

His face was calm, but she was sure he was furious. "What can you do with your alleged comprehension that I can't do with mine? Show me one thing."

"I can talk to the Traveler," she said.

"To be sure. I can even talk to my foot. But what kind of a *reply* do you get?"

She concentrated all her attention and will-power on this one effort, knowing that her thesis, her one superiority over Schön, depended for its proof on the performance. "Traveler," she cried, "Traveler, can you hear me?"

Nothing happened. Schön gazed at her with a fine affectation of pity.

Was she wrong? She had been so certain—

"Traveler," she repeated urgently, "do you hear me? Please answer—"

Y E S

It came from every direction, that godlike response. It assaulted her senses, scorched her fingers, swelled her tongue, blasted her eardrums, lanced into her eyeballs

466

with letters of fire. *Was this what Moses had experienced on the mountain?*

Schön stood dazed. He had received it.

"What are you?" she asked, frightened herself but aware that this might be her only opportunity to make this contact. Only while she rode the crest—

And it came at her again, a torrent of information, projected into her mind in the same fashion the melting cycle had acted on the cells of her body. The passing portions of the Traveler beam triggered nerve synapses in her brain and spoke to her in true telepathy.

In essence, this: Just as interstellar travel required the reduction of solid life to liquid life, and thence to gaseous life, so true intergalactic travel required one further stage: radiation life. The Traveler was not a broadcast beam; *it was a living, conscious creature*. Originally it had evolved from mundane forms, but its technology and maturity had enabled it to achieve this unforeseeable level, freeing it of any restraint except the limitation of the velocity of radiation through space. Even that could be circumvented by using the jumpspace technique—once space had been cartographically explored by lightspeed outriders.

There was nowhere in the universe this species could not range.

But very few life-forms ever achieved this level. Why? The Travelers investigated and discovered that in the confined vicious cauldron that was the average life-bearing galaxy, the first species to achieve gaseous-state jumpspace capacity acted to suppress all others—then stagnated for lack of stimulus. The problem was that technology exceeded maturity. Only if more species could be encouraged to achieve true maturity could universal civilization become a fact. They needed time—time to grow.

And so the Travelers became missionaries. Each individual jumped to a set spot in space and underwent the transposition to radiation, retaining awareness throughout. Physical synapses became wave-synapses, thought occurring from the leading edge backwards, but lucidly. And each individual personally brought jumpspace capacity to Type II technologies resident in individual galaxies.

It was the Milky Way as a whole that was being cultivated. The Traveler beneficence resembled that of the destroyer: it seemed cruel, but actually fostered an acceleration of maturity. *Species* might suffer, but *galaxies* were prodded into growth. Those galaxies that achieved control over their immature elements—so strikingly defined by their actions in the face of jumpspace temptation—were on their way to success. The Milky Way, after several failures, had finally gained that self-control, and was on the verge of true maturity—as an entity. This was the gift of the Traveler: the passport to the universe, and to universal civilization.

"The white man bringing his god to the ignorant natives," Schön muttered. "Big deal." He stepped into the next chamber.

"It *is* a big deal, even if you're too immature to admit that extragalactic aliens can do things *you* can never hope to do," she cried, pursuing him. "And mankind, too, may share in that distinction, if it survives its own adolescence. Not by becoming smarter, but by maturing. We—"

SATURN

♄

Schön was in a soldier's uniform, unkempt, and in his hand was a bottle of cheap whisky. If he had a post to guard, he was derelict in duty. Somewhere he had made an error, a nondiscriminating decision, and the consequence was upon him.

Afra was in a glorious gown, a golden-haired goddess, as she swept into the room. She observed banks of computerlike machinery, and took it for the sensitive, quality-control mechanism of the station, but she was intent on her personal opportunity. Schön's deviation was her reward, his faithlessness to the common welfare her good fortune—so long as she proceeded with confidence.

He lifted the bottle to her in a drunken salute. "My candle burneth over," he said. "You won again."

Then that elusive special memory unlocked itself and emerged from its dungeon of security: something Bradley Carpenter had told her. In times of stress it had pushed up, only to retreat before scrutiny. Now at last she had it. "Schön is dangerous—make no mistake about that. He has no scruples. But there *is* a way to bring him under control, if the need exists and the time is proper. Now I'm going to describe it to you, but I want you to tell no one—particularly not Ivo."

"Who is Ivo?" she had inquired, for this was before it all had started.

"He's my contact with Schön. But this is the one thing about Schön he doesn't know. I'm going to implant in you a hypnotic block against divulgence."

And he had done so, skilled as he had been in such matters. She had not remembered it until this moment—this moment of discovering Schön in his weakness, knowing that his vulnerability was temporary, dictated only by transitory animation of symbols. Schön still led her in points, and she knew what tremendous resources he possessed; she would never overcome him if she did not finish him now. Uranus or Neptune might swing the pendulum back to him, and with it the initiative and the final victory.

"Do you remember Yvonne?" she asked him.

The image vanished. Schön turned on her, the bottle in his hand replaced by S', and it was as though the fire of his essence took physical form. "Brad, you bastard!" he cried. "You told!"

But he was in his weakness, she in her strength. "You have a memory like mine, one you can't face," she said. "It is the reason you could not take over control from Ivo, whatever else you managed. It is the knowledge that gives me power over you." But only if the circumstance were appropriate—and that could be a matter of definition.

For there had been a third genius of the project, one falling between Brad and Schön. Yvonne—"The Archer"—and there had been intense conflict.

They were five years old when the culmination came, both having experienced more of life in all areas than had most adults, but both remaining children emotionally. It was the classic case of two scorpions in a bottle, two nations with nuclear overkill and insufficient patience: two children with the powers of adults. Because they were male and female, there was a certain mitigating attraction; but their rivalry was stronger, and when the camaraderie ended they put it on the line: a game, a contest, more than physical, more than intellectual, whose precise rules no other person comprehended. For a day and a night they had faced each other, locked in a private room, and in the end Schön had won and Yvo had committed suicide.

Then Schön, protecting himself, had operated on the body and made it resemble a mutilated version of his own in certain ways that would deceive the outside world. He had arranged an impressive "accident" of conflagratory nature that made the deception complete, and had then assumed her place in the project community. Thus he had become Ivo, and somehow managed to alter the records to confuse the prying adults. It seemed to them that a male child had died, yet the count did not confirm this; instead one male had been mislabeled female. Yet if a female had been lost, which one?

Schön had gotten away with murder.

But he had not confused his contemporaries. They were not as clever as he, but they knew him, and they knew the score. They were his peer-group, and it operated with unprecedented force. They did not report his crime to the adults, for that was not the peer-code; they *did* pass the word informally and judge him themselves and impose a sentence on him. He *became* Ivo, then. No longer could he masquerade as another person by choice and convenience. For the group had this special power over its members, part ethics, part force, part religion, part family: what the group decreed, the individual honored. It could not be otherwise, even for Schön.

The secret had been kept, but he had been punished. Even after the project disbanded, the peer-power remained, the inflexible code, a geis on him he could not break.

Only Ivo himself could set him loose when the need arose—and Ivo had never known the truth, and was stubborn to boot. Ivo had thought it was the tedium of daily existence that kept Schön buried originally. He had never heard of Yvo.

As the Traveler disciplined the universe; as the destroyer disciplined the galaxy; as circumstance disciplined mankind; so the peer-group disciplined Schön.

And nothing else! Schön still had the galactic instrument, S', and this was not Earth-locale, and Afra was not a peer of the project. "You cannot get home

URANUS

without me," he said. "The sentence cannot be invoked, here; there is still need for me."

So the grand ploy had failed, and now that pendulum was swinging back, restoring his power, diminishing hers. It was her turn to retreat.

The next room was another highly technical one: a strange conduit admitted something invisible, and stranger equipment manipulated it.

"Conversion," Schön remarked with some of his old confidence. "Channeled gravitrons adapted to macrons for the broadcast." He touched S′.

Five people stood on an Earthscape in the sunshine. A woman and two men faced south; two women—one older, one younger—stood fifty feet away, in the trio's line of sight.

For the first time Afra saw the symbols and remained in doubt as to which one was hers. The woman in the northern group might be herself; the men might be Schön and Ivo. One of the southern pair was an old-fashioned woman; the other was an up-to-date girl. The one pinched, stiff; the other alert, open-faced. Their clothing and manner identified their types—but which of the three women, really, was Afra?

This seemed to be the time for indecision, and Schön evidently shared the mood. "Am I so bad?" he demanded somewhat plaintively. "I never tortured to death an animal, and not many who pass through conventional childhood can say that. I never shot a man, and not many who served in the armed forces can say that. All I did was play a fair game for high stakes and win. Had I lost, *I* would have died. I have always abided by the rules of the game."

Then Afra knew that the woman between the two men was Yvo, as she might have been at maturity. Schön was bracketed by his past, and by competing demands, and it was not in her to condemn him out of hand.

But Afra was bracketed too. She had witnessed the history of the galaxy and absorbed its significance. Was she now to return to her old, narrow ways and attitudes, or was she to open her mind and personality to change, movement, spontaneity? Which woman was she? There was advantage in conventionality, but also in initiative.

She had never realized before that her own prejudice against Negroes stemmed at least in part from that chase in her childhood by a well-meaning supermarket employee. She had remembered that pursuit subconsciously and associated it with the sudden, crushing death of her father, fatally wounded that day, and she had somehow blamed all Negroes for it. Yet it had been a white man who fired the shot, attempting to hold up the cashier. It had been a Negro who had tried to help, even to the extent of expressing an unjustified confidence in her father's health. The strongest elements of the experience had been the killing and the Negro, and her subconscious had made a connection her conscious had not. No doubt the climate of her upbringing had promoted this, too. . . .

There were no answers for either of them here. They moved to the next room.

NEPTUNE

Maintenance: cleaners, repair machines, testing robots. She walked down the aisle, Schön following several paces behind. At the far end was a spherical dance of light, communicating in the galactic code. She studied it—and understood that it was warning all comers that the next compartment contained the destroyer programming mechanism.

The other chambers had not had warnings; why did this one?

She was sure she knew. Theoretically, any creature who was able to travel to this station had achieved the maturity to be immune to the destroyer concept. But there could be less mature associates, as in the case of the species that had actually emplaced this unit; the truly mature individuals were not capable of violence, however practical its application. Younger species would have to maintain the equipment and do the work.

472

Or—there could be children, recapitulating evolution, poking aggressively into dangerous nooks. So—a warning. There could be stray destroyer emanation here.

"This is the end of the line," she said, showing him the warner. "We have to go back. Why don't we stop this foolish contest and try to help each other?" And she wondered whether her distaste for him had dissipated with her fear.

He brightened. "We are prisoners of what we are. These symbolic animations are only projections of our two personalities. We are Neptune now, planet of obligation ... and such. For you this is A HOUSE RAISING, helpfulness, cooperation, joy in common enterprise. That is why you have spoken as you have."

"Then what is your symbol?"

"A MAN IN THE MIDST OF BRIGHTENING INFLUENCES."

She saw that the game was not over, and that he had almost won. Beatryx was dead; Harold was gone; Ivo had been replaced by this stranger—and she was ready, in her overwhelming spirit of helpfulness, to give whatever she had to offer to the victor. Perhaps there had been a time when she would have felt otherwise; intellect told her so. But not at this moment.

"The score stands at 78 to 69, my favor," he said. "If we stop here, and I agree we might as well—"

She tried to reach the Traveler again, but that wave of ability had subsided. She might never again achieve the peak of awareness and drive necessary to call it forth directly. No help there.

Without letting herself consciously realize what she was doing in her desperate effort to stave off defeat, Afra stepped backward into the destroyer-room.

"Hey!" Schön called, taken by surprise. He dived for her, astonishingly swift on his feet—but too late.

P L U T O

Ivo resumed control as the destroyer sequence hit. A rainbow of color/concept threatened to overwhelm his perception, building with merciless velocity toward oblivion—

but he had had long experience diverting it. He deflected the impact and concentrated on Afra.

She was kneeling on the floor, trying to cover her face, but the emanations were everywhere. They leaked out in forms susceptible to reception by ears and skin as well as eyes. There was no physical way to block the destroyer off, this close.

He reached her and clamped both hands on her wrists, hauling her around and up and back through the doorway. Her eyes were fixed, her lips parted in the obsessive rapture of assimilation. As they passed from the chamber the barrage stopped, sealed off by some unseen shield.

Afra slumped into unconsciousness. He propped her up against an inactive scrubbing machine and peered anxiously into her face. Had he brought her out in time? If he revived her now, would she awaken to personality—or mindlessness?

She had won the game with Schön. Her daring had scored a clean sweep of Pluto, for she had survived where he could not. It was the one situation where lesser intelligence was an advantage. The extra minute she had withstood the destroyer was the same as a knockout victory.

Schön had had to have her help, if he were ever to leave the station, since only by burying his own personality could he have faced the destroyer. He could have fashioned an idiot personality for the purpose—but then the geis on him would have taken effect, keeping him bottled. Only if another person released him could he reemerge, in the absence of Ivo. A simple request would have been enough: "Schön—come out!"—but it had to be from someone who acted independently. Someone outside the bottle, for the seal could not be broken from within. Someone who knew him and knew what the request meant.

Certainly Schön would never have let Ivo resume control. Not when both knew that Afra was in love with that alternate personality. But an idiot—capable only of a directed reception of the Traveler—she would have had to banish that. Her temperament would have forced her to uncork the responding mind, even though she hated it. And of course she would have felt obligated to honor the terms of the agreement, having lost the game.

But she had won. Ivo was sure of this—because he had

been the referee. Had it been otherwise—that is, had Schön not arranged to *make* it fair—the results would not have been binding. A legitimate win for Schön would have forced Ivo to return control to him, even after saving him from the destroyer. Ivo, too, was bound by the geis, having agreed to arbitrate the contest.

As it was, that intervention to save their mutual mind had cost Schön all ten points of the final round, putting Afra ahead 79 to 78, and it was over. She had won the right to choose her companion on the way home. She had made the nature of that choice plain during her dialogue with Schön.

Provided she retained, literally, the wit to make that decision. Otherwise, she too had lost, and rendered the round a tie that was meaningless. A mindless Afra could not serve Schön's purpose.

Ivo contemplated her face, so lovely in its repose. He had longed for this from the moment he saw her the first time. He had traveled the galaxy only to please her.

The surface of the machine against which she leaned was reflective. He saw in that mirror the head of a man. It seemed to smile knowingly at him. He knew, as the gift of one of Schön's conscious thoughts during the contest, that this was Afra's symbol in Pluto—A MAN'S HEAD—just as the rainbow he had seen as he took over had been Schön's. But whose head was it to be?

Had all his life been leading to this crisis, this empty vigil with an unconscious girl? If she were gone, what was left?

Ivo held her, afraid to wake her, and remembered.

There had been the project breakup, thrusting them all abruptly into the massive, confused, tormented world—yet most had greeted it as a release and a challenge. They had exploded across the planet, three hundred and thirty eager youngsters seeking experience ... and had been absorbed by it without a ripple. Brad had gone to college; Ivo had followed the melody of the flute, searching out the obscure monuments of the life of Sidney Lanier. Quite a number of the others had married nonproject people. All had sworn to keep in touch forever, but they were young then, and somehow had forgotten. There had been some almost-random encounters, however—enough to circulate news of most. From time to time Ivo had dreamed of a grand convening, a project reunion—recognizing the very desire as a reflection of his inadequacy, his poor adjustment to the world of the '70's.

Then Groton, on a hot Georgia street, and adventure had been thrust upon him. Brad needed Schön! Afra, vision of love, bait of trap—would he have stepped into it had he not wanted to? The proboscoids of Sung, overrunning their world heedlessly, and mankind doing the same. Human organs, black-market. Plump Beatryx, wife of an engineer. Image of a school crisis: boy in classroom, cigarette, smirk. Senator Borland, man of ambition, power. Destroyer image: one dead, one ruined, one untouched? Sprouts, a winning configuration, S D P S, Kovonov, who had meant to go himself. . . .

Joseph the rocket, accommodations for five. Learning to use the macroscope, that instrument of galactic civilization. Astrology: "The complex of your life and the complex of the universe may run in a parallel course." UN pursuit. Image of a living cell. The handling—identity confirmation or sexual experience? The melting—skull canting, gray-white fluid coursing out eye-socket. Reconstitution—from cell to self in four hours.

Mighty Neptune, sea-storm world of methane. Triton, where Tryx found a bug. Schön, moon of a moon. There he had come to appreciate real people, to know the meaning of friendship, its prerogatives and its miseries. Terraforming: a joint effort. Poetry, prejudice, a chess analogy. Starfish. Afra's horoscope, the chart that defined her. The flip of a bus token. Trial: another case of handling, really. Spacefold diagrams. Visual penetration of Neptune—dwarf with the breath of a giant, yet more ancient than Sol. Gravitational radius.

Tyre. Mattan, talking of superpowers. Baal Melqart, hungry for children. Swords and torches in the night. Aia: "We shall have joy in one another, while both being true to our memories." Image of Astarte, milk spurting from her breasts. Stench of rotting shellfish, for purple robes. Gorolot, offered an imperious housemaid. Afra, volunteering in lieu of Aia, comfortable harbor for ships. All because Schön craved freedom.

Well, Schön had lost, whether Afra had mind or not.

Suddenly Ivo could stand the suspense no longer. He put his hands under Afra's arms, drew her to her feet against him, and kissed her with all the passion he had suppressed for so long. Try *that* for handling!

She woke abruptly. She brought her arms up outside his, wedged her stiffened fingers against his cheeks, and shoved back his head. "Get away from me!" she exclaimed angrily.

Ivo released her with guilty haste. *She had not chosen him!*

Then he realized with shivering relief that she thought he was Schön. She had no way to know about the contest result and changeover. He opened his mouth to explain.

"Don't be ridiculous, Ivo," she snapped. "I can tell you two apart easily. Aside from that, I knew Schön couldn't get me out of there. It had to be you—or nothing."

His feeling of stupidity was back in full force. He tried to speak again.

"You thought if only Schön were gone, everything would be just fine. Boy gets girl, curtain lowers on happy sunset. Sorry—when I want a lapdog, I'll whistle."

What had happened? Her dialogue with Schön had suggested that she was in love with Ivo, but now she was treating him with greater contempt than ever before.

"Schön was right about one thing," she remarked, adjusting her clothing. "You certainly aren't véry bright—and I do dislike stupidity."

Was she saying she wanted Schön back? That made no sense to him. But if she didn't want Schön and didn't want Ivo—

Afra faced about and began to walk away, back toward the chamber where the visions had started. Somehow he knew that if he let her go, he would never recover her—yet he could not act. He had lost her without ever speaking a word.

Jumps of thousands of light-years, until they stood outside the great disk of the galaxy itself, and returned—that he remembered clearly, yet he could not bridge the gap of a few paces between two people now. A history of the Solar System, billions of years strong—yet seconds were undoing him. Where had he gone wrong?

Approach to the destroyer complex: "It's tracking us!" His foolish jealousy of Harold Groton, returning his concept of the man to the impersonal surname. Afra's excitement at the element display. The final chamber. S′.

477

Wheels on wheels, symbols meshing in "The Symphony." Simultaneous yet chronological adventures of galactic history. Schön: "That means our daughters get dinked." Beatryx: "You were *not* wrong, Dolora." Harold: "I had thought it was an insult to serve under Drone command." Where had he gone wrong?

Now Schön had been nullified, Beatryx was dead, Harold was seeking the Traveler, and Afra disliked stupidity. Yet he remained, and so did his responsibilities. Where had he heard that? Promises to keep, and miles to go before . . . He had to do something for the gallant Groton couple, sundered so unfairly; then—

But I love you! he cried subvocally at Afra. Imperious she might be, problems she might have—but underneath that surface beauty was an extraordinary woman. She had fought Schön. . . .

She continued walking, culottes shaping a trim derriere, bright hair flouncing loose.

Afra, whose Capricorn history segment had slipped somehow, throwing her instead into a savage personal conflict. Yet that program error had saved her—and him— from a dream-state that might have endured until their bodies disintegrated. The normal person did not emerge from that slumber, as Harold and Beatryx had shown. That, apparently, was the final test: only a mind that could survive and finally break the stasis was fit to go free again. The human mind lacked that capability. Even Schön had been trapped.

Strange, fortunate coincidence, that Afra should have been evicted from that clinging mold. And that she alone, subsequently, should establish a momentary rapport with the supercreature, the Traveler. The Traveler: nerve impulse between galactic cells, whose capabilities spanned from macrocosmic to microcosmic with equal finesse.

Coincidence? Perhaps the Traveler *had touched her intentionally!* This was easily within its compass. To nudge her just enough to break the trance, and then again to win a vital point from Schön . . . and it could not touch Schön himself—or Ivo!—because of the mind-block against the destroyer-concept Schön had so carefully arranged. Afra had been the only one available with an open yet sharp enough mind. . . .

Why? Why interfere at all, this creature with a galaxy

to supervise? Could it have seen some hope in her, in humanity? Did it want them to return to Earth with their message of galactic and intergalactic culture? Yet Afra could not return to Earth by herself, and she had turned her back on him.

At least, he thought with transitory irony, he didn't have to worry about Schön interfering. Geis apart, Schön could not take over again, since Afra wouldn't cooperate with him and the destroyer fields suffused all the galaxy. Schön was barred from space. He, Ivo, could now draw freely on any or all of Schön's talents as required without risking his identity. He could get home. He had only to reduce his personality when actually dealing with the destroyer, protecting his immunity; at other times he could, literally, be a genius.

Fat consolation, he thought, watching Afra's dainty feet moving. *You can use it to fathom why you lost her.*

Yes—the genius of Schön would clarify that, at least. Ivo reached . . . sunburst! He understood exactly what Afra was doing.

"Girl," he said clearly.

She halted. She had not been walking rapidly and had not yet entered the adjacent chamber. She was still, in the imagery of the recent contest, in Pluto or Neptune. Obsession, obligation—yet so much more, positive as well as negative.

"What the cloud doeth," he said, "the Lord knoweth; the cloud knoweth not."

She turned slowly. "I don't understand."

"It's a quote from Sidney Lanier. The course of the cloud may be predestined, but Man possesses free will." He had spoken in Russian.

Her capitulation was as sudden as her awakening. She skipped across the room and threw herself into his arms. "I knew you weren't a cloud, Ivo!" she murmured before she kissed him.

Further explanation was unnecessary, yet the hard-core Ivo in him ran it through during their extended embrace. Afra had wanted neither the omnisicient supercilious Schön nor the stodgy ignorant Ivo. She required compromise: Ivo's personality with Schön's abilities. For neither identity alone represented the complete man. Schön had never grown up, while Ivo had shied away from the exercise of his rightful talents. How could a woman really love half of a schizoid personality?

But the destroyer had shifted the balance and broken the stalemate, making Ivo the artist. He could unify and control—and time and experience had made his identity the more fit of the two for human intercourse. A child normally grew into an adult—and to abolish the adult Ivo in favor of the child Schön would be a foolhardy inequity.

Thus the personal equation. Boy had not won girl; man had won woman.

What, now, of Earth? Mankind was a child-culture with adolescent technology; were they to present it with devastating *adult* technology? Or would it be better to stay clear and allow natural selection to function, as it did elsewhere in the galaxy?

"What the artist doeth," he murmured, "the Lord knoweth; knoweth the artist not?"